From Heaven Fought The Stars

Joanne Szedlak

DEDICATION

For my children, David, Abigail, Eleana and Alice.

ACKNOWLEDGMENTS

Thank you Jesus, my inspiration and source, my hiding place and high tower, my love and best-friend, for giving me the imagination and insight to write this book.

Thanks to my husband, for his strength of character, wisdom and integrity, for his love and support, for believing in me and encouraging me in my writing. To my children for their love, patience and for making every day wonderful. Thank you Abigail, my daughter, for your inspiration on the character of Deborah and your artwork on the book cover. Thank you David, my son for your brilliant creation of the map and your militant faith which is such an example to me.

Thanks so much to my parents, for being my refuge and security in the midst of life and teaching me about the mother/father heart of God and the virtue of standing and fighting for what you believe in and walking in integrity. And to my brother, the most noble and virtuous of men, a true warrior in his integrity and generosity to those who know him.

To Sarah, for her friendship and inspiration on the character of Jael and help with editing and Naomi and Paul for their inspiration of Abraham and Naomi – their integrity, humility and theological grounding leave me inspired and humbled.

To Wilma, for her friendship and encouragement, for the discussions and input in the early stages of the book; for teaching me humility in adversity and its application to Deborah. Thanks too to Alex and Becky, for their encouragement and helping me publish the book . Also, a massive thank you to my dear friend and prayer partner Shaz, for her initial editting. To my friends: Anne-louise, Ayo, Becky, Carolyn, Claire, Daphne, Elke, Holly, Katie, Karen, Kelsie, Kaz, Libby, Mel (for proofreading), Naomi, Natalie, Pauline, Priya, Rowanna, Sarah, Shaz, Wilma, Veroniqua. Shelley and my other dear friends at school, spiritual mothers who fight militantly with strength and compassion for those they love and helped inspire this book. Many thanks for all they do, the example of integrity they set and in knitting the fabric of our world together with their love, wisdom, grace and strength.

To The King's School, Fair Oak, the wonderful teachers and Heather Bowden, a true Deborah in a real community.

To Durban Christian Centre and CI international, where I gained my initial passion for Deborah and theology. To Dr Fred Roberts who taught me to turn deeper in Christ in adversity and about a faith that aims for the stars. To John Torrence for believing in me and teaching me transparency, integrity and humility in leadership.

.

Prologue
1262 BC

Deborah was eight the first time Yahweh spoke to her.

As the day began to fade and evening's gentle, amber strokes painted the sky, Deborah celebrated *Pesach* with her family. Amos, her father, recounted the narrative of their ancestors, who had fled Egypt. He spoke with a passion that wove around their hearts, drawing them on a journey of Israel's faith and trials and leading them, inspired with awe, into the Promised Land.

And so, as they joined with their fellow Israelites, feasting on roast lamb, lentils and unleavened bread, washed down with wine from last year's harvest, they remembered how the Angel of Death had passed over their people, delivering their nation from Pharaoh's oppression. As her father spoke, a deep sense of belonging and strength were embedded in Deborah's heart birthed from a shared spiritual and cultural history. Finally, Amos ended by thanking Yahweh for Ehud who had delivered their nation and now judged with Yahweh's wisdom and love.

Her mother blew out the oil lamps and as darkness rolled across Shiloh, it seemed a blanket of contentment had enveloped them. Her mother bent down and tucked her in, moving onto the pallet next to her where her brothers Enoch and Isaac lay. She stretched out on her straw pallet as the new moon smiled down upon her and, in the distance, Mount Ephraim protectively loomed over them, like a watchful parent.

As she slept in this warm embrace, Deborah saw a tree, tall and ancient, from which grew twelve strong branches. Each branch was weighed with such delicious fruit, that the creatures of both air and field were drawn to it; thus it seemed alive, as butterflies, honeybees and birds thronged to the tree. The roots of the tree were spread wide and deep, feeding into a sparkling river that flowed to its own peaceful melody. It seemed to dance as it journeyed around the tree before disappearing into the rolling hills and verdant grasslands beyond. As Deborah trailed her feet in the cool water, she was enveloped in the hazy bliss that emanated from the tranquil shade of the tree.

Without warning, a storm cloud appeared, dark and oppressive; it shrouded the tree, filling Deborah with a deep sense of foreboding. Lightning struck from nowhere, hitting the tree at its core. She hurried in panic to see what devastation had befallen the beautiful tree. Relieved to see that it seemed unharmed, she once again sat down, hoping to regain the serenity of her previous memory. But the sense of impending doom hovered and she could not shake it. As she stared into the face of the clear waters, she had begun to regain her previous calm - when she was startled by a splash. Looking up to see what had caused it she noticed that the fruit had begun to die and was falling from the tree. As it fell, the water turned black, poisoned by the dead fruit.

Horrified, Deborah watched as the dark, miasmic cloud began to rain down its torrents and stood aghast, as winter crept across the tree. With it came a sense of deep terror. When the tree was finally bare, she was able to see the damage that the lightning had done: it had struck the core of the tree, dividing the branches and penetrating to the depths of its roots, poisoning the air as it exhaled. Deborah wept.

Sitting up and wiping her tear streaked cheeks, she was aware of a presence in the room, as powerful and terrifying as the memory of her dream, but its source and overflow carried a deep sense of goodness and love. The air seemed to vibrate, with a heavy pressure of purpose, conviction and glorious authority.

Her father's story of Moses meeting with God invaded her thoughts: *could this be HIM? Surely he wouldn't find me, a girl, would he?* She looked around the room to the sleeping forms of her brothers and parents. *Why haven't my family woken up? Maybe I'm still asleep.*

And then suddenly, a thought entered her mind, both quieter and clearer than her own questions. It seemed to breathe, like the softest wind *"Who am I?"*

Hesitantly, she whispered "Yahweh? Are you Yahweh?"

A warm swirl...a breath...a smile, answered her thoughts, encircling her, cocooning her in a sense of peace...and....love. With this presence she was aware that the fear had left, as though it had been defeated by a greater master. She sat motionless, concerned lest she disturb the sacred air around her; that HE might leave.

When morning thrust its rosy fingers through the window, His presence was gone.

Yet the imprint of the previous night was firmly embedded into her being. For all her eight years, Deborah knew, irrefutably, that she had met with Yahweh: that he was ultimately powerful and loving. But also, that change would come and bring with it pain and death.

1

Today I have given you the choice between life and death, between blessings and curses. Now I call on heaven and earth to witness the choice you make. Oh, that you would choose life, so that you and your descendants might live! Deuteronomy 30:19

1258 BC - Deborah

Fear, raw and brittle, clung to the roof of Deborah's mouth. Her heart pounded like the cadence of the approaching chariots.

Deborah knew she should be running. She could hear the panic in her father's gentle voice and desperately sought to let his words filter through the tempest that threatened to consume her. It called her, like a hand, grasping to prevent her from falling over a precipice of her own fear - but the words fell before they reached the quiet refuge to which she had retreated within her mind. Her eyes darted to where the rising dust in the distance drew closer.

As though in a dream, she could hear her mother's voice, shrill with barely restrained hysteria and the look of hopelessness reflected in her eyes as they flitted wildly, seeking some solution to the inevitable. The long mournful pitch of the ram's horn being blown echoed the dread that had pitted in her stomach.

Her father was kneeling down and had grabbed her arms, but it was the sound of her brother crying that finally penetrated the world she had drawn around herself. "Deborah! You are to take your brother and go to the mountains: go to *your* place. Stay until I come for you. You must hurry now! Keep low in the wheat field until you come to the olive trees. Do not stop, whatever happens, keep running!"

She looked into his deep, brown eyes and wanted to beg him to let her stay. Her eyes pleaded silently with him; she wanted to tell him she wasn't a child -she was twelve years old – she should stay. But the fear she saw reflected, silenced her. She nodded quietly, tears rolling down her cheeks as he embraced her in his strong arms. He had always made the world right. Surely it would all work out well, it had to - Abba always had a way of making things right. Everyone knew that. She tried to look brave as he released her and she took her younger brother's hand.

Amos lay his hands on his children's heads. "Yahweh bless you and keep you," he prayed. Hot tears pricked his eyes and he blinked them back. "Yahweh make his face to shine upon you and be gracious to you." His throat constricted and he swallowed the sense of dread that had gathered in his gut. "Yahweh lift up his countenance upon you and give you peace." He removed his hand from Deborah's head and as he did the absence of the warm, steady hand that bore such weight seemed to Deborah like a portent of calamity.

Amos pulled his wife back from the children. "Be strong, run fast, Yahweh is with you."

"Yes Abba." She grasped his words, allowing them to form a path of deliverance in her mind: *Yahweh is with me.* He squeezed her arm and nodded, affirming her confidence.

She grabbed Isaac's hand and pulled him from their home. As adrenalin coursed through her body, an instinctive compulsion to survive now drove her forwards. They quickly covered the short distance to the field to where the tall wheat, almost ripe, undulated gracefully in the mounting wind. She ignored the pain that ripped into her legs and hands as she forced a path through the dense, prickly crop and set her eyes on the slopes of the olive grove, and beyond that the rocky path up the mountain. Pulling Isaac behind her, she was increasingly aware that his breathing was becoming laboured. She had seen him like this before, usually at its worst in winter. He stopped, bent over, struggling to draw breath. "It…. hurts, my…. ch…"

"I know! We need to get clear of the wheat: it's making it worse. Can you still walk?"

Isaac nodded weakly.

The familiar, leafy boughs of the olive trees welcomed them into their protective embrace. Isaac collapsed into Deborah's arms. His lips had gone blue and each breath was a struggle to draw in.

Deborah fought the urge to cry as she struggled with her own sense of helplessness. Peering out from their wooded fortress, she immediately regretted her impulsive behaviour. Her father had positioned himself in the village centre, beside the well - *for that was what her father was: the heart of their village.* He was one they turned to for both blessing and consolation, the one from whom they sought advice and wisdom. He was the leader, or judge, of their community, according to the Mosaic order. Now, he was mediator to the Canaanites, the 'traders', whose reputation as cruel oppressors was notorious; for they went from village to village, taking whatever they wanted. Their military might made them invincible.

The iron chariots thundered closer, each drawn by two powerful warhorses. On the side of each chariot, Baal, the god of storm and war, was portrayed as a bull, casting lightning down before him -his threatening grimace defined his intent. Each chariot carried two men: a warrior, carrying a bow and arrow on his back and an axe at his waist, and a driver. As the chariots came to a stop the warriors stepped down. Over their blue, knee-length tunics they wore bronze chain mail, indicative of their higher rank. They were clothed to resonate fear. Their iron helmets and breastplates gleamed in the midday sun, making them look like the gods of destruction depicted on their chariots. Their muscular arms were adorned with bronze arm bands, their faces and bodies grotesquely decorated with red war paint.

Most of the village had retreated to their huts. Only Menachem, a recently married man, twenty-two years old, and Tobias, her father's oldest friend, stood by him. They held no weapons.

Amos stood motionless, tense with anxiety as he recalled the stories of destruction and horror he had heard from other villages that had been 'visited' by the Canaanites.

"What can they want?" Menachem whispered, his voice trembling.

Amos's expression was dark "I don't know, but I pray that our village will not suffer as others have."

The warrior strode toward them with the confidence of a man who already knows he has won. Sisera's dark eyes were cold, piercing with a chiseled hatred, as he paced the village, peering in through window openings like a predator, marking his claim and purpose, while drinking in the scent of fear. His right hand rested intimidatingly on the hilt of an axe at his waist. It seemed he held something wrapped in cloth in his left hand.

The second chariot had come to a halt, and the man who dismounted towered head and shoulders above his superior. His face was contorted by a scar that ran the length of his face, making him look more like a mythical beast than a man. He took mighty strides, drinking in the cringing fear that his presence evoked, until he stood next to Sisera.

Amos stood his ground. He noted the cruelty in the man's eyes and something else that he had never seen before and was therefore unable to identify.

They are men. You are Almighty God. He forced his faith to push back the tide of fear, and anchored himself on the stories of his people; of Joshua who had forced the sons of Anak to leave the land. Legend had it that these giant men were descendants of the Nephilim. He shuddered inwardly at the thought.

Sisera was ambitious: he would rule King Jabin's army - in that he was determined. Subduing the Hebrews would move him further toward his goal, and he would enjoy it. He despised these people with their pious pride and narrow-minded faith that judged his nation. But his hatred was not based on religious, nor political passion. His father had been General before him, and he had been raised on stories of Yareah, centre of Canaanite moon-worship. He had been defeated by the Israelites after 'their God' pulled down its walls. His father had been killed that day, along with every other person in the city. His mother, young, beautiful and bitter, had remarried; but she had moulded Sisera as her weapon of revenge. When he came of age, he was sent to Egypt to receive military and academic training. He would not make the same mistakes his father had. He had come to know these people, learning their language, their customs and their God – to find their weakness; for all men's strengths and weaknesses are closely united. And their strength was their faith and their unity. To compromise their faith, to divide these people would therefore be their downfall. And, as he knew, every man's greatest hope and fear is for their children.

"There have been raids on our farms; it would seem they have been carried out by Hebrews."

Amos waited for the man to finish. He spoke Hebrew; this man was educated, intelligent and practical.

"No doubt you have heard we have been *visiting* your villages," he added, quietly assessing the character of the three men and quickly determining Amos to be the one to whom his conversation would be directed. He read the compassion and courage in the man's face. He was mindful that he, too, was being examined and his lips curved slightly, knowing that what this man saw would fuel the fear he sensed.

Amos nodded, but said nothing. Only yesterday a family had arrived in the village seeking shelter. Their village had been burnt to the ground, several of the women raped, men murdered and many of the children taken as slaves where they would be sold at market to the highest bidder. The leaders had been brutally murdered.

Amos' attention was drawn away by movement behind one of the houses. It was out of the view of the Canaanite warriors. Enoch, his eldest son, was clearly urging his wife to flee. Keziah shook her head, her hand protectively resting on her stomach over their unborn child.

He stepped aside, keen to distract the soldier. "I am sorry to hear that Israelites have been responsible for raiding your farms. It is not our way. Stealing is forbidden in our Law. We are farmers."

"Don't you people believe that your God has given you this land?" His lips curved as he began to unwrap the item he held, and then laid the weapon flat on his calloused palm. "Do you recognize this?"

Amos paled and his expression told the hardened soldier more than dialogue ever could have.

"So, you recognise it." It was a statement that required no explanation.

A wave of nausea hit Amos and he swallowed the bile that rose in his throat. His mind flashed back five years. After an abundant harvest, he had travelled to Gibeah to sell their olive oil. Amos had traded a hin of olive oil for the knife blade and later whittled the handle from acacia wood, engraving Enoch's name on the handle. He had presented it to Enoch to celebrate his thirteenth year. He recalled how proud his son had been as he danced around the well, pretending to be Ehud attacking Eglon king of Moab, his right hand tucked up his sleeve to emulate the warriors mutilated hand, while his left wielded the dagger.

Amos' eyes darted to Menachem and Tobias; his panicked, adrenalin-fuelled thoughts clawed desperately to find a solution that would not end in destruction. But even as he tried, he saw the inevitable outcome reflected in the eyes of his friends: their recognition, terror and hopelessness. Menachem looked away. His shoulders had slumped as though seeking to retreat within himself. Tobias' face was etched with deep compassion and pain as he perceived his friend's despair and burden.

Amos cast a look towards his wife, as though to convey his love for her and remorse over the inevitable outcome of what he was about to do. She shook her head, her eyes wide with horror as she silently acknowledged the certainty that either her son or her husband would pay for the attacks on the Canaanite farms. She clapped her hand over her mouth to prevent herself screaming and staggered back into their home, her knees buckling beneath her as she sunk against the wall of their home and her Amos stepped toward the Canaanite.

In that moment Amos knew a courage that was greater than his own capacity. "It is mine…." His eyes held the warriors scrutiny.

Sisera's eyes narrowed as he probed Amos' soul for the truth. "*Yours?*" His voice had lowered dangerously.

"Yes….I carried out the raids on your farms… Only me… I accept my life as forfeit." His eyes held Sisera's scrutiny and he willed himself not to show the fear that pressed against his chest.

The Canaanite's mouth twitched and Amos realised what he had previously been unable to perceive: the man was amused. He took joy in his brutality. Sisera turned to Menachem. "What is this man's name?" Menachem glanced uneasily at Amos, looking for explanation. He found only resolution and hopelessness, and his eyes betrayed him. He knew that this man of God, whom he had looked up to his entire life, was asking him to lie, and in doing so to deliver his death sentence - or to disobey him and condemn his son. The silent plea was returned by Amos.

"His name is Enoch," his voice trembled, as his eyes shifted nervously to the ground.

The warrior smiled, his head tilted with fascination. He sighed patiently, as he leaned toward the two men and then, speaking in a whisper: "And I thought your God forbade not only stealing, but lying. It seems I find both here." He sighed thoughtfully. "But the question is, who are you protecting?"

He paused, turning around to face his second in command, Talmai. His hands behind his back, he spoke to the village. "Bring me this man's sons!"

Enoch, realising the inescapable conclusion that must shortly unfold, emerged from behind the small hut that had been his and Keziah's home for the last eleven months since their marriage. He glanced backwards at Keziah, who was stumbling across the field, her hair blowing like a dark flag over the sea of ripe wheat.

Sisera's eyes followed Enoch's, his smile widening in his amusement, as though the game had just become more interesting.

Keziah had stopped, the weight of the baby made running over the uneven ground laborious and painful cramps were now racking her body. As she glanced back to the village, she spotted Enoch and the soldier watching her and naively ducked beneath the golden horizon, hoping she had not been seen. Frowning now, Sisera turned to Enoch.

Amos stepped forward, tears filled his eyes as his broken voice pleaded "Please, I told you it was me...it was me!"

Enoch stepped forward, realising that Keziah's escape had been discovered. He looked into his father's eyes, drinking in his father's love as he sought to convey his gratitude and his resolve.

In his mind was their journey to Bethlehem, eighteen months ago, three weeks before Passover. Ehud, the revered judge of Israel had asked each village to send a representative that they might collectively remember the commandments and promises given to Moses by the Lord. His father had decided to take the family to stay with old family friends. During the evening meal, they discussed the day's events and Obed had revealed that there were young Israelites who felt that the Lord's command to Moses and Joshua to 'possess the land' was being forgotten and had begun raiding Canaanite farms and villages.

Something had been birthed in Enoch's heart that night: a zeal for the Lord, for his kingdom, and a passion to be a warrior as their great judge Ehud had been. When they had stopped at Ramah on the way back from

Bethlehem to visit relatives, Enoch discussed with some of his cousins what he had heard.

A week later, under the cover of night, the group of five boys had stolen onto a Canaanite farm. They did not harm the sleeping family, but they had set fire to their fields and killed several of their livestock. They had justified their killing of pigs as 'unclean' animals that the Lord forbade his people to eat. The adrenalin, comradeship and adventure that they had experienced fuelled several similar ventures. They encouraged each other that, like Ehud, they were great warriors, carrying out the Lord's will. One night, the farmer had awoken and had found Enoch struggling with a large pig as his friend slit its throat. On seeing the angry farmer wielding a huge iron axe, the boys realised they had met their match and fled for their lives, the advantage of their youth making them swift on their feet. It was only later that Enoch realised he had forgotten his knife.

That had been his last raid. He had married Keziah a few months later, and that part of his life had been left behind.

He now closed the space between Sisera and his father, glancing at his father before he spoke "No, stop! It was me. Didn't Moses and Joshua say we should possess the land and He would give us the victory against these vermin?" He spoke to his father, but hoped he would redirect the soldier's anger towards himself.

Amos paled as he suddenly recalled the conversation in Bethlehem, the way his sullen son had suddenly become so impassioned. How had he not noticed? Had he been blinded by his parental love not to have seen that his son was secretly carrying out raids on innocent farmers?

Sisera motioned to the giant, Talmai, who, kicking the back of Enoch's knees, forced him into a kneeling position, grabbing Enoch's hair as he gripped him around the neck in his vice-like hold. The name of Joshua, his father's nemesis, fuelled his conditioned hatred.

"The truth, at least. So, we have a fool, a thief, but not a coward." He looked again to the field that Keziah was now half-way across.

"What is it you Hebrews say: An eye for an eye? You burnt our fields, didn't you?" He nodded to the other man, who was waiting.

A strangled cry escaped from Enoch's lips as he perceived Sisera's intention and fell to his knees "NO! NO! Please! I beg you now; take my life, not hers. Please!" Enoch felt the darkness close in around him as the Canaanite soldier set the burning torch to the field.

"Oh, you will die! But first, you will watch – let us see whose God will have the victory today." Sisera grabbed Enoch's hair in his strong grip, forcing him to look as the dry wheat was consumed by the hungry flames.

"Keziah! Run!" Enoch shouted seeking to alert his young wife who lay hiding, cradled in a wall of wheat. Hearing Enoch's voice, she ventured to look from her hiding place. She screamed, scrambling clumsily to her feet.

Turning to her husband, she saw Enoch held in the lock of the soldier and was immobilised by her fear; her instinctive desire to rush toward him, to try and help him warred with her fear.

And then she saw the fire, burning a path toward her. The soldier watched her as he calmly lit the wheat in different places, then stepped back as it blazed to life, a living mass that swirled. It was as if hell's hordes had been let loose: the flames moved with such speed. She began to run. The dry, uneven ground and the child's weight in her stomach slowed her progress as she pushed aside the thick wheat. She could see the edge of the field in the distance, like a horizon of hope, and the sturdy olive trees beyond it and she strove to reach it.

Enoch watched, helpless, as Keziah tried to outrun the blaze, staggering, falling and then moving forward again; willing her to run faster, to save herself and their unborn child.

Isaac's breathing was less laboured now; no longer the painful, wheezing gasps, though his lips were still an unhealthy blue. Deborah held him, as much for her own need to feel safe as for his.

She felt certain they were safe in the trees, for now. Resting her head against the broad twisted trunk of the olive tree she took comfort in its shade. The leaves above her quivered in the summer breeze, as though they, too, sensed her trepidation. Their fruit would not be ready for a couple of months yet, Deborah mused, remembering the annual ritual of pounding and crushing the ripe fruit. Little by little, the oil would drip onto the large stone with a rim chiselled out of it, leading to a clay bowl. It took several weeks to complete, and every family member participated in the laborious process. Finally, the precious oil would be sealed in clay pots before carrying the pots onto the housetops to store them.

Deborah was roused from her thoughts by the smell of smoke. She peered out from behind the tree and stared mutely as panic seized her.

Keziah saw her, and suddenly survival seemed possible. She ignored the pain ripping through her body and lungs as a wave of thick, dark soot and smoldering ashes covered her, singeing her clothes and choking her. She stumbled through the thick stalks of dry wheat, unthinking in her panic as she attempted to push against the tide of dense wheat. All the while, the wave of fire seemed to move like a starving animal, craving its kill.

Deborah's eyes darted to the burning field and her heart raced with her own impotence. *If Keziah made it to the trees she would stand a greater chance of escape The fire would slow down when it reached the wood. Could she help her now? Or, should she take her brother to higher ground as she promised her father? If she stepped into the open field, she would risk endangering Isaac by exposing their whereabouts, and she still had no idea what she could do to help Keziah!*

Isaac began to cough as the smoke irritated his lungs. Decided, she remembered her father's last words and turned to Isaac. "We need to move, can you continue?" He nodded and stood to his feet. Casting one last look back to Keziah, Deborah grabbed Isaac's hand and half-dragged him through the olive grove, until the village was obscured and only Keziah's screams lurched in her mind...

Keziah could feel the heat from the fire now. It was nearer, and it was moving too fast! She looked up to see Deborah running. *"She knows it's hopeless, that I cannot make it,"* she thought as deep, helpless sobs shook her body. She staggered forward, but her body was spent. She collapsed for the last time before the fire seized her dress and the pain enveloped her.

Enoch screamed, his body arching and twisting, as he violently tried to fight off the strong grip of his captors. He freed one arm and used it to elbow one of the guards in the jaw. Enraged, the soldier swung his fist into Enoch's jaw. Rage and grief consumed Enoch. Sisera turned, wearing the same satisfied smirk as he strode over to Enoch.

Amos instinctively ran forward, grabbing Sisera.

"NO, please, it's enough, take my life. Please!"

Without warning, Sisera punched Amos, who crumpled to the ground. The soldier mercilessly delivered kick after kick to him, until no more sound could be heard except the desperate sobs of his wife.

Maya stood, helplessly watching the events unfold. Only an hour ago everything had been fine. She had been resting from the midday sun, eating bread, with her friends Shayna, Raisa and Aaliya and talking about the birth of her first grandchild. This couldn't be happening! Standing watching, futility and despair seeped into her bones and her mind until it possessed her, unable to move, unable to leave.

Sisera pulled his axe from where it rested at his hip and teasingly ran his finger over the blade. As he stepped nearer, Enoch arched his body, using the guard's hold on him to his advantage. He kicked the warrior with both legs. Sisera staggered backward, the smirk leaving his face momentarily. But as he regained his balance, the resolute fury in his eyes left no mistake as to the outcome of his vengeance.

Maya watched as Sisera swung his axe deep into her son's young body, his chest ripped open. His lifeless form fell into a pool of his own blood. Her son, her first born was dead. The darkness mercifully enveloped her.

A stunned silence fell over the village as Sisera wiped the blade of his axe on Enoch's tunic. It was as though time had stopped, the horror of the scene imprinted on their minds as they struggled to make sense of Sisera's words.

"The farmers who have been stolen from will be pleased to know that justice has been served. However, there is still the matter of their financial loss. This village will provide compensation from their harvest in spring and autumn for these farms. I will return in six months. If your recompense is not deemed sufficient, your children will be taken as payment." He nodded to the other soldiers as they stepped onto their chariots, and left.

2

*Then the sons of Israel again did
evil in the sight of the Lord, after
Ehud died. And the Lord sold them into the hand of Jabin King of
Canaan, who reigned in Hazor. Commander of his army was Sisera.
Judges 4:1, 2*

1258 BC - Deborah

Deborah didn't look back until she could no longer hear Keziah's screams. Scrambling up the rocky path, she allowed the desperate rasps of Isaac's breathing to focus her thoughts away from the horror that threatened to master her.

Get to my place, keep Isaac alive' pounded in her mind like a war drum, its rhythm keeping pace with the rise and fall of Isaacs's laboured inhalation.

When she finally saw the looming limestone rock formation, set back slightly from the path, she was bearing most of Isaac's weight.

She looked at Isaac "We are here Isaac. We just need to climb around this rock and you can rest. I can't help you here. Can you make it?"

Isaac nodded weakly "I'll...try," he said, in between rasps of breath.

"Look where I put my feet and follow me."

She pulled herself up, her bare toes instinctively finding the familiar foot holds that had become like her own secret staircase. When she reached the top, she watched as Isaac followed her steps.

"It's easier on the way down," she smiled.

Isaac looked at her, the fear plain in his eyes. "I'm...scared," he wheezed.

"We're nearly there and you can rest, see: climb down to the smaller rock and then you can slide down the rest of the way on your bottom," she encouraged him. But she was scared too. The idea of Isaac dying in her arms, all alone, was too real, too unthinkable. She pushed the thought aside.

Deborah had found her mountain retreat by accident two summers ago. The looming rock face dipped backward, and was overshadowed by a larger rock on the left side and the mountainside on the other. It was only from the other side of the path that one was aware that a type of cave existed. She had always referred to it as her fortress, her place, where she would come to escape family feuds or village politics. But never had she felt the sense of refuge quite as she did today. Clutching Isaac, as he once again fought for his breath, she offered up her silent pleas to Yahweh: "Let him live, please let him live; not him too."

Finally, Isaac's breathing softened to a gentle whistle, and as his body relaxed in her arms, she acknowledged that he had fallen asleep.

She wondered how long they must wait until someone came for them? Her mind was turbulent with anxiety for her village, and ravaged by the memory of Keziah's screams. Huge tears rolled down her face, and she felt the pressure in her chest build as grief and fear assailed her. Desperately, she forced her thoughts to change direction; to journey back to the safety of her memories. She recalled last year's Feast of Tabernacles, when the first fruits of their harvest were offered to the Lord at Shiloh…

Deborah smiled sadly, remembering how Enoch, betrothed to Keziah, had been miserable at their separation. The ten-mile journey had been a happy blur of laughter and chatter with fellow pilgrims taking the same mountain path toward the holy city. She recalled her mother pointing out the old terebinth tree of Deborah, who had been Jacob's nurse, the daughter of Uz, the son of Aram, the descendant of Shem, her mother's ancestor and Deborah's name-sake. She mentioned it every year without fail, but Deborah didn't mind. She loved to be reminded of her heritage.

The road rose to meet the busy market that sprawled outside the city walls, spilling out of the gates to greet the bustling throng of visitors who sought to enter the city. Heckling stall holders and livestock mixed with the praises of the priests and Levites as their voices rose in a holy chorus that trickled down the crowded streets.

The Feast of Tabernacles was a holy convocation in which the Lord had told Moses that every male should appear before him (though many had not observed this ordinance since the days of Joshua).

Deborah looked forward to seeing relatives and friends that she had not seen for a year. As they built their *sukkot*, bringing olive, myrtle and palm branches from the forests to roof their temporary homes, they chattered and sang, remembering their relatives' wilderness years and the Lord's faithfulness in bringing them into the Promised Land. In the evenings, having offered their first fruits at the temple, they would sit around open fires, feasting, talking, singing and laughing as they thanked Yahweh for the harvest. Finally, they wearily snuggled up in their *sukkot* with their families, peering through the leafy branches as heaven seemed to gaze back at them.

Deborah was reminded of that day, the fifth day of Tabernacles. She had grown weary of the busy chatter that surrounded the celebrations and yearned for the quiet mountains of her home where she could disappear to 'her place'.

Her mother was discussing items they would purchase from Shiloh's market with her friends, Raisa and Aaliyah. When Deborah had asked if she could take a walk, her mother had smiled, understanding her daughter's need for her own space, but reminding her not to venture too far. Deborah had wound her way through the maze of *sukkot*, people, fires, animals and water jugs until she came to the grassy slopes, dotted with sheep and goats lazily grazing in the gentle autumn warmth.

Running across the parched grass, she felt elated to be away from the crowds and slowed only when she began her ascent up the rocky hillside. Almond, fig, sycamore, oak and terebinth trees were scattered across the terrain, which became denser as she climber higher. She popped a couple of ripe figs into her pocket, and was soon lost in her own sense of wonder and adventure, heedless as to where she was going.

She paused at a spring that gushed out of the rocks, dancing down its own rocky path before disappearing back from whence it came. Thirstily, she placed her mouth under the fountain, letting the ice cold water run over her face and down her throat. It suddenly occurred to her that she had lost all sense of time, and as she had searched for the sun through the trees, she realised that it was well past its midday climb. She ought to begin her way back lest she get caught in the dark.

Hit by sudden anxiety, she tried to recall the direction of her travel. If she could see over the trees, back to their camp then she would know which way to walk, but she didn't want to walk further up the mountain and risk getting more lost. Fighting the urge to panic she decided that climbing a tree was possibly the wisest thing to do, giving her a better view. She picked one with low branches and, hitching her dress, she effortlessly pulled herself up the first few branches. As she reached out for the next branch, her acknowledgement that her hand had gripped something other than the tree and the unexpected stab of pain were almost simultaneous. Looking to see what had caused the pain she saw the snake, its zigzag patterns on its scaled back rubbing together, forming a rattling war chant as it prepared to attack again. Her only thought of retreat, Deborah lost her footing and fell from the tree, hitting the branches on her descent.

She recalled that moment, where her death had seemed inevitable. She had been unable to put any weight on her left foot, and her hand had already begun swelling. What she had really wanted to do was sit down and cry, but as her adrenalin raced, her desperate desire to survive overcame her fear. She found a stick she could use as a crutch, acknowledging that she needed to find help quickly, and that she stood more chance of finding help at the bottom of the mountain. She painfully began her descent, and it was not long before she had started to shiver uncontrollably and weakness overcame her. She recalled the sickening fear of seeing blood oozing from the wound, and the taste of it seeping from her gums.

When she fell to the floor, futility and fear overwhelmed her. She drew her knees up to her chest, wishing only to see her mother and father. As her feverish thoughts consumed her, she waited for death to enfold her, praying that somehow Yahweh might still save her.

And then, in the midst of the dark nightmares that took hold of her, she had been aware of a voice, as though from far away and arms beneath her, lifting her.

Her family had remained in Shiloh for two weeks, while she regained her strength. Initially, she had floated in and out of a fevered delirium, faintly aware of her parents' desperate prayers as they battled for her life. And then, in her darkest hour, she felt hands resting on her head, infusing her with life and pulling her back from the abyss upon which she teetered.

After three days, she opened her eyes and saw her mother's face, weary and tear stained, smiling as she leaned over her. She stroked Deborah's hair. "Welcome back, darling. You've given us all quite a scare."

Deborah weakly returned her mother's smile. "I'm glad to see you again... I prayed...I was so scared...I thought I would die."

Her mother nodded as tears poured freely down her cheeks. "You were found just in time."

Fragmented memories skittered across Deborah's mind as she tried to recall her rescue.

Responding to her thoughts, her mother explained: "Lapidoth found you – he had been searching for wood. His grandparents live here and they let us stay. They've been so kind."

"How did they find you?"

"When you didn't return, we were worried. We began looking for you. Well... word travels quickly amongst our people, as you know. It wasn't long before we heard you were here."

The door opened, and a woman around her mother's age bustled into the room. She introduced herself as Hannah, Lapidoth's mother, and talked incessantly as she packed a poultice of maidenhair fern and honey on her hand. In the first few days of her recovery, Deborah would feel exhausted by the time she left the room.

Lapidoth came to visit her twice. She estimated him to be a few years older than herself, closer to Enoch's age. His voice had broken and his shoulders slouched slightly, as though he was not yet used to his sudden growth and he had a mop of curly black hair that fell across his eyes. On the first occasion, she had been barely conscious. After the fourth day, she had been able to sit up.

"How are you feeling now?" He smiled, an easy, warm smile, pushing his hair carelessly out of his deep, brown eyes.

"Much better. Still a bit shaky, but better every day." She returned his smile nervously. "I don't remember much about being found. But thank you...you know...for saving my life..." She shook her head, as though to clear her embarrassment at the memory.

He shrugged. "You must be tough. It was a miracle, really - it looks like it was a saw-scaled viper. He frowned, his curiosity getting the better of him.

"Did it have zig-zag patterns on its back and make a rattling sound?"

"Yes, I think so. Is that important?"

"No, probably not. " He smiled apologetically. "I was just curious.... But it does make your survival more incredible," he admitted, suddenly seeming lost in his own thoughts.

The memory of her despair and her last desperate prayer surfaced in her consciousness. "My memories are so vague; it's hard to recall what was real and what was part of my nightmares. But, there was a point I felt Yahweh near to me, and I knew, even in that place of darkness, I would survive."

Lapidoth seemed thoughtful, as though considering his response.

"Well, you've certainly created a bit of excitement in Shiloh," he chuckled.

Deborah rolled her eyes. "I'm delighted my near death experience has enlivened people's otherwise dreary lives."

His eyes shone mischievously. "Of course, you'll need to find something better to do on your next visit."

"I've got a year to work on it, maybe an encounter with a wild mountain lion?" she grinned.

"That's fine." His eyes glinted playfully. "Although I'd like to make clear my responsibilities in our heroic escapades: I rescue you *after* you have been mauled and the lion has left."

Deborah sighed with mock disappointment. "I clearly need to look for a new rescuer."

"...or a less dangerous scenario," Lapidoth suggested, catching her eyes as they laughed.

Throughout her delirium, she had been vaguely aware of prayers around her. She later discovered the faces behind these voices: Lapidoth's grandfather, Josiah, an elderly man with a bushy grey beard bent low over a walking stick. Yet he clearly carried great authority in the family. He had a serious disposition that was not without compassion. He had spent a life devoted to making torches to service the tabernacle, a trade he had passed on to his sons. Lapidoth's father, Abinoam, being the second son, had not taken over from his father when he retired but married a Naphtalite and sold torches to the public. Lapidoth's grandmother, Yemina, was a tiny lady, with a gentle spirit but a shrewdness that immediately warmed Deborah to her. Abinoam and Hannah had been visiting from Kedesh in Naphtali, Hannah's home town for the Feast.

A week into her convalescence, she was introduced by Isaac to Rebecca, Ruth and 'little' Josiah, Lapidoth's younger sisters and brother. They had been banned for the first week, and had been desperate to see their mystery guest. Isaac burst in first, throwing himself on Deborah. "I missed you so much. We were so worried about you."

She ruffled his hair. "It's lovely to see you, too! Do you have some friends to introduce me to?" she laughed; the three children heads peered cautiously around the door, as though their visitor might be a dangerous predator, waiting to pounce. Rebecca, the oldest girl, smiled shyly. She was the same age as Deborah, but had a more timid disposition. Turning back to her younger siblings, she whispered to them before they promptly tumbled into the room.

Ruth, at ten years old, looked like she had been in a fight. Her hair and clothes were askew and she seemed like she would burst with excitement. Deborah was immediately drawn to her. Josiah, the youngest of the children at eight years old, stood with his back straight and his hands behind his back, clearly doing his best to seem grown-up and sensible, although Deborah's suspicious nature was inclined to think he was hiding something behind his back.

"Hello," Deborah said. It was nice to see children her own age again; she had begun to feel bored now that she was feeling better. But her legs were still unpredictable in their strength and so she had grudgingly obeyed her mother's orders to rest.

Ruth strode impulsively forward and sat on the side of Deborah's bed. "Is it really true you were bitten by a snake?"

"Yes, it's true," Deborah laughed.

"Can I see it? How did it feel?" Ruth quizzed.

"Ruth!" Rebecca scolded, looking embarrassed, and a little curious.

"How did it happen?" Josiah asked, his little face screwing up in horrified curiosity.

The three children listened in awe as Deborah dramatically expounded her adventure and near death experience. When she had finished, she felt exhausted, and Rebecca sensitively began to usher her siblings out of the room. A moment later, she poked her head back around the door.

"Oh! I forgot! Grandmother thought you might like to join us for dinner this evening, if you feel well enough."

"I'd love to," Deborah yawned, determined to leave the confines of her room, despite her weariness.

Over the next week, Deborah grew slowly stronger. Her parents forged a strong friendship with Abinoam's family. Lapidoth had taught her brother how to make pitchers for torches, and how to mould the clay and fire it so that it did not crack in the heat. Deborah began to see the flickering traces of maturity in her headstrong, irresponsible brother.

She loved shopping at the market with her mother, Hannah and Rebecca, who taught her the best places to shop and how to barter with the stall keepers. Isaac had become inseparable from Ruth and Josiah; the three of them would play together all day, only returning for prayer and meal times. During the latter, they would conspiratorially huddle together, making plans for their next great conquest.

"Today, we will go to the Tabernacle of Meeting," her father exclaimed. "We will offer a burnt offering to thank Him for the life of my daughter." Enoch had chosen to go with Lapidoth.

They went first to the market, where her father picked a lamb, inspecting it thoroughly before he handed over his money.

"Without blemish, we give Yahweh our best." He smiled, ruffling Isaacs's hair as he stared with wide eyed curiosity.

They paused before the tabernacle and a shiver ran down Deborah's spine. She was filled with a sense of reverent awe. She looked at the pale linen panels, the bronze pillars and silver sockets that held such mystery. The day was still young and as they approached the entrance, the first rays of the morning sun lingered symbolically over the ornately woven panels that were upheld by four pillars.

Her father spoke softly, as though the very air around them was holy. "Yahweh told Moses: 'My presence will go before you and I will dwell among you... I will give you rest and show you my goodness.' This is our inheritance, children, if we obey his word."

"Why four pillars?" Isaac asked, with childlike interest as they stepped into the outer court.

Amos smiled as though he was delighted with the question.

"Yahweh gave Moses exact instructions as to how he was to make the tabernacle, and every detail had a special meaning. Four is the universal number: Yahweh desires that all should come to him. We are his chosen people, but He loves all men, never forget that. Yahweh provided the plan, the people provided the materials and He filled Bezaleel with His spirit to create the Tabernacle. It begins and ends with Yahweh." He pointed to the elaborate panels that formed the entrance to the court. "It is a beautiful interwoven relationship, in which every thread is vital and held in place by his great design and love." Inside the courtyard, many knelt, worshiping Yahweh. They approached the brazen altar, and the priest smiled kindly at

Deborah as her father showed them how to place their hands on the head of the lamb.

"The lamb is a substitute for us. Our sin separates us from Yahweh, because He is holy. The price of sin is death and the life of the flesh is in the blood. This lamb will die today in our place so that we can live for Yahweh."

Tears ran down Deborah's face as she acknowledged what must be done. Her father grimaced as he slit the lamb's throat and the priest caught the blood that flowed into a bowl. To Deborah's disgust, the priest then sprinkled the blood around the altar.

Amos put his arms around the shoulders of his children. "Remember the story of Passover: the blood of the Lamb. It is shed for our sins, and the angel of death passed over."

Deborah and Isaac nodded somberly, watching with both awe and morbid curiosity as the priest skinned the animal and then dissected it.

"What's he doing?" Isaac asked, his nose wrinkled in disgust.

The priest spoke as he worked. "The sacrifice must be perfect, not only outwardly, but inwardly. Yahweh judges the thoughts and intents of our hearts and minds, not only our behaviour. Each part of the animal is representative." He examined the head and placed it to one side.

"The head represents the mind and intellect."

He lifted the inner organs. "The will and affections." His eyes turned to heaven.

Next he held up the legs. "Our outward walk and conduct."

Finally the fat. "The health and virility."

"It is the consecration of all we are, offered to Yahweh," he continued.

"It is perfect; a worthy sacrifice for Almighty God." The priest spoke softly, his worn eyes were kind. And then he placed each part onto the fire of the altar.

"Your offering is a sweet sacrifice to Yahweh," he smiled.

Deborah imagined the aroma of the burnt offering, its smoke bleeding with the chants of the priests into the wispy pink clouds of autumn. She heard her father thank Yahweh for his daughter's survival, and she slipped to her knees, reverently looking at the tent raised at the back of the courtyard. She knew that only the priests could serve ensuring the golden lampstand, lit by Yahweh and maintained by the priests, never went out. The table of showbread and the table of incense also stood here, where the sacred mix of spices were offered to the Lord. Beyond that was The Most Holy Place, where the Ark of the Covenant and the mercy seat resided. Her heart yearned for the presence of Yahweh once again.

Deborah had no idea how long she had sat without moving, but the sun had almost retreated to its place of rest and the sky was blood red, streaked with the first signs that darkness would soon settle over the land.

She was roused by the sound of voices. Leaping to her feet, adrenalin reacted to her state of shock; her responses were instinctive, driven by her will to protect and survive. Frantically, she looked around her whilst her panicked mind tried to focus on what she needed to do. Isaac stirred in his sleep, moaning.

Mechanically, her heart pounding, Deborah reached for a rock which she tucked into the folds of her dress before climbing silently to the top of the rock face. She could hear men's voices approaching, but the fading light made them impossible to distinguish. She realised they were speaking Hebrew only moments before the reality of what they were saying hit her: "…Let them come back to the village first…they'll be tired and hungry," Gershon suggested, his eyes drawn into their customary frown.

"We can't let them see their father this way." Hillel's shoulders were slumped, weighted by the tragedy of the day.

"Menachem has offered to look after them tonight. I'm more concerned about telling them what has happened to Enoch and Keziah." Gershon replied grimly.

"Enoch!" Deborah said, as her mind stumbled and then floundered on the truth: "NO! Not Enoch!!"

With that she lost her footing and slid clumsily, down the rock face, scratching her back as she did so and landing painfully in front of the two men. She looked up at them, as icy shards of shock stormed her senses. Then she broke down, pulling her knees into her chest, willing the world to recede, to discover that none of this had been real…it couldn't be…

While Hillel went for Isaac, Gershon sat down quietly beside her, his arms around her. He said nothing. He knew that there was nothing to be said that could help with the pain she must feel.

Darkness had swallowed the village, only the faintest glow of light spilled from the mud and daub houses. Everyone seemed reluctant to turn them out this evening, as though they represented the very hope and life of the village. The sense of despair and loss seemed like a physical cloud that had sunk, like a winter mist: entering homes and clinging to its occupants so that their very hearts ached with its chill. The quiet sound of tired, strained voices drifted into the night air as people struggled to contemplate sleeping, when their future suddenly seemed so bleak.

As they reached the first house, Deborah was aware that they were not walking towards her family's hut. An inexplicable feeling of deep unease began to grow within her.

Tobias came out to meet them. He exchanged an unspoken message with his son, Gershon, as he placed his hands on the children's shoulders.

"We think it is best if you go to Menachem's home tonight. You'll be needing something to eat, drink and then some sleep and…your father was hurt and needs to rest. Your mother is with him." His eyes were lined with compassion and sorrow.

Isaac spoke first, his voice trembling as he asked: "Hurt?"

"What do you mean hurt?" Deborah probed, the panic barely restrained in her own voice.

"He was very brave. He tried to save Enoch…The Canaanite soldiers hurt him. He will take a while to get better, that's all, and your mother and Raisa are with him now…He'll be fine…but he needs rest and you need rest, too, and some food."

"And Mama?" asked Deborah tentatively, her unease growing.

Tobias paused, a little too long. "She's fine, very tired and…shocked, of course…It's been such a terrible day…" His voice trailed off as if he was drawn back involuntarily into his own nightmare of the day's events.

Menachem's wife, Nissa, came to the door. She pulled them into her arms and held them for a moment before drawing them into her home.

That night, Deborah slept fitfully, her dreams filled with screams, fire and terror as she desperately strove to outrun the grimacing, bronzed face of Baal. As he stood over her, his sword drawn above his head, she mercifully awoke, her heart racing and her body trembling. She tentatively touched the rough walls of their wattle and daub home, grounding herself in reality as she tried to find that place of peace: to find Yahweh as she had known him before. But a gnawing sense of doubt battled against her experience of Yahweh as loving and powerful, silenced only by the promise: *Abba will know. He'll make sense of it.*

The next day, Isaac and Deborah were allowed to visit their parents. Her father's face was cut and swollen, his left eye was completely closed under blue and purple bruises and strips of cloth lay over his body. He lay curled on his side, laying so still and looking so frail, Deborah feared his spirit had left him. Suddenly, his legs twitched and Maya, who sat at his bed side, fell to her knees beside him, clutching his hand.

"Abba" Isaac spoke, the shock in his voice evident.

Deborah stood motionless as though assimilating the destruction of her family: her mother, her eyes hopeless and desperate. Enoch: dead. Isaac's voice beside her.

Maya stood, tears rolling freely down her face. She looked at Raisa, hoping to draw some strength from her friend as she bent to embrace her children.

"He'll be fine, you'll see. He'll be fine."

But he wasn't fine. Two days later, his spirit left his broken body, and it seemed to Deborah that her mother departed with him; though her body remained warm, she no longer engaged with this life but sat pale, her eyes staring into an empty world of desiderium.

It was agreed that Amos, Enoch and Keziah's bodies should be buried together in a cave near their family home. According to law this needed to be done immediately. It had been delayed already due to Amos' deteriorating health.

The grief and loss that saturated the village was nothing compared with the guilt and gratitude: that they had survived. Her mother laid 'the knife' next to her son's lifeless, bloodied body. She bent double, huge sobs racking her body as she knelt before their bodies. A future without them was inconceivable, stretching before her like a long dark road, bleak and futile – if she could have remained in the tomb, she would have, but a small part of her mind acknowledged that Deborah and Isaac still needed her.

Deborah stood beside her, wrapping her arms around her brother as though she could shield him from his loss. She felt numb, as though everything had stopped inside of her. She was watching the events unfold, her mother's cries, her brother shaking in her arms. The sun that would not venture into the depths of the cave, but blast down its unsolicited fury. The grass, verdurous and still, while a lamb gently bleated for sustenance from its mother. As the stones were piled over the cave mouth, the finality of her loss hit her: *never* to feel her father's arms around her, or hear his stories, his gentle laugh and reassuring eyes telling her that her world was safe. Never. She recalled how Enoch, Isaac and she would run through the forest to escape the heat of the summer and would throw themselves into the stream. Enoch, never content to simply languish, would splash them and duck their heads under the water. She could hear their laughter now, its painful vibrations scorched the lining of her soul, but she would not give her pain a voice, for she was terrified of falling over a precipice of her own grief and there would be no one to catch her. She must be there for her mother and Isaac.

The village drew around them, their own tears falling freely as they sought to comfort her family. Her friend, Miriam, came and took her hand - but even touch seemed uncomfortable. "…It is with the greatest sadness that we lay our beloved family and friends, Amos, Enoch, Keziah and their unborn child, to rest with their fathers. May Yahweh lead us through this difficult time with His mercies and wisdom…May You forgive us our sins and show Your servants the path of righteousness to lead Your people forward through this dark and uncertain time." Her uncle's words picked holes in her deadened mind, like vermin in the roof of a house that filled her with a deep sense of unease.

In those first early days, the responsibility fell to Deborah to look after Isaac and her mother. Whilst many brought food gifts and offers of help, their village had changed - life was harder now - every able-bodied person was needed to farm the land. The realisation that next winter would be a harsh one, and the threat of the children being taken into captivity had changed the attitude in the village. There was a gradual shift that grew without anyone really noticing it. It was fuelled by a primal fight for survival and protection of one's own. Deborah acknowledged that their goal had changed: no longer were they living for Yahweh, but living to survive - and within that reality, cracks emerged in their tight knit community.

There was no leader in the village now, which added to the uncertainty of their existence. Although Tobias would never have suggested that he desired, or would accept the position, many felt he should assume the role: he had been Amos' best friend and confidant, and had the maturity and compassion that made him an obvious choice. However, Deborah's uncle, Jared, asserted his claim as Amos' next of kin. His wife Shelimoth, the stronger character in the relationship, was clearly the unseen hand that pushed for her husband's rule. Jared was younger than her father by three years. He had a mop of wild grey hair and thick eyebrows that met in the middle. He reminded Deborah of a storm cloud, and had the disposition to match. His wife, Shelimoth, was a head taller than Jared, both physically and in temperament. It was clearly she who pushed for Jared's leadership, and she who would lead the village if Jared were accepted. Aunt Shelimoth, with her religious fervor that lacked all compassion, was fuelled by her own need for control.

3

After him (Ehud) was Shamgar the son of Anath…
Judges 3:31

1253 BC - Shamgar

Shamgar plunged his head into the water trough. The summer heat was already upon him, and he still had to drive the ox another *parasang* until he reached home. He began to imagine the faces of his children, standing at the end of the dirt track, waiting for him. He wondered if he would see them there. And Sarai, his beautiful wife, her long dark hair, tied back under her head covering, as she ran to greet him. Stripping to his waist, he splashed the water over his body before tying back his thick mane of red hair. His beard had grown during his absence. Sarai would laugh and tell him he looked like a fiery lion. He grinned, suddenly missing her infectious joy and warm nature. He put his tunic back on and set to work, rounding up the oxen, prodding them with his goad until they were all moving north. He had stayed clear of the Patriarchs Highway, a road he would have used a few years ago. It had become notorious for bandits and robbers, and whilst he was confident of his ability in battle, he would not risk the cattle.

He thought of his father, Anath, a Canaanite warrior, and how he had made him train day after day with sword and lance until he had defeated his teacher. As his father's third son, he had not been forced to follow a military career. His mother had been a Hebrew, taken in the spoils of war. But his father had loved her and had allowed her to teach their children Hebrew law; she had died giving birth to his youngest sister several years ago. When the time came for him to find a wife, he had taken Sarai, also a Hebrew; partly out of respect for his mother and her God, but also some deeper conviction in the authority of this god over others. In the ten years of their marriage, he had taken the Hebrew faith as his own, even submitting himself to the unpleasant ordeal of circumcision. He winced grimly at the memory. Yahweh's demonstrations of faith were definitely not for the fainthearted, nor the undecided, he concluded.

His farm was outside of Beit Shemesh, a Canaanite city, named after the sun god, who legend said had once worshipped there. When the Israelites invaded they took it as their own and set it apart for their priests and forcing the Canaanites and Philistines into the hill country. In recent years, their religious fervor had waned and they had become more accepting of their neighbours, particularly in relation to the trade and affluence that they brought. His father, a retired general, owned a large property on the side of the hill and had become a respected member of the city council. Due to its proximity to the northern border of Judah and Canaan, it attracted a mixed culture. In recent years intermarriage had become more and more common and so, too, a tolerance and compromise of each other's beliefs.
Shamgar saw smoke rising on the horizon ahead of him. At first he dismissed it as domestic use. But as he drew nearer, a sense of foreboding rose within him, thick and suffocating as the black smoke that filled the air. It was too big to be a cooking fire. He quickened his pace, driving the cattle at a run, as anxiety induced adrenalin coursed through his body.

Before him stood the remnant of his home. He stood momentarily incapacitated as snarling red flames wrapped around the exposed beams, engulfing them until they collapsed. Then he saw Sarai, half naked, beaten, and her throat slit. Near to her were the bodies of two of his servants. He fell to his knees, roaring with rage and grief as he clasped her broken body to his own. As he stood, deep guttural cries tore their way from his gut as he called the names of his children. He stumbled, consumed with fear and grief as he repeated their names. And then he saw a small form lying some distance away, as though he had tried to run, three arrows protruded from his back. He removed the barbed arrows, and lifted his son, Samuel's, lifeless form in his arms before placing him next to his wife. Hearing a scream he spun. It was coming from the house.

"Manoah!"

The scream sounded again, this time from where the bedroom had been. Another beam crashed to the ground sending sparks and ash billowing into the air. Panic and hope warred within Shamgar. He called again. This time, there was no response. He grabbed the old tunic he had taken off earlier that day, and plunging it into the water trough, wrapped it over his face and hair. The heat besieged his flesh before he even entered the house, but his desperation drove him in. Unable to see through the thick smoke, he allowed his knowledge and intuition to lead him to where he thought he had heard the sound.

"Manoah!" he cried again.

Nothing sounded back. He sobbed as hopelessness began to take hold of him. And then, a small figure emerged through a doorway. A beam creaked overhead.

"Abba?"

"Manoah!" Covering the gap between them, he threw his eight-year old son over his shoulder and ran through the house as the timber beam collapsed behind him.

Shamgar carried his son out, carefully avoiding the bodies of his brother and mother. "Your sisters, are they in there?" he coughed, gasping air into his burning, smoke-filled lungs.

Manoah shook his head, tears marking a path through his soot-stained face. Shamgar read the fear in his son's eyes before he spoke.

"Philistines…took them. I saw them, I saw them hurt Mama and kill Samuel." Shamgar's body shook with emotion as he held his sobbing son in his arms; there were no words of consolation that would not be empty.

Shamgar swore under his breath, the blood burning hot in his veins as he thought of his two daughters in the hands of the soldiers. He swallowed tears of impotent rage and fear for what his daughters would be going through if they were still alive.

"Manoah, how long ago were they here?"

Manoah was silent for a moment. His young son seemed to age before him as he relived the last few hours. Finally, he spoke. "When the sun was at its highest." Shamgar pulled his son into his arms.

He debated what to do; he needed to bury his wife and son and yet he was aware that every moment he lost lessened his daughters' chances of survival. He decided on a quick, temporary burial.

"Manoah, I need you to stay here while I bury them. Promise me. I won't be long."

Panic flooded Manoah's deep brown eyes "Don't leave me! Let me go with you."

Shamgar stroked the hair away from his son's face, noting the amber eyes; his mother's eyes. "I need you to be brave. I won't be far. I need to honour your mother and brother and the servants. I don't want you to see them now. The Philistines are gone now, but if they came back you could call me and I'd be there."

Manoah nodded, drawing his knees up to his chest and wrapping his arms around them.

Shamgar quickly buried the bodies under a heap of stones - remains from their home – and secured the cattle in the fenced paddock. He would return once he had found the girls, and give them a proper burial.

He quickly found the tracks and determined that the group had headed to Gezer. Gezer, positioned at the crossroads of the Via Maris and other important trade routes, including the Great Sea, was a strategic city of trade. Historically, it had known the rule of Canaan, Egypt, Philistia and Israel. Israel, acknowledging Gezer's prominence and Canaan's economic dominance and skill, had allowed them and the other nations to dwell in the city. With the desire to maintain their own spiritual purity, Israel had largely made their own occupancy outside of Gezer, only holding government in the city. Now that Canaan's power in Ephraim was restored, the Hebrews had largely fled to the hills.

Shamgar slung his bag with water bottle over his shoulder, grabbed his ox-goad and lifting Manoah onto his back, he began to run.

4

They went and served other gods and worshiped them, gods whom they have not known and whom He had not allotted to them.
Deuteronomy 29:26

1257 BC - Deborah

As the days grew slowly longer, Deborah worked harder than she had ever known possible, driven by the need to survive and protect her mother and brother. She spent hours, searching for herbs and wild vegetables on the mountains and tending their small garden patch. She would wake early, lighting their fire, grinding the wheat and mixing it with water she had collected from the well. Afterwards she would sweep the beaten clay floor before going to help the other members of her village farm the land and tend the animals.

She worked silently, as though frightened she might unleash the torrent of emotion that she had locked within. And so she ignored her inner screams by observing those around her, all the while seeking to understand what was happening to her world. Deborah noted what pain did to people: many sank into their own dark worlds, compromising their faith to cope with the difficulties, and looked after themselves and their own. Others locked themselves behind the high walls of their religious zeal that left no room to help others. A few clung to Yahweh with desperate and honest vulnerability, and found the strength to open their world to any who needed them.

She was about to pass the courtyard of Shayna's house. Shayna's daughter, Batia,fourteen years old, was talking to Hagar's son, Edom, a year her senior. They were behind the wall, and their low voices drifted through the still heat of the morning air.

"Ima says Enoch brought this on the village and that if Amos had dealt with him more sternly, Sisera would never have had reason to come."

There was a pause, as though Edom was deliberating on his response. "Seems the family has paid for his mistake."

"It's not just his family though, it's all of us. What happens if we don't have a good harvest? And where were Deborah and Isaac when it all happened? Amos had the good sense to send them to the mountains. It was selfish at best."

Deborah felt the venom of Batia's words spread through her mind. The worst part was their truth. The acknowledgement that her family had inadvertently caused the suffering of their village and the others Sisera had visited was too horrendous to consider. Did all the village feel this way? Edom had seemed hesitant to place blame, hadn't he? She felt herself shrink inwardly. Suddenly she felt no right to the grief that she felt, and the blame and accusation of Batia and Shayna's words formed a wall that alienated her from many in her village. She resolved to find a way to make amends and to restore her family name.

She popped her head through the door-opening of Raisa and Tobias' home. Due to her age and ailing health, Raisa had been excused from working in the fields, but instead watched over the young children, while their parents worked. She was sat with Judah, Hannah, Eber, Isaac, Tebah and Gabriella, telling them the story of Abraham, when Deborah passed. She looked up and smiled. Deborah noted how tired she looked.

"Are you ok, honey bee?"

"Yes thank you." Deborah didn't mean to lie; she just didn't want to talk about how she felt, and neither did she want to add to Raisa's burden. She had spent the day pulling weeds out from between the fledgling plants and watering them and was exhausted, with the only relief being her lack of time to think.

There had been very little wheat left after the fire, and what there had been was sown as seed for next year's much needed harvest. Fortunately, the barley harvest had been taken in and stored before Sisera came.

Rekindling the fire from the morning, Deborah began the labour-intensive process of grinding the barley until it was in fine, powder form. Then, mixing it with water, she formed them into small, round balls before placing them in the oven. Her mother and Isaac would return soon, and they would be hungry. She collected firewood and refilled the water bucket from the well, fighting the fatigue that dragged on her feet and weighted her eyelids.

"Deborah. I was just coming to find you."

Deborah smiled, turning to see Nissa standing next to her, holding a plate of food.

"I made your family some pistachio cakes." Nissa smiled. She had been married to Menachem for five years now and as yet they had no children. She bore her longing by reaching out to those around her.

Deborah hugged her, and the silent message behind the act sent a warm glow thorough her heart. "Thanks Nissa, you are the most beautiful person I know. Menachem is so blessed to have you for a wife."

Nissa blushed. "So he tells me." She smiled sadly, and then brushed the thought aside, aware of all that Deborah had been through. She took her young friend's hands in her own.

"You are beautiful, too, Deborah. You have a sense of greatness about you. When I look at you, I often wonder what you will do in your life. We are here for you and your family. Know that."

Two faces peered around the corner of the door opening; it was Asher and Edom, Hagar's son and Shayna's son.

"Hello, sorry to interrupt. Our grandparents wondered if you would like to share dinner with us tonight. It's deer. Abba caught it today in a trap," Asher announced.

"We'd love to. Thank you," Deborah answered. Meat had become something of a rarity, and though she found social occasions uncomfortable of late, she knew that Isaac and her mother would welcome the company as well as the food.

During the evening, it was announced that Reuben and Shayna were expecting another child. Everyone congratulated them; the idea of new life entering the village was seen as Yahweh's blessing upon them.

Summer's morning chorus awoke Deborah. She sat up, taking small pleasure in those moments before the rest of the world stirred: when she was alone. In those moments, the air seemed fresh and alive and whispered the promise of a new day. She moved quietly, desperate not to wake her mother or brother and made her way past her aunt and uncle's home to the village centre. She lowered her bucket into the well, drawing it as she had a thousand times before.

As she again passed her aunt and uncle's home, she heard their hushed voices. She peered in, ready to greet them, but they had their backs to her. They were leaning over something. She knew it was wrong to spy on them, but her curiosity got the better of her. She ducked as Ariel moved from the courtyard to join her parents. When she looked up again, she saw the three of them bowed before a statue of Baal, Dagon and Asherah.

She leaned against the wall of their home, catching her breath. *Surely she must have mistaken what she saw? Surely Abba's brother would not serve Baal? For how long had he been doing this and were there others in the village?* She felt giddy, as though the foundations of her world were crumbling faster than she could adapt.

"May El, the great and almighty bless us. Oh great El, help us to lead this village and grant us the wisdom and authority, as you did Joshua and Moses. Baal, may you bless our harvest and turn your servant Sisera from our path." Shelimoth's whispered voice rose to a furious crescendo while Jared grunted his agreement.

"Praise their holy names," the three agreed.

"As we offer our sacrifice, may you bless our harvest." Deborah heard liquid being poured, and her mind spun as she sought to contain her fury. Her father had died to protect the village from Canaan, and now her uncle invited it into their midst. Her chest felt tight with emotion and hot tears stung her eyes.

There was a shuffling sound as Shelimoth hid the statues.

"I think you need to address the village, Jared., They are lost and looking for direction. The hand of almighty El, our great lord, is clearly upon you. Now is your time to lead his sheep."

"Shelimoth…I'm not sure people are ready for a leader. My brother was greatly respected. I am not my brother." Deborah wondered if she detected reluctance or bitterness in Jared's hesitation, possibly both.

Shelimoth sighed impatiently. "No, you are not your brother, but he is dead and the village will not survive another encounter with Sisera if someone doesn't organise them. He will be here in six months, whether we do nothing or prepare. What makes more sense to you?"

"I'll speak to them," Jared sighed.

Shelimoth's voice softened. "The village is in shock and chaos. They need you as Amos' brother to lead them now. When the village is saved by your brilliant leadership, they will naturally look to you."

Deborah crept away. She felt as though a stone had been dropped into her soul, and she was drowning as the truth of its inevitable consequence sunk within her. And the question that reverberated in her mind: *what should she do? What could she do? Who would listen to her?*

Leaving the water bucket outside their home, she peered in the window opening of their home. Her mother was still sleeping. Like Deborah, her dreams had been troubled; she moaned in her sleep and often woke up sobbing or screaming. It was hard seeing her mother so distressed. She had always been so strong and optimistic about life.

Feeling suddenly overwhelmed, Deborah slipped into the covering of the trees, winding her way downward to the brook. She broke into a run, partly because her mood dictated it, but more because she was desperate to find Yahweh and His peace. The brook that would be deep enough to swim in come autumn, was shallow. She dipped her feet in, its coolness acting as a balm. Then she splashed the water over her face, before leaning back against a sycamore, her eyes closed.

"Yahweh," It was a whisper that echoed the scream in her heart. She waited silently until…He was there, and the air around her became still, yet fused with energy. She wrestled for a few moments with the angst and confusion within. She knew Yahweh wasn't blind to what was happening in her village – she felt no need to tell Him. But it helped to say it out loud. And when she had finished, she waited until His answer came.

"Wait… and pray."

When her uncle called a meeting of the village, she knew what would be said. The atmosphere was subdued. Nobody wanted Jared to lead them, but nobody had the conviction, or the cruelty, to tell him otherwise. He had been Amos' brother, and people felt a loyalty to his memory.

Shelimoth nudged Jared, who cleared his throat nervously. "I have called you all together to discuss how we will deal with the return of the Canaanites. I am suggesting we organise working parties; we will need to work harder, with the destruction of the wheat fields. We will then put most of the produce into a central store house, but each family is to take some and hide it on their roof, or in their homes. That way, if Sisera and his men empty the storehouse we will not be left to starve come winter. Does this seem good to everyone?"

The logic of his argument was obvious, even to Deborah, and so it was agreed upon.

As the work load increased, people's energy and focus were consumed with the need for a good harvest and the fear of the Canaanite return. Deborah worked her mother's shift as well as her own; she was still not well enough to take on responsibility and Jared insisted everyone needed to do their share. When she finally collapsed into bed each night, she would fall into a deep sleep, only occasionally awoken by nightmares.

Isaac was the one person who had the ability to penetrate her world. She smiled as he came toward her, with his usual lightness of spirit. She envied him that. He grinned and bending down next to her, he began to help pull weeds from the soil around the young pea plants.

"Have you heard about Shayna and Hagar?" he said, referring to Tobias and Raisa's daughter and daughter-in-law.

"There's not much that gets missed in a small village."

Shayna's patience has been a little unpredictable since she had Ephraim. "I heard Ima speaking to Raisa. Apparently she's not sleeping and Raisa said 'at her age', it's hard work with a baby and big family. " Deborah smiled grimly, recalling their heated debate.

Isaac gave a snort of agreement. "She snapped at me the other day because I took too long drawing water from the well." He paused thoughtfully. "Hagar's got a point though. I mean, we could send the children to the mountains to where we went, Debs?"

Deborah snorted cynically. "And what do you think the Canaanites would do to those who remain if they knew what we had done?"

Isaac was obviously playing out the likely outcome to this possibility. He hung his head in defeat, before looking up at Deborah remorsefully.

"They would kill everyone left if they found out, wouldn't they?" Deborah said nothing.

"Couldn't we all go?" Isaac suggested, returning to his usual childlike optimism.

"To where, my dear brother? The mountains, with no food? We wouldn't survive winter. They would find us. You can't just hide an entire village. We have worked hard; we must have faith it will be enough."

There was a pause as they both worked silently, absorbed in their own thoughts.

"How does Mama seem to you?" Isaac asked, breaking the silence.

Deborah glanced up at him. His eyes, usually light-hearted and cheerful, revealed the depth of his grief and concern.

Deborah hesitated in her response, wiping her brow with the back of her hand as she decided how to reply. She sighed inwardly.

"It's going to take time, Isaac...She's probably doing as well as she can with what's happened. All we can do is pray. How are you managing?" She felt a pang of guilt, and chided herself for not having noticed Isaac's pain; of course he would be struggling. She was a fool to think he would just breeze through the death of his father and brother.

Isaac closed his eyes and swallowed, unable to speak.

"It's alright to cry. You need to. I do. It's too much, isn't it?"

Isaac nodded, burying his face in his hands as he gave in to his sobs.

Deborah took him in her arms, remembering how their mother would silently stroke their hair, quietly singing to them of Yahweh's faithfulness. It seemed a lifetime ago. She missed her mother's strength and love, and silently pleaded for her recovery.

Deborah had recently begun her monthly course and had enjoyed joining other women in the Niddah retreat, for her seven days of separation. As women who live in close community tend to, many of the women in the village overlapped this period and so it was seven-day break from usual chores; a place and time that necessitated rest, where grandparents, fathers and siblings would take care of the younger children.

As a young child, she had watched enviously as the women disappeared into that special place. A spire of smoke would puff into the sky on cooler evenings, while the sound of laughter and tears would trickle down the hillside like a bubbling brook from a hallowed fortress. In this place, cakes would be baked, new recipes would be tried and clothes made.

But something deeper, more miraculous occurred: as they shared their lives in openness and vulnerability, counsel and wisdom would be shared, the problems in the village would be discussed and prayers would be offered. When two women were in conflict, they could find a safe place to vent their feelings amongst the counsel and support of those who knew and loved them; and before the seven days were over, there was almost always a restoration of relationship. Within true community, where each person is needed and valued, it was in everyone's interest to solve conflict – for unity was survival.

In the evenings, they would rub olive oil into each other's hands and feet, discuss husbands and children, village politics and proposals of betrothals were considered. As they brushed each other's hair, they would reminisce over shared history and listen to the stories of those who were new; in this way the fabric of the village, the underlying foundation of their community was made strong.

In their last two days, when their bleeding had stopped, they would relax and tend the beautiful garden, which was fruitful with both flowers and vegetables. Its outer perimeter was marked by a row of fig trees that partially hid it from the village. When their time of separation was over, they bathed in the *mikveh* situated near a fall of water that flowed down the hillside, thus keeping the water pure.

The men of the village knew that what happened in the Niddah retreat was sacred, for when their wives returned with baked treats, they were revived and loving. The insight and wisdom that came from their conversation flowed not only into the family, but into the wider community. And the husbands, having helped take care of the children for seven days and managed the house, would have a new-found appreciation for the role of their wives. They respectfully acknowledged that a unity was created in the retreat that had a deep impact on the village: a social foundation that knit the village together.

———

As summer's full heat beat down upon them, the gruelling work-load took its toll. Deborah was increasingly aware of subtle changes in the village. Many people had silently retreated into their own worlds, their own homes: united only in their need to work. From the outside, things looked the same: people were friendly and considerate, as they had always been;

referred to their faith in Yahweh, as they always had - but the lines had been drawn. There was an awareness that choices may eventually need to be made: one person's children over another's, which created an underlying tension that nobody had the time or the energy to see growing. It was exacerbated by lack of food and anxiety for their future.

Shelimoth's monthly course had become erratic as she went through the change, and she had the temperament to prove it. She, Shayna and Uriel were sitting together at the table in the Niddah retreat when Deborah arrived. They had been discussing the recent betrothal of Shelimoth's daughter, Ariel, to Shimon. They acknowledged her presence without greeting, and returned to their conversation, their voices now lowered .

Deborah sat alone, feeling the quiet hostility of the women and wishing she could run away.

"Deborah!"

She felt her heart pick up a notch. "Yes, Aunt?"

Tight lipped, her arms folded, she nodded to the fire. "You should start on dinner if it's to be ready on time."

Deborah noted the eyes of the other women on her. They were watching for her reaction.

She felt her pride war within her like the heat from a furnace that craves oxygen. And all the words were on her tongue to put this woman in her place, to tell her the truth of who she was and how others saw her. All her grief and anger could unleash themselves on this woman, who had continually taunted and provoked her. But in the same instance, she recognised that in doing so she would harm herself more than Shelimoth and she would not compromise her integrity for the sake of this woman, she simply was not worth it.

"As you say, Aunt."

Shelimoth watched her walk away.

The following evening, Shelimoth left, and to Deborah's relief, Miriam arrived. When Orpah arrived the following morning, she was fuming. Glancing over her shoulder at Shayna and Uriel, her eyes burned with anger, and the indignation in her whisper was barely restrained.

"Jared has announced that we should no longer be given seven days separation as Moses said, but that five days would suffice! There is too much work to be done, he says!! We know where he got that idea from!"

However, on the last day of Deborah's separation, Nissa and Maya joined them, and it was in that place that the women decided that the 'old ways' were Yahweh's ways. On their return, Shelimoth was told that if she felt she wanted to work an extra two days then she could, but they would take the rest Yahweh had given them and trust in his wisdom and laws. Deborah resisted the urge to smirk.

Now, more than ever before, she often felt that she was on the outside of the village looking in, though her manner and behaviour appeared largely unchanged. She felt a deepening void of pain and confusion that hungered for answers. She enjoyed the company of the children; she found their uncomplicated thoughts and transparent behaviour refreshing and saw that their parents no longer had the time or energy for them that they had once had. And so, she would make up games and tell them stories of Hebrew history and Yahweh's laws, as her father had once told her.

Some of the women had come together to prepare the figs to be dried and then stored for winter. She listened quietly as their conversation fluttered in and out of her own anxieties. There was a quiet intensity and strain in their voices while they worked that had replaced the laughter and singing of previous years. It troubled Deborah to see the emotional strain on the faces of those she loved, and it frustrated her that she could not help them.

"I'm worried about Emunah. She's not coping with this pregnancy," Aaliya confided. Her usually rosy complexion and cheerful expression were replaced with pallor and lined with anxiety.

"Is she unwell?" Raisa asked, reflecting her friend's concern.

"It's not that. There's not enough food to go around and she insists on feeding the girls and Ahron. He's working in the fields, she says. But the baby isn't growing. Then the other day, Netanya let the bread burn. It was a small thing. Ahron lost his temper and hit her because they all had to go hungry that day. Emunah stepped in and told him to stop, but he was so angry and frustrated. It's too much; you work so hard with no certainty of what will come. He said if Yahweh wouldn't help them, then perhaps Baal would. I see his faith wavering. He walked away and didn't come back until the next day and I fear he went to Ramah." She looked up meaningfully at her friends.

Raisa sighed. "Let's hope he just went for a walk in the hills. More and more are turning to the ways of the Canaanites." She looked at Maya and Aaliya. "It was going on before Sisera came as we know, but it was under the cover of pretending to worship El as Yahweh, and more subtle."

"People are becoming more influenced. They refer to our worship of Yahweh as the only God as 'the old way'. They say he is El, the Canaanite father of all gods and then justify their worship of Baal, saying they are doing it to ensure a good harvest," Aaliya agreed.

"Worship of Baal! They just want to justify their desires," Raisa flared.

"I do miss our trips to Shiloh though. They always reminded me of Yahweh's sovereignty and power," Aaliya smiled wistfully.

"And the sense of belonging...to something bigger than ourselves," Maya sighed.

"And the feasts! Remember the feasts: everyone, all together, a lovely ensemble of love, laughter and Yahweh." Aaliya laughed as her stomach rumbled loudly.

"Roast lamb, new wine, fresh figs, spiced bread and vegetables," Raisa reminisced with a deep sigh.

"Stop!" Aaliya cried, laughing, clapping her hands over her ears.

"I wonder how many more there are in the village that have turned from Yahweh?" Maya mused.

"Uriel has turned back to her Canaanite roots and she influences the children." Aaliya anxiously twisted her greying hair between her fingers until a tiny knotted spiral had formed.

"I'm concerned for Reuben and Shayna. He's always had a need to understand the world. He's drawn to the Canaanite religion because of their knowledge and trade; their farming practices and language are advanced and he argues we should be learning from them." Raisa sighed.

"I fear the time is coming when our village will be divided." Maya added. Deborah noted her mother's comment, pleased to see her engaging with the women's conversation. She had shown steady improvement over the last few months, though she still seemed to drift in and out of deep melancholy, as though a shadow would fall upon her.

She wondered if she should mention that she had seen Jared and Shelimoth worshipping Canaan's deities. It seemed so dreadful that she feared she would not be believed. She looked up, wiping her hands as she hung a string of figs from the beam of the ceiling.

"That's a deep frown, Deborah. What's on your mind honey-bee?" Aaliya smiled, her warm brown eyes creased by years of sun and life.

Deborah liked Aaliya. She was the same age as her mother, but where her mother had always been level-headed and pragmatic, Aaliya was creative, tactile and intuitive. Her husband had died ten years ago, shortly after the birth of Hannah, and the village had drawn the family into its warm embrace. The lines between individual families had always merged in times of difficulty as extra love and practical support were poured in to assist them. Now that everyone was struggling to survive, many lacked the emotional or physical ability to help others, and Deborah was grateful for Raisa and Tobias. Their consistent love for her mother and Aaliya was a mark of their strong character.

She spoke hesitantly, feeling foolish. "I saw Jared, Shelimoth and Ariel worshipping Baal, Asherah and Dagon recently."

The three women looked at each other silently, as each contemplated the implications this had for the village, and what should be done with the information. Finally, Raisa spoke.

"I'll speak to Tobias."

"You did the right thing, Deborah, telling us." Aaliya patted Deborah's hand affectionately.

Maya said nothing, but the furrow on her brow deepened as though she was deep in thought.

"I wonder how long this has been going on?" she choked. "I'd thought Enoch brought this pain into the village...But, Yahweh said, if we turn away from Him, He will send those who will oppress us."

Deborah saw emotion flicker in her mother's eyes.

"Why would he do this? He shared the same father as Amos, he knew it was wrong," Raisa asked.

"He's always been resentful; there's been an underlying bitterness. Shelimoth fuels his anger. I suppose, if you feel you are failing and are angry, serving Baal and his cohorts requires less accountability with more physical reward." Aaliya raised her eyebrows as she spoke.

"They refer to worship of only Yahweh as 'the old way'. By referring to him as El, the father of all gods, they justify their worship of Baal, saying that they are stock piling fertility to insure a good harvest." Raisa wiped her hands roughly on her apron with indignation.

Aaliya frowned. "You don't think..."

"I don't want to think," Maya replied grimly, as she hacked an onion into pieces and added it to the pot for dinner.

Deborah didn't ask what they were referring to; she had heard conversations about Canaanite worship involving temple prostitutes before.

As summer gave way to autumn, the toil increased as they brought the harvest in, drying and storing the food that would see them through the winter.

During this time, Deborah's thirteenth birthday came. Raisa had gathered her own family, Aaliya's immediate family, including Deborah's best friend Miriam and her mother and brother. She beckoned them into her courtyard. Maya congratulated her daughter; holding her in her arms. She smiled, but the sad, distant look in her eyes betrayed her: there were so many faces absent from this celebration. She handed her a bag.

"We bought the material together darling, do you remember?" she asked, her glazed expression intimated that she had wandered into the past.

Caught off guard, Deborah swallowed back her tears; the sudden flood of happy memories of her family promised to overwhelm her.

It was less than a year ago that they had all journeyed to Gibeah, but so much had passed since then: there was no remnant of that child left.

She silently mourned the death of the carefree girl that had been as she recalled their excitement walking up the hill toward Gibeah; its raised embankments surrounding the wall adding to its sense of opulence. The fields were quiet; it was winter. The harvest was in and families were enjoying the rest after all the work bringing in the harvest. Small houses dotted the landscape, and smoke could be seen lazily drifting into the mild winter sky. From open doors, smells of fresh bread and lentils spiced with herbs made their mouths water as they tiredly approached the gates of the town.

A group of small boys were laughing and playing with wooden swords, while their fathers discussed politics at the city gates. The market sprawled outside the city walls: traders selling fruit, bread, sweet fig cakes, material, bowls and wine. Other stall holders sold knives, axes and plough shears. The market holders' voices could be heard now mingled with the sounds of the animals and her mother's infectious laughter as she bartered over the price of material with a stall holder. She handed him the money and took the material just as her father had come, put his arm around her waist, and drawn them into a tavern.

"Look who I found, Maya!"

"Abinoam! It's so good to see you!" her mother said, embracing him. "What brings you to Gibeah?"

"Actually, business," Abinoam replied. "We have a few clients here, mostly rich noblemen. Lappi is running a stall at the market. Did you see him on your way through?"

"No, we didn't see him, but that's wonderful. Are you all here?"

"Yes, we are. Hannah wanted to come to the market with the girls." Abinoam rolled his eyes in an expression of mock irritation.

"Perhaps we can meet here for dinner later?" Amos asked.

"We'd love to, but please come and eat with us. Our clients are wealthy and have offered us rooms for the duration of our stay. You would be very welcome."

"Once again, you offer to take us into your home. Your hospitality is overwhelming – we cannot," protested Amos.

"But you must! Hannah would never forgive me if I tell her that we met and I did not bring you home," he laughed. "So you see, it is you who would be doing me a courtesy."

"Your hospitality is outdone only by your graciousness, my friend. We are forced, with the greatest of pleasure, to accept."

Enoch smirked, his eyes shining playfully. "Now isn't this wonderful? You'll get to see your Lappi again," he whispered. Deborah had glared at him and tried to kick him under the table, but missed and kicked Isaac, who angrily kicked her back.

"He's not *my* Lappi!" Deborah hissed as she recalled her humiliating rescue on the mountains in Shiloh by Abinoam's son, Lapidoth. When her family had returned to Shiloh for the Feast of Tabernacles last year, they had extended their stay and joined Lapidoth's family for an extra week. Deborah thought that the annual reminder of her stupidity and humiliating rescue, in which she had no doubt dribbled blood and pus all over their son, was in some way a punishment for her having left the holy festivities. She had begged her parents to let her go home with Tobias and Raisa. Reluctantly they had agreed. It seemed, however, that fate was humouring her; she would not go unpunished. Only three months later, here she was!

As twilight covered the tel with its muted shroud, they had made their way to the address Abinoam had given them. Her father tentatively knocked at the door. A moment later, it was opened by Lapidoth. He was taller than she remembered, and broader. His face had lost its boyish form and taken on the strong lines of manhood. His eyes contained a solemn depth, like a forest pool in the shade of an ancient terebinth tree, catching the rays of sun that pierced the leafy boughs.

"Great to see you all again, please come in." His voice was deep, gentle and self-assured. He greeted Deborah's parents with a kiss on each cheek, and Ethan and Isaac with a slap on the back.

"Congratulations Enoch and Keziah on your marriage, it's so good you can both be here. Deborah, welcome. We are so pleased that you can be with us today."

Deborah smiled, her sense of etiquette allowed her to respond naturally: "As am I."

As Lapidoth led the way down the long corridor, Deborah took in the luxury of Abinoam's client's home. It was adorned with woven carpets strewn over tiled floors, couches draped with thick, colourful coverings and ornately carved furniture decorated with vases of fresh flowers.

They were greeted by Hannah, warm, tactile and demonstrative with her characteristic display of affection and inability to finish any sentence, or allow anyone else to finish theirs.

"My darlings, so wonderful to see you all, what a delightful surprise...Maya, have you seen these carpets? I'm so jealous, I want to take one back to Shiloh," she giggled conspiratorially "How have you been? Just awful about Ehud, isn't it?"

Maya spoke with her usual pragmatic calm. "It is dreadful. Who will Yahweh raise up now do you think? We haven't been affected too mu..."

"Well, I don't know, but in the cities we see the degeneration already. Many of our people have begun to look to Canaanite gods and practices. Temple worship has already begun to decline but Abinoam fears it's only the beginning."

Maya nodded thoughtfully and was just about to ask Hannah another question, when Hannah spotted Enoch.

"Enoch, it's lovely to meet your beautiful wife. How long have you been married?"

"Three months…"

At that moment, Rebecca, Ruth and Josiah raced into the room, Abinoam and Hannah's other children. Rebecca smiled shyly, "*Salam alahum.*" Ruth, in contrast, rushed forward, hugging Isaac and beckoning him to follow her into the courtyard, where she had apparently trapped a gecko.

"Can I offer you some water, or a glass of wine? " Josiah asked, formally, leading them into a dining area.

The table was already laden with dishes of goat, cooked with spices, a roast chicken, beans and vegetables, bread flavoured with cumin, and honey donuts.

Abinoam thanked Yahweh for the provision of food and for bringing their friends to them, and Amos prayed blessing on Abinoam's family for their hospitality. Deborah fell into her usual contented pattern of watching the interaction of those around her, laughing along with the happy flow of the evening, but volunteering little of herself and thereby avoiding her older brother's teasing. She listened to Lapidoth's voice, curious to dissect his character, to weigh him, to assess him for insecurity or honour. His voice had a gentle depth, reminding her of a brook as it rushed over the stones, sure of its own journey.

"Tell me, Enoch, Keziah, about your wedding feast?"

"It was wonderful! My family is from a village near Enoch's, and there was music and food and dancing! It was such a wonderful time."

"It was the happiest day of my life," Enoch agreed, stroking the back of Keziah's hand.

As the table was cleared, Abinoam and her father began to discuss the recent death of Ehud, former judge of Israel. Deborah recalled how pivotal that conversation had been. "It seems strange to think that he has been dead nearly two summers now," Abinoam reflected sadly.

"Have you noticed a difference in the other towns, in Kedesh and Shiloh?" her father asked.

"Yes." For a moment Abinoam lost his happy demeanour. He rubbed his brow as though forcing the frown to leave his anxious expression. "It began before Ehud died. As he aged, his influence decreased, but it's worse now than ever. Shiloh is not only the resting place of the tabernacle; there are other influences. As Jabin's power grows, so does his pagan influence. In Kedesh, we see it more because of its proximity to Hazor, Jabin's capital. Sisera rules this territory with an iron hand."

"There is a couple who came to our village after their town was raided. The man is Hebrew, but his wife is Canaanite. They had lived near the cross roads, between Beit Horon and Ramah - one of their four children had been taken into slavery and their youngest died shortly after they arrived. Tobias and I made it clear: they were welcome, but they needed to leave their idols outside the village. The threat of stoning for idolatry has not needed adhering to for as long as I can remember, but it's still acknowledged, and as such acts as some deterrent." He leant back in his chair, exhaling deeply. "But we aren't naïve, we realise you can't just force people to abandon their beliefs – you just force them into secrecy; and you can't fight what is unknown." Amos' frown deepened as he anxiously considered the future of the village.

Abinoam nodded in agreement. "It's like an invisible cloud that permeates our consciousness and we aren't aware of what is happening. Last year was a hard winter, as you know. When Ehud died people became…susceptible," Abinoam explained.

"Susceptible?"

"Yes…to Canaanite influence. Their wealth and ease of life is attractive to poor farmers, especially when they are watching their families go hungry. The Canaanite religion is attractive after all."

Abinoam raised an eyebrow meaningfully.

Amos snorted in disgust. "Yes, to believe that by visiting a temple prostitute you are stock piling fertility for next year's harvest would appeal to the flesh of most men." Deborah acknowledged that her father was clearly unaware that his daughter was listening.

"It's not just the northern tribes of Israel; you can see their influence in the towns of Ephraim too. People are lost without Ehud, desperate for something physical to trust in; it's like a poison that is slowly defiling Yahweh's people. They have twisted the truth, choosing to believe that Yahweh is El, father of all gods and therefore to worship Baal, Asherah and Dagon." Abinoam shook his head.

"What caused it initially, do you think?" Amos asked.

"It made sense, economically, to trade with the Canaanites; they are advanced in so many areas. That is where compromise first came in, and then, changes in mindset were advantageous."

And that was when Deborah remembered her dream. She looked up to see her father watching her as they exchanged their unspoken revelation.

Deborah suddenly felt weighted, as she saw the truth of her dream begin to unfold. She wanted to escape, to a place where she could reflect and process and most importantly, to pray. She needed to find peace before it overwhelmed her.

Standing up from the table she picked up plates and took them through to the kitchen. Her mother was deep in conversation with Hannah, and so she wandered into a small 'L' shaped courtyard, enclosed by vine-covered brick walls. Seeking the darkness of the furthest corner, she sat on the stone bench, drawing her feet up to her chest. The familiar sound of chirping crickets and the cool winter breeze rustling in the trees comforted her. The moon gazed solemnly back at her, while the stars set their own course, unconcerned with the turmoil in her heart. She sighed in exasperation. "Yahweh! Be merciful to us, I pray."

She was quietly contemplative for some time, until the sound of footsteps drew her out of her thoughts. She sighed inwardly at the intrusion and shrunk back into the stone alcove, trying to make herself small. Lapidoth stepped into the courtyard and sprawled himself out so that he was lying on his back, covering the length of the wall. It would be impossible for her to leave now without being noticed. However, it felt equally rude and lacking in decorum not to let him know she was there.

She coughed nervously and heard Lapidoth laugh.

"Deborah? Are you seeking refuge from the depressing conversation too?"

Deborah smiled. She liked Lapidoth's way of making light of life.

"I'm hiding from imminent Canaanite invasion. And you?" she responded, moving herself about so that she could see him. He had his hands behind his head and turned toward her.

"Why, I'm protecting you, of course."

She rolled her eyes. "My hero, of course, how could I forget."

They both laughed and then sat in a comfortable silence, looking at the night sky.

"The stars always remind me of how very small and insignificant I am."

"Can that be helpful?" she mused.

She heard his low laugh. "Anything that helps me remember how small I am and how great Yahweh is, is infinitely helpful."

She respected his answer, and was enjoying their game, and so she continued: "How can it be helpful to know how small you are? Did Yahweh not tell Joshua that we should be conquerors?" she provoked.

"Without a doubt. But I am just a small piece in a large picture that is drawn by Yahweh. The stars remind me of my great dependence on Him and that it takes many stars to light the sky."

"That's true!" she whispered. "But even the smallest part of the picture, even the smallest star holds light, and must play its part to bring everything to completion."

"Yes," he whispered quietly, almost to himself. "And heaven commands the stars - I wonder what our part will be?"

Deborah fell silent, her thoughts returning to the dream.

She shuddered, and was brought back to the moment by Isaac, who had proudly presented a wooden bowl that he had made with Tobias. "Happy birthday, Deborah! You're the best," he grinned, hugging her. Isaac, with his charming smile and gentle nature, had always been able to bring the best out of her. The bowl was filled with pistachios, honey cakes, and raisins.

She smiled. "Thanks Isaac, that's amazing – I love it!" She quickly glanced at Tobias to show her appreciation, without wanting to take anything from Isaacs's sense of accomplishment.

"The contents of the bowl are from me," Raisa said, offering her own warm embrace.

"Look on the bottom of the bowl!" Tobias urged, his hand on Isaac's shoulder.

Deborah lifted the bowl over her head, careful not to empty the contents out. She gasped in delight.

"It's a honey bee! It's your name!" Isaac beamed with pride. He suddenly looked apologetic. "I did get quite a lot of help with that," he confessed humbly.

Deborah fought the urge not to laugh; Isaac was an open book: he was pure-hearted and his thoughts were always transparent.

"Well," said Deborah, "I am impressed, not only with your excellent craftsmanship, but also your ability to take instruction and your humility; that shows true character. Abba would be proud of you." She glanced at her mother as she said it, unsure how her mother would react. She was pleased to see her smile, the first flicker of her mother's former self.

The Sabbath had ceased to be a day of rest. There had been heated debate about the breaking of this law. Once again the village had been divided, but finally Jared declared that there was too much work to be done - and his logic was undeniable. Finally, it was agreed that those who did not feel they should work, would not, and would work an extra shift another day. After finishing her shift, Deborah allowed herself for the first time to go to *her place*. She wondered if she would be reminded too much of that day, and chose a different path to her rocky retreat.

A gecko had taken up residence on the flat stone in her sanctuary, and was basking in the midday sun. She carefully maneuvered herself around it, careful not to disturb it, hoping it would stay. Finally, she pushed her body into the smallest part of the rocky indent until she felt cocooned by the vertical faces around her. Above her, the overhang partially hid her view of the sky but satisfied some inner need for seclusion. As Deborah pulled her knees up to her body, wrapping her arms around them and sighing deeply, she uttered her single-worded prayer: "*Yahweh.*" It was a visceral utterance that reached out to find Him. And in the same breath, He was there; and in

His embrace, she wept, her body shaking as she sobbed uncontrollably. When she finally finished, she rested once more. In His peace and in that place, and for that moment, she was able to let go of her need to understand.

5

...who struck down six hundred Philistines with an oxgoad.
Judges 3:31

1253 BC – Shamgar

Gezer rose imposingly before him, its four meter-thick stone walls protected by a five-meter earthen rampart. Houses and shops were built on structures on the slope of the tel. By the time he reached the south gate, the sun had dipped behind the northern walls. Grey and white clouds hovered over the city, casting dark shadows like the hand of judgement. Shamgar slowed his pace, getting in line with the other travellers as they filed wearily into the bustling city. As he started up the steps, he noted the deep limestone shaft leading to a water tunnel. "It doesn't have its own water supply," he mused. His father's military training instinctively invaded his thoughts as he acknowledged its significance.

He took a moment, then, to consider what he needed to do. He sighed as he considered the ox-goad in his right hand, the pointed nail at one end and the spade at the other. He shook his head at the absurdity of what he needed to achieve, and the weapon that he would need to use.

He set Manoah on his feet and grasped his arms. "I need to go and find your sisters, and I can't take you with me. Once I've found them, I will return." Manoah nodded, swallowing and blinking back the tears that threatened to disappoint his father.

Shamgar paused briefly, acknowledging that he had no plan and no weapon. He looked at the ox-goad in his hand: the metal blade that would be used to till the earth, and the pointed end that would prod the cattle in a direction. He sighed, silently praying: "*Yahweh, be my sword and shield and lead me into battle. Give me the victory, and I will give You the glory.*"

A woman before him travelled with two small children. He watched her attentively dealing with her children, though she was clearly exhausted. He tapped her shoulder, speaking a greeting first in Hebrew, then in the Canaanite tongue. She replied shyly in Hebrew, responding to her son as he tugged on her arm whilst eying the huge farmer with curiosity.

Shamgar smiled at the small boy, thinking sadly that he was about Samuel's age. He wondered if the woman saw his pain. Her own eyes were shadowed with fatigue - perhaps she carried her own burden. "I have business in the city to take care of." He removed a bag of coins from the sack across his shoulder. "I will give you more when I return. Can you take care of my son, please?"

She looked hesitant, drawing her daughter closer. Shamgar understood her reluctance to help a stranger, even for money. These were such dangerous times. The wise did not trust lightly. Each person looked after their own and did what was necessary to survive.

"Please," his voice broke, "they have taken my daughters. I need to find them." He regretted being so open about his intent, but he had no other choice. His emotions were raw and his need desperate.

The mother's eyes softened, reflecting her empathy and understanding that were born out of her own sorrow and brokenness.

"Of course. I have come to stay with relatives. Village life has become too dangerous. My husband..." Tears rolled down her face as her expression told the familiar story. She quickly brushed them away, her eyes flitting to the children.

She told him where she would be staying and took Manoah's hand. He whispered now, only for her: "If I do not return, please find someone you trust to take the boy to Beit- Shemesh. Ask for Anath, he is known there. You will be rewarded richly for the safe delivery of his grandson."

Taking his leave, he pushed his way through the heaving mass of people, his eyes scanning the crowd for Philistine soldiers. *'Yahweh, let it not be too late, help me to find them.'* His silent prayer pounded like a war drum to the thud of his heart. Near the apex of the tel, he noted the roof of the white palace housing the Canaanite governor, and the smaller, but no less impressive Hebrew, Philistine and Egyptian governmental buildings, surrounded by large walled and guarded courtyards.

He decided his daughters were more likely to have been taken to the market.

The mighty stone peaks of the *mazzeboth* could be seen in the northern part of the tel: a row of ten tall monolithic stone tels ran from north to south, representing the ten Canaanite cities. It was here that cultic rituals relating to treaties between these cities would be performed.

Shamgar knew there were a number of possible ends that his daughters could meet: in the governor's home, a brothel, a sacrifice to Baal and Dagon, or sexual fodder for the soldiers. But his gut led him toward the market. If they were sold, it would be harder to track them down and the fact that they had been brought to Gezer, rather than the other Philistine cities, was most likely for a quick sale. The towers that flanked the central gate of the city marked the beginning of the market but he was guided by the flow of people, travellers, merchants and residents of the great city. It looked out onto the Via Maris, the great highway that linked Gezer, Megiddo and Hazor and brought trade from the merchant ships travelling from Greece, Crete and further afield. The road ran to the south, bringing linen, gold and spices from Egypt.

On any other day he would have felt his senses inspired by the variety of culture and produce. But today he was desperate, driven only to where his daughters were. He went to the first stall.

"Where would I go to buy girls?" he growled. When the man looked confused, he repeated his question, first in the Philistine tongue, then in Hebrew.

The man laughed, raising his eyebrows knowingly whilst making an obscene gesture. Shamgar prodded him impatiently with his goad and the man lost his smile. Looking affronted, he jabbered a few directions. Shamgar left him, shoving his way forward now, ignoring the indignant protests of the throng. The frightened screams and crude heckling warned him he was near before he even saw the slave stand. On a raised platform stood a young boy, who had been stripped to his waist. Shamgar judged him to be eleven or twelve. He stood trembling while a bulbous man, wearing extravagant robes that gathered under his overhanging belly, ran his hooded eyes lustfully over him. A small smile played at the corner of his lips as though lost in his own perverse fantasy. Next to him was a man in a plain, linen tunic. He seemed more serious, and Shamgar judged him to be a servant in a wealthy house, looking to buy a household slave. He was guarded by two soldiers, while the auctioneer, an effeminate, jewel-bedecked man crudely advertised his new sale. Shamgar forcefully made his way towards the guards who blocked the way to the tent where the slaves awaited auction. He knew that he could take on most men in battle, but recognised he had had no time to find out how many guards there were, and that he was armed only with the goad. He could see four outside the tent. Likely there would be armed eunuchs inside. Furthermore, he still had no actual evidence to suggest that his daughters would be here. He was following an instinctive guess.

"Harela! Itiya!" he shouted out their names. A pause, and then…

"Pap…!" and the muffled sound of screaming.

Adrenalin coursed through Shamgar and drove him forward. He saw the raised swords of the guards, acknowledging their hesitation and angst as they took in his size and fearless rage. They quickly recovered, hiding behind their soldiers' masks. They charged toward him as one, their swords raised for attack. He swung his ox-goad with such force that he knocked them to the ground in one motion. Then, using the metal pointed end, he stabbed each of them quickly, pulling his goad free ready to face the next assault.

He heard the two guards that had been standing with the young boy rush towards him, and turning, he gored the first in the neck with the metal blade. Without removing his goad, he used the other end to knock the second guard to the floor. He stamped his foot hard onto the man's chest, breaking several ribs before ending his life. The auctioneer had disappeared into the crowd, as had the young boy. He used his goad to pull back the curtains of the tent. It was quiet inside. Too quiet. He knew, of course, that they would now be waiting and organised. He picked up the body of the guard he had killed, and letting out a loud guttural cry, hurled it through the doorway before charging in after it.

"Papa…! Watch…" Hearing movement behind him, he thrust the shaft backward using his strength to wind his opponent, and then impaling him before he could recover.

Two more came at him. The first he killed quickly; the second was harder. He had a long sword and though not as tall as Shamgar, he was athletic and quicker on his feet. Shamgar felt the metal slice into his lower arm. He needed to focus. He drew on his military training. Looking for weakness in his opponent and using his strength, he hurled a table at the soldier. It created the distraction he needed. Leaping onto the up-turned table, he thrust the goad down, skewering his assailant through the top of his head. The last remaining eunuch, seeing the horrific end of his compatriot, fled through the tent door, stumbling over the bodies of the dead guards. Shamgar knew he would go for help, yet he had to get his daughters out. He saw Harela, who at aged fifteen had the curves, beauty and gentle nature of her mother. His eyes searched futilely for Itiya, his thirteen year-old daughter, who was tall and striking with fiery red hair and a temper to match it.

He grabbed Harela, clutching her to him, kissing her hair and telling her she needed to be strong, they had to leave. He noted with fury that her eyes had been painted with kohl, and she was scantily clothed for a better sale.

"Where is Itiya?"

"She was taken when we entered the city. I told her to be quiet but… you know how Itiya is…she found a knife and stabbed one of the guards. They hit her, and then they said they would take her to the palace…for sport. I heard him say that the Philistine lord was here from Ekron."

Tears streaked the kohl down her face.

Shamgar dug his palms into his eyes. It had been a long day. Anxiety, rage and adrenaline battled against his fatigue.

"We need to leave."

He turned to the other slaves, mostly young girls, and a few boys.

"You are all free to go. You must go quickly, reinforcements will come soon. Do not try and leave through the south west gate. They will expect that and come looking. There is a water tunnel; does anyone know where it starts?"

One of the prisoners nodded.

"Go now, take the others with you!" He searched the bodies of the dead soldiers and handed out money pouches and a couple of knives.

"Take these, stay together. Buy water and something else to wear. Wait until nightfall to escape and do not stop until you reach Beit-Shemesh. On the outskirts of the city, find my father, Anath, and present his grand-daughter. He will take care of you until I come."

Drawing his daughter into his arms, he crushed her to his chest, as though to infuse her with his courage "I need to get Itiya. I will come for you when I have her."

Offering up a prayer to Yahweh, he led them out of the tent. The market had grown suddenly quiet in anticipation of coming trouble...

He stopped with the group briefly as they chose suitable clothes from a skittish stall holder, and then watched as his daughter became lost in the crowd.

He would soon lose the light completely. He knew that wisdom dictated that he wait until morning, that the Philistines would be waiting for him. But his own experience as a soldier taught him that come evening, the men would drink, and after that they would bring out the slave girls. He would need to use the cover of night to his advantage whilst also distracting them.

By the time he reached the palace, Shamgar had killed thirty more Philistine soldiers. The moon was a hazy sliver in the black sky, and the clouds that had dappled the sky grey earlier, now hung low, blotting out the stars. He heard the distant rumble of thunder and felt the first drops of rain on his bare skin. He welcomed it. The air had cooled and was waking him up, helping him to think. He climbed to the roof of a nearby house, enabling him to see the palace and judge the height of the walls. As lightning flashed in the hills, he saw that they were ready for him. Waiting. He judged there to be over one hundred Philistines, half lining the tops of the walls and half below. They were distinguished by the colour of their skirts. He was suddenly overwhelmed by the impossibility of what he needed to do. It was hopeless. The heavens opened and rain fell in torrents as if to confirm his gloom.

Shamgar bent low, drawing in deep breaths in an attempt to slow his pulse. The cool breeze acted as a balm to focus him: channelling his rage. Again he offered a silent prayer: *Yahweh my enemies are Your enemies. May we fight as one.*

The air grew static, as though charged with electricity, raising the hairs on the back of his neck and fusing him with strength. *Yahweh had answered him.* Words formed an impression in his mind, *Though the darkness surrounds you, and the storm rages around you, My light will be with you, My love will shelter you. Use what is in your hand.* His lips curved into a peaceful smile that came from the assurance that victory would be inevitable. He offered up his silent thanks. He still had no idea what he would do, but knew unequivocally Yahweh went before him.

He turned the corner of the street. Light, laughter and chatter spilled from homes into the night air reminding him of the natural absurdity of what he was about to attempt. *I should be home; with my family… this should not be happening.*

He walked forward. The darkness enveloped him. He walked closer still, waiting for them to notice him. His mind and body alert, for the battle cry and arrows that would rain from above, while he was attacked by fifty trained swords-men. He was close enough now to hear their conversation; the vulgar comments of their intent at the end of their watch and discussion over his capture and death.

He stepped closer until he could smell the stale sweat and wine on their breaths.

Though the darkness surrounds you and the storm rages around you, My light will be with you, My love will shelter you. Use what is in your hand.

Shamgar avoided the urge to laugh out loud - they couldn't see him! He looked to the ox-goad in his hand and, with smug confidence, ran to the first men who stood in formation against the wall. He leapt from the shadows, skewering three men, and panic broke out next to them as they searched for their unseen foe. Shamgar quickly ducked back into the shadows created by the houses, and sprinted nimbly to the other end of soldiers, delivering the same judgement. Terror had seized the men, who had broken their ranks and were searching wildly for their assailant. All the while, the driving rain spewed its fury upon them. As strength coursed through him, Shamgar effortlessly killed the first fifty men, spearing one with the nail end and stabbing the next with the flattened spade end in a fluid action. He could hear the shouts of the men above him,as they prepared to release their arrows, their burning tips aimed into the darkness. Lightning flashed around him, followed immediately by deafening thunder and a shower of fiery arrows. As Shamgar held back in the shadows of the street, he noted that the houses had grown quiet; shutters and doors had been closed extinguishing their light. He smiled inwardly.

And he waited.

Fear and confusion had spread like a plague on the parapets. He had fought many times in battle under excellent commanders. He caught himself unconsciously appraising the excellence of Yahweh as both his General and rear-guard, and gave Him the honour and glory of this battle. The reflection was both humbling and empowering.

Exulted anticipation flooded Shamgar's senses as he continued to wait.

Thunder and lightning crashed simultaneously, violently splitting the sky with its charged branches while thunder exploded; a crescendo that rolled from the vaults of heaven and roared for justice. It took
Shamgar's eyes a moment to adjust from the intensity of the flash. He blinked and laughed out loud. The gate to the palace had swung open, left dangling from its hinges. The men who had stood guard could be seen running toward the palace sanctuary.

Shamgar released a triumphant battle cry. "In the name of Yahweh, you will be defeated this night!"

The sound of marching filled the night as men abandoned the parapets to defend the palace. As they positioned themselves in battle formation Shamgar observed the men make way for their general. The man had a commanding, intimidating presence that filled the space between them. On either side he was flanked by soldiers bearing torches.

"What is it you want, farmer? You must know that you cannot possibly win this battle." His face was chiselled; hard lines accentuated his piercing demeanour. His visage was framed by an imposing red plumed helmet while his bronze breastplate gleamed in the torch light.

His red skirt defined him as a Philistine.

Shamgar ran his fingers through his wet hair, pulling it away from his face. He kept his voice low, steady, though he could feel the desire to battle flooding his senses "I want the death of every Philistine in this place."

His grip tightened around the wooden shaft. "But you are right. I cannot possibly win this battle…But Yahweh can. He is the true God." He knew better than to let them know that he was coming for his daughter. They would use her as leverage to weaken him. The rain continued to fall in sheets. There was a pause while both sides waited for the thunder and lightning to pass.

"We will see then, Hebrew, if you will avenge your family today, or die trying."

"I am the son of Anath," he stated, defining his Canaanite parentage and his rank as a soldier, "…and vengeance is Yahweh's." Shamgar wiped the rain from his eyes and tightened his grip on the goad. He knew that he needed to remain in the shadow of the night; darkness was the protection Yahweh had provided for him.

"The Philistine army is no match for Yahweh," he challenged. "One man can defeat an entire army. What will your enemies say to your defeat today: that all were too feeble and afraid to fight?" He knew the general could not afford to let this accusation pass. Though shutters and doors had been closed, ears and mouths were not. He listened with tense satisfaction to the quiet movement of the soldiers: they were readying to charge. Quickly, he padded back to the rooftop he had begun his evening on.

The Philistines moved forward with skilled caution in three rows. They carried spears in one hand and swords in the other. These men were not novices, Shamgar observed. He looked again at the goad in his hand. His military logic told him to exchange it for a sword and spear, but the same voice told him to always follow his General's orders.

"Where are you, Shamgar, son of Anath? Have you come to your senses, hiding like a girl?" the general taunted. They knew who he was. Shamgar lifted his goad above his head, ready to release it. The general turned toward him. The rain continued its assault, black and forceful as thunder rumbled overhead. The General saw the goad in the lightning flash, centimetres from his head. His jaw dropped open in shock as the pole entered his mouth, protruding from the back of his head. There was a stunned silence amongst the Philistine army as their revered general fell to the ground. In that moment, Shamgar leapt to the ground. He used his strength to break the neck of the first warrior he encountered; then, taking the soldier's sword, he hacked a path to retrieve his goad. A terrified frenzy had broken out in the ranks, and many of the Philistines were blindly swinging their swords, killing and maiming each other.

Shamgar surveyed the carnage around him before racing into the palace. Most of the soldiers had been defeated on the palace walls. Hearing shouting, he followed it to its source - behind ornate double doors. He pushed it aside cautiously, his ox-goad held as a lance, ready to attack.

He took in the scene before him: the young girls barely dressed, tied to a post and on a cushioned divan lay a man, his lavish robes and jewel bedecked hands defined him as the Philistine lord of Ekron.

Unaware of the defeat of the army, he had the confidence and arrogance of one used to being unchallenged and undefeated.

Shamgar took in the golden goblet of wine in the man's chubby fist as he sized Shamgar up, noting the ox-goad and the man's face and clothing both dripping with fresh blood. For a moment his composure slipped, and Shamgar knew his fear. He slipped behind his political façade, gesturing to the five attending guards to hold back. Shamgar noted one of them slip through a door, and he smiled inwardly knowing that he was going to get reinforcements, but would discover they were all dead. He let him go.

"What can I help you with?" His tone was helpful, almost fatherly.
"Where are the slaves?"

He looked surprised, but smiled. "Of course." He answered, gesturing to one of the guards. "Take him to the slave quarters."

Shamgar looked at the two young girls. They looked terrified! They were younger than Itiya and they were someone's daughters.

"I'll take those two as well." He nodded toward them.

The lord smiled, understanding registering on his face as he gestured to a guard to unchain them. The guard who had left a few moments ago returned, his face pale. He glanced quickly at Shamgar before whispering to the lord, who was silent. His mouth set in a line as he acknowledged his situation.

When he turned back, his smile was tight, forced.

"My guard will show you the way and find you wagons to hasten your departure, only spare my life."

Shamgar looked at him, and his face twisted with contempt at the man's selfish cowardice.

"I'll find my own way," he answered, hurling his spear through the air and splitting the lord's skull in two. He turned to the remaining guards, who were closing in on him. He felt Yahweh's strength upon him as he ended their lives.

Turning to the girls he stepped back a pace, aware that they must be frightened by his bloodied appearance, and watching him kill their master. He lowered his voice, his heart suddenly full of fatherly compassion for them.

"I am here to rescue my daughter; she was brought here as a slave. Can you show me the way? I mean you no harm. When I find her, I will take you to a place where you will be safe…and free," he added.

He noted the eyes of one of the girls darting nervously to the younger slave beside her, her voice trembled as she spoke. "I.. think I know where she will be."

Shamgar nodded, tearing a sheet from the divan and handing it to them to cover themselves.

Leaving the room, the girls lead Shamgar through a maze of corridors and doors. Finally, they stood before a thick, bolted door. Shamgar pulled the bolt aside, suddenly feeling sick with anxiety at what he would, or worse still, would not, find.

Inside were children ranged in age from eight to sixteen. The room stank of human waste and sickness. His stomach twisted with anger as he scanned the room. The children were huddled against the cold, stone walls in terror. When they saw Shamgar standing in the door, some of them began to whimper, while others were mute with fear. Shamgar felt pity and rage well up within him.

"Abba?"

His head turned, a spark of hope flickering within him. He saw a girl his daughter's age, her clothes torn and her face swollen. She looked so vulnerable and weak. That spark of life that he so loved was a fragile thread that he was afraid would snap.

"Abba? It's you. It's you!" Her voice broke as she began to sob.

"Itiya." He barely recognised her. He fell to his knees, holding her gently for fear she might break. He sighed, allowing himself a moment, in which he thanked Yahweh for Itiya's life. He took her hands in his, searching her eyes for her hidden strength. She smiled faintly.

"I'll be fine."

"We need to leave. Can you walk?"

"Yes, but we can't leave them." She gestured to the other slaves, cringing in the darkness.

"No. We can't."

He turned toward the girl who had led him here. "What is your name?"

"Carmela."

"Carmela, do you know where the stables are?"

She nodded, "I think so."

He turned to the children "I'm going to get you all out of here. But you need to make it to the stables. Can you all do that?"

"My brother can't sir. His leg is broken."

Shamgar nodded, lifting the boy in his arms.

As they made their way through the silent passages, Shamgar was mindful of their vulnerability and listened for sound in the empty corridors. His anxious thoughts wandered to Harela. He had told the group to leave at nightfall. If their escape had been successful, they should be somewhere between Gezer and Kiriath by now, hopefully in the cover of the hills. He hoped they had had the good sense to stay off the roads.

He felt a wave of fatigue and nausea sweep over him.

"We're here, sir." Carmela pointed to the stables, drawing Shamgar out of his troubled thoughts.

He harnessed two of the horses, attaching the cart with automatic efficiency, his thoughts still on Harela, whilst acknowledging that he needed to find Manoah before he left. He lifted the boy with the broken leg on first, before helping the others.

As he drove the cart through the city, the streets were empty and silent as though the air itself had retreated behind locked doors. And yet, the rain had stopped and the air was fresh, purged.

When he finally found the address he had been given, he knocked on the door. He was unsurprised by the silence that greeted him; nobody with any sense would be out on a night like this, nor answering their doors to strangers. He didn't want to draw attention to this family for harbouring his son. Instead he went around the back of the house and tapped on the shutter, whispering Manoah's name. When the window shutter was opened by the woman, it occurred to him that he hadn't even asked her name. He had trusted her with his son, but had not asked her name. She smiled wearily, nodding as she hastened to awaken Manoah. Behind her, he saw her family, crowded around a table; their faces looked drawn and pale. They looked at Shamgar, his clothes and skin splattered with dried blood and then at the girl. Shamgar thanked her, handing her another pouch of money. He didn't mention that he had taken it from the guards he had killed.

Lifting Manoah, still half asleep, through the open window, he sat his son next to him in the cart and held Itiya on the other side, pushing the horses until they were out of the city. The guards on the gate were Canaanite: they took one look at him, covered in blood and the children behind him, and ushered him through. Canaan had supremacy in Gezer, and whilst it tolerated the presence of other nations for the sake of trade, there was no loyalty that would cause them to risk their own lives – word had already travelled of this man's defeat of the Philistines.

As they reached the base of the tel and picked up the road to Beit Shemesh he heaved a sigh of relief; he hated killing and had left the army because it never seemed right to him. Tonight was different, he acknowledged grimly: he would have killed as many as he had to to bring his children home.

He pushed the cart as fast as he dared. He had hoped they would pass Harela on the way, but he knew it was unlikely, and he needed to find help and refuge for the children in the cart, including Itiya. He sighed. He had been frightened to ask what she had been through, and she had not asked about her mother or siblings. He was aware that they were both teetering on a chasm of raw emotion and trauma, held back by determination and hunger to survive. She seemed as desperate as he to hold back thought tonight. They travelled silently.

6

....all the people did whatever seemed right in their own eyes.
Judges 21:25

1256 BC – Deborah

The first signs of autumn were beginning to colour the landscape. The sky was pale grey, like new ash, with warm, gentle hues of smoldering embers. The village was tense with trepidation; everyone was aware that the Canaanite return was imminent. They had gleaned all that they could from the fields: many of the grapes had been crushed and their juice stored in sealed barrels, others had been carefully dried and sealed in clay jars. The olives had been pressed for their oil or preserved for the winter. However, there was none of the usual joy that ended this season: no Feast of Tabernacles, that joyous holy pilgrimage which reunited their family and friends. It was a sobering thought that for all their hard work, there would most likely not be enough food to see them through the winter. Jared had suggested that everything allotted to the Canaanites should be placed in a central storehouse, but that each family would make some provision of their own. That way, if the Canaanites took everything, they would not be left to starve in winter. This had seemed good to everyone. And so barley, dried figs, olive oil, wine, dried beans and lentils were stored under rugs and wood on the flat roofs of the homes.

None of the men travelled to Shiloh for the Feast of Tabernacles for the first time Deborah could remember: there was too much work to be done. The roads were deemed dangerous and they had begun to forget why they would want to. Their need to survive consumed their thoughts and Yahweh became a memory that was clung to as an identity, but not a reality.

Deborah remembered that night, over five years ago, when she had met with Yahweh; it was a dim memory, veiled by darkness, pain and confusion. But it had been a reality.

This is what Egypt did to the Israelites: we live for ourselves and we are divided and weakened by it, but how to find our way back? Deborah mused.

Deborah was returning from the forest. Winter was almost upon them, and the last brown leaves drifted down from the trees. She had been clambering up the slope, her arms heavy with firewood, when she heard the sound of shouting. Assuming that the commotion heralded Sisera's return, she dropped the firewood in panic and broke into a run, her heart pounding furiously.

She came to an abrupt halt, and stood immobilised, her mind raced to comprehend what she saw. In the centre of the village four statues had been erected: Baal, Dagon, El and Asherah were positioned next to the well.

Only six months since my brother and father were killed here. Is that how long it takes to forget? What has become of us?

"I'm not suggesting we bow down and worship them! I'm suggesting it might be wise to appease the Canaanites," Jared implored. But even as Deborah watched, she knew that there was more to the idols than placation: before their wooden feet, fruit, and other offerings had been placed. Her eyes slipped to Uriel as she recalled her reluctance to part with the household gods. She had conceded at the time because of Amos' insistence and their vulnerable state. But how long had they been in the village, for how long had she been worshipping them secretly? She had, after all, seen Jared and Shelimoth worship the statues.

"It's idolatry! We are putting our trust in them saving us rather than Yahweh, whether we bow down to them or not. Are we suggesting that Yahweh, who made heaven and earth, needs our help?" Tobias reasoned. His family had drawn around him.

"Did Yahweh save Uriel's village? Did they not trust him?" Hillel, Aaliya's son, bitterly accused. Uriel put her hand on his arm, but he shrugged it off, his voice thick with emotion as he looked at her.

"What do I have to do, watch as my wife is raped and my children are killed…? Because I can't. I can't! I'm sorry, I just can't."

"We feel the same," Ephraim agreed. "We, too, have seen the violence of the Canaanites, we have had a child taken into slavery and feel that we will do what we must to protect those we have left. My wife is Canaanite, and we have learned to accommodate each other's beliefs. We believe that Yahweh is El, Almighty Father – there can be many ways to one god."

Ephraim and his family had arrived in the village following a Canaanite raid, which had destroyed their own. They had lived in a village on the outskirts of Beth-Horon, where inter-marriage was more common. Ariel stood, her hands on her full hips, her long hair falling at her waist and

Shelimoth, her lips in a tight narrow line and arms folded, nodded their agreement with Ephraim. It was as if a line had been drawn in the dirt, and Deborah watched in unbelief as her close knit village divided. Nissa's father, Joshua, younger sister, Yudit, and brother, Levi, had recently joined them after the destruction of their village and family, which had ended the lives of their mother and three brothers. They, too, stepped forward, despite the hushed protests of Nissa. Joshua looked up; his tired eyes looked pained as he turned to Nissa.

"We have seen too much loss, Nissa. I just feel tired. Surely the Canaanites will fear their own gods." His voice trembled as he spoke.

Something began to stir within Deborah as the memory of the dream filled her mind: *Watching, as the fruit falls from the tree and the water is poisoned.* She felt a holy fire grow within her that caused her heart to race and filled her mouth with words that would not be restrained. They were driven by a power that made her forget her fear and pain, as righteous anger consumed her. As she spoke it was with an authority that was not her own.

"My dear family and friends, did Yahweh not say: if we diligently obey His voice and His commandments, then He will set us high over the nations of the earth? Have our ancestors been misled? Is our faith in vain? There can be no road of compromise. It is cowardice and we become blinded by a deception that poisons our nation. We **must** obey Yahweh. We have been given a choice, but there can be no true victory without Him." Deborah paused, her stubborn resolution was now swathed with compassion and understanding of the deeper conflict in the hearts of her community.

"We have suffered, we grieve and we seek consolation. But because we do not understand the ways of Yahweh, we cannot turn away from Him. We must seek His will now more than ever. He will deliver us if we trust Him completely." There was a silence that had covered the village. The truth had been made manifest, and it wrestled with their hearts. But whilst the truth freed some, it enslaved those whose hearts were already embittered.

Gershon stepped forward. "Jared, she's right, we cannot do this. We can't change the truth just because it might help us," he admonished gently.

Tobias met Jared's glare and allowed the rare display of his spiritual authority to bear down on Jared. "You need to remove these. They are not the answer."

Jared's face reddened and eyes narrowed with unconcealed fury as he acknowledged his defeat. "Do what you will, and let the destruction of this village be on your own heads." He turned, and pushed his way past Hagar and Tobias through the crowd. Deborah stood next to them, and he saw the opportunity to maintain his pride and allow an outlet for his rage and bitterness. He jabbed his finger in her face. "Who do you think you are?

Your father would have done well to have rid us of you when he had the chance!"

With that he thundered into his house.

Deborah stood motionless as the crowd dispersed. Only Tobias remained. She was suddenly aware that she was shaking, and now that the moment was over, the reality of what she had said hit her: *who did she think she was? She had insulted the leader of their village, her father's brother.* As she battled with shame, a part of her realised that she had had no choice and that, whilst they may have won this fight, the real battle was in people's hearts.

Tobias walked toward her, lacking his usual certainty: he was a thoughtful man, but not given to spontaneity. Action usually followed careful reflection and prayer. Thus, he was nervous as he reached out and placed a gentle hand on Deborah's shoulder. She searched his eyes, confused as her mind raced to make sense of Jared's remark. She had tried to dismiss it as a spiteful comment without meaning, but Tobias' concern and pain confirmed her suppressed suspicions. And now, it was as though she was teetering on a mountain crest, knowing that she must inevitably fall.

"Shall we walk?" Tobias smiled grimly.

She didn't answer, but kept pace silently next to him.

They walked away from the village, passing the firewood she had dropped earlier, and back through the forest until they came to the brook. As he sat down on the rocky bank, he motioned for Deborah to sit next to him.

"Your father and I used to come here to fish when we were boys," he smiled sadly.

"What was father like when he was young?" Deborah asked. She suddenly needed to hear his name, to talk about him.

"Well now," Tobias chuckled, "we all have a mixture of mischief and goodness, don't we?" He stroked his grey beard. "We used to have plenty of adventures alright. One night we crept out when everyone was asleep, snuck onto the roof, and we switched all the barrels around so that when Amos' Abba went to get wine, he poured oil!"

Deborah giggled. "What did Grandpa do?"

"Oh, your grandpa Isaac was clever. He feigned ignorance, and said to Amos: do you think this wine tastes funny, son? He made Amos drink until he owned up and apologised." Tobias' chuckled sadly; his face suddenly seemed to age with sadness. He turned away. "They were easier times," he sighed almost to himself, as though he were alone, wandering in the catacombs of his own memories: that sanctuary of peace and torment.

They sat silently for some time, both reluctant to take the walk back to reality, until finally Deborah asked the question that had formed in her mind: "Why?"

Tobias turned to her, confused, as though trying to recall their earlier conversation. "Why?"

"Why were they easier times?"

Tobias paused. Gathering his thoughts, he sighed, "Times were simpler, I suppose. We trusted in Yahweh because we had experienced Him, and our shared belief and experiences in him knitted us together as a people. We built houses, farmed the land, people married, had children, and looked out for each other. We passed on His Laws to our children and they grew up safe, within that security. When things went wrong, we knew to seek Him and that the fault was with us, not Him. When he showed us, where we had sinned, we repented. This way of living kept us free and in peace. If there was a dispute we couldn't work out among ourselves, we spoke to the village elder; and if they didn't know, they took it to whoever was judging. But it was a tapestry woven out of love and respect."

"So, what went wrong?" Deborah asked.

"When Othniel, Jared's brother died, people were lost – he was the last of the wilderness generation. When difficult times come, we discover how much of our faith is personal relationship, rooted in faith and how much is religious ritual."

"Like when Moses went onto the mountain top and was gone too long, the people made a gold calf. They thought Yahweh had abandoned them because they didn't have Moses."

"Yes, faith relies on what we cannot see. But people look to the tangible. When Othniel died, people stopped attending the festivals at Shiloh; they became isolated in their villages and susceptible to the beliefs of those around them. Without Yahweh's guidance, we made decisions that seemed 'sensible': Marriages were made to settle trade and land agreements and so compromises were made. Slowly, our thinking changed, people began to worship El as Yahweh, and then began worshipping Baal and his cohorts. Building high places, sacrificing their children and temple prostitution progressed naturally after that. After a while, there was no one to remind us that we were breaking Yahweh's Laws. We started thinking it was acceptable."

Deborah leaned back against a sycamore tree. She had heard the stories before, but never had she understood the importance of them, as she did now. "Then what happened?"

"When Moab began to oppress us, we had forgotten the way back to Yahweh. Sin and apathy are great allies; they feed off of each other until Israel no longer had the strength, nor the will to fight, despite our oppression. We had lost our way. Many died because of the annual tribute that Eglon demanded of our people. There was never enough left over. People starved during the long winters, while Eglon kept getting fatter and fatter. In His grace, Yahweh would not let us go. He created opportunities to teach us to trust Him again. Eventually, when we reached the end of our own strength, in desperation, we called out to Yahweh. And He sent Ehud – you know the story. For as long as that generation lived, we had the painful lesson to remind us of God's truths, and we had seen His power and love for us. Very few of us are left to remember how awful it was, or the miracle of Ehud's deliverance, now.

"The new generation, they don't see the lessons that history can teach us. As the Canaanites grow in power, so does commerce and trading, they thrive and we look to them. Over the last few years, your father and I were aware that people were returning to the old ways. We have been protected to a large extent in the village. But there are those who visit the cities, even in this village, it's like a spiritual sickness that weakens us."

"Why does Yahweh allow it? Why doesn't He just kill the Canaanites, or drive them out of Israel."

Tobias frowned. "Well, that was His initial plan. When Yahweh told us He would give us this land, we were commanded to kill all the inhabitants of the land. But we were disobedient. Many thought the Lord was uncompassionate to ask us to kill innocent men, women and children. But He loved them too. We live in a spiritual world: sometimes evil is so strong, you have to kill something at its root or it will just shoot back up... He had warned them for hundreds of years what He would do. He wanted to permanently end child sacrifice, temple prostitution, to end all that would cause wars for hundreds of years and the suffering of many, not only Israel, His chosen people. But most importantly, He wanted to stop people being lost to Him for eternity, through being misled by false gods."

"Wasn't there an easier way?"

"It's important to understand the nature of Yahweh and His relationship with man. He is just; but He is also loving. Men were created for relationship with Him. He desires our love, but love is a choice. And choices always have consequences attached to them. Choices and consequences are natural laws."

"How do you mean?" Deborah probed.

Tobias stroked his beard thoughtfully. "Well now, let me see. If you are staying in my house and I say to you: as long as you stay in my house, I will protect you - you will be safe. But outside there are bears. One day you get bored and decide to ignore my warning, and go outside. You see the warning on the door as you go out, but still you choose. Outside a bear sees you and kills you. Whose fault was it you got killed?"

"Mine...I understand. Abba used to say that Yahweh works with men, and He won't take away our choice. He wants relationship, our love but you can't force someone to love you, or it isn't love." Deborah smiled sadly. "But why, is this happening now? Can't Yahweh just send someone to kill Sisera?" she insisted with child-like simplicity as she threw a stone into the stream. She watched it skip three times across the surface of the water before disappearing into ripples of perfect concentric circles.

Tobias let the moment pass silently.

"Do you think, at this time, it would really help us?" Tobias questioned.

Deborah wanted to blurt out, "Of course it would help us!" but she knew Tobias well enough to know he was making her think.

Finally she answered tentatively, as though she was still forming the thought in her mind. "If Sisera were not a threat, people would continue down their own path and our nation would die. So, this way, when things are bad enough, they will eventually turn back to Yahweh. Then He will raise up a deliverer."

Tobias nodded sadly. "Pain is there to show us something is wrong."

"But why did my father and Enoch die? They weren't worshipping Baal."

"No, your brother wasn't worshipping Baal, nor was your father." Tobias swallowed. He looked down at his feet, and when he met Deborah's eyes she saw the depth of his pain.

"The truth is never simple. Sometimes we have to let go of the need for answers and be content with the fact that He is God and we are not. That's real faith. But the reality is that we are fighting against a far bigger enemy than Sisera."

"Satan." Deborah had loved Abba telling her the story of Job.

"That's right. There is a battle between Yahweh and Satan, and man's choices are a part of that battle, because we are made in His image and because we are destined to rule with Him in eternity. Satan hates us and fears us.

"But let's begin with the choices part, because it will be the hardest to look at, and the most important lesson to learn. Let's go back to the house. Let's pretend that I am superhumanly strong and kill bears. Does that make you a bear-killer?" His eyes twinkled, playfully.

"No," Deborah answered, trying not to giggle as she imagined elderly gentle Tobias as an angry bear-killer.

"Good. If you wanted to kill that bear, what would you have to do?"

"I'd need to ask you to go with me. You'd do the killing and I would watch," Deborah laughed.

"Right!" Tobias paused, waiting while Deborah pieced together the truth of what he was trying to tell her.

"Enoch didn't ask Yahweh, did he?" her face fell as the truth sank in.

"No, I don't think he did," he smiled sadly. "Unfortunately, it's not enough to have the right intention. That's why Joshua always consulted the Umin and Thummin before he went into battle. Yahweh sees the whole picture; we see only a small part of it. That's why we need His direction. He doesn't punish us because we don't do things His way, like some overcontrolling parent. We simply step out of His realm of protection when we try and do things our way."

"So Baal is the bear; if we invite him into our village, we are going to see him hurt people." Deborah closed her eyes as the truth sunk in. Her eyes filled with tears, and she wiped them away. "But then why did my father die? He didn't do anything wrong."

"Your father chose to defend his son. That was his choice, and had it worked, Enoch would still be living. He didn't deserve to die." He swallowed back his tears, trying to check his emotions for Deborah's sake: he could tell she was not ready to grieve yet.

"But...sometimes Satan's will prevails and nobody has done anything wrong. You remember the story of Job?"

"He lost everything, except his wife."

"Man views success differently to Yahweh. Because we do not fully understand the concept of eternity, we grip hold of this life as though it will never end. We are God's great creation. Satan hates us and a battle rages in the heavenly realm in which we are both the warriors and the targets. Remember how Satan appeared before God, and asked to test Job? When we remain faithful under temptation and attack, we win battles in the spiritual realm. Your father understood that."

Deborah nodded. She remembered her father once telling her the same thing.

"How can we be so stupid?" Deborah asked.

"The answer is human nature. We're a foolish and stubborn breed, and I sometimes wonder how Yahweh puts up with us. Your father used to say we were like sheep, but that it was no compliment; they are the most foolish creatures you could imagine. The moment they lose sight of the shepherd they get into all sorts of trouble, wander off, roll onto their backs to get comfortable and then get eaten by foxes."

Deborah smiled sadly remembering. "Yes, but Abba would turn aside and search for even one that got lost."

"He was a wise man, I miss him greatly. You are your father's daughter, Deborah. I see him in you: his wisdom, his passion and his strength of character."

"If I were a man, I would fight the Canaanites."

Tobias chuckled. "If Yahweh had wanted you to be a man, you would be. Our nation needs a mother, to knit it together, to heal it, to show it Yahweh's love and wisdom. I think that was part of your father's plan." He picked up a stone and let it skip four times across the water. He laughed, "I never grow tired of doing that! Years of practice." He was silent for a moment.

"Abba always said our lives were like those stones: they create splashes and ripples that have lasting effects."

Thinking of her father made her recall her uncle's last words to her. She felt a knot twist in her stomach, and as she looked at Tobias, she knew he was thinking about it too. She wanted to stand up and go back to the village and not ask, for she knew that her personal strength was already floundering.

But the youthful mind is like a rushing river, seeking to force its own course and never mindful that the destination may lead to its own destruction. Almost as a whisper, she looked up at Tobias, meeting his sad eyes. "Why? Why did Jared say Abba should have got rid of me when he had the chance?"

Anger flickered across Tobias' face, and for a moment, Deborah wondered if he was angry with her for asking. She waited.

Finally, Tobias spoke, slowly, as though he was struggling for the right words to say: "Deborah, I don't know the entirety of this story and it's likely I never will. Your father came to me about a year ago. He told me about your dream..." He paused, waiting for Deborah to acknowledge what he had said before he continued. "Your father was concerned about what he saw happening in Israel. When you were in Bethlehem, your father sought the counsel of Ehud. He told him about your dream. Ehud said the dream spoke of his death, and that the time would come when Israel would be divided and oppressed again. He said that you would have some part to play in Yahweh's plan for restoration, but you were young...too young. You were only eleven. It was decided that a marriage should be organised, for when you came of age...someone suitable".

Tobias frowned. "I did not ask, because he did not offer the information. I knew Amos well enough to know that he would have told me if he'd wanted me to know. It was never discussed again and possibly nothing was organised yet...So I don't know if a husband was found for you or if it was just spoken of. I'm sorry. It was agreed that nothing would be said... until your thirteenth birthday. Your mother would know of course, but..."

"Now's not really the right time to ask, is it?" Deborah smiled sadly, suddenly feeling tired as though she had aged in the last few months.

Tobias squeezed her hand. "You've done so well Deborah...with everything that's happened. You must feel a bit lost- but remember, God's plans remain constant through the storms."

"Why don't you become leader of the village? People would follow you and then you could keep people right with Yahweh – you could talk to people quietly at first, or we could do it for you, I know they would stand with you."

Tobias chuckled. "Well, I suppose the easiest answer is because Yahweh hasn't told me and I'm not about to go and take that on by myself. I can't make people follow Yahweh; it's between their hearts and His. It's part of

Yahweh's sovereignty and power that He sometimes uses the difficult people in the world to accomplish is plans."

"Then you think I shouldn't have argued with Jared?" Deborah asked, defensively.

Tobias' eyes appraised Deborah kindly. "I think you know you had to do that, don't you? There's a difference between rebellion and standing against ungodliness," he reasoned.

He patted her knee with fatherly affection. "I suppose I ought to be getting you back to the village. Shall we see what Raisa and your mother have made for dinner?" Standing up, he straightened himself slowly.

In the following weeks, an apprehensive calm seemed to hover over the village. The air had cooled and it was ordinarily a time when life would quieten down. They would light fires, sing songs and enjoy the new wine with the other fruits of the harvest. However, the knowledge that the Canaanites could arrive at any moment, and the threat of their previous violence, created an emotional cauldron of tension, in which life could be ended at any time. Each moment became precious in its fragility.

Deborah sat with Tobias and Raisa's twin grandchildren, Tebah and Gabriella, who were ten years old. Tebah was a stocky and boisterous character, with a mop of unruly hair and two missing teeth that rather suited his character. His sister, Gabriella, bore little resemblance and was thin. Her long waist length hair seemed to look too heavy for her tiny body and she had a squeaky, timid voice. Deborah had always wondered if Tebah had somehow wrestled with Gabriella and taken all the strength from his sister in his mother, Orpah's, womb. Isaac joined them with Hillel and Uriel's son, Judah, and his younger sister, Hannah. Judah, aged twelve, was an intelligent, thoughtful child, with a high brow and an athletic build. He had a natural charisma, and gentle confidence that set him apart as the leader in their group. His sister, Hannah, was no less strong, at least in will, despite her size and being two years younger. She had learnt at a young age to use her younger-sibling-power to full advantage by telling tales on her brother if she felt she was not being treated well. Thus, the two had a grudging respect for each other. Judah picked up a sword he had carved out of a piece of wood.

"Hey, let's play a game! Isaac and Tebah, you pretend to be Canaanites, and I'll be an Israelite warrior."

"What shall I be?" squeaked Gabriella.

"You can be a woman, crying to be rescued," her older sibling sneered.

Gabriella's face reddened with indignation. "That's boring! How come the boys get all the fun jobs?"

"Well, it would hardly be a woman who defeated the Canaanites, would it?" Tebah smirked, glancing at Isaac and Judah for support. They laughed fawningly.

Hannah put her hands on her hips, looking at Reuben.

"Girls can be strong too. Anat is a woman."

Reuben glared at Hannah. "Remember what Mama said, big mouth."

Hannah stuck out her tongue, taking the tearful Gabriella by the arm and marching purposefully to her parents' home.

Deborah was feeling tense, and Tebah's brutish insensitivity niggled her. "That was unkind, Tebah. Ehud might not have been a woman, but he wasn't a bully either! Why don't you…" Her voice trailed off.

All of a sudden, there was a hushed silence, where time seemed to slow. Sound and movement diminished as their panicked senses sought to hone in on the source of the fear – to define and certify their legitimacy. When Deborah considered it later, it was as if terror had arrived before any physical, audible warning and people seemed immobilised by it.

7

And Jael was the wife of Heber the Kenite.
Judges 4:17

1257 BC - Jael

Jael muttered furiously under her breath as she fought to dismantle her family's heavy goats hair tent.

"There's no point getting angry with the tent, Jael," her mother sighed.

Jael spun around, her rage as wild as her thick, waist length hair. She glared at her mother. "I won't marry him! I won't! I don't love him, I could never love him. The man is a snake. I can't believe Papa would force me to marry him."

"Jael!" her mother cautioned. She kicked dirt over the open fire, sending ash and dust into the morning air. It was still cool enough to work, but the sun, a hazy ball of fire that lazed on the horizon, would soon blaze its full fury. "We are women. We rarely have any control over the choices in our life. Your father made this decision because it provides our family with stability. He will not always be able to work so hard, and he has only daughters. Life is difficult!" Her voice was edged with bitterness as she turned Jael to face her. "He does believe this is best for you, you know. Heber is a man of some wealth; he will provide for you. You are always wanting adventure and excitement - well here is your chance. You of all people don't want to spend your life making tents, setting up tents, cooking, carrying water."

"I'm hardly marrying into royalty!" Jael spat with disdain. "The man's a Kenite: he mines copper and iron."

"Perhaps not, but Heber has slaves. You will have an easier life – if you can learn to make the best of it. And he's still a Midianite - he is one of us," Kiya tried to reason.

Jael put down the wooden poles she had collected. She faced her mother, her hands on her hips, her voice level, though the familiar fire burned with intensity in her eyes.

"Father is doing this so that it will make his life easier! Please, at least, do me the courtesy of being honest. And I...I am a commodity to be traded. Well, I will not compromise who I am...Not for father, not for you and certainly not for Heber! We are Midianites. We belong here, in Midian. This is where our people have always dwelt!"

"Well, you know little of our history then, Jael. Midian was a child of Abraham through his concubine, Keturah. The Israelites are the children of Isaac and therefore are our distant relatives. You see, our relationship with them goes back long before Jethro."

Jael rolled her eyes with irritation, noting with satisfaction her mother's ire and pretending not to listen – her mother loved to talk about their history.

"After Hobab, Jethro's son, led Israel through the wilderness, he was given an allotment with Judah, which makes him as much Midianite as us! The Midianites have been mining at Timna since the metal was first discovered.

"We must travel to Arad; there's simply no point in arguing about it."

Jael thought about walking away, but she was still angry and scared for her future and needed to let off steam. "Heber's heritage does not alter that well-known fact he shows no allegiance to anyone other than himself and his ambition! How could you expect me to marry such a man?"

Kiya met Jael's glare, lowering her voice in a way that warned Jael that she was on the brink of losing her temper, and Jael knew from past experience that her mother's fury was the only force she could not stand against.

"You will marry Heber! Or you will be left to wander the wilderness alone, and believe me, far worse things wait for you out there. And when you are married, you will use that great will of yours and your good looks to help him understand our heritage." Calmly, she picked up the water bucket and walked to the well.

Jael willed her pride to push back her tears. She began to round up the sheep and goats, the final preparation before their caravan moved on...on to Judah, to where Heber awaited. Leaving behind Midian, and all that was familiar. With all her heart she feared her future; she felt it, like a dark cloud of vultures, hovering over a dead carcass - her dead carcass - and she was being driven into it.

"Jael!"

She spun round. She knew that voice.

"Jael!"

Her eyes searched between the chaos of semi-dismantled tents, and camels and donkeys protesting as they were attached to loaded caravans and strapped down with luggage. At last she found him. He stood tall against one of the caravans, watching her, smiling, as he had that first time two years ago. The desert wind blew his linen robes against his muscular form. He would almost have been camouflaged against the pale sand, were it not for his dark skin and long black hair that fell in thick tendrils to his waist.

"Zimran!" Casting a quick look around her, she ran to him, throwing herself into his arms. His dark eyes held hers for a moment, and as he took her face in his hands, his lips found hers.

"I missed you." She rested her head against his solid chest, the steady rhythm of his heart an elixir to her turmoil - and yet with it came the pain of knowing this was the last time he would hold her.

"Where have you been?" Jael asked. She loved hearing about his adventures as a caravan driver, travelling to other countries and fighting off bandits.

"We have returned from Egypt, with linen, gold and..." he delved into his pocket and held a small packet on the palm of his hand. He flashed her his beautiful smile, his full lips parting to reveal his perfect white teeth. He was beautiful, his features so strong and chiseled it was as though he were made of finest black marble. She felt the familiar emotions of awe and desire.

The smell told her before she opened it. "Frankincense!" Her eyes shone as she unwrapped the tiny parcel. A small amount of frankincense was worth a great deal, not only for its medicinal qualities but also for its aroma. He knew her so well: gold would never have delighted her in the same way.

"I love it! Thank you!" she exclaimed. She looked up at him from beneath her thick black eyelashes, and the love she saw in his eyes pushed away her fear. She would forget Heber for today.

"How long are you here for?" She pulled on his hair playfully, forcing his face downwards to meet hers; forcing her to face reality in the sorrowful reflection of his countenance.

"Alas, fate is playing a cruel joke on me: I have been ordered to drive your caravan to Arad tomorrow."

The familiar feeling of nausea, fear and sadness took hold of her until she felt that she would drown in it. She looked up at him silently, waiting for him to offer her another road.

"What do you want, Jael?" His eyes, black as the night, were solemn.   "Do you want to leave? You know I love you, don't you? We could go to the desert and live as we were meant to."

She wrapped her arms around him, as though he were a rock in the midst of a storm.

"I love you too…" She wanted to tell him that they should leave now, mount a camel and ride until Midian and Arad were far behind them. They could live as nomads in the wilderness; they would never be found. They knew how to survive the desert. She could be his: to wake up to him each day, to bear his children, to travel and grow old together.

Everything in her longed to go with him and he was giving her a choice. The choice she had longed for and never had. She had always been sure of what she would do, if she were she able to decide for herself. But now the bitter reality of life confronted her: choices were never that simple, because her choices would inevitably affect others.

She was furious with her father for selling her like a prize camel which could so easily be traded. But to leave with Zimran, and reject Heber's marriage proposal, would bring humiliation to her family. Her father was relying not only on Heber's generous dowry, but also on the business he gave them. Her betrayal would force them into poverty. Then what would happen to her young sisters, Cozbi and Sera? At worst they would starve or be sold into slavery to pay for her father's debts. To be responsible for knowing that her parents and sisters would grow old under the curse of shame and destitution - was she that angry with them, could she do it? And to never see her family again. Her family was not affectionate, neither in word or touch, but they had an unspoken bond.

Yet to consider the alternative: to live apart from Zimran forever. For every moment not to be measured until the time he returned. To let go of the future that she had dreamt of, could she do that and still survive? And, not only to let go of Zimran, but to commit herself to a man she neither loved nor respected. And what of Zimran and his loss?

Suddenly, choice seemed a curse: two roads stretched before her, both seemed full of pain and sorrow, either to herself and Zimran, or to her family.

His eyes held hers, searching her thoughts. She pushed her palms into her eyes, pushing back the tears and the pain that had formed in her chest. He held her and stroked her hair, but said nothing.

Finally, she looked at him. "Everything in me wants to go with you Zimran, but I cannot do that to my family. I love you…I know that I'll always love you, but…it would be too selfish. I would never be free of the guilt of knowing what I had done to my family."

She buried her face into his chest, her body shaking with the weight of her decision. She felt the rise and fall of his chest as he, too, struggled with the pain of her answer.

Finally, he lifted her face to his, imploring her as he drank in her beautiful features. The idea of Heber touching her made him feel sick.

"Jael, do you know what you are doing? Because I do. I work for Heber, I know what the man is like – I am not sure he is capable of love or kindness."

"I know as much." She placed her hand on his chest. His heart beat wildly and his expression was one of desolation. She felt her resolve wobble, and she lacked both the conviction and strength to fight it. She mentally shut the doors to her heart, and forced herself to walk away with the briefest of farewells.

As she entered their tent she was met by Serah. She shoved heatedly past her.

"So, you've told him," Serah stated.

Jael nodded, throwing herself onto the cushions, and giving in to her sorrow.

Jael pushed aside the curtains that separated the sleeping area from the living area of their tent. She tiptoed past her sleeping parents and sisters, dreading the thought of company on this day. The sun had just begun to rise, like an angry ball of fire that promised to show no mercy.

She stoked the remains of last night's fire to flame, taking comfort in the familiar ritual and smell of wood smoke. Taking a handful of grain, she began pounding it angrily between two stones until it was fine enough to mix with water and oil. While it cooked, she walked to the well, drawing water and carefully avoiding looking toward the large tent, with its sumptuous, exquisitely designed curtains over the doors. Next to it was another tent, smaller, though no less elaborate. Surrounding them were plainer tents that she assumed belonged to her future husband's slaves.

The city of Arad with its large fortress rose in the distance. Though the Kenites dwelt amongst the Hebrews and were under their protection, they had maintained their nomadic culture, preferring to live in tents rather than the mud-and-daub or rock structures of the Hebrews.

Hearing movement from the slaves' tents, Jael ducked back behind the goats-hair flap of their shelter.

She submitted herself to having her hair brushed, and bathing 'to be prepared like a lamb before it's sacrificed,' she contended sulkily. Her mother, aware of her temperamental daughter's mood, had been surprised that Jael had suffered the traditional henna party the night before. While the women in her family and Heber's retinue sung, Jael's face, hands and feet had been decorated with henna for her wedding. For Jael's part, she had made the greatest sacrifice, and it had left her feeling resigned and dead inside; making a fuss about a henna party seemed of little consequence. Zimran had left after the caravan arrived, and she did not know if she would see him again; yet he was there, in every thought.

In the distance she could hear the celebrations of Heber and his friends as they gathered around him. To Jael they sounded like howling wolves.

Finally, Jael stood in her red bridal dress, embroidered with gold and purple. A purple veil, fringed with tiny gold bells, covered her long, dark hair, which had been pinned back. She took the gold bracelets from her sister, Cozbi, and slipped them over her henna-decorated hand. The women in Heber's entourage had given them to her.

"He has no family here, don't you find it strange?" Cozbi asked as she placed a simple gold band around her sister's neck.

"It says something about a person's character," Jael shrugged. She had noted that Heber's family had been absent, and whilst she was curious as to their absence, she was also relieved at the prospect of their lack of involvement in her life after she was married.

"Yes, and nothing good." Her sister met her eyes and smiled sadly. "Are you going to be alright, Jael?" she added after a moment.

"I'll have to be, won't I?" Jael shrugged, turning away from the conversation and the panic that rose in her throat.

When she was finally ready, she felt like an alabaster statue: cold and without feeling. Her father held her, and through his tears, told her how beautiful she looked and that he was proud of her. Jael smiled dutifully back, as she felt herself recede behind the mask.

The curtains were pulled back, and light flooded in, exposing her to the waiting guests. As nomadic tradition dictated, Jael mounted the waiting camel that would take her to Heber's tent. The journey took only minutes, and guests followed, singing and dancing, while musicians played; to Jael it sounded like a funeral dirge. She took in the man who stood before her: double her age, his dark hair and beard stood out in contrast to the linen robes he wore. His thin lips were curved in a half-smile that dissolved before it reached his eyes.

As the camel bent down to allow her to dismount, Heber approached and took her hand. Ignoring the gesture as an act of defiance, she slipped gracefully to the floor, feeling a small twinge of triumph. She snatched a glance at her husband; the smile had slipped from his face. He bowed stiffly, his eyes cold and in a moment of realisation, she knew she had made the wrong choice. She wanted to run - she had changed her mind; this wasn't a game in which she played a hero. It was life, her life! Everything within her recoiled from this man. She felt nauseous and dizzy with fear, aware that everyone was watching her, and she scanned the crowd looking for Zimran.

What was she thinking of? He wouldn't have stayed for this!

Blinking back the tears, she held her head high, mechanically forcing herself to step toward him.

As though watching events unfold, she saw herself handed over by her father. She was speaking - agreeing to spend her life with a man she neither loved nor respected. She saw the girl congratulated by family and friends. She acknowledged the sadness that shadowed her mother's eyes. Then she was aware of Heber, leading her into his tent, and slaves closing the curtains behind them like doors to a prison. Their voices grew louder as they began the celebrations that would continue without them. He led her to the cushions, and she knew what was expected of her. She would show no fear; give him no sense of owning her...so she receded within her mind, shutting down thought and feeling until the girl was no more.

The next morning, she was led to her tent by slaves; her husband had business to attend to at the mines in Timna. Of that she was glad. She pushed aside the thick curtains that hung over the entrance. The tent was divided into two sections: the first being the living quarters, where she would be expected to entertain guests. A low, flat table was positioned in the middle of the room, surrounded with cushions and carpets. The sides of the tent were decorated with hangings and drapes, and small lanterns hung from the ceiling. More thick, embroidered curtains divided the front section from the back where she would sleep. Her sleeping area was layered with animal skins, cushions and brightly coloured coverings above which small lanterns hung from the roof poles. On a carved wooden table lay a basket of figs, a plate of biscuits and a jar of water. On the opposite side of the room a shrine had been erected in which statues of Asherah, Baal, Dagon and El watched her mutely.

She knew, had she been an ordinary woman, she would have been seduced by such opulence; and certainly there was a part of her that could appreciate its beauty. But she was in no mood to enjoy comfort. The tent made her feel like a caged animal that would tear off its own limb to be free. As she carefully pulled the curtains behind her, she sank into the cushions and sobbed until her grief was spent and all that remained was the smoldering fire of her anger - that familiar feeling of comfort.

It was that anger that made her purpose to overcome, to survive and to find some way to remain true to herself. In that moment she realised that the strength that flowed through her, which defined her, remained. It would sustain her and guide her. She would not be overcome, nor subdued. Neither would she allow herself to be compromised by Heber, or life.

8

They chose new gods. Then there was war in the gates
Neither a shield, nor a spear was seen among forty thousand in Israel.
Judges 5:8

1255 BC - Deborah

The winter sky was pewter. Dark rain clouds could be seen as block sheets over mount Ephraim, sullen and threatening as they poured out their fury.

The moment was here. They had dreaded it and planned for it for so long that it seemed surreal: the reality of the invasion and their impending doom fought their innate human desire to hope. And the unconscious knowledge of their helplessness warred with the revelation that to hope for mercy from men who know no mercy was futile, bearing its own crippling despair.

Deborah's first instincts were primal and instinctive; her body shook with asphyxiating fear as she beheld the man who had murdered those she loved. A thought pricked the walls of her terror and quickly intensified until it was a resolute, inner scream – she must save her mother and brother. She half ran, half stumbled into Raisa's house where her mother spent most of her time. They were talking as they sliced leeks and adding them to soaked chickpeas. Her mother turned as she burst through the doorway. She took one look at Deborah's face and her own face drained of blood.

"They're here." It was a statement.

"Where's Isaac?"

"He's by the brook with Tebah."

"There's no time. You have to hide." Her eyes flashed to Raisa, who still stood with a leek in her hand. "Tell the others to hide!" she urged.

Her mother looked at her, her eyes suddenly overcome with a resignation that was as hopeless as it was peaceful.

"I won't hide Deborah. If Yahweh wills that I should die today, then so be it – I am ready this time." She spoke with her former levelheaded pragmatism that Deborah had so missed in her mother, but which left no room for question. Her eyes flitted imploringly to Raisa and back to her mother as decision became impossible.

"Find Isaac…Go now darling." Raisa's voice was decisive yet sad, for she sensed the frustration and helplessness of Deborah's dilemma, even as she recognised her friend's stubborn nature and weariness of life.

Everything in Deborah warred against leaving the cluster of houses.
The last time she had left, she had returned to the death of half of her family. She knew it was irrational of her, that she could not have done anything had she been there, but the guilt of having escaped was a persistent ache in her chest that grew and fed her need to protect.

Making her decision, she embraced her mother and left the house. She broke into a run, fuelled by the panic that was spreading through the village and passed Shelimoth, who was hurrying Ariel into their home. She stopped when she saw Deborah and tried to grab her arm, but she tore herself away and plunged into the cover of the trees. She quickly wove her way through the dense pine and eucalyptus. Shafts of light pricked their way through the dense foliage. The air was still and eerily quiet, as though nature, too, held its breath in helpless terror.

Finally, the trees thinned out to sporadic oak and sycamore trees which were bereft of their leaves, so she was able to see the stream winding below her. It was swollen and dark from the winter rains and surged violently on its journey to freedom. When she didn't find the two boys, she decided to follow the brook down-stream, knowing that there was a deep pool half a mile away where the boys liked to fish. She pushed her aching legs to keep moving, nimbly avoiding the roots that had prised their way free of the soil. Her breath was hot in her lungs and her chest ached by the time she finally heard Tebah's voice and scrambled down the rocky embankment.

"Isaac…Tebah!" her voice came out in breathless gasps.

Isaac turned, the blood draining from his face as he read his sister's wild, panic filled eyes. "They're here!"

Deborah nodded gaining her breath. "I didn't want you to walk in… not knowing. Stay here until they've gone." She dug her palms into her eyes as panic tightened its grip on her senses.

Isaac looked at her. "And Mother…?" His brown eyes looked haunted.

Deborah shook her head, her brow creased with anxiety.

"She wouldn't come…I need to get back, but you stay here. Stay here…" She caught her voice, before it broke.

Isaac searched her eyes, as though looking for the answer to his indecision. His innate and desperate will to survive battled with the knowledge that if his mother and sister were killed, he would be alone…

"And what if something happens to the two of you…do you think I could live knowing I had escaped? I…I need to be with you and Mother, no matter what."

Deborah nodded in resignation. She could not argue with him - his argument was her own.

Sisera felt that pleasant pull in his gut that he experienced from the knowledge of his control and fear-induced dominance. It was like a drug that fuelled him, and its lust made him complete. He never knew exactly what he would do when he arrived at a village, but his actions were driven by his sadistic fantasies. The 'fear game' he liked to call it; he was driven by the response of the victim.

He strode into the centre of the village, Talmai beside him. The soldier's face bore none of the chiseled, handsome features that Sisera possessed. He was a head taller, and his girth was like that of a mighty oak. A scar ran across his eye and down his face, giving him the appearance of a perpetual sneer.

This time there was no welcoming committee, the General mused with satisfaction; *they are without a leader and their strength and unity is compromised.* Whilst he purposed his next step, the old man he recognised from his previous encounter stepped out of one of the houses.

"Welcome." Tobias cleared his throat. "We have all that you requested; it is ready for you to…to take."

Sisera was silent as he looked the old man up and down, his gaze roaming the village. He knew that all the while he was silent, terror was building in the hearts and minds of the people.

"I was lenient with you when I came last time. You escaped as few other villages have."

Tobias' heart pounded. He leant against the well, willing his knees not to buckle beneath him. He had always known that Jared would have neither the courage, nor the compassion, to speak for the village; but he had been unable to mentally prepare himself for this inevitable encounter.

"My lord, we have worked hard to give you all that you requested."

Tobias searched the soldier's eyes for any sign of appeasement or mercy, but his hope slid from the forged iron of Sisera's countenance and withered before him.

His face was inches away from Tobias' as he spoke in a snarled whisper. "But will it be enough? We'll see." He beckoned to the other men; there were eight of them this time, four soldiers and four drivers, each one responsible for one wagon that would carry away the fruit of their labours.

He smiled like an indulgent father playing with a child. But the set of his jaw and the unveiled contempt in his dark eyes exposed his true intent.

"You." He gestured to Tobias. "Show me what you have prepared, and while you do so, I require any weapons or shields that you have to be collected and relinquished."

It was at that moment that Tobias acknowledged that whatever they delivered to the soldier it would not be enough. He was here to play. And their lives were the game.

"Are the women hidden?" the old man whispered.

"They are." His son's face was pale, his expression grave.

Tobias felt righteous anger rise up within him as he beckoned Gershon and Menachem to help him with their produce. His silent prayers went up to Yahweh as he asked Jonah and Reuben to organise the collection of anything that might be seen as a weapon.

Four of the soldiers came with them into the storehouse. They began helping themselves to the sealed barrels and bags before loading them onto the wagons. Talmai kicked and beat the bleating, whining animals as they hesitated to mount the wagons. The distress and anxiety of the village was a heavy, tangible presence that made one silent and another scream. Talmai walked to the first wagon, and as the doors were closed, it seemed they would leave. A sense of relief rippled within the village, its fingers of hope teasingly caressing their torment - and yet, Tobias was aware that the four soldiers still remained. It was then that the revelation of Sisera's game unfolded: he was allowing them to hope, but there was more to come. He glanced with scorn at the small pile of rudimentary knives and weaponry that were piled before him, and the village watched as their final hopes of defending themselves were loaded onto the last cart. Trepidation, like a thick, oily smoke began to coil itself around Tobias as he felt darkness descend upon his people.

Sisera beckoned Tobias to him.

"Sir?" Tobias raised his eyes now to meet Sisera's. The General met his righteous defiance with a raised eyebrow. "I find human nature such an interesting study: at first you want to hide, to do anything other than embrace your fear and possible death. Eventually, when your fear is ripe, you want only to know what your end will be." His lips curved but his eyes remained hauntingly cold.

"Sir?" Tobias repeated, refusing to give this man anything more to feed on.

Sisera genuinely weighed Tobias, although he had several ideas as to the outcome, it was only now he was decided.

"It was NOT enough," he whispered, and nodding to his men, the four of them began to storm the houses. The men watched frantically, and it seemed that their efforts to hide the girls had been successful.

"The girls. Where are they?" Sisera hissed.

Tobias was silent. He swallowed his fear. He would not lie, but neither would he fear death. Sisera perceived his resolution, and turning slowly, his eyes rested on each man in the village, waiting for the one who would show him. There were many things he could have done: tortured their leader in front of them until they spoke, or burnt the houses to the ground, but this way would do the most harm. Blame. Blame that leads to division. Division causes weakness. Weakness allows itself to be ruled.

Finally, his lips curved and Tobias felt his gut twist as the soldier's eyes settled on the roof of the threshing floor. He gestured to his men and they ran up the stone stairs reappearing moments later with four women, the youngest of whom was Ariel, at fifteen years old. She was whimpering hysterically. Sisera walked up to her. His lustful eyes took in the feminine curves of her body and her long dark hair.

"This one will be mine." He gripped her face in his hands, marking his claim. "A treasure for Canaan."

Jared rushed forward, throwing himself at Sisera's feet as he pleaded for mercy.

"No! Leave her!" Shimon, Aaliya's son and Ariel's betrothed, reacted with the fearlessness and passion of youth. Grabbing the plough shear that rested against his home, he rushed at Sisera, the rudimentary weapon raised above his head.

His protest was abruptly silenced.

Taking his axe from his belt, Sisera moved with the speed of a seasoned warrior, his axe deftly shattering the wooden pole and in the same fluid movement, his second blow sliced through Shimon's neck. The boy's head lolled to one side as his body collapsed and his life ebbed into the ground.

Aaliya's bereft sobs merged with other parents' and the screams of the terrified girls as they were dragged into the forest.

Deborah, Isaac and Tebah recognised the helpless, terrorised cries as they clambered silently up the wooded slope. Leading the way, she caught a glimpse of the men as they violently threw their victims to the forest floor. Their struggles were silenced by the brutal blows of the men before they violated them. Deborah threw herself instinctively to the ground and heard the boys follow suit behind her. She clapped her hands over her ears as the screams of those she loved seared her soul and helplessness tortured her. The image of their defilement seared itself into her thoughts as tears of impotent rage bled into the earthy mulch; Yahweh seemed far away.

An icy shudder gouged the air as the girls' wails turned to desperate pleas for mercy, and then something worse than the screams: silence.

Only one voice could still be heard, a desolate whimper that curdled the forest air with its horror. Deborah raised her head to see Ariel, half naked, being dragged away by Talmai and packed onto one of the carts.

After a long time, Deborah felt Isaac's hand on her shoulder. "Hey, sis. Let's go home now. Ima will be waiting." The empty brokenness in Isaac's voice reflected her own fragile state.

Their eyes involuntarily sought out the horror that Sisera and his men had left behind; the bodies of those that they had grown up with, disgraced and butchered, their faces contorted by their violent end.

They staggered from the forest, sullied and distraught.

When Maya saw her children, she ran to them, pulling them into her arms. "Thank you, Yahweh." No other words could be said, for while her children had escaped, the rest of the village grieved.

Deborah nodded mutely. There was a hollow silence in the village, broken only by the desperate sobs of grief. It was a void that words could not fill, nor attempt to make sense of.

"Come into the house," Maya said. The winter air was cool and a fine drizzle of rain had saturated their clothes. Deborah's body was shaking uncontrollably as her mother wrapped each of them in a blanket, stoking the fire that had died to glowing embers. Some part of Deborah's mind acknowledged that in the midst of their horror, in which each family had lost at least one member, her mother had returned to her, and was looking after them. For that small mercy, she was grateful.

9

Declare me innocent, O LORD, for I have acted with integrity; I have trusted in the LORD without wavering.
Psalm 26:1.

1253 BC – Shamgar

As they pulled into his father's estate, Shamgar could feel exhaustion threatening to take hold of him. It had been a very long day. He handed the reins to one of his father's servants as he was met in the courtyard.

His father met him in the entrance hall, having been awoken by the servants. Despite his age, he still walked with the strength of presence of a military leader. He took in his son's blood-stained, battered appearance and the bedraggled, traumatised children in his wake and grimly noted the absence of Sarai and Samuel. His son's weary eyes met his, and he read the pain and loss that was too raw to verbalise. Gripping his son's shoulders, he silently led the exhausted group into his home. Some of them staggered, without hope, whilst others were skittish, their eyes constantly on the lookout, unable to adjust to the idea of safety.

"We will talk tomorrow. Tonight you will eat something and sleep. I will send out servants to look for Hariya. You can do no more tonight." He nodded to Shamgar decisively, but his expression was not without compassion.

Shamgar nodded gratefully, laying Manoah gently down. Itiya was wolfing down a plate of bread and olives, slurping wine in between mouthfuls. He smiled slightly at the sight, sadly imagining how disapproving her mother would be of her manners. But it was good to see she still had an appetite; it had to be a good sign, he concluded. He took the glass of wine his father handed him, suddenly realising he had not eaten or drunk anything since he set out toward his farm this morning. It seemed a lifetime ago. He felt fatigue engulf him as he sank into the luxurious purple and red coverings that were draped on the couch.

Shamgar awoke with the optimism that flickers at the beginning of each new day, before the conscious mind has fully awoken. And then the events of the previous day besieged his mind, a visual bombardment of memory that ended with his daughter Hariya, and the awareness that when he had slept last night, she was still not home. Adrenalin flooded him until he felt nauseous with anxiety. He groaned as he forced his aching body into an upright position and staggered through the corridors of his father's house, calling his daughter's name. He was met by the servant he recognised from the courtyard last night.

"Sir, your daughter has been found, she is safe..." He shifted nervously "Your father felt it was better that she and the others.... and you, slept."

Shamgar realised he had just been bellowing her name. He grunted, as relief washed over him.

"When you are ready, sir, breakfast is waiting in the dining room." He paused, clearly uncomfortable.

"And?"

"Your brother, Balak, and father are there too, sir."

"My brother?" Shamgar mind raced. His brother was a Canaanite army general. He hadn't heard from him since leaving the army. He frowned inwardly as he entered the room. Barak was of the same imposing height as Shamgar, but a smaller build. His intimidating stature was compensated for through his resolve and forcefulness. Few men opposed Balak, and fewer lived to tell of it. The compliance of those around him was not only anticipated, it was expected.

He paced back and forth, in heated discussion with his father: the two were a formidable force. Shamgar sighed, any thoughts for an easier morning quickly pushed aside.

"It's a mess. We've had peace with the Philistines for years. Gezer has been a successful trading centre for both our nations. And now we are on the brink of civil war. Shamgar walks in announcing he's your son and kills two hundred Philistines."

"You could hardly have expected him to leave his daughters to the mercy of Philistine soldiers."

"They're women! They're the spoils of war! You should know that, of all people, Father!"

Shamgar felt his blood boil. "Then perhaps you should offer your daughters to the Philistine soldiers as compensation, Balak. I see you still have the sensitivity of a rabid dog."

His brother turned, the vein on his neck pulsated like a viper threatening to attack. "You should know, brother, that there is a price on your head. By being here you endanger not only yourself, but also our father and his household. Your children are not safe yet. It is only by my influence, and my men that guard this house, that the Philistine army is not here already. I cannot hold them back forever; nor will I risk the peace between Philistia and Canaan for your sake."

Shamgar sat, his head rested in his hands. For the first time, he felt futility tearing at his inner resolve. When he looked up, the fire that had blazed a path before him yesterday was barely an ember, dying in the wind of the mounting opposition he faced.

"What do you suggest?" he asked, his voice barely audible.

His brother sighed, lowering his voice, still authoritative, still lacking all sentiment, but confident in the face of submission.

"Join the Canaanite army, brother. Fight with us and we will guarantee the protection of your children."

"I'll not fight against the Hebrews, Balak. They are our mother's people...they were Sarai's people...and they are mine." His tired eyes were set with resignation.

Balak's expression was icy. "I will give you one day to reconsider, brother, and then *you* will decide your own fate, and that of your children."

He turned, giving a brief, expressionless nod to his father by way of taking his leave.

Shamgar pushed the heel of his palms into his eyes as he tried to think. He needed to see his children. He needed to find the families of the children from Gezer; but now all their survival depended on the decision he would make.

He felt his father's hand on his shoulder.

"Whatever you do now, son, there is no going back. Whatever has happened, whatever choices you have made, it doesn't matter. It's what you do now that matters… I'll leave you to think…You did well yesterday, son."

Shamgar sat in the silence; the cold marble floor and sterile bench accompanied his mood. His father's words ricocheted off the corner of his mind before it coiled itself into the dark places - the places to which pain and fear are banished. The words tugged on doors long rusted shut, and retreated. Too quickly. They were looking for weaker entry points.

He thought about his father: his military career had consumed him. He loved his father; he hadn't been a bad father, just preoccupied. His position, reputation and desire to conquer took precedence over family and integrity. He had watched his mother die while his father was out defeating the world. For whom had he fought? For what, if not his family? He had seen what ambition did to people, to families and nations: six different nations fighting for one piece of land. Driven to the point where reason and compassion became mute, and people were mere instruments to be used in pursuit of the goal. The compromise of morals and integrity were deemed acceptable in the name of success. Thus ambition had become a swear word in Shamgar's mind. He equated it with greed, and saw the wars it fuelled.

He had turned away from his military training and chosen farming when he married Sarai. He had been determined that his wife and children would be first. Only once a year he left them to sell cattle in Hebron. In that week his wife and son had been killed. He considered the bitter irony of his life, and now he felt less inclined to consider an alternative. It was too damaging to contemplate that his choices had been ill-considered at such cost. He stubbornly changed the course of his thoughts, forcing the barrage of questions into submission.

Crossing his arms, he rested his head on the table. He felt suddenly old, and wanted nothing more than to recede into the unreal, if fitful, realm of sleep where the assault of questions and challenges ceased. But he knew that to do nothing was not an option. He strove to find a place of peace. His thoughts of Sarai were now marred and filled him with bitterness. Finally he found the place, a rooftop in the midst of a storm: *Yahweh*.

"What! What do I do now? Direct me as you did. Protect my children. My life is yours. Protect them, Yahweh, and guide me." It was a desperate prayer, without eloquence or reverence, to which he was not expecting an answer. When an answer came, he was both astonished and grateful. A whisper in the depths of his mind of a place he had once heard Sarah speak of: *Shiloh*.

10

Village life ceased, it ceased in Israel.
Judges 5:7
1253 BC - Deborah

Deborah handed Isaac bread, giving him some of her own share. At thirteen years of age, he had grown suddenly tall, making him look almost skeletal. She had grown used to the constant hunger that gnawed within her, but her heart ached for Isaac. His previous energy and optimism had developed into a dark humour that, whilst making her laugh, had a tendency toward cynicism, which concerned her.

He smiled gratefully at her. "Are you going to the mountains today?"

"Yes," she replied, quickly twisting her hair into a braid and throwing it carelessly over her shoulder. "I'll see if I can find any food...there were wild strawberries last week, not yet grown...maybe they will be ready now."

Maya looked up from the loom. The mustard coloured wool that they had dyed the previous week was now ready to be spun. She smiled gratefully as Deborah silently sat down next to her and began rolling the wool into balls.

"I noticed you and Miriam have taken Hadas under your wings," Maya commented, her expression mixed with approval and curiosity.

Several other families had joined them in the last year, many of whom had brought their gods with them - and the lure to follow the carnality that their beliefs encouraged was drawing more and more away from Yahweh.

Hadas had been one of six children, three of whom had been killed along with their father when their village was attacked eight months ago. The village had subsequently been abandoned. Her two older brothers, Salmon and Adiel, of seventeen and nineteen, had survived with her. Hadas' mother, Tamar, had an extensive knowledge of herbal medicine, which she had passed on to her daughters. They were one of the few families who still followed Yahweh, despite the pain they had experienced.

Hadas and Deborah had instantly connected. She had a hidden depth that Deborah respected, and a transparency that warranted her trust.

"I really like her; she has a quiet strength and stands for what she believes, and…she has a different way of looking at the world, that's refreshing," she mused.

"It's all those strange mushrooms she eats," Isaac teased, joining in with the conversation. He wiggled his eyebrows comically as he grinned.

"Hadas knows which mushrooms are poisonous and which aren't!" Deborah replied defensively. "At least I hope so. You are eating them," she chuckled, looking at his soup with mock concern.

"Maybe." Isaac's eyes glinted playfully and pulled a 'crazy' face.

Deborah poked out her tongue at Isaac, who laughed, looking over his shoulder as he left the house.

Her mother kissed the top of her head as she stood to place the balls of wool on a shelf, and Deborah inwardly acknowledged the act as a small sign of her mother's engagement with life.

"You've been teaching the younger ones the Torah," Maya commented. "Your father would be proud of you, Deborah."

Deborah shrugged. "If they grow up not knowing the truth of their history, of who they are, of who Yahweh is, what hope is there for the future of our people?"

"People are so tired. Before, everything would revolve around Him. I hate what I see happening, but I lack the energy, or perhaps the conviction, to stand against the storm. It is good that you do it."

"I can't very well complain if I won't do anything about it. Still, there are many that don't want their children to learn the old ways. They say that I should teach about Yahweh as El, as well as Baal, Dagon and Asherah." She stood up, placing another ball onto the shelf. "I won't!" she asserted.

"Does Hadas talk about her village, about what happened?"

"Not about her family. But, she did tell me about a man in Philistia. He goes by the name of Shamgar, and is said to have killed three hundred Philistines and many Canaanites with just an ox-goad! There is hope Yahweh will use him to deliver southern Israel from the Philistines," Deborah mentioned, careful to restrain the excitement in her voice lest she give her mother false hope.

"Is he Hebrew?" Her mother asked.

"Apparently not, though his wife and mother were – he is a Canaanite by birth; his father was a war lord."

Maya frowned skeptically. "It all sounds unlikely, don't you think?" A deep sigh escaped from her lips before she added. "But let's hope it is true. We need hope."

Three years had passed since Sisera's visit, and it had been eight months since the last Canaanites had come for 'taxes'. There was an understanding that as long as their quota was reached, they would be left unharmed. Deborah, for her sixteen years, was astute enough to see the outcome of this situation: they were survivors. Their thoughts and energy were spent surviving, rather than living - as they once had. Sisera had them where he wanted them: devoid of hope and imprisoned by fear. They would not rebel, for he had shown them the price of non-compliance, and thus they were his slaves, bearing the illusion of freedom whilst they worked tirelessly to provide food for his army.

She picked up a bag, and disappeared through the door, slipping behind the other houses in her need to escape. Deborah wished she found it easy to talk about her feelings and thoughts as her friends did. They would discuss their hopes and dreams while they brushed each other's hair, twisting and plaiting in different styles, talking about betrothals, weddings and running homes of their own. Deborah would politely submit to their preening and compliments, offering her own thoughts when asked, but she always felt like an observer, on the outside looking in. She didn't have romantic feelings for any of the boys in the village and was not aware that any of them felt that way toward her. Her mother was not yet in a place to be left alone, nor to organise betrothals anyway. The whole thing was best left alone.

As she climbed the familiar path, she was greeted by the familiar sound of the sheeps' gentle chorus as they navigated the steep hillside. A sparrow hawk was perched on the rocky crag of *her plac,e* watching her ascent like a feathered sentry. Its haunting screech filled the air. She clambered up the rock face and nimbly climbed down the other side. She had named the gecko that frequented *her place* Joshua, and he was the only one that was party to her conversations with Yahweh.

Her trips to this sacred place had been her anchor during the past years: it was where she poured out her heart to Yahweh and listened to His. From this place she had begun to see the world through His eyes; to see someone's anger as frustration, and to quietly allow Him to show her the source. She had learnt when to see withdrawal as rejection, and to understand when to offer comfort and when to speak truth. Most importantly, she had learnt to wait. She sat quietly, her legs drawn up to her chest, her chin rested on her knees. At once, she knew that He was there, and His quiet voice spoke to her - a strong impression rather than audible words. This time, she felt arms around her, and His compassion flooded her until tears poured down her face. She began to see what would come, and she knew that He would be with her; but the reality was still hard to bear. Sisera was returning - and in that instant, she had come to understand her enemy. She felt both fear and hatred.

11

Now Heber the Kenite had separated himself from the Kenites, from the sons of Hobab the father-in-law of Moses, and had pitched his tent as far away the oak in Zaanannim, which is near Kedesh.
Judges 4:11

1259 BC - Jael

Despite Heber's indifference to her pregnancy, Jael found she was happier than she had been for some time. Her husband's increasing absence was a relief, and during those times she was able to spend time with her sisters. She had also grown to cherish the friendship she shared with Adva, and was hungry to hear her stories of Yahweh, the Patriarchs and their wives.

In turn, she would tell Adva stories about Jethro, the Midianites and how they had been able to survive in the wilderness.

Whilst Kiya had never spoken of Yahweh as Jael had grown up, there was a pride attached to their cultural history that had been passed down. She had spoken to her daughters of Jethro and his journey with Moses through the wilderness. Both women were fascinated by the facts that were the same in their cultural history, but told from different perspectives. Jael had heard of the struggles of her nomad ancestors as they sought to find food and water for such vast numbers of Israelites. Understanding first-hand the scarcity of food and water in the desert, she was enthralled when Adva told her how Yahweh had instructed Moses to hit the rock, and water had flowed; and when she learned how He had provided quail and manna, tears had sprung to her eyes. It had spoken to her deeply of Yahweh's goodness in hardship.

She had shared with Adva the sense of responsibility, and at times frustration, Jethro and Hobab had faced whilst leading a divided nation. She had explained how nomads have a clear sense of responsibility and unity, because, for desert nomads, all are needed for the survival of the tribe. When Israel first escaped from Egypt, they were a people lacking national identity. They were fragmented, united only by the base need to survive. In understanding how instrumental Jethro had been in helping Moses, she acknowledged how Yahweh was in the detail, as well as the big picture. She saw His grace and sovereignty in using their disobedience as an opportunity to unite them, and knit them to Himself. For, during the wilderness years, an entire generation grew up on the Torah, far from the distraction or pollution of any other nation. As Adva and Jael talked, they realised that the wilderness years of wandering were in fact years of foundation-building for the nation of Israel. Had they not had that time, she wondered if their conquest would have been successful.

Thus, as the baby within her grew, so did Jael's understanding of Yahweh, and herself. She began to understand that Yahweh was all-powerful because He could use life's hardships for good. Within that thought, she found great peace in the midst of her difficult relationship with Heber.

Her relationship with her mother had begun to grow, too. As she asked her mother more questions, she began to realise the hidden strength that her mother carried, and whilst she could be volatile and chaotic, she had survived in this way. Jael respected her for that.

She held one of the goats between her legs, while Kiya cut the hair from its body. It bleated momentarily before realising the futility of its efforts.

Cozbi collected the bags, grumbling about the heat, and took them back to the shade of the tent to be spun and woven into panels by Serah.

Previously, it had been Jael's job to sow the panels together, and though she would never have thought it, there was a part of her that missed the laborious task.

"Why did you never speak to us or teach us about Yahweh if you knew Him to be the true God of Jethro, Mama?" Jael frowned accusingly at her mother.

Her mother looked up wiping her brow with the back of her hand. Her dark hair was wet with perspiration as the heat of the day beat upon them. She placed the hair in the sackcloth bag, and poured water over her face before drinking from the goats-hide container.

"I told you," she fought the urge to react, "your father was opposed. He wasn't from my tribe. Remember, not all of the Midianites turned to Yahweh, only our tribe: Druze. Many of the Elders followed the old ways, and were opposed to the Israelites coming into our land."

"They asked Balaam to curse Israel, didn't they?" She remembered Adva telling her the story of Balaam's donkey. She had laughed so hard her belly had hurt.

"Yes, and the death of the five kings and their people is still a painful memory. He felt that it would cause trouble and be bad for our family and…for business."

"Right." Jael resisted the urge to give her opinion, and congratulated herself on her newfound self-control. "You should tell Cozbi and Serah though. They need to know."

Kiya shrugged defensively. "I will, when the time is right."

As Heber's baby grew within her, Jael was anxious over her indifferent, and at times negative, emotions she felt toward her unborn child. She sadly remembered how she had once dreamt of carrying Zimran's child, of being *his* wife, and the joy she had felt. She felt as though her life had been stolen from her, and wondered how she could ever reconcile herself with her reality.

But when the baby kicked for the first time, something changed within her – suddenly, the realisation that it was *her* child sparked a tiny ember of warmth within her. From then on, her love grew with every passing day, warming the cold ache of her heart and creating a fire that burned hot with protective passion.

She avoided Heber whenever possible. But whilst his derision suggested he did not desire her company, her indifference irritated him.

He had begun to insist that she welcome him dutifully on his return from the mines.

Jael laughed at Heber scornfully. She knew she shouldn't, but when she felt angry, her senses were clouded.

"And may I ask why?" she asked, with mock courtesy.

"You may not, no!" He snarled with contempt, grabbing a fistful of her hair. He stunk of stale sweat and wine. "You are my property. I bought you from that worthless man you call your father, and I paid more than you were worth – you're mine to do with as I please!"

Jael lowered her voice in measured control, though the truth was that the river of her wrath had burst its banks. "My father is loved and respected, things you will never be," she sneered.

Heber's face turned red with unrestrained fury. He turned silently away from her, and something within Jael knew she had gone too far. She tried to back toward the door, but he caught her arm, throwing her onto the cushions. He had picked up a rope that would have been used to secure the tent.

"Perhaps not love, but respect can be taught; when my animals misbehave, I know how to teach them obedience." He was doubling and twisting the rope as he spoke, his dark eyes were narrow slits of unmasked rage.

"What a man you are! You must feel so proud of yourself – are you going to stoop so low as to beat your pregnant wife?" Jael knew that she was prodding a vicious snake, but her pride and anger silenced any wisdom or caution she may have felt.

Heber's thin lips formed a snarling smirk as he lifted the rope above his head and brought it down with full force. She forced her scream inward, as the thick rope bit into her skin like a red-hot brand. After the first few blows, Jael crumpled to the floor, instinctively covering her swollen abdomen and praying that she and the child might survive.

Finally, he stopped, and stooping over her, he grabbed her bloodied, swollen arm. "You will welcome me and you will show me respect as your husband. Are we clear?" he hissed.

Jael turned her face from him but remained silent; she had not thought it possible to hate him any more than she had before.

When Adva came to visit her in the evening, she had done her best to cover her bruises, draping a long headdress across her face and shoulders. But Adva was no fool. She pushed aside the flap of the tent and reappeared a moment later with the prickly leaf of an aloe vera plant, which she snapped in half and proceeded to wipe the gel onto Jael's cuts.

"Jael, I know him. I know what he is capable of. Please talk to me. The baby - is the baby alright? Have you felt it kick?"

Jael turned to her, not wanting to verbalise the anxiety she had been feeling. "Not since before." Her eyes welled up now, allowing her sorrow to find their vent. "I was stupid. I shouldn't have argued, I know what he's like…But I hate him and he makes me so angry. But now, I just want the baby to be alright…"

"Pray, Jael," Adva urged, clutching her friend's hands.

"I did," Jael pouted. "Perhaps it is Yahweh's will to teach me the consequence of my bad temper."

"You still have a lot to learn about the heart of God, my friend – He's not a tyrant like Heber at all. He cares for you." She smiled, squeezing her friend's hand.

"I hope so," Jael yawned. Now that her adrenalin had calmed down, her body suddenly felt weak beyond exhaustion. She lay back on the cushions as Adva placed another blanket on top of her.

"Good night, my friend," she whispered.

"Good night Adva…Adva?

"Yes, Jael?" her friend sighed.

"I want a Hebrew midwife," Jael smiled, as she felt the reassuring, gentle kicks of the baby stirring within her.

Adva laughed, "Do you never give in?!! Sleep!"

When Jael's time came, Adva called for the midwife. She was a small, frail-looking lady whose face was as care-worn as a crumpled parchment, etched with wisdom and experience; her eyes were sharp and perceptive. The woman introduced herself as Bracha, meaning 'Blessing', and she proved to live up to her name. Despite her apparent fragility, she bore a gentle authority and compassion that Jael trusted and yielded to.

The sun had just dipped under the horizon when the first contractions began. Nothing had prepared her for the pain that ripped through her body, or for the exhaustion that would disempower her. Her entire body was drenched with sweat as she tried to breathe through the agony. Looking up at Adva, she saw herself, wild with fear and pain, reflected in her friend's eyes, and with it the acknowledgement that she may not, could not, go on much longer. She could feel her body warring to give up and end the pain, against her instinctive desire to survive. But over-riding them both was the overwhelming and triumphing force of her love for the child she had never seen, and the determination that it must survive.

"It's time. You need to push," Bracha gently encouraged. "It will be over soon." Bracha's voice was a caress as she moved Jael's thick, sweat drenched hair away from her face.

Screaming as she bore down, searing agony consumed her, drove her to end the pain and then groaned with relief as the downy black head, and then the shoulders, emerged from between her thighs. She sunk back on the bed in exhaustion.

"It's a girl," the midwife said, wrapping the baby in swaddling and handing her to Jael.

A tiny smile of exultation and joy parted Jael's lips. She stared at the tiny, perfect fingers, the full lips and the dark eyes that stared back at her, and swallowed a surge of emotion that threatened to overwhelm her.

Bracha squeezed her hand. "Yahweh be praised for new life. You did well, Jael, she's a beautiful babe. You need to put her to your breast as soon as you can."

Jael nodded and, placing the baby to her breast, she felt the bond between her and her daughter grow - a surge of love that was defensive, sacrificial and unconditional.

"Do you have a name for her?" the midwife asked.

Jael nodded, her eyelids suddenly weighted. "I will call her Meira, for she is God's light to me in the midst of darkness."

"We should let the father know he has a daughter." Bracha handed Jael a drink of milk, sweetened with honey.

Mention of Heber almost destroyed the perfection of the moment.

She clutched Meira to her protectively. "Give me a short time, please," she pleaded.

The closed curtains were shoved roughly aside in the next instant, and Heber entered the room, ignoring Bracha's indignant protests with a crude profanity. Jael watched as his snake-like eyes scanned the tent. He gave no indication that he was either surprised or indifferent to find that his wife was holding their baby. Beside him stood a man. His attire suggested he was military – a Canaanite. He made no apology for his presence, but instead his eyes intrusively and hungrily roamed over Jael's semi-naked body before Adva could pull the sheets over her. His behaviour was an utter violation of propriety and nomadic culture: to enter a woman's tent. Jael knew that Heber would relish her discomfort, and that she would only gratify him further were she to protest - and so she remained silent.

Heber's mouth curved slightly as he acknowledged her humiliation and vulnerability. "Well?" he sneered.

"It's a girl," Jael replied, trying not to sound defensive.

He swallowed, as if to rid him of an unpleasant taste and said nothing.

Her eyes flitted to the soldier, his eyes were hard and dark, the colour of slate. He looked at her baby in a way that made Jael's stomach twist: she saw a level of cruelty in the man's eyes that not even Heber possessed. She glared at him until his gaze shifted to meet hers. Bored amusement flickered in his eyes as he looked purposefully at the child and then back to Jael.

"I must begin preparations. I will leave you to discuss matters with your wife." He nodded to Heber, then turned to Jael. "I'm sure I will see you both again soon." With that he turned and left the tent.

"Preparations? What was he talking about Heber?" Jael hissed, a sense of dark premonition rising from the pit of her stomach.

"We will be moving to Zaanannim, near Kedesh. I have instructed the slaves to have our tents packed and be ready to go in two days."

Jael was speechless as her tired mind vainly tried to piece together what Heber had said: *leave, he said leave, I can't leave, not now, not with him, there has to be a way out! My family, they won't want to leave...* She realised that her mouth was open, and that her obvious shock had given Heber a moment of victory.

"Why now?" she spluttered, resisting the urge to defy him. It was a week's journey travelling through the Negev wilderness. It was not only impractical. It was dangerous to attempt such a trek with a newborn baby.

"Business." He turned to leave.

"And my family, our people…What do they say? You cannot expect everyone to pack up on such short notice. Many of them have been settled here their whole lives!"

Heber breathed out through his nose as his eyes rolled in contemptuous derision. "Your family have not been asked, nor will they be. My business does not concern them, and frankly, their opinions are neither valued, nor required. Your father has given me all I require of him, and I will find new tent-makers where we settle. You *will* be ready in two days. She will come, to help with the child." He nodded to Adva, without looking at her and left the tent.

"He can't do this!" Jael was wide-eyed with panic, her emotions raw as they battled with her post-birth hormones. She looked wildly from Adva, to Bracha to Meira, her mind trying to forge an alternative path, an escape. This unseen current that she had birthed no longer fought its own course, or demanded for its own destiny. It was wild and furious and powerful, both liberating her and terrifying her in its intensity to protect. For she knew that she must firstly protect Meira from her father, and then from the world. And she knew that her acquiescence and seeming compliance at this moment were her shield and sword.

Bracha, who had been quietly tidying away the blood-soaked linen, sighed as though responding to an unheard voice. She washed her hands and drew up a stool next to Jael. She rested her weathered hand on Jael's, her watery eyes holding the young mother's before she spoke.

"Life can be hard, can't it dear child?" she smiled sadly, compassion spilling from her expression. "Your name, it means wild mountain goat, doesn't it? Goats long for freedom, you know. But remember, Jael: freedom isn't something we can find in our circumstances. It's a place we find in Yahweh, under the shadow of His wings. I pray you might find that place." She laughed kindly, as though responding to the inaudible voice. "Goats are clever and strong, they are survivors. Yahweh has made you a survivor." She patted Jael's hand and left, leaving Jael feeling as though she were floating in a gentle rock pool, surrounded by a raging river.

True to Heber's word, two days later, the caravan was packed, their tents and possessions loaded on donkeys and camels. There were two Canaanite soldiers with them, although Jael was glad not to recognise the man who had come to her tent. Their military presence was supposed to be for protection against bandits who patrolled the highways. But Jael couldn't help feeling that they were there to ensure their compliance.

Many of the tribe had come to see their families off: wives, saying goodbye to their husbands who were helping drive the caravans and Adva's family through the Negev desert.

Jael had been dreading saying goodbye to her family. The uncertainty of seeing them again was as bleak as the track before them as it disappeared into a haze of dust. Her mother embraced her, kissing her hair. "You will be a good mother, Jael. Know that. You are strong, but wisdom knows when to yield. We will pray for you."

She clung to her mother, suddenly feeling like a small child. "Promise me you'll tell Cozbi and Serah."

"I promise," her mother whispered through her tears.

And then her father joined them, tears glistening in his eyes as he kissed Miera's tiny, closed hand, and then his daughter's cheek.

"You were right, Jael, about Jabin and Heber. I'm sure you were."

Impulsively, she gripped her father's arm. "Find *good* husbands for Cozbi and Serah."

He didn't answer immediately, as his eyes filled with tears. "If I could turn back time, I wouldn't have le…"

"What's done is done," Jael silenced him. His regret was impotent as far as it concerned her. "Don't make the same mistake again." Jael knew she sounded harsh, but she needed to leave feeling that her sisters were safe. The sudden revelation that she would not, in all probability, see him again this side of eternity transcended her resentment. With the same impulse, she threw her arms around him.

"I love you, Abba. I know you did what you needed to for the family."

She hugged her sisters, with whom she had worked her entire life. They had shared secrets, dreams and tears together; and now, to imagine the loss of their bond, she felt bereft. Unspoken words clung to the roof of her mouth, unable to find their expression. She pulled herself away, forcing the tide of emotion into submission. Handing Meira to Adva, she pulled herself onto the shaded platform and beckoned the driver to move away.

As first her family, and then the dark cluster of tents, disappeared from sight, she allowed the hot tears of grief and anger to find their release.

Later, Miera's cries pierced her grief. Wearily, she took Miera from Adva and placed the baby to her breast. She closed her eyes. She was exhausted. But, in symbolic defiance, she opened her eyes to look at the road ahead; it was her last remaining act of control.

Jael was jolted awake by the lurch of their camel over the dry rocky road. The sun glared down at its apex, proud and merciless in its assault. Jael and Adva had retreated under the linen canopy, shielding Meira from the sun. Meira was fractious, fidgeting and crying; the heat was unbearable. Jael had taken off all of Miera's clothing and kept wiping her with water, feeding the child to keep her hydrated. Adva's creased brow as she fanned Meira's tiny body told Jael that she was worried for the child, too.

They were alone now. The desert stretched out to the west, a furnace of russet and amber, as though the sun had forsaken its boundaries and sought to consume them. To the east towered the Judean mountains: giant, cracked rock fissures that rose and fell in staggered steps, to the salt sea. Their path was mostly in dry riverbeds that snaked their way across the landscape, before disappearing into the ground. It was as though they, too, sought to escape the constant barrage of the ruthless sun. Only the occasional weathered acacia tree and wild brush decorated the otherwise bleak terrain. They did not follow any known path; they were nomads, and whilst their people had lived with the Israelites for several generations, survival in the wilderness was handed down. It was what defined them.

As the afternoon drew on and the sun began its descent, Meira had finally cried herself to sleep. Jael looked at Adva, and thought how grateful she was that she was here.

"How is it you came to be a slave for Heber, Adva?" Jael spoke into the silence.

"My father had been ill for as long as I can remember. When he finally had to stop working, it was impossible to make enough food to survive. I was the plainest of three girls; my parents would get less dowry for me. And so I was sold so that my family could survive."

Jael snorted. "Our stories are not vastly dissimilar, then. How long have you been with Heber?"

"Three years."

"I'm sorry that you were sold, Adva. Though, given the nature of my own life, I am pleased you are here with me." She clasped her friend's hand.

Adva grinned. "I'm sorry I was sold as a slave, too, but I'm glad I'm here. All things considered, it could have been worse."

The caravan had entered a rocky canyon. Tall, almost vertical sandstone rock formations loomed above them on either side, giving them welcome relief from the sun.

Jael's thoughts wandered as she pondered Heber's reason for leaving Arad. She was certain that his motivation would be business, or self-preservation. *Why was he moving to Kedesh? What was there for him, and what part did the Canaanite soldier play in his decision? The only obvious answer was her father's suggestion: he had formed an alliance with the Canaanite army.* She toyed with the idea of discussing her thoughts with Adva, but decided against it. She was ashamed at the thought of her husband betraying their Hebrew allies, and she was also fearful for Adva; the less she knew the safer she would be. As she felt her curiosity grow into irritation, she remembered Bracha's words and sighed: *Lord, if I'm meant to know, I trust you will show me.*

Finally, the canyon came to an end and opened up into a curved ridge with a caved indent at its base, suggesting the erosion of water in the past. She saw Heber barking orders at slaves as they tethered animals together, securing them before beginning to feed and water them. Occasionally, she would catch him watching her. His piercing eyes seemed to be scrutinising her, no doubt waiting for an opportunity to criticise and humiliate her. By the time fires were lit with cooking pots suspended over them, the night air had brought its desert chill. Jael and Adva huddled near to the fire, listening to the chat of the women as they cooked. She appreciated the lack of segregation that desert life brought – in which all people seemed equal.

"This is how I was meant to live," she sighed quietly, almost to herself. Her thoughts drifted unconsciously to *that other life* she had been offered with Zimran. She felt the dull ache of their sweet pain amass in her heart, and dragged herself back to reality.

"Last time we were here, my husband got us lost. I knew the way! But would he listen? What can you do? " The woman pulled her headdress around her hunched shoulders, and gave the fire a prod.

The other woman scoffed. "They don't listen to us. You just have to hope another man comes along to tell him, before you die of thirst!"

The first woman laughed, tasting the contents of the pot and adding more spice.

Meira began to cry. She was hungry, too. Jael shivered, reluctant to leave the warmth of the fire. She pulled the blanket over her shoulders and picking up a torch, made her way toward the sleeping area that had been set up for the women.

Laughter trickled through the air, sending a warm shiver down her spine. Her senses pulled it away from the other sounds, seeking its source. Her reaction was visceral, creating a cyclone of emotion that she could neither comprehend, nor halt, creating in her the desperate need to see him and the strongest compulsion to run. It was Zimran.

As though drawn by some unseen gravity, his eyes found her, framed in the glow of the torchlight, his tall, muscular form and his thick, matted hair. Everything else seemed to dissipate around her as their eyes met, that silent exchange of souls. He seemed older, more serious, but the same strong jaw line, full lips and deep brown eyes. And then, as though the tension splintered and its tiny shards pierced her heart, he turned away from her. The low sound of his voice filled the night air, coiling around her until she felt it would suffocate her.

Jael clasped Meira to her. *What did she expect? That he would still love her? And what if he did? She was bound to Heber; there was no escape. She had known that.* And yet, she had selfishly hoped that he still loved her. That hope and the memory of him were glowing embers that she warmed herself by. *Of course he would despise her; she had walked away from him.*

When Adva came to bed, she found Jael asleep with Meira tucked in tightly next to her.

Jael slept fitfully. She dreamt she was walking in the desert of Midian. She should have felt peaceful; it was her happy place. But something was wrong. She had the sense that she was being tracked by a predator. As panic set in, she tried to run; but the ground beneath her had become thick and fluid, her feet were sinking and she was helpless.

She jolted awake, trying to steady her breathing as she established where she was, and then recalled seeing Zimran again. The dull ache in her heart began to throb, growing until she felt it would swallow her. She shut her eyes tightly, forbidding herself to shed another tear.

Standing up, careful not to wake Meira, she tiptoed over the sleeping forms of the other women. The camp was quiet, save for the occasional movement of the animals and snoring of exhausted travellers. She cautiously made her way through the dull glow of fires, using their light to map her path. Seeing a ledge some way up the verge, she clambered up to it and sat, her knees drawn up to her chest, watching her breath coil into the cool night air. The waxing silver moon had asserted its victory over the canopy of stars that had punched their way through the darkness. Their glow illuminated the giant rock formations that contrasted against the vast and empty desert. She breathed in the cool air, and allowed the majesty of the evening to rebalance her ragged emotions. In such splendor, she saw Yahweh and thus found reason to hope.

As her eyes grew accustomed to the darkness, her attention was drawn by movement across the canyon. She squinted, wondering if her mind was playing tricks on her: it was virtually impossible for any animal to survive the harsh conditions of the desert, and the animals that they had brought with them were tethered. At first, as the creature moved slowly along the thin ledge of stratified rock, Jael panicked, fearing that it was a mountain leopard. Her first thoughts were for Meira as she lay asleep in the cave. However, as the creature leapt from rock to rock with sure-footed ease, there was no doubt as to what it could be. She smiled as Bracha's words came back to her: *you are a wild mountain goat that will survive anything.* The significance of the moment enveloped her and comforted her, for she knew that Yahweh was speaking to her. She knew, by His grace, that she would survive the wilderness and difficulty of this time. She allowed the knowledge of this thought to spread through her, strengthening and reassuring her.

As the caravan worked quickly to continue their journey, the morning sun promised another day of merciless onslaught. Everyone was keen to leave the Judean wilderness behind them. The path they travelled along was formed of russet and sedimentary rock, and steeped downward toward the salt sea. Their water supply was now dangerously low, and they needed to reach the Wadi of En Gedi before nightfall. However, despite her thirst and blistered feet, Jael felt a quiet peace that she had not known for a long time. She felt, for the first time she could recall, that she had the strength to adapt and survive in her own wilderness.

12

Thus let all Your enemies perish, O LORD; But let those who love Him be like the rising of the sun in its might.
Judges 5:31

1253 BC – Deborah

They were in the month of Tammuz, over two months into the dry season. The leaves on the vines were withered, and the grapes shriveled from lack of water. Yet everyone was aware that a good grape harvest was essential. They had once sung as they laboured. The motivation of celebration at the Feast of Tabernacles, and the promise of quiet winter evenings and dining with their families and community, had made their labour meaningful and joyful. It was now about survival.

The water in the well was lower than anyone could remember, and the heat unbearable. Reuben had suggested an irrigation system such as the Canaanites had implemented. However many felt that this was a pagan tradition and would be tantamount to idolatry. Reuben was an intelligent man and said they were being ignorant; not everything the Canaanites did was evil. After heated discussion, in which neither side yielded, it was agreed that water should be carried from the brook to water the vines. Thus a chain was created, and the younger, strongest people, aged between fifteen and thirty, were given the midday slot.

Deborah had returned home with dreadful blisters. She covered them with aloe vera gel and wrapped linen around her hands before returning to work the next day.

It was her job to collect the water from Hadas and hand it to Tebah. She was grateful that most of the time she was under the shade of the forest. As she handed the bucket to Tebah, she was alerted to how pale he looked, and that he had been standing under the vicious glare of the sun since the morning.

"Are you alright Tebah? Have you been drinking water?"

He swayed in response, muttering something unintelligible, and rubbing his head.

She lifted the bucket to his mouth. "Drink," she urged.

Seeing his eyes roll back, she steadied him as he staggered, drawing him under the cover of the trees. She poured some of the water over his head and, leaving him with the rest of the water, ran to Hadas.

"I'm worried Tebah has sunstroke," she explained to Hadas. "Can you let Jonah and his mother know? I'll try to get him back to his house. He's weak."

"Of course!" Hadas replied, beginning to hasten up the hillside.

"Hadas!" Deborah shouted back over her shoulder, feeling suddenly unsure of herself.

Hadas stopped, turning back toward her friend and wiping her brow.

"Soaked Fenugreek leaves with honey?" her brow creased with uncertainty.

Her friend smiled. "You know it is! Have confidence my friend. Mother has an infusion prepared. If she's still in the vineyard, take it. It's on the shelf, next to the oil."

Deborah nodded and hurried to find help. A grazing goat looked up at her, its lazy eyes following her for a moment before returning to its patch of withered grass. Fortunately, Menachem was the next person in the chain, as Tebah was barely able to hold his own weight and she knew she was not strong enough to support him alone. Tebah was delirious by the time they returned and had to be half-dragged back to the village.

Shelimoth and Shayna sat under the shade of the latter's courtyard, talking in low voices. Together they were splitting chickpea pods, and placing the dried legumes in clay containers where they would be stored for winter.

The horrific rape and loss of her daughter had left Shelimoth understandably and inconsolably bereft. For this, Deborah had great empathy. However, she noted that people dealt with their pain very differently, and for that they must carry some responsibility. That Deborah had once again been absent during the violence of Sisera's last visit, meant she must be punished in other ways.

Shelimoth was waiting, her hands on her hips, her lips pursed in disapproval. Deborah groaned inwardly. "Aren't you supposed to be with the other young people…working?" Her tone was neutral, yet Deborah noted the underlying insinuation. Shayna glanced up and gave an awkward half-smile that was neither friendly, nor unkind, and returned to her work.

Deborah felt Shelimoth's fury and intimidation reach out and choke her. She struggled to find the words to defend herself.

"I'm helping Tebah - he has sun stroke," she spluttered, endeavoring not to increase Shelimoth's ire.

The older woman clicked her lips with disdain. "Helping Isaac, helping Tebah. At least try and be truthful to yourself, Deborah. You don't actually believe that, do you?" She smiled with feigned concern. "You just want to survive, don't you? If you need to feel noble about it, to persuade yourself it was an act of altruism, then feel free, but you're not fooling anyone but yourself."

Deborah felt Shelimoth's words drive like a knife, thrust into an old wound. For a moment, she felt disabled by the cruelty of Shelimoth's accusation; she remembered her drive to survive that had led her up the mountain path, and winced as she recalled her decision to leave Keziah. She had been thinking of Isaac and obeying her father, hadn't she? Self-doubt and shame assailed her thoughts, and she blinked back the hot tears that welled up within her. Turning, she fled stumbling into the sanctuary of Tamar's house.

Grabbing the labeled pot, she raced to Orpah and Tebah's home, careful to avoid Shelimoth. Tebah was vomiting, his face pale and his hair wet with perspiration.

"I did what I could, laying him in the shade and stripped him to his undergarments." Orpah anxiously wiped her son's neck with water as he lent over the clay basin.

"I brought this from Tamar's house," Deborah explained. "Give him half of this now, and half again in two hours. I can make up some more for you when it's gone."

Deborah was about to set off back to the forest, but was prompted to fetch water for everyone. She lowered the bucket into the well, once again aware of how long it took to reach the bottom. She lifted up a silent prayer to Yahweh for Tebah. Then, hearing footsteps behind her, she looked over her shoulder. It was Jared. She forced herself to remain calm, aware that her actions would look like 'another example of her attempts to escape social responsibility'.

"Deborah!" His greeting had the tone of mock approval. "Why is it, when the rest of the village is working, I find you lazing about by the well?" He looked disheveled.

Deborah repressed the desire to ask him when was the last time he worked, realising that this would only fuel his acrimony.

She sighed heavily, meeting his eyes. "Tebah has sunstroke, I brought him here, and now I'm taking water to the others…so that we don't lose any more workers," she added hastily, hoping to appeal to her uncle's practical mind.

His face reddened, the bulging vein on his neck warning Deborah that he was not appeased. His eyes darkened as he stepped toward her. "Do you think I only care about the work people do? I'm trying to save the village… Not just myself and my family…"

Deborah stepped back, shocked by the candor of his insinuation. Shelimoth's accusations had caught her off guard, but now she could feel Jared's bitterness fuelling the spark of her own rage and grief, and she longed to give vent to it, to defend herself.

Her voice was steady. "Then I am sure that you will begin to pray to the right God for your village, rather than invite Baal and Dagon in and wonder why He reaps destruction on it. I believe you were brought up by the same wise man that taught my father that idolatry was wrong, and would be punished."

She watched Jared open and close his mouth, reminding Deborah of a fish that her brother caught and then thrown onto the bank. A part of her knew she ought to stop, but she was furious. Her tone remained calm, though inwardly she trembled. "And since you care so much for the village, I suggest you rethink your work plan. Let people rest in the midday sun, and if necessary, work a little later in the evening. They will work faster when it's not as hot. And perhaps you and Shelimoth could show your deep compassion by passing out water while the people work, since you seem to have time on your hands."

Jared stepped toward her. She acknowledged she had been disrespectful to her elders, and that punishment would follow.

He grabbed her shoulders in a painful grip, his face twisted into a snarl. "You know nothing about leading a village. Well, we'll see when there's not enough food, maybe it will be your family that starves."

"Deborah!"

She turned, and was relieved to see Tobias walking toward them, his eyes were fixed on Jared, and though he smiled, she noted his quiet indignation.

"I hear you've been looking after my grandson?" He put his arm around her, meeting Jared's glare with his gentle, authoritative eyes.

It occurred to Deborah at that moment that leadership was an anointing from Yahweh, not dependent on position. If you have it, people will follow you, as they did Tobias; if you don't have it, you have to control people in order to maintain order.

"Thank you," she whispered to Tobias as he led her away from Jared.

"You're shaking. Come back and let Raisa get you some goat's milk and a honey cake."

"Honey cake!! Where did she get honey from?" Deborah asked.

Tobias chuckled rolling his eyes. "Raisa has her own rules. She says, as long as she's doing right before Yahweh, she's not giving everything to Jared while he gets fatter and we're starving. There's a hive in the forest and she smoked those bees out herself; says it was a gift from Yahweh, and what Jared and the Canaanites don't know about, they can't ask for."

By the time Deborah had devoured her second honey cake, she felt much better. Her mother had popped in, too, and as she and Raisa curdled goats' milk, they began to discuss what was happening in the village.

"It's grief, of course. They're angry and looking for someone to blame. But it's not right to take it out on Deborah," Maya reasoned, as she podded peas, smiling affectionately at her daughter.

"I know. They've been through a terrible time. I understand," she empathised. It wasn't that she was angry with Jared or Shelimoth, it was that their words had created a cyclone of self-doubt and guilt that she was too ashamed to voice.

"Jared's insecurities go way back. Even before you and Amos were married and you joined the village," Raisa remembered.

"Amos loved Jared. He always defended him. How could Jared be so unkind, with all that's happened?" Maya fumed with frustration.

"I think he always stood in Amos's shadow. As the younger brother, he never seemed as fast, as clever, or as strong." Raisa's eyes were soft as she laughed. "Amos always had a way with people; he warmed to them and they to him. I think that was the hardest part for Jared to understand as a boy. Then he married Shelimoth, and her iron will prevailed. When Amos died, I think Shelimoth hoped she would be able to rule the village through Jared. And, to some extent she does, of course. But for Jared, it's just reinforced how far short he falls of Amos."

"Suffering seems to highlight people's weaknesses doesn't it?" Maya mused, thinking about her own struggle.

"I suppose it does, but it can make us better, too. I'm worried about Jonah, at the moment. Orpah says he has nightmares, and lives in constant fear of Sisera's return. I mean we all do. But I'm worried he will…" her voice trailed off.

"Will what?" Maya quizzed her friend.

"I don't know. He just seems a little unpredictable…jumpy, and I'm concerned."

Her mother and Raisa's words seemed distant to Deborah as she struggled in her own dark battle. Had their words not had an element of truth, she would have been able to shrug them off. But now, all she could see was Keziah, burning in the field - as she ran. And her friends raped and murdered in the forest- while she hid. She felt sick with the revelation of her self-centred nature. Had her father been alive, she would have poured out her heart to him, and he would have known what to say. She felt alone. She knew her mother loved her, but her shame and guilt were buried deep. To bring them to light and to acknowledge them was too painful. She felt herself recede further within. Her self-accusation burned like a fire within her, consuming both sense and reason, and creating a path before her: next time, she would be the one. She would not run, would not hide again!

When the evening shift came to an end, Hadas, Miriam, and Deborah wearily made their way back to the village. Her small family often ate with Raisa and Tobias. The empty spaces were particularly felt at meal times, where her father had told stories and made them laugh. On certain evenings, the elderly couple's children, grandchildren, great grandchildren and other village members would gather in and pour out of the courtyard. In those moments, despite their lack, it was almost possible to forget that life had changed. Songs were sung and conversation and laughter flowed freely, creating a brief respite in the midst of their hardship. Towards the end of the evening, Gershon and Hagar arrived with Edom and Miriam and announced that they would be having another baby. Tobias opened a skin of wine, declaring a cause for celebration.

When the next Sabbath came, the air was still, and the sun beat down relentlessly, despite the fact that the day was still embryonic. Perspiration pricked her skin and Deborah warred with the idea of making the climb up the mountain. But her desire to escape and the need to find Yahweh's presence drove her from the protective shade of her home. She grabbed her water bottle and bag, kissing her mother as she patched a hole in Isaac's old tunic.

Leaving the olive grove and vineyards behind her, she began the ascent up the steep hillside. The white, chalky path, which had been bordered with prophet's clover, lupins and kehla a few months ago, was now bare, save for withered, ashen grass. Being careful not to drink too much, Deborah took sips of water. She wistfully slipped into the comfortable world of her memories, recalling how Tebah's father, Jonah, had taught them how to identify poisonous mushrooms from non-poisonous and taught them how to hunt. There were long sunny days where they would camp out under the stars, cooking their kill proudly over open fires, without fear.

She was almost at her rocky retreat, and longing to seek the respite of its cool shade, when her attention was drawn to the hovering mass of black birds soaring and swooping above the summit. When she later considered what had drawn her to continue her climb, she was unsure if it had been a spiritual prompt, or simply her own insatiable curiosity.

She concluded that Yahweh works with men in their humanity.

Her breathing formed a chant that set the pace of her climb. However, it was soon drowned by the unmistakable sound of vultures; their mournful, extended squawks defiled the air as though they had been created to be oracles of death. Her stomach twisted inside of her and she wished again that she had stopped at *her place*. She felt a growing sense of dread warring within her: she willed it to be a dead goat or sheep, yet her pounding heart and sense of unease warned her to anticipate the worst.

She staggered back; nothing had prepared her for what she saw. She heaved, vomiting up the little breakfast she had eaten, and willing the scene to leave her mind. The eerie cackles of the carrion seemed to follow her as she stumbled down the mountain. She slipped and fell on the loose stones, heedless of the cuts and scrapes in her desperation to flee the image of the tiny child she had seen laid across the broad stone, its charred remains overshadowed by carved stone statues of Baal and his cohorts. She reached the overhanging rock that marked the location of her rocky retreat and paused, sobbing as she took in deep breaths. She was torn between her desperate need for the comfort of Yahweh and her desire to leave the mountain; it seemed defiled.

What would she do when she returned to the village? What, if anything, would she say? Whose child had it been? Theirs was the only village near this mountain: did that mean it was someone she knew?

Her mind slipped back to the image of the shrine. She swallowed, fighting the urge to vomit again and willing her mind to think on anything else. Resolved, she rapidly climbed the familiar overhang and pushed her body into the corner of the cold rock. She pushed the palms of her hands into her eyes, taking in deep breaths to steady herself.

"Yahweh! What is happening?! Yahweh, we need you, yet they do not understand!" She spoke in desperate, whispered gasps. As she spoke, she felt emotion welling up, like a river of fire that rose within her, uncontainable and uncontrollable. She clutched the rock face on either side, aware of Yahweh's presence and His grief and anger, but also His comfort that wrapped around her and stilled both thought and feeling. In this place she sobbed, not only for the child she had seen, but also for what her people had become and the consequences that would inevitably follow.

"Lord, show mercy, show mercy... Expose unrighteousness!"

Opening her eyes, she saw the image of a void in space, a swirling, coiling cyclonic spiral of dark colour, with black at its centre.

"This spinning vortex, what does it mean?"

And then, the answer came:

In our darkest hour,
We feel what is unknown.
We grasp at reality,
Bound by fear.
We refuse to let go, of what's safe and near,
Yet we are drawn,
Pulled relentlessly,
Each to their destiny.

But what is unseen is shrouded in mystery;
Colours, though inspiring are uncertain.

And Deborah spoke: "And so my thoughts are driven,
My confusion shadows this prophetic vision.
Is this a chasm full of anguish and pain?
Or a portal to heaven, where our destiny reigns?
But what can draw me but Thee?
For you are my gravity,
My inner horizon.
And so, letting go...
I trust...
In nothing but Thee..."

Looking up, tears poured down her face. A messenger of the Lord stood before her, framed and radiating light and glory. He leaned down, touching her mouth, her eyes and ears with his hands. She trembled as power coursed through her body, leaving no room for fear or grief.

"You will lead your people into freedom. You will be a mother to them. I will be with you in all that must come first."

"What must I do now?" she whispered.

"Let dark and light divide. Wait." The messenger smiled, compassion pouring from his countenance, and a fire-like intensity burning in his eyes that reassured her and communicated His will.

"Can I warn them? Surely we must destroy the high place."

"Do what is on your heart Deborah. Time will show men's hearts."

Reluctant to leave the mountain, yet driven by the spirit of Yahweh within her, Deborah walked back down the mountain, her steps lighter as she pondered the angelic visitation. She found her mother tending a lamb that had hurt its leg, and waited for her to finish. When she eventually turned to Deborah, she took a moment to speak, as though she was puzzling over an unseen factor.

"What happened?" her mother whispered as confused awe flooded her countenance. Her brother, too, stood looking at her, his mouth agape.

Deborah took a deep breath, wondering how one conveys a meeting with a supernatural being that doesn't make one seem insane or deluded. "I was on the mountain. A high place has been built." She recalled the image. "A child was there, and vultures. It was awful! But then, I went to *my place* and a messenger from heaven appeared to me." She paused, her eyes shining with the recollection of their meeting. "He spoke to me." It seemed understated, and she wondered if that was how Jacob felt after his encounter with an angel. She half expected them to laugh at her, yet clearly they saw something she did not.

"Isaac, run and get Tobias," Maya instructed, releasing the bleating sheep without letting Deborah out of her gaze.

Tobias took one look at Deborah and beckoned her and Maya to sit down. Isaac joined them. "Can you tell me what happened up there?" the old man asked.

Deborah nodded, recounting her horror at finding the high place on the mountain, the child sacrifice and the carrion. She went on to describe her vision and seeing the Angel of the Lord, telling them what the Angel had said.

Tobias listened quietly, stroking his beard thoughtfully. "And you say the Angel told you to do what is on your heart?"

Deborah nodded.

"Well, that's indecisive," Tobias chuckled, raising a quizzical eyebrow. "I suppose then the question is: What is on your heart, Deborah?"

"Well, clearly we need to destroy the high place. I'm worried it was set up by people in the village." She hesitated before adding: "I saw Jared and Shelimoth...and Ariel...It was before...They were worshipping Baal in their home."

Tobias nodded sadly.

"They're not alone," Maya blurted. She looked down at the floor and bit her lip nervously.

"I don't want to gossip, but we know there were others that day..." She referred to the day that the statues of Baal and Dagon and Asherah had been erected in the village centre - though allegedly only to appease the Canaanites. "But it's happening, and people seem to be more open about it. As others come from villages where it's more acceptable, they bring it with them. It would be easy, if Jared met with them while we were out in the fields, that one of their children...we would never know they had existed. We don't really know who serves Baal."

Deborah, spoke quietly with a gentle assurance of what she must do.

"We must expose what has happened; let dark and light divide. We must destroy the high place. We cannot ask Yahweh to save us when we are worshipping Baal – while such defilement rests above us."

She stood, her back to the well, and waited, thinking of all that had happened at this place in recent years: her father and brothers' deaths, the raising of the false gods, Jared's accusations.

"There had better be a good reason for calling us away from work," Jared grumbled, looking to a few of the other villagers. He gripped a plough shear in one hand and wiped his forehead with the back of his hand.

A sense of divine judgment lingered in the air, as though the messenger moved among them; and whilst many were unable to define the atmosphere, they were nonetheless unnerved by it.

Miriam and Hadas came and stood next to Deborah, as did her mother, Raisa, Aaliya and Tobias.

Tobias cleared his throat, his tone was uncharacteristically subdued, and the brooding sense of anticipation grew denser.

"I pray that each of us might listen with open hearts to what will be said. Let us consider carefully what is the truth, and take great care with the decisions we make, for they will determine our future and that of our children." He gestured to the dark cloud that hovered over the mountain.

"The messenger of the Lord met with Deborah today on the mountain and spoke to her. I plead with you, that we all might listen to Deborah, to what she found, and what He said." He motioned to Deborah.

The sun had begun its descent, and yet still it was a fiery ball of intensity that pricked their skin, persistent in its onslaught. As the eyes of the village rested upon her, Deborah felt a surge of panic as she acknowledged that what she would say was already being weighed by their perception of who they believed her to be. Some looked on her with curiosity, others openly, but many were cynical as to whether anything worthwhile could come from the mouth of a girl. Her heart pounded and her thoughts betrayed her: *I am just a girl, they won't listen to me. I can't do this.*

Deborah later wondered whether it was the unconscious nature of humankind to seek out that which they fear the most; to tempt that which they know can destroy them - or whether it was the hand of Yahweh that caused her to seek out Jared and Shelimoth.

She noted Jared's dark frown, and Shelimoth's mouth twisted with humorous disdain as she turned to whisper to Shayna, and her words clung to the roof of her mouth. She bowed her head, forcing her gaze inward - an act of surrender, and a plea to He who is greater: *Yahweh, Holy and Mighty Yahweh, help your servant to speak.* The image of the altar flashed into her mind, and with that fuel, she heard her trembling voice cut the silence.

"I walked to the mountain today, as I often do. When I was half way, I saw…carrion, I continued to the top of our beloved mountain." She faltered as the memories of the darkened corpse assaulted her composure. Taking a deep breath she continued: "There I found a high place…a child has been sacrificed there…We all know there are no other villages so near to the mountain as ours." Righteous anger had triumphed over her fear, and now it was her turn to pierce their souls. "Have we forgotten that Yahweh hates idolatry? Have we stepped so far from the truth that it no longer leads us? We…we need to repent of our sin and destroy the high place. If we remove Yahweh as God of this village, how can we complain when Sisera comes again that He does not protect us?"

There was a stunned silence.

As she expected, Jared and Shelimoth stepped forward. Deborah had naïvely hoped that they would be the first to relinquish their hidden idols. However, Jared's rage contorted face and Shelimoth's religious disdain spoke louder than the verbal onslaught that would follow:

"Who do you think you are?" Shelimoth spat, her control barely constrained. "You are a sixteen year old girl. You are *not* the leader of this village. You are *not* your father. And you certainly have *no* right to tell people what to do!" She stepped forward, and the expression on her face changed so that it was one of feigned compassion. As she spoke her voice was level with the pretense of compassion that made her flesh crawl.

"Deborah, we know you've been through a dreadful time, as we all have. We all wish someone would come and make sense of what has happened. But we can't just go around making things up because it makes us feel better, honey-bee."

Deborah felt the barrage of Shelimoth words buffet the wall of her convictions. She saw the eyes of people on her, weighing her. *Had she made it up? Why would Yahweh choose to speak to an insignificant girl?*

Their silence spoke volumes and she felt her resolve shrivel within her. She wanted nothing more than to run, to bow her head in shame and walk away.

Hadas and Tobias stood by her. The old man's voice was steady, but his underlying ire was apparent. "I, for one, believe her. Let us not think that Yahweh cannot use Deborah because she is a girl. I saw the Glory of Yahweh radiate from her when she first returned from the mountain, and you would see it too if you had the eyes to. Or, am I deluded too, Shelimoth?"

"No, Tobias, I don't think you are deluded, simply gullible and prone to thinking the best of people." Shelimoth smiled sweetly with the patience one might show a small child.

Deborah had begun to move away, and Shelimoth, clearly feeling smug, believing Deborah had listened to her, also stepped back folding her arms. But Deborah stood in the doorway of her home, her fingers tracing the etched words that marked the doorpost. She realised that she had come too far to back down now. She would throw herself into the chasm that taunted her, and trust Yahweh to catch her. Mentally silencing the inner voice that told her she had stepped out of line, she allowed herself to be driven by the righteous anger that had risen within her. She raised her voice so that everyone could hear her.

"You shall write My Laws on the doorpost of your home and teach them to your children…" Her voice sounded stronger in her own ears.

Jared opened his mouth to speak, and then uncharacteristically closed it again.

She did not look at the engraved words, for they were written in her heart. "You shall have no other gods before Me. You shall not make for yourselves an idol. You shall not worship them or serve them. You shall not take the Lord's Name in vain. You shall not murder. You shall not commit adultery. Did He not say that if we did, He would allow us to be oppressed by our enemies in order to show us the falsity of their gods; that we might turn back to Him? Can we not see what is happening, my dear ones?" She could feel tears of passion sting her eyes, and blinked them back lest she now end up looking like a foolish girl.

There was a moment's silence in which the curtain was held back, hearts were weighed and lines were drawn in the dirt.

Joshua slipped quietly away from the crowd. His head was hung low with the shame and grief of a man who has seen too much sorrow. He disappeared. When he returned a few minutes later, he held in his arms the carved wooden idols of Baal, Dagon, Asherah and El. He paused for a moment as though wrestling with letting them go, tears rolling down his face, as he faced the magnitude of his loss and sin. His children, Nissa and Levi, came and embraced him.

"We will," Menachem said grimly, clutching Nissa's hand as they stepped forward to stand next to Joshua.

"I will too," Gershon volunteered.

"And I." Deborah was surprised to see Miriam's younger brother, Josiah, stepped forward. She also noted how many had not chosen either side, and that the divisions between families, friends and village that had previously been a faint line that no-one wanted to define, were now walls that separated them.

"Then let us go now, while there is still daylight." She cast a look towards Jared and Shelimoth, and saw that Uriel and Hillel, with their children stood by them. Judah looked decidedly awkward. When Reuben and Shayna stepped forward, with their youngest son, Ephraim, aged six, Tobias staggered backward, his expression one of shock and sorrow.

"My son, what are you doing?"

"I'm sorry, Abba, we should have spoken to you first. We've been worshipping with the others for some time. I love you, Abba, Mama, please try and accept our decision. It's not that we don't believe in Yahweh, we just feel…the ways of Yahweh are too prescriptive; we are ignoring some important lessons because of our fears…We can't think that everything the Canaanites do is wrong…their agricultural methods, their understanding of trade are far better than ours to name but a few. We feel we can worship Yahweh as El Elyot – god most high, creator and father of all gods. We do not need to be divided over our faith."

Shayna completed his sentence. "Why do you think Canaan is so lush? See how they live with abundance. We need rain. If we honour Baal, god of storm, he will send it. We need to assure a good harvest – surely you can see the logic in this? Did not Abraham refer to Yahweh as El? Did he not offer his son?"

"Yahweh defined himself to Abraham as El, the only God, as a way of leading him away from the gods of his father and his people," Tobias pointed out raggedly. "Surely you can see that a god who demands that we sacrifice *our* children to him is unworthy of our praise? You speak of Canaanite intelligence as though it were admirable, and perhaps their ideas of farming are worthy of consideration, but will you stock pile fertility by sleeping with temple prostitutes? Does that seem intelligent to you my son?" Tobias spoke gently, but his voice shook with emotion as he looked at his grandchildren.

Reuben had his head bowed, when he looked up, his eyes pleaded. "It won't come to that, Abba."

"Would a loving God command the genocide of other nations, including, women and children?" Uriah sparred.

"You do not understand the heart of Yahweh. It grieves Him that any should die, but better that the essence of all who would cause the slavery and prostitution of innocent people should once be removed, than thousands of innocent children murdered and years of wars, death and separation from Him, which will happen if we fail. Yahweh warned them for many years of his judgment on their actions and they ignored him," Tobias urged.

As he spoke, Deborah saw Shelimoth motion to Jared.

"And yet, it is not they who suffer now, but us. Does that show you nothing? You cannot pull down the high place! You will call down the vengeance of the gods!" Hillel pleaded.

"We suffer *because* we have turned from Yahweh! We have taken ourselves from His protection, and in doing so we surrender ourselves - not to Baal, who is made of stone, but to Satan, the enemy of our souls," Deborah insisted.

Jared stepped forward, a muscle twitching at the side of his mouth. He looked at Shelimoth, who smiled almost imperceptibly as she nodded her head in affirmation.

He cleared his throat. "I believe I speak for many in the village when I say there can be no tearing down of the altar. It would invoke the wrath of the gods. We will fight any who attempt to do so."

Those who had sided with Deborah looked to her now, then at Tobias. A few of them had come from the fields and carried plough shears and trowels, but nobody wanted a bloody battle amongst their friends and family.

She wasn't a leader. She had no right to challenge Jared; she was just a girl. What had she been thinking of? She had said what was in her heart. She could do no more.

She hesitated, feeling uncertainty tug on her resolve. Tobias was quiet and reflective; he laid a gentle hand on her arm and waited as long moments passed. Finally, He whispered: *wait for Yahweh*. She heard the words of her prayer echo in her mind: *let unrighteousness be exposed*. It had been.

And yet, as she walked away, she acknowledged how the burden of failure weighs heavier than the satisfaction of success.

Her desire to recede enveloped her as isolation sought to silence her. She mentally retreated to *her place*, where her fortress became the arms of Yahweh, embracing her and reassuring her.

13

…and pitched his tent by the great tree in Zaanannim near Kedesh.
Judges 4:11

1255 BC – Jael

During her life, Jael had often wished she had been born less complicated, able to bend in the storms rather than trying to fight them. The simple truth was that she hated Heber. The more she tried to tolerate him, the more he would tighten his control and the more she resented him for it. Her father had once told her that a fox caught in a trap would chew off its limb to be free - freedom being a higher necessity than comfort. She knew that she was that fox.

The situation had worsened at En Gedi. She often slipped through the open gate that sealed the fortress of her carefully guarded inner world, where her memories and daydreams gave her respite from Heber's growing ambition and cruelty.

The date palms and lush vegetation were watered by springs that fell over towering rocks into pools, sparkling and pure. Natural caves with smooth, rounded mouths flowed with the formation in the rock as though they had been lovingly caressed into shape by the hand of God. Jael found herself wondering if this was what Eden had looked like. She cupped water into her hands, careful not to drink too much after her dehydration. Breaking off a piece of aloe vera, she rubbed its gel-like sap onto her blistered lips.

Without warning, Heber viciously pulled her back to reality, his fingers digging into her arms as he hissed in her ear: "Serve the men...and make sure you're polite. I'd hate for them to have to see me teach you how to curb your foul mouth." His nails dug into her flesh.

She swallowed, trying to keep her voice from shaking, though her heart thumped wildly in her chest.

She had considered telling Heber the truth: that Miera needed feeding, but decided against it. "I should change first. Meira has been sick over these clothes."

He eyed her with disgusted disdain, but released her. "Then hurry!"

Jael exhaled with relief and fled. Taking Miera, she put her to her breast, thanking Yahweh that her milk had returned. She took the cup that Adva gave her; drinking small sips as the baby thirstily choked on the milk. She asked Adva to find a change of clothes for her, constantly looking over her shoulder for Heber lest he should discover her deception.

The servants had cut up fruit and were offering it to the Heber's caravan drivers, guards and soldiers while they waited for a goat to be roasted. Later as she helped, she filled their glasses with wine, ignoring their crude suggestions and leering glances.

Heber sat with the soldiers and his senior caravan guard. When she passed, he grabbed her arm and pulled her onto his lap. She fought the urge to free herself, knowing that her non-compliance and his embarrassment now would be punished later. He stank of sweat and wine.

The day had begun to take its toll and weariness sunk in when Zimran arrived. He had spent the day herding the weary, dehydrated animals along the final stretch of the way. When they arrived at En Gedi, Jael had noted how he had made sure they were taken to the water before he drank anything himself. Now, here he was. Heber was already drunk and loud. He called Zimran to come and sit with them. Zimran darted a glance at Jael and she felt the dull ache within her heart re-open, a deep cavity she tried to ignore.

"Thank you, I'll keep an eye on the animals," he answered with quiet conviction.

"Nonsense, come and have a drink. Jael! Pour the man a drink!"

She stood, her hand trembling as Zimran took the glass from her. Their eyes met for a fleeting moment before he looked away. The hole within her grew like a desert sinkhole, and she felt herself slipping, unable to withstand the avalanche of emotion that threatened to suffocate her. Heber barked her name, and as she returned to his side, he grabbed her face, kissing her. She felt hot tears of shame and humiliation sting her eyes, but worse than that, the knowledge that she was betraying her heart.

When Heber finally staggered to his sleeping quarters, Jael slipped away. She felt exhausted and dirty, as though his hatred and control had seeped into her pores and was poisoning her system. She crept to the cave where Adva, Meira and a few of the other women were sleeping and picked up a torch. She longed to run, but was aware of the open holes that dropped hundreds of feet into underwater pools and rivers, and so instead she walked cautiously, placing her feet down warily.

The moon gave its crooked smile as it ducked in and out of smoky white clouds, faintly illuminating the towering rocks. Finally, she found what she was looking for: a pool about eight feet wide and deep enough that she could step in and still feel the bottom with her feet. She stripped off her clothes and stepped into the water – it was deliciously warm. She sighed, submerging her head under the water and raking her fingers through her knotted, dusty hair. The water had the cathartic effect that she had hoped for. Folding her hands on the side of the pool, she rested her head and closed her eyes, allowing her legs to float behind her. She felt weightless, peaceful. She stayed in the water, watching the stars danced on the rippled water as the moon continued its journey toward the horizon. Time had stopped, and she was free. Her thoughts gravitated to Zimran, his smile, his gaze, his care towards the animals. How could she feel so much pride and respect for someone who was not hers?

It was the thought of Meira that eventually dragged her back to reality. Reluctantly, she clambered out of the pool and got dressed. She realised then that the torch had gone out, only a glowing ember remained. She tried, unsuccessfully, to blow it back to flame but in doing so, extinguished the ember. Her heart picked up a notch as she tried to focus her eyes on the stones around her, looking for some sign as to which way she needed to go. Dark looming shadows that had offered solace and privacy now seemed walls that imprisoned her. She had no idea where she was placing her feet. Her palms were clammy; the night air suddenly seemed too warm. Hearing movement behind her, she fought the urge to panic. She knew better than to wonder about being unable to see. She would have to wait until morning. No doubt Miera would awake, but Heber would not for some time, of that she was certain. Adva would have the sense to go for help. She found a comfortable place and pulling her knees up to her chest, rested her head on her knees. Jael sat like that for some time, hoping she would sleep, but the cold rock dug into her back and the night air had cooled on her damp clothes so that she was soon shivering. Once again, she heard movement behind her. This time it seemed closer. Her heart raced; whatever it was knew she was here. She stood up, and began to feel her way along the side of the cliff. She had come in from the East with the Salt Sea behind her. If she used the North Star to guide her, she could surely find her way back to camp. Each time she put her foot down she felt the ground cautiously beneath her.

She continued in this way for some time until the first tips of sunlight caressed the soft rocky verges. Jael squinted, hoping to recognise her surroundings, but nothing seemed to be the same as it was last night. She chided herself for being so foolish as to wander off alone. In another hour, people would begin to awaken and somebody would be sent to look for her. She was angry with herself for being so foolish, and yet resolved to find her way back to the camp. She looked up at one of the rocks and realised that from the top of one of them, she would be able to make out the smoke from fires. Decided, she began to climb one of the rock faces. Jael discovered that she enjoyed climbing, and that she was able to scale the rutted surface quickly.

When she looked down, she was jubilant at her achievement, and the view before her. Sequins of sunrise dazzled on the surface of the Salt Sea reflecting the molten copper of the sunrise. To the north, the rust coloured rocks of En Gedi were contrasted by the verdant paradise of exotic flowers and fruit trees, waterfalls and streams. To the south lay the vast and barren desert from whence they had come. Beyond that was home: Arad and Midian. She breathed in the view as though to imprint its magnificent splendour upon her soul.

A thin line of smoke coiled into the cool morning air and she smiled inwardly with relief, knowing now that she would be able to find her way back.

The climb down was more difficult than her ascent. She nearly slipped and fell a few times, and by the time she reached the bottom, her hands and knees were scraped and bleeding. She hobbled toward the direction of the smoke. Finally, she could smell it and hurried now, ignoring her tiredness and pain. When she rounded the corner, she expected to see the camp. But the fire had been stamped out and the occupants left. Panic set in. *Had Heber ordered them to leave her? Would he do that to her? Of course he would.* She kicked the ashes and screamed in frustration and self-pity. The dust and smoke made her choke. Finally, she sat down and cried.

"Still getting yourself in all kinds of trouble, Jael?"

That voice.

She looked up.

It was him.

Everyone was gone, and he had remained. Why?

She was staring at Zimran, and he was laughing his deep, beautiful laugh. His full lips and perfect white teeth.

Why was he laughing? At her?

She wiped her tear-streaked face with the back of her hand revealing her soot-covered face. Of course. She must look a vision.

Her emotion swung between joy at seeing Zimran, and embarrassed indignation and humour that bordered on hysteria. She succumbed to the latter, laughing until her sides hurt while he laughed too, his deep carefree laughter.

And then, they sat, neither moving, nor speaking; only holding each other's gaze, as though to remember everything about the other, lest the memory fade. The space between them remained, and yet their unspoken words were imparted. Neither dared to move closer, the gravity between them was too strong and neither one had the strength to fight it. They remained that way until the invasive sun prodded them back to harsh reality.

She pulled herself away from his eyes. She could live now, knowing he loved her, and he knowing that she still loved him.

"Heber told me to find you. He needed to take the caravan to Shiloh. Sisera is waiting." His dark eyes scrutinised hers for response.

"Of course." She looked away.

A camel waited, tethered to a date palm. Zimran unpacked one of the saddlebags, handing her a goatskin flask and a strip of linen. She drank some and then used a little of the water to wipe the soot from her face.

"An improvement?" she grinned, grabbing her long hair and tying it back.

He smiled back at her, watching her movements as though he were drinking them in. He pointed to the space beneath her nose and then forced his eyes away, stroking the dusty neck of the camel.

The camel was loaded for one rider.

"Ride with me Zimran. We'll never make it to Shiloh in time to meet Heber otherwise."

He nodded; she was right. Yet, with every moment they shared, it would be harder to hand her over to Heber. He'd seen the way the man treated his animals and slaves. He would make sure their conduct was above reproach, for both their sakes. But he longed to hold her in his arms. He longed to take her away with him. He re-arranged the saddlebags and then spoke softly to the camel who obediently lowered himself into a sitting position. Jael gripped the saddle and adeptly swung herself onto its back, behind the second hump, so that Zimran could lead. She was used to the animals, of course, having grown up with them. She and her sisters had raced them in Midian when her father was away.

Now he was near to her, she breathed in his scent of spices and desert - of home and freedom. She longed to reach out and touch him. It was as though the air between them was charged with a force that connected them, while the walls of her vows to Heber rose impenetrably between them.

She consciously pierced the power of the silence. She had to.

"Heber is meeting Sisera?"

"Yes. He's made some sort of alliance with Jabin."

"Is that why we are going to Kedesh?"

He turned his head to her. "Do you not know?"

"No, he doesn't speak to me."

"About work?"

She shrugged. "About anything. Unless it's derogatory or a command."

Zimran paused. She wondered if he was deliberating about whether to break Heber's confidence, but he wrestled with the anger that rose within him. He stopped the camel, swinging his leg around so that he was facing her.

"The man will stoop as low as he needs to in order to get what he wants. Rumour has it that Sisera has offered him money and slaves, Hebrew slaves, and access to the mines at Gerasha, in return for production of nine hundred iron chariots."

Jael felt giddy as the blood drained from her face. She thought of Yahweh, of Adva, and her Hebrew friends. Zimran must have noticed because he caught her arm. His touch brought her back to reality. She gripped hold of the saddle.

"He cannot do this. Yahweh will avenge his people and we will be killed, too. I won't let it happen. I won't."

Zimran watched as Jael grew distant, the way she did when her mind was seeking a solution to a problem. He smiled, raising his eyebrows.

Finally, she broke the silence. "Zimran, how can you work for such a man?!" her voice sounded incredulous if not condemning.

"How could you stay with such a man?" he retorted bitterly.

"I have no choice. You do," she contended, defensively.

"There are always choices, Jael." He paused as though choosing his words. "I chose to remain in Heber's employment because it was the path that brought me closest to you," he smiled bitterly.

She allowed the truth of his words to sink into her soul, creating a bittersweet maelstrom of feeling that brought both elation and misery.

"I stay with him because I know it is the will of Yahweh, for now," she replied quietly, giving voice to her inner conviction.

"Yahweh? Since when did my wild desert girl fear Yahweh?"

She laughed half-heartedly, as she realised Zimran knew nothing of her recent journey with Yahweh.

"You drive the camel, and I'll talk."

By the time they reached Shiloh, the sun was beginning to dip below the horizon, and Jael had told Zimran all about her mother, her secret faith and her conversations with Yahweh.

As Tel Shiloh rose before her, it sent shivers of wonder down her spine. Adva had told her that Joshua Ben Nun had discovered the city, taking it from the Canaanites, when he entered the Promised Land.

Their camel easily climbed the gradual southern slope to the mighty gates of Shiloh. The other sides were protected by steep rocky cliffs, ending in mighty stone walls, over twenty four feet high and eighteen feet wide in some places. At the top, the tabernacle dwelt, from whence the chants of the priests and the smoke of sacrifices arose. Homes and public buildings rose in a maze of streets and stone buildings around it.

The city resounded with the holiness and majesty of Yahweh, that was unmarred by the hectic market place that sprawled outside the city walls.

Zimran helped Jael dismount from the camel, and paid a slave to tend to the animal. Together they made their way to the address Heber had given. The sense that their time together was coming to an end, created the pain of anticipated loss, as though their hearts were knitted; and to separate would leave both irreparably torn.

Heber had dressed in his finest clothes: a white linen robe, with an embroidered purple sash. He leaned back in his chair, his one arm draped over the back of a chair ostentatiously, whilst he used the other to dramatically emphasise the importance of his speech. A long wooden table stood between him and Sisera, who stood looking out over Shiloh.

Jael turned to Zimran, aware of the sanctity of their last minutes together.

"You know, it will always be you…" she whispered.

"I know…" He looked away. "Try and be good…and…stay alive," he smiled sadly, before walking away.

As she turned toward Heber, she noted that he had been watching them. She disappeared once again behind the wall, pushing emotion and will into the dark corners of her mind, until their voice was nothing more than a muffled scream deep in her chest.

Sisera stood with his usual composure, one arm rested on his sword, the other hung loosely at his side. His smile was a social tool, another muscle of control that assured his victory and his prey's compliance as his internal jackal assessed for weakness. Jael knew that Sisera was appealing to Heber's need for approval from those he deemed 'successful'. She almost pitied him. Almost.

"Ah, Jael. Come here. Sisera, I believe you have met my wife already." He beckoned her with a flick of his hand that indicated his possession, and demanded her submission. Of course he would try and show his dominance over her to hide his fawning sycophantic behaviour and personal weakness. She recalled her last meeting with the man, now identified as Sisera, when she had just had Miera and blushed, pushing her embarrassment into the same dark cavity as her other emotions.

She smiled sweetl., *Fine - if that was what he wanted, she would play.*

"Darling, I'm so sorry I'm late." She turned to Sisera lowering her head respectfully. "How wonderful to see you again, my lord. However, I fear that I am still inappropriately attired after my long journey. Perhaps my husband will allow me to go and change?"

Heber looked at her suspiciously, motioning with his hand to dismiss her, while his usual look of distaste twisted his mouth.

Jael found Adva pacing the room with Miera, who was sobbing for all she was worth.

Adva let out a relieved sob when she saw Jael and flung her arms around her. "I'm so glad you are safe!" she gushed as she handed her Meira.

"She's had boiled water, but she's hungry. It's been nearly twenty-four hours. I've been so worried; I daren't hire a wet nurse until it got desperate, because of Heber's reaction." Adva's voice shook with emotion.

Jael placed Meira to her milk- engorged breasts with relief, the familiar and overwhelming sense of love coursing through her as she looked at her child. She looked up gratefully to Adva.

"Thank you, my dear friend. I knew you would look after her."

"I found a woman in En Gedi, another group of travellers; she fed her this morning before we left. But she's had nothing but water all day."

Adva sank onto the straw pallet, exhausted. As the baby greedily gulped down the milk, Jael relayed to Adva how she had gone to wash and got lost. She did not mention anything about Zimran, partly because she did not want to compromise Adva's loyalties, but a small part of her did not want to open the sacred chamber within her heart, where her love for Zimran remained hidden.

14
Until I, Deborah, arose.

Judges 5:7

1252 BC – Deborah

"Miriam! Have you listened to anything I have been saying?"
Deborah laughed, suppressing her irritation at her friend's glazed
over expression. The three of them were sitting in the Niddah
retreat, where Deborah was weaving wool on a loom. Isaac had shot
up another few inches, and his old tunic was threadbare. She had
been working on it in secret and hoped to present it to him for his
birthday. She popped one of the fig-cakes that Hadas had made the
previous day into her mouth. They were discussing Miriam's recent
betrothal.

"Sorry, Deborah, what were you saying?" Miriam played with a
strand of hair that had fallen from her headdress.

Hadas groaned. "It's only half as bad for you, Deborah. I've got it
at home as well. Nobody listens to *anything* I say. Adiel is dreaming
about the day he weds *his beloved Miri.*" She cast a lovesick look at
Miriam, who gave a smitten grin.

The three girls had all passed their eighteenth birthdays, and in
previous years they would be married with children by now. But life
had changed; people no longer travelled between villages as they once
had for fear of attack. (It wasn't just the Canaanite warriors). As
people turned from their Hebrew roots, their integrity was
compromised and each man lived for himself. Under the oppression
of the Canaanites, they took to robbing travellers to provide for their
families.

"Mother is busy making preparations with the other women."

"And Salmon?"

"He's just enjoying the sport of teasing Adiel. Can we not move this wedding forward, Deborah? Something MUST be done!" she exclaimed with mock frustration.

"I'm just pleased we're having a wedding. There have been too many funerals lately," Deborah grimaced with mordant humour.

Miriam sighed sadly. "Amen to that. Well, what about you two? I've seen you and Dan talking a lot lately, Hadas." She raised her eyebrows questioningly.

Hadas blushed furiously. "We were just talking!" she retorted defensively. But her colour and expression gave her away.

"It's hard for me to think about a betrothal or having a husband," Deborah said uneasily, with an uncharacteristic and forced openness. She struggled to speak of matters of the heart; they always felt locked deep inside her. However she empathised with Hadas' apprehension regarding the future, and hoped to spare her friend the awkwardness of explaining, so she told them about the plans for betrothal that her father had made for her..

"So, now I don't know who he is, or was…In any case, they're probably married now." She bit her lip introspectively, allowing herself a moment to follow a different path. She shrugged as though to dislodge the thought.

"And I have no idea how far the discussions went; I have no father to arrange these things for me or to provide for me. I've just decided its best not to think about it," she concluded pragmatically.

Hadas nodded in empathy. However, Miriam the romantic optimist, was not discouraged. She sat forward on the bench, her head resting on her hands and the formidable spark of romance in her eyes.

"Just think, though, he could ride into the village at any moment, or perhaps he's here." Her eyes flitted around the room as though someone might pop out of an alcove.

Deborah laughed, grimacing as she glanced over shoulder with dramatic concern. "I sincerely hope not."

"But you should ask your mother! She'd know! And aren't you just the slightest bit curious?" Miriam persisted.

Deborah sighed, picking at a broken nail in an attempt to avoid eye contact with her persistent and perceptive friends. "I am just the slightest bit curious. But firstly, Ima is more herself lately and for that I am *so* thankful. I will do nothing to risk her relapse - neither of us can afford to focus on what has been, or might have been. The other possible scenario is that she may feel the need to honour my father's plans and set about trying to organise a wedding for me, and I won't feel I have any say in it, because it was my father's desire. Besides, there is nobody in the village I have *any* romantic feelings for. In short the whole thing is best left well alone!"

"Oh. I see." Miriam looked momentarily disconcerted. Then, her head flicked up. "*In the village.* Is there someone *outside* the village then?"

A memory of warmth and laughter flitted into Deborah's mind, as the boy pushed his wild, dark curls from his deep, brown eyes. She felt a sudden wistfulness and a desire for the presence of the boy who had saved her life. Warily, she allowed the locked door of her heart to open a fraction, exposing the girlish daydream that lingered beyond. Then, quickly recognising the futility of such thoughts, she slammed it again, sealing it with her bleak resolve. "To be honest, most of my thoughts are focused on us all surviving at the moment." She pushed the loom away and stood up, signifying the end of their conversation.

The grapes had been pressed and were fermenting. The figs were dried and stored, and Deborah acknowledged the passing of her nineteenth birthday.

As the days grew shorter and the air cooled, Deborah noted the continued change in their community: the work that had forced co-operation and communication had calmed and the village grew quiet, as it always did in the winter months. The division in the village was once again reinforced, as people withdrew into their own homes. There, they could live as they wished, doing what was right in their own eyes. And if their isolation deprived them of the community and fellowship that had brought support, they were also free of judgment and criticism. If they met with others, it was with those who reinforced their actions and beliefs, and there was no longer any shadow of pretense that things were as they had been.

Deborah, her mother and brother met for prayer and study of the Torah with those who followed Yahweh. Deborah watched the file of those who worshipped Baal make their way to the high-place, her stomach twisting with sickened apprehension at what would occur there.

She awoke the next morning with the same dark foreboding that hung like a cloud over the village.

It was not until the following evening that her feelings were explained. The sound of a woman's sobs pierced the dusk. Both Deborah and her mother looked up, turning to each other: they were Raisa's. What would make her cry like that? They ran toward the grief that splintered the air.

Tobias was crossing the village, entering the home of his son Reuben, his face was red with fury and grief. He did not look at them as he passed.

Deborah felt terror grip her as she entered the room; *something terrible must have happened to have destroyed the peace of this man and woman of God.*

Tobias' voice pierced the air, and the fact that she had never heard this gentle man raise his voice in anger before made it sound terrible.

"...My grandson...you have murdered an innocent child... how could you...?" She heard his voice break with emotion and the gravity of what had happened sunk like a lead weight in her own soul. Raisa was on the floor; deep sobs racked her body as she buried her face in her hands. Maya took her in her arms and wept with her.

"He was not murdered...how dare you accuse us? He was sacrificed to Baal as an act of devotion. Do you think it was an easy decision?"

"Has your mind become so blinded with deception that you no longer remember the Law? Do you no longer remember who you are? You will bring the judgment of Yahweh on our village!"

"No, I am ensuring the blessing of Baal on our village's harvest. We will not listen to your religious ranting anymore. Leave my home, Father. Now!"

Tobias' face was grey, crumpled with sorrow as he took his wife in his arms. He turned to Deborah, Maya and Gershon, who had now appeared from the fields.

"Let us pray as we never have."

"I fear things must get worse before they will get better," Gershon replied with grim reflection.

Spring poked its downy head into the valley and the rains came; with it went the peace of knowing that Sisera's chariots could not come yet. The fragrance of narcissus, the bleating of new born lambs and the verdant fields of green wheat that were yet to ripen. They enjoyed the first fruits of the barley harvest, celebrating separately.

Many people had begun to speculate that the Canaanites would not return. Even Reuben, practical and prone to see the negative, had pointed out that the barley crop had been taken in and had been bountiful, and that they would have 'a little extra'. Jared attributed this to his leadership and the rituals and offerings that had been offered to Baal.

As the violence and hardship increased in Israel, people fled their towns and villages, seeking refuge in the hills and mountains and bringing with them their spiritual beliefs and gods. There was a wild desperation to survive at any cost that numbed people's senses and diluted their memories of their Hebrew roots. The physical pleasures of Canaanism offered consolation and gratification, while the deified statues offered clear religious satisfaction. There was the sentiment of righteousness without the constraints of the Law that they had forgotten was sent to protect them, not to bind them. Like any moral decline, it began with a small step and further compromises were subsequently easier to justify, until the life and God they had once loved was a hazy shadow, obscured by justification, pain and shame.

Deborah felt her concern and sadness grow as those she had grown up with abandoned Yahweh, and her village became divided and weakened, possessing a fragility that was brittle and raw.

It was three weeks later; everyone was working to harvest the wheat. At the end of the day people trawled home exhausted, to find a family in the centre of the village. A man, stood with his two young sons and daughter. For all that they had seen in Ephraim, Deborah had not seen such desperate hopelessness as she did now. It saturated them; an invisible cloud that stirred both empathy and antipathy, for it threatened the precarious cauldron of emotion over which they teetered.

Jared spoke with heated compassion. "We understand what you have been through, we have suffered here too. But there is barely enough for our families. Perhaps in the cities they can help…"

Tobias stepped forward. He rarely challenged Jared's authority and his voice was gentle, barely above a whisper, lest he humiliate Jared publicly.

"We cannot do this Jared. I will not do this. If you will send these people away, then I will invite them into my home, to share our food." He spoke without anger, nor pride, only the deepest compassion.

"Then do what you must Tobias. We have sacrificed enough." Jared's answer was without malice, but his own despair and loss left little concern for others.

Gershon had arrived on the scene, and now stood with his son, Edom, next to him. He leaned on his ox-goad, shading his eyes from the glare of the sun as he weighed up the situation. Finally, he sighed. "We have taken in an abundant harvest, are we not to bless those who have nothing, since Yahweh has seen fit to bless us?"

Reuben spoke now. "Baal has been appeased through our efforts, brother. But if Sisera returns, he will expect the same harvest we have all always given. He will not be ignorant of the fact that the harvest has been bountiful this year. We have taken in many families, now. With every family that comes, we must spread the food thinner. Sisera will not be sympathetic to our compassion. Do you want your children taken or killed? We must do what is best for ourselves before we extend charity to others."

Gershon bowed his head. When he lifted it again, he smiled, but his eyes glistened with tears as he acknowledged the gulf that had grown between him and his brother. They had been so close growing up, both logical and practical, with a need to understand the world. He recalled how the two of them would make dams in the stream to catch the fish, proudly taking them home for supper.

"As always, my dear brother, your logic is undeniable. But I cannot ignore my conscience. What if it was our family here?" He motioned to the man before them.

The wretched family stood silently, their faces drawn and expressions desolate. The father fell to his knees, in desperation and exhaustion, his voice shook with emotion. "Please, I understand your dilemma..." His eyes flitted with desperate anxiety, aware that his family's survival now depended on the good will of this village. "I will work hard," he swallowed.

"We left Issachar with my wife, my sons and three daughters. It's dire there. They live among us, they rule over us taking whatever, whomever they want - and we are powerless. We live with constant terror and subjugation. They have become known as 'the traffickers'. They take our young children and sell them as slaves, as temple prostitutes or sacrifice them to their gods - but they are never heard from again. I took my family and ran. Perhaps I was foolish. We made it through the mountains and thought we had escaped. But we were attacked along the road. They took my wife and two older daughters and left me badly beaten. We kept walking for four days. We heard it was better further south..."

"Please, I ask nothing of myself, but please feed my boys and daughter and I will be your slave." He fell to his knees, his head bowed to the ground. Jared stepped forward, his bushy eyebrows met, like an angry cloud, hovering over his reddened face.

"I'm sorry – my answer is final!" He turned and stormed away.

Deborah felt compassion and pity for the man; his head now slumped in defeat. She felt the man's desperation, as one who had suffered too, and she knew he must be helped.

Tobias stepped forward, the compassion and concern etched clearly on the man's face as he watched the humility and sacrifice the man made for his children. His heart ached for the pain they had seen. He clasped his shoulder.

"You'll do nothing of the sort. You're a Hebrew. Come into my home. You are welcome to share all that we have."

The man touched his forehead to the dust, sobbing as his children clung to him, grubby-faced and distraught.

It was not long before Tamar had brought ointments, Orpah had taken her children's old clothes and Joshua brought bowls that he had carved. Deborah brought her father and Enoch's blankets at her mother's suggestion. The man told him that his name was Manasseh; his children were Othniel, Gad and Eliza. He slept soundly that night for the first time he could remember, his children curled next to him on a straw pallet in Tobias' courtyard.

Morning came late to the village; menacing rain clouds hung low blocking out the sun. Spring seemed to be hesitant this year. The wheat was almost harvested and Deborah was aware that this would be the sixth year that they had not celebrated Passover. She sat on the wooden bench in the courtyard of her home, shelling peas with her mother.

"We'll have grapes next month."

"Hmmm," Deborah answered, her own thoughts far away as she pondered Hagar and Shayna's recent argument. It typified a growing tension in the village related to the food shortages and added numbers. Edom, Shayna and Reuben's son, had apparently caught Asher taking vegetables from their garden. Four years Asher's senior, he had grabbed the guilty boy by the arm and dragged him over to Gershon and Hagar's house to demand an apology and appropriate restitution. Horrified at the treatment of her son, Hagar had immediately called for Shayna, anticipating her understanding. However the argument had escalated, and now neither parties would speak.

The truth was that years ago, they would willingly have shared all they had, but now walls had been built and people looked after their own - and even then, not always. The core values and beliefs that had knitted them together had been eroded by hardship, and a belief system that was individualistic. Where once these quarrels would have been settled during Niddah, Shayna did not come; she and Reuben had agreed that the practice was an outdated tradition. The cord that held the village together was badly fraying through friction; its loosed threads indicative of its fragility.

Her mother put down her bowl and looked at Deborah.

"You're lost in thought, honey-bee. Is everything alright?"

Deborah sighed, smiling up at her mother. "Yes, just village politics. I've been thinking how much I miss our trips to Shiloh. I miss the tabernacle, the worship, the sacrifices; I miss seeing people, finding out what's happening in their lives. I miss the journey and the feasts, the way everyone came together – they united us aside from the day-to-day squabbles. I miss…" Her eyes welled up, as she tried to suppress the happy memories of their family.

Maya leaned forward and grasped her hand, her own eyes glistening with restraint. "Yes, I miss them too," she sighed, embracing her daughter. "Yahweh will deliver us and we will go again once the roads are safer." She tried to sound hopeful.

Deborah nodded. She wondered if she should warn her mother about what would come. It would surely be better for her to know, but she couldn't bring herself to think about it, let alone talk about it.

She took a breath. "Ima, I need you to know that whatever happens in the future, I will be fine and Yahweh will look after me." She looked into her mother's eyes and read the fear, the old shadow that hid in the darkness, which had slowly receded over the years. She watched her mother's battle of faith and the stoic smile that swept aside her maternal anxiety.

"Of course you will, darling; I know Yahweh's hand is upon you. You will be fine." She squeezed her hand and returned to shelling peas.

Miriam and Adiel's wedding was the happiest week anyone could remember. As dictated by tradition, nobody knew the day or hour that the bridegroom would come. However, the seasons dictated that autumn was the best season for a wedding: the harvest was in, the work was done and food was most plentiful. Adiel's brother, Salmon, took the role of the bridegroom's friend and traditionally announced the coming of the bridegroom to the bride. A goatskin canopy had been erected outside the newly finished mud and daub hut of the bridegroom, where the feast was laid out and the ceremony was conducted by Tobias. As Miriam was escorted to their new home, where Adiel waited, she looked beautiful in pale linen dress, her hair held back with a veil that had kindly been donated by Nissa.

Jared felt that Baal had accepted their sacrifices and that Sisera would not return. Thus, it had been agreed that a feast was well overdue. Deborah kept silent about her prophetic knowledge of the future, knowing it would only cause further schism and strife, and could not alter what would come. The festivities lasted a week, as was tradition, and during that time, it seemed the divisions between the village blurred.

Autumn's warm colours lingered, and there was a sense of holding on to those last days of warmth after the new seed had been sown, and people entered their rest. The betrothal of Hadas and Dan had been agreed upon, with the promise of another celebration and the distraction of planning. Miriam and Hadas spoke excitedly together about marriage and preparations, and Deborah felt herself shrinking back into her introverted cocoon, where the outside world seemed distant and her inner thoughts and dialogue with Yahweh became her reality. In this place, the world was safe and the moral and spiritual divisions in the village affected her less.

People clung to the hope that life had got better, would improve and that Sisera had forgotten the village. But the underlying tension revealed the fragility of their optimism. Whilst many still professed to follow Yahweh, the moral banner that had once guided their behaviour had faded and choices were driven by selfish motivation and carnal desires. As people became more selfish, they became more aggressive as they sought to defend and protect their own family, their own rights. Traditions had been abandoned and those who maintained their faith did so with the desperation of a young doe in a mountain landslide.

Deborah saw the purpose of the commandments: a social and moral code that was Yahweh's gift to protect them. But He had not been concerned for their social and spiritual well being only, for He had given to Moses instruction on hygiene and food preparations, and treatment of the dead that prevented the outbreak and spread of disease. As many forgot Yahweh's laws, or the 'old ways' as they were known, sickness had become more common. In the chaos of surviving, they had failed to pass on God's truths to their children.

Hence, as each person began to do what was right in their own eyes, they destroyed their own world.

"What has she been eating and drinking?" Gershon wore his usual frown as he felt Eliza's head.

"I don't know, she was with Eber yesterday," replied Judah.

"And do we know how he is? Have you spoken to Jonah or Orpah today?"

"I'll go and see them," Judah volunteered, his brow puckered as he looked at his sister whose eyes were sunken and devoid of their usual childish joy. Manasseh had been up with her all night while she feverishly struggled with vomiting and diarrhoea.

Gershon turned to Othniel, Eliza's older brother. "Would you be able to go and fetch Tamar, she may be able to help."

He nodded and left hurriedly.

Orpah arrived a moment later with Eber.

"We went down to the stream," he explained, looking remorsefully towards the floor. "We followed the stream to the pool where Tebah and Isaac fish. Eliza was thirsty and so she drank from the pool. I said not to, it looked dirty, but she did anyway."

Tamar arrived as he was speaking and asked him to repeat what he had said. She rubbed fresh hyssop between her hands as she spoke.

"It sounds like the water was bitter," she explained, her hand resting on the child's forehead.

"Can you help her?" Manasseh's eyes flitted anxiously between Tamar and his daughter.

Tamar looked up, her eyes filled with compassion as she empathised with Manasseh's pain; it was difficult having faith when you had lost people you love.

"I think so, yes. I need to go my home and pick up a few things."

She left the hut, her mind racing as she mentally scanned the ingredients on her shelf. She would need white onion juice, but did not have any, though she had seen them growing in Hillel's garden. She paused, acknowledging the underlying awkwardness that had arisen between people because of their beliefs. When she arrived, Hannah, their daughter, was in the garden with Reuben's son, Asher; they were talking with their backs to her.

"Can I help you, Tamar, is everything well with you?" Asher's intense frown bore shocking resemblance to his father's.

"I wondered if you could spare a couple of white onions." She looked awkwardly at the garden as she unconsciously scanned it and hastily added: "Deborah mentioned that you had found some growing wild and been able to cultivate them. Eliza is poorly. I think that she drank bitter water, and white onion juice should help her fever."

Hannah had her mother's mild, warm disposition. "Of course. I'm sure that will be fine. Do you know what you are looking for?"

Tamar smiled gratefully, pointing to the tufts of white foliage that poked out of the earth.

Taking the precious vegetable, she hurried back to her home to prepare the medicine, before returning to Eliza who was leaning over the bed, retching green bile from her empty stomach.

"What is it?" Manasseh asked when she returned, eyeing the concoction suspiciously.

Tamar smiled sympathetically. "It's juice of bitter gourd and white onion. She hasn't been poorly long. I'm hopeful that this will help."

Tamar's convictions proved correct, and Eliza recovered after a few days. However, her sickness was typical of a growing number of incidents that had been avoided in the past because of their strict adherence to the Law.

Winter had arrived and after several days of rain, Deborah had been desperate to escape the confines of the village. A fresh breeze blew across the hills while the sun hung low, playfully dipping in and out of feathery white clouds. Deborah ran until she reached the mountain. The atmosphere of the village had become like a stagnant pool of underlying stress that was held together by common suffering and fear.

Both her close friends were married now. It wasn't that she was jealous, as such - she had no feelings for any of the men in her village - but at twenty-four years old, that she had not married was a reflection of the isolation and lack of direction that marked her life.

The only thing that was certain, that marked her life with meaning, was Yahweh and the promises He had given her. Thus, all of her frustration, remorse and hope were driven to one goal and purpose: praying for her people. Everything she had heard from Judah about the atrocities occurring in northern Israel had filled her with the deepest sadness. Lapidoth and his family came to her mind, for they had come from Naphtali; she prayed they had not been harmed. Her thoughts lingered on the boy with the dark curls and lighthearted nature who had saved her, and she wondered if she would ever see him again.

She had received neither visions, nor revelations for almost a year and was beginning to question her previous experiences and her relationship with Yahweh: *had she displeased Him? Had they been the imaginings of her youth, as Shelimoth had suggested?* As she sat with her back against the cold stone, winter wrapped its cool fingers around her, causing her to shiver. Gideon, her gecko, had gone into his winter seclusion and she felt lonely. She struggled to pray, her mind wondering into the past, trying to work out the future and what Yahweh would do.

Finally, cold, discouraged and confused, she began her descent down the mountain. Smoke curled into the cool winter air, and the promise of warmth and her family hastened her descent.

She had no warning, no sense that anything was amiss. As usual she avoided the village centre, skirting around the houses before entering her family's hut. When she didn't find her mother and Isaac at home, it did not dawn on her to think further. She went to Raisa's. The first scream alerted her, followed by the familiar feeling of terror that flooded her senses. She fought the urge to panic, taking in deep breaths to control her breathing.

He was here. It was time. That revelation she had had, years ago; a faded picture on the wall of her mind, now defined itself, first in colour, then in form.

She reeled, slamming her back into the wall of Raisa and Tobias' home and feeling the world spin around her. She willed her inner world to encompass her - for panic to recede to the outer boundaries of her consciousness. Closing her eyes, her prayers were desperate, gasped, rather than spoken: "Yahweh! No! Please! No! Please! Let it not happen! Help! Please help!" She felt herself drowning as the world threatened to close in around her.

The second scream chilled her blood and quickened her senses as her fear grew outside of herself to cover those she loved. She had to end it.

If she stepped out, she might end it. Perhaps her village would be spared.

"Courage! Please, Yahweh, courage." Fear still pounded on the walls of her conviction, but now she felt a quiet strength war with it, compounded by the knowledge that if she failed, every life in her village would end.

She forced her fear and will into submission, leaving the frightened girl clinging to the walls of Raisa's home and stepped out.

There he was: the man who had killed her father and brother, who had been responsible for the rape and murder of her friends. Beside her stood the brute Talmai. The last time she had seen him, he had violated and murdered her friends. Her fear was once again championed by a greater emotion: righteous anger. She felt it seep into her blood, swathe her mind and silence reason as she stepped forward. She had seen this moment, had played it over in her mind until, at times, it seemed more real than her daily life.

Tobias stood in the village centre, his back against the well, as her father had stood twelve years ago. His eyes were empty, tear-filled. His face, which usually carried a peaceful wisdom, now looked like a man burning. She followed the direction of his gaze, suddenly feeling sick with instinctive horror. And then she saw Jonah lying face down, three arrows in his back, his legs twitched and he groaned as Orpah and Tebah held him. Deborah watched as the archer restrung his bow, preparing to fire, this time his arrow pointed at Orpah. The arrow flew through the air, piercing her lung. Tebah screamed, throwing himself onto his mother's body as it collapsed over her husband's, choking on the blood that spurted from her mouth. Gabriella, at fifteen, and Eber at nine, were held back by Gershon and Manasseh, their bereft screams muffled as the men buried their faces into the folds of their tunics.

Raisa had fallen to her knees, weeping as her son and daughter-in-law lay dead. Deborah turned to Tobias, who looked at her with dead, empty eyes. Seeing this man, who was a father to their village, reduced to such brokenness, yet drawing on a hidden well of courage and faith made her heart ache with compassion and her resolve harden. She noted that her mother stood next to Aaliya and Raisa, who was on her knees weeping, and frantically scanned the village for Isaac. Finally, she spotted him. He was standing next to Asher, Reuben and Shayna's son.

"You have taken me for a fool. I am aware that your harvest has been plentiful this year." His lips curved, though his eyes remained dark.

"Yours is not the only Israelite village we have visited." He scanned the faces like a predator marking its kill. "During our postponed return, others have also thought they could defy me." His voice remained level, without inflection, nor emotion, suggesting a boring dialogue before the sport began. His delay had been intentional, Deborah realised, and part of his game was to instill false hope, whilst testing their obedience. But it wasn't their compliance he was looking for: it was their destruction, not only of their lives, but their spirits.

"And now, you will see how Canaan responds to rebellion. What was your remit when you entered our land: to kill every man, woman and child?" He paused, turning to the soldiers, who had unsheathed their swords and held burning torches in their hands.

Your children will be taken; the youngest will be offered as a sacrifice to Baal for your sin against him, and the oldest will be sold as slaves, to be broken and used in any manner their owners see fit. Your women will be raped and murdered while you watch, and then you, too, will die. When we have finished, your village will be burnt to the ground – I will erase the name of your people and your God, forever."

Terror stormed the village and children clung to their parents, who fell to their knees weeping. The archer had restrung his bow, this time pointed toward Tebah.

"No, no, please help, Yahweh!" Deborah knew she must act now. Suddenly, desperation triumphed over her fear. If she failed she would die anyway. She heard her voice, low and steady, as though it belonged to a source outside of her. Its strength surprised her.

"Stop, Sisera of Harosheth Haggoyim." The archer pulled back the arrow and held it taut. "Stop, in the name of Yahweh, you who brandish fear, and kill innocents. You have spoken of the doom of my village, and I will tell you yours. Yahweh knows you; He has weighed you and numbered your days. He knows the nightmares that grip you, when darkness envelopes you, and the walls around your fortified cities are torn down as they were for your father. Hear now Yahweh's word to you: If you continue, He will destroy you and your legacy. Your shame will be worse than your father's, and your death will be remembered as one of weakness." She saw hesitation flicker in Sisera's eyes. She had touched a nerve. He stepped toward her. She forced herself not to move. He ran his axe across her collarbone: *the axe that killed my brother.* Fear, sharp and brittle, poked holes in her chest, and now she was immobilised by fear, unable to breathe. A tiny voice, like a thread of reason, coiled its way through the darkness and she clutched it: '*Yahweh*'. The thread expanded into a cord and grew into a rope, until she felt herself being lifted to safety as Yahweh's promise wrapped itself around her mind, enveloping her: *she would be a mother to Israel.*

Sisera noted the confidence in the girl's eyes; it was unnatural, and he had never seen anything like it. It unnerved him, and he wanted to break it. Yet knew he could not retreat, he could not be seen to listen to a Hebrew girl. He had never spoken of his nightmares to anyone. They were a sign of the weakness he despised. He semi-disregarded her prophecy with the naive arrogance of one used to winning. But his dreams betrayed him, and he knew it was the nature of fear to fulfill it's own silent prophecy.

Hence, he was faced with a dilemma: he could not leave the village unpunished, but neither could he destroy it. In the midst of this, he knew that the power this young woman had could not be left here, unrestrained. He had always believed the Hebrews did not accept women as spiritual leaders, unlike his own people. Yet her spiritual authority and insight clearly identified her as a spiritual leader – the Canaanites would have called her a priestess. Why else would she have confronted him?

He leaned closer to her; she could smell his sweat and the oil on his body. *Courage Deborah.*

"Your name?"

The words Yahweh had spoken seemed a lifetime ago, yet they appeared clearly in her mind now. She looked at him, and saw the fire that burned in her eyes was reflected in his.

"My name is Deborah, meaning honey-bee. I am not the wild goat who will trample the image of your name into the ground; the one who haunts your sleep. But we serve the same God." Sisera's face paled. He staggered backward, as though he had been hit, before retreating behind his stiff military composure. And then he knew what he had to do. Whilst his initial plan satisfied his need for vengeance and instant gratification, he could argue that it was not profitable in terms of produce yield, nor would it prolong their pain. Crippling them was a far better long-term goal, and one that kept his own demons at bay.

He beckoned Talmai to organise the loading of the barrels and animals onto the carts. While the terror in the village continued to build, they waited for Sisera to act on his word.

Several of the women had fainted, and children were clinging onto their fathers as they finally loaded the last barrel. Nobody forgot Sisera's last visit.

Deborah stood next to Tobias now. She gently laid her hand on his arm. He turned to her, and she saw the hopelessness in his eyes.

"Yahweh has shown me what will happen now…But the village will survive; it was the only way." Her eyes filled with tears. "Look after them, Tobias, instruct Isaac in the ways of Yahweh, and tell them I love them and…I will be fine." Tobias looked at her. Confusion and resignation filled his eyes and tears ran silently down his face. He clutched her in his arms. "Yahweh be with you, Deborah."

Sisera returned, Talmai next to him. He whispered something to the giant man, and Deborah felt a kick to the back of the knees. She fell to the ground and Talmai was upon her. Images of his previous violence flashed in her mind and panic rose within her. The warrior grinned; a twisted, contorted expression that was demonic, and his gaze darted to Sisera for consent.

Sisera tilted his head, as though deciding, and then shook his head almost imperceptibly. "Not yet."

Talmai scowled.

"Bind her and load her in with the animals."

There had been no time to say goodbye. As grief and fear tightened their grip on her, she wondered if she would ever see her mother and brother again.

Sisera stood one foot on the chariot. "Your prophetess belongs to Canaan now!" She turned to see Jared and Shelimoth standing with their mouths hanging open.

In years to come, the memory of their faces would make her laugh, as her last memory of her mother would make her weep. She closed her eyes to shut out the picture of her mother as she crumpled to the ground. Gershon held Isaac back as he tried to run after her, his screams finally fading as she watched the village, and all she held dear, disappear behind her.

15

... For there was peace between Jabin the King of Hazor and the House of Heber the Kenite. Judges 4:17

1255 BC – Jael

The final stretch of their journey took them through the valley of Jezreel. Its vast, ragged terrain reminded Jael of home. Zimran left them at Shiloh to travel to Joppa. They pitched their tents outside of Jezreel for the night before continuing on the last leg of their journey. As they travelled through Issachar and Naphtali, Jael was horrified to see the level of oppression that had been afflicted upon the Israelites under the hand of Jabin and Sisera. Whole villages had been burnt to the ground, people slain as they ran from their homes, their possessions strewn on the ground and bodies left rotting, feasted on by carrion and flies.

Even Heber looked shocked by the level of atrocities that had been committed. Hazor, Canaan's capital city, had been burnt to the ground by Joshua, but rebuilt by his namesake and great-grandson, Jabin. The palace on the acropolis of the *tel* was majestic by all comparison; Jael had never seen anything like it. One of the soldiers proudly told them how the decorative zigzag-shaped wall, decorated with basalt orthostats, were of Syrian design. They crossed a paved outer courtyard with a cultic platform in its centre, bearing a golden statue of El sitting on his throne, his raised arms indicative of his supremacy and authority over the other Canaanite deities. The priests bowed down before him, laying food and jewels before him as they chanted.

Two massive columns held up the impressive porch. They walked up the steps, passing the guardrooms that flanked the entrance. From there, they entered the palace core and the throne room. Its floor was made of finest Lebanon cedar, and its walls adorned with basalt orthostats depicting Canaan's triumphs. Jael shuddered as she looked at the grotesque images of Canaan's massacres. This was the home of the man who ordered the destruction of innocent families. Her mind involuntarily replayed the atrocities she had seen on her journey here: babies lying in their mothers' arms as both were shot down and left with no one to bury them. With it came the sickening revelation that her husband would create this man's weapons of destruction.

Jabin sat while his cupbearer replenished his drink. His ornate golden throne was decorated with depictions of Baal. He had a natural beauty that was almost effeminate; high cheekbones, full lips, deep set eyes and long, dark, wavy hair that flowed over an embroidered purple cloak. On his head, he wore a gold crown, encrusted with rubies, diamonds and emeralds. His beard was shaved in the Egyptian style. He sat with poise and a masculine vanity that was edged with hidden cruelty, and he was flanked by a beautiful woman in a flowing, low-cut, purple robe. Her jewellery and headdress defined her as a priestess.

"This is Heber, your Majesty." Sisera bowed low to the floor, but his facial expression was not one of subservience.

"Heber." He purred the name in such a way that he sounded bored.

"Your Majesty, it's an honour." He bowed to the ground, and Jael and the others followed suit.

"Please allow us to present our gifts to you." Heber beckoned one of the servants, who came forward with carved wooden boxes.

"Frankincense and fine linen from Egypt, and pearls from the Great Sea," he proudly stated..

Jabin's lips curved almost imperceptibly, as though to express that his favour would not be so easily won. "Your gifts are gratefully received." He beckoned one of his guards to take them away, and taking a piece of pomegranate from a servant bearing a gold platter, he popped it into his mouth. His eyes moved slowly over the group as though he were assessing them. Finally, he took a linen serviette that was offered to him and dabbed his mouth with small, deliberate actions.

"You will no doubt have heard; we have taken control of Gerasha."

"Yes, your Majesty." Heber kept his eyes lowered.

"Hazor imports tin from Babylon and Syria, with whom we have strong commercial ties. And your mines in Timna supply copper."

"But iron is stronger, harder and lighter." Heber's eyes glittered with excitement.

It wasn't just the money, Jael realised; he was excited by the project. Yet he was too deceived. Too in awe and in need of Jabin and Sisera's approval of him to realise that he was being used. She decided that she hated Jabin even more than she disliked Heber.

"Exactly." Jabin threw his arm carelessly over the armchair of the throne, revealing his jewel-bedecked fingers. His expression was one of contemptuous pride that made Jael want to slap him. But Heber looked only in awe. "Of course, iron chariots are not something new to Canaan. My ancestors have used them since before the Israelites came; our allegiance to Egypt is not without benefit. Whilst the old chariots were fine for the plains and prevented Israel from defeating us in Jezreel, we were still made to pay tribute." His eyes narrowed and Heber was conscious that he was being weighed. "But now is Canaan's time. We grow stronger and our territory expands; we need better-designed, lighter chariots that will enable us to access the hill country. I desire an army of chariots through which I can extend and secure Canaan's territory. I am relying on your expertise to exact this task. I believe the payment was agreed with Sisera and found favourable?"

"Yes, certainly. It would be an honour, your Majesty."

"You will answer to Sisera, then. He oversees the production of the weaponry and chariots at Harosheth. Will you be taking him with you?" He raised a lazy eyebrow as he glanced at Sisera.

"No. Whilst we will still continue to import iron from the sea people with whom we have been historically allied, we have our own source now. I will continue to use the smithy at Harosheth for weaponry only. The scope and magnitude of our vision requires larger and more organised facilities, such as are available at Tel Hammeh. Its location is also favourable, being between Hazor and Gerasha."

"Good. Then we are agreed, the chariots will be ready before next spring."

Heber swallowed. "Your Majesty, that is less than six months away. It simply cannot be done."

Jabin, who had been about to pop a grape into his mouth, paused, his expression hard, as though this was the first time anyone had ever questioned his demands. His tone was calm but resolute. "Spring is the season for battle; I will not wait another year. My guards will see you have as many slaves as you require."

He popped the grape into his mouth, as though to signify his closure on the subject. He chewed slowly, his gaze passing over the small group. "I don't cope well with disappointment. So don't let me down." He gave a barely perceptible nod to his cupbearer, who gracefully refilled his cup. His lips curved. "Until spring, then." He raised the cup to his lips and waved his hand in a gesture that told them it was time to leave.

When they left the palace, Heber was pale and uncharacteristically speechless as Sisera spoke to him.

He's just realised he's in way over his head, Jael acknowledged. *And he's alone, and he's scared.* Despite all her anger and misgivings, she felt pity for him. For the first time, she found herself wondering *how had he ended up here?* It was a question that coiled around her mind, demanding answers.

Heber took the caravan to Kedesh. His expression was taut, as though he might crack if pressed. They pitched their tents by the mighty oak in Zaanannim, overlooking Lake Huleh. The oak was somewhat of a landmark to travellers due to its enormous size and the history that went with its considerable age.

He sat quietly, seemingly disengaged with the caravan; and for a while, nobody did anything for fear of Heber's wrath. Finally, Jael began to organise the pitching of tents, wondering how long they would remain here. As she drove the tent pegs into the earth, it gave her a small sense of home and the history of her people. She had made a temporary resting place.

Jael was nervous. Everything in her wanted to avoid Heber and yet he was like a stupid animal that you both wanted to slaughter and protect, if only for your own perverse sense of achievement. She recalled how unnerved he had been in Shiloh when she had shown him kindness, albeit in pretense.

She would try. Once.

She walked to his tent.

"Heber?"

There was no answer.

"Heber?"

She hesitated, the urge to walk away growing within her.

She pulled aside the flap and stepped inside. It was dark. She noticed Heber's form lying on the straw pallet without a covering. She stepped closer. He was sleeping. She looked at his face, it was contorted. He looked as though he was in inner torment. Part of her hoped he was. But a very small part of her wanted to reach out to him, and she was afraid of that voice - afraid that in doing so, it would cause her more pain.

She picked up a blanket and laid it over him. *Yahweh help me to do Your will,* she grudgingly prayed, torn between a genuine need to please Yahweh, a gnawing sense of pity, and her distrust of Heber.

Jael woke early to the sound of birds. The air smelt earthy and fresh. Meira was awake and gurgling softly. Jael lay there for a moment, marveling at her baby's first smiles as she kicked her little legs freely.

She once again felt the overwhelming flood of love for her as she kissed her soft, downy cheeks.

Finally, she decided to walk the short distance to the lake. Leaving Adva to sleep, she put Meira in a sling on her back, and wandered through the canopy of oaks and myrtle trees, their leaves taking on the first colours of autumn. The air smelt moist and earthy, so different to Midian or Arad, while the chorus of birds and crickets played their symphony around her. Even the sun seemed a gentler shade as it cast rosy shadows on the forest floor. When the trees finally thinned out, she discovered that she was standing before a sea of long, thick grass and poppies dancing in the morning breeze. A herd of deer, grazing peacefully, looked up at her lazily as she passed. Beyond lay Lake Hulah, framed by tall reeds. It lay like a silver platter of tranquility stirred only by the kingfishers, herons and cranes. She stood, marveling at the scene before her, and appreciating a rare moment of time alone. Raising her head at the noisy sound of quacking, she watched as a gaggle of geese fell out of their perfect formation and alighted on the water. Having grown up in the desert, where food had often been scarce, this place seemed like paradise. By the time she returned to the oak, she had already decided that she would grow vegetables and learn to hunt.

Heber was sat outside his tent, his head in his hands. He looked up at Jael suspiciously.

"Where have you been?" he growled.

"To the lake." She forced a smile and sat on the bench next to him.

"What do you want?" he barked, shooting her a sideways glance.

She avoided the urge to answer that she wanted to know what made him such an unpleasant man, who made such stupid decisions.

"You seem worried."

"So? What do you care?"

She shrugged. She could feel her ire rising. She bit her lip. It was so, so hard to be nice to someone *so* dislikeable.

"You are worried about how you will complete the chariots in time?" she offered.

"Jael, if I want to talk to you, which I don't, I will tell you. Now get me some food and then get out of my sight," he gestured with his hand, his lip curled in disdain.

She stood up, sent a servant for some food, and spent the rest of the day thinking of all the bad things she wished would happen to him.

When she saw Heber later, he was talking to one of the Canaanite guards. He needed to travel to Tel Hammeh tomorrow to begin the oversight of the iron smelting and smithing. She overheard the guard tell him that the first caravan would be arriving from Gerasha the next day.

"Jael!"

She turned and walked reluctantly toward him, the familiar anxiety- induced adrenalin pounding through her.

The shadows under his eyes were dark, and his face carved into tight lines of anxiety and intolerance.

"I'm going to Hazor tomorrow. Ensure the slaves have my things packed." He rubbed the back of his neck. It was as though he was being held together by fine pieces of thread, and was trying frantically to maintain control, lest he completely unravel.

"How long will you be gone?"

"I don't know, do I!" he growled. "What do you care? Just pack for a week!" His voice sounded empty, and she knew that, for all their sakes, he needed to believe that he could accomplish what he had been asked to do.

She leant forward and squeezed his arm in an attempt to show affection that she did not feel. It felt alien, like stroking the rear of a horse you knew would only kick you in the head.

"You can do this Heber. You're great…at what you do."

He looked at her, his eyes narrowed with suspicion; she had the sense of a viper coiled, ready to attack. He searched her eyes, and when she looked steadily and reassuringly back, he looked uncharacteristically confused.

"Right," he stammered.

There was a long pause, in which he seemed to be deliberating.

Patience and kindness were not qualities that Jael was most familiar with. She found herself wondering what Adva would say now.

"What is it?" she tried again, whilst inwardly retreating.

He sank back onto the seat, and she bridged the gap by sitting next to him, silencing the inner voice that sought her own preservation.

He stood up, and began pacing like a caged animal.

"It's too late!" he snarled angrily. Jael could feel herself reacting to his tone. She wanted to find a reason to walk away. She wanted to tell him what an idiot he was, but she forced herself to remain calm.

"I didn't mean it to turn out like this; I don't know how this can be done…Now I have no choice, they've left me no choice!"

"You have no choice?" Jael repeated, completely confused.

He looked at her, and vulnerability flitted in his eyes, almost imperceptibly, before the viper regained control.

"That's it. I have no choice," he spoke mutely, before walking away.

Jael sighed inwardly with relief when Heber left the next day. His absences marked her freedom, when she and Adva would talk openly about life and the children could run freely outside, without fear of Heber's control and cruelty. During the journey she had become acquainted with some of the other slaves; in particular, Mary, an older Hebrew woman, who had worked for Heber's family since she was a young girl. Jael was surprised and intrigued by this. She had never heard Heber talk about his family, and she had never asked, nor cared. (It wasn't that she now cared, so much as a morbid fascination into what had made him into the man he was.) She sat down, placing Meira on her lap. One of the slaves, Hati, a Philistine, had carved a little wooden horse for her which she passed from hand-to-hand now, smiling and babbling away as she performed her new trick. Meira had stolen everyone's hearts, excepting Heber's. He barely looked at her.

Mary smiled. Her hands had become twisted with age and she winced each time she stood up. She had a certain wisdom that Jael admired, and a gentle nature. But it seemed to Jael to be born more out of weakness and self-preservation than personal strength or compassion.

"So what were they like, his parents, his family?" Jael enquired.

"They live near Beersheba. They're still alive. Well, his father and brothers are." Her eyes held Jael's for a second, as though to convey some hidden question.

Jael held her gaze for a moment as she pondered the question that had risen in her own mind: *do I want to know? Do I want to understand him? In understanding him, will I have compassion for him? What if I find a person I hate more, but worse still, what if I find a person I want to help?* Her hatred of Heber had kept her strong. She battled for a moment, until her curiosity got the better of her.

"Tell me about them," she demanded grudgingly.

"Heber's mother, Elke, was a wonderful woman. She was a warm, generous, mother; we all loved her. His father was rarely around; he was a merchant, selling tools in Arad – they did well, too, a wealthy family. Heber's four brothers were older than he, the youngest by five years. When Heber's mother discovered she was pregnant with him, it was a surprise for everyone. She had thought that she wouldn't have another child. Heber was the apple of everyone's eye. He was a beautiful child and had a sweet nature, though used to getting his own way." Mary chuckled as she replayed scenes from her memory, and she drifted away momentarily. Jael found herself wondering if old age was affecting Mary's memory. Could she possibly be referring to the same Heber?

"And so?" she asked after a few moments, her impatience getting the better of her.

"When he was five years old, Heber made a friend with one of the servant's children. His name was Malachi, and he was two years older than Heber. Malachi was an energetic child with a wild imagination and propensity for adventure and mischief alike. The two were inseparable, but nobody minded, as long as Heber was happy, the boy was favoured.

One day, Malachi hatched a plan: they would go to the river, make a raft and he would teach Heber how to fish."

Mary's face had become pale. "When Elke went to look for the boys, Malachi's older brother told them where they were. She naturally panicked. Heber was too young and the autumn rains had left the river swollen. Of course, she knew better than to go off alone, so she took my husband and another servant with her. When they got to the river, the boys were nowhere to be seen. It was agreed that they would split up to search. Heber's mother found them. The raft had been poorly made and fallen apart. Heber was holding onto a branch. He was terrified, of course and the river was carrying him down stream. As mothers do, without a thought for her own safety, she rushed into the river. We don't know what happened then. It's thought she caught her foot on weed and was dragged under by the weight of her dress and the current." The old woman's eyes glazed over. "Heber watched helplessly as his mother died.

"Everything ended that day. Malachi was beaten and then sold. He had run for help, but nobody had believed him. Heber never saw him again. The adoration that his brothers and father had had for him turned to resentment, and as Heber withdrew, they came to hate him. Heber never spoke of that day. He mourned alone. He tried to win their favour. It was pitiful to watch. But nothing he did would change what had happened. When he reached manhood, his father sent him to oversee the work in the mines, and I was chosen to join his household there. He did well, but soon grew tired of working to send money home to the father who never acknowledged his effort. He slowly established his own contacts, and broke off contact with his family. He's pushed people away ever since. He anticipates rejection. I think he hoped…" She sighed and left the sentence unfinished.

"So, you see how I am able to love him despite the man he has become?" She looked sadly at Jael through her care-worn eyes.

Jael sat in silence for a moment, trying to process her feelings about what she had heard. She did feel some pity for Heber. But she knew, too, that people have choices, and their reactions were partly down to attitude. She could have been selfish, and she could be resentful and unkind, now, because of the way Heber treated her, yet she chose not to.

Finally, she looked up. "It helps to understand. But it can't justify his cruelty. People still have decisions to make."

Mary nodded. "That's true, Jael. We all do." She had a look in her eyes as she spoke that hinted to another story. Jael was tired and confused. Hating Heber had been easier, less complicated, than feeling sorry for him.

She deliberately allowed her thoughts to drift to Zimran, and wondered where he was now and whether he too was thinking of her. She tried to picture his face, his smile and his eyes.

Heber returned a week later; his face was grey and slack from stress.

"Jael!!"

She gritted her teeth - he was *so* rude. "Yes!"

"We need more tents! Jabin has given me slaves to make the chariots. The furnaces are in Hammath. The rains will come soon and I need tents for myself and the slaves."

"And what do you want me to do?"

"Do I really need to spell it out to you? I want you to organise tents to be made. You worked with your father and mother, didn't you?"

Jael paused while she processed what he was asking her to do, and how she felt about it. Strangely, she noted that she was excited by the return to her old life. And yet, this time she would be in charge of the process. She knew better than to let Heber know how she felt. She needed to use it to her benefit.

"Well?" He was obviously trying to curb his ire, but the impatience in his voice betrayed him.

She smiled sweetly. "If this will help you, Heber, then I will do this for you. Of course, I'll need looms. And goats, we'd need goat hair, a lot of it." She spoke as her mind formed a list.

"Right...good." He looked disconcerted as he left the tent. She sighed inwardly, hoping he would leave now, but he returned shortly with three soldiers, carrying three looms.

"The goats will be brought here in the next few days."

Jael stood, her mind reeling as she contemplated what she was being asked to do, and the speed with which she would need to work. She would need to train every available slave and servant they had. The challenge excited her. She smiled inwardly; they would have goat's milk too. And when she had finished, she would make tents to sell at market so that she could have a little money for herself.

"Jael - come to my tent later!!" he barked.

Turning, she did not answer, but walked away; he had made it clear that her acquiescence was not open to discussion.

16

The commander of his (Jabin's) army was Sisera, who dwelt in Harosheth Haggoyim.
Judges 4:2

1250 BC - Deborah

The cart bumped violently over the rutted limestone road as Deborah was jostled between the frightened animals. She finally found a corner next to one of the sheep, that had by some miracle fallen asleep, and wedged herself next to it.

The animals remained her last familiar contact with her village, and despite the fact that they were covered in fleas and bruised her with their kicking, she found their presence a sole and desperate comfort.

As darkness crept closer toward them, Deborah drifted into a fitful sleep. She dreamt of her family, her father and Enoch, all sitting around a table, laughing. It seemed so real that when she awoke in the darkness, it took her a few moments to realise where she was. Fear-filled adrenalin jolted through her and the cool darkness smothered her. The cart lurched from side to side, and she felt the damp stench of animal excrement pool beneath her. She unsuccessfully fought the urge to vomit.

Deborah gave in to the silent tears of loss, fear and self-pity that welled within her and clutched her arms around her knees.

I need you Yahweh. I really need You now. I feel so alone.

She felt His gentle assurance pierce the darkness.

The grey light of winter poked its gloomy shadows through the slats of the cart, heralding the beginning of a new day. She pulled herself up, and peered out. The dark shadows of Ephraim's mountains lay far behind them, and the road was flatter now that they were travelling north. She had never travelled past Shiloh before. She felt sick with fear and loss as she forced herself, past despair and sorrow, to cling to Yahweh's promises.

She could hear running water, not like the stream, not even as it grew in winter; it had to be a river. A cold wind seemed to travel with it, sending icy blades through the wooden floor, numbing her to her core.

She tried to remember her father's stories of Israel's victories. She knew that Manasseh lay north of Ephraim. They must be in the valley of Jezreel. She recalled her father telling her that the Israelites had never been able to drive the Canaanites from Jezreel because of their iron chariots. At their strongest, they put the cities to tribute. She pictured her father, drawing in the dust as he unfolded the story and his words: "Yet Joshua had spoken to the house of Joseph – to Ephraim and Manasseh – saying: "You are a great people and have great power. You shall not have one lot only. But the mountain country shall be yours and its farthest extent shall be yours; for you shall drive out the Canaanites, though they have iron chariots and are strong."

"Why did they not defeat them, if God had told them they could?" Isaac had asked, with his simple, childlike faith.

Amos had smiled with satisfaction, as though that was exactly the question he wanted Isaac to ask. "Because they looked to the natural; to what they could see, instead of looking to Almighty Yahweh. As soon as we take our eyes off Him and His promises, we start to doubt. Fear and apathy defeat us long before our enemies do."

Deborah let her father's wisdom sink into the recesses of her mind, nourishing and strengthening her waning resolve. So this was Jezreel, which meant that the river that she could hear was the river Kishon.

Daylight made a half-hearted attempt to announce its presence, but dark, grey clouds pushed back any hope of the sun's warmth. Finally, large drops of rain thudded onto the goatskin roof of the cart. It quickly intensified to a moody deluge; an outrage that formed a background to the cadence of the cart's wheels as they propelled thick, wet mud through the wooden slats. The sound of the river rushed beside her; they were headed east, toward the Great Sea, toward Harosheth-Haggoyim, Sisera's province.

Shivering uncontrollably, Deborah pushed herself into the midst of the animals, craving their warmth and oily coats. She hadn't eaten or drunk anything for almost a day, and her mouth felt dry. She wondered how her mother and Isaac were, but that thought, too, pained her: images of her mother's grey, hopeless face after the death of her father and brother flashed uninvited into her mind, twisting her stomach with worry. Tears rolled down her face, and she once again gave in to the sobs that racked her body until she dosed into a fitful sleep.

She was awoken by hands gripping her and dragging her from the wagon. Lightheaded and exhausted, she staggered and fell onto the stone path. A huge courtyard lay before them; it was part of a much larger area protected by a huge stone wall. Behind them lay a large house that was ornately designed, making it just short of a palace. Grey stone steps ascended to a large entrance supported by four imposing columns, each guarded by a Canaanite deity.

Sisera spoke to one of the guards; his cloak and bronze armbands defined him as a man of some standing.

"She's a prophetess from one of the villages."

"Should we kill her?"

"No. I have personal reasons for keeping her alive, at the moment."

The man's lips curved as he looked over Sisera's shoulder and ran his eyes over the length of Deborah's body. He turned away, the confusion and disappointment clear in his expression.

"Surely you could have found one better than her from our own, my lord?" But perhaps under all the mud, she might make a worthwhile prize.

Sisera's jaw worked as he sought to curb his impatience.

"Have her taken to the fortress."

The man nodded, beckoning to the two soldiers. "Sisera's got plans for her. See you don't touch her, and have the servants get her new clothes and feed her." His face twisted in repugnance.

Deborah willed herself to remain standing. The fear of what awaited her hung like jackals in the corner of her mind, but her faith was a torch that she brandished, though her arm grew weak and her spirit tired. She longed to give up. A weak voice coiled out from beneath the debris of her futility: *Help! Please help, Yahweh!*

The Canaanite soldier took one look at her, and took her arm, not unkindly, as he led her toward the fortress. He gave brief commands to one of the women servants, who looked at her, and then each other with the same disgust. Grabbing her arm, they climbed several floors until Deborah felt she could not go any further. Finally, a door was opened and she was ushered inside. She heard the door shut behind her, and the sound of a bolt sliding into place.

The room she was in had whitewashed walls. An icy sea wind blew through the window opening, and underneath stood a small, crudely built wooden table upon which sat a clay jug and washbowl. Teeth chattering, she dragged the table under the window and climbed onto it, hoping to find some possibility of escape. Her heart sank with the disappointment that hope had not birthed, for her prison was situated high above a stone courtyard, and there was no way down. And beyond that, the fortress was set upon a double mound, making it virtually impenetrable and almost as difficult to leave undetected. Tall stone walls flanked each of the two risen hills, while passageways ran within the width of the mighty walls and stone watch towers. Below the walls stretched a road which ran from Megiddo, alongside the river Kishon, to the Great Sea. In summer, the river would be little more than a stream. But now it was swollen, and snaked its way through the ancient oak forest like an angry leviathan, twisting and writhing until it vomited its froth and waste into the Great Sea, while the statue of Asherah, walker of the sea, Mother Goddess and wife of El, stood watching at the opening of the river mouth.

Deborah curled up on the mat, wrapping the blanket around her and drawing her knees up to her. When the servant returned, she darted a fearful look as a plate of honey cakes and dried figs were left on the table. A skin of water was placed next to it and a new linen, patterned tunic with purple sash in the Canaanite style. As soon as the door was shut behind her, she hurried to the skin, gulping down water until her stomach hurt. She paused, knowing she had drunk too quickly and prayed she wouldn't bring it back up.

Stuffing a honey cake into her mouth, she stripped off her wet, muddy clothes, and scrubbed herself clean, her eyes flitting nervously to the locked door, before hurriedly throwing on the new clothes. She took the cakes, figs and water to the bed and wrapping the cover around her, she sat in the corner, waiting.

Yahweh, I need to know that You are here.

A sense of calm invaded the room. It carried a thick, tangible peace and an aroma, sweet, like incense.

Thank you Yahweh. I am afraid of what will come now. Help me.
In the midst of her desperation He spoke: *You will be a mother to Israel. What Sisera intends for bad, I will use for good. Do not be afraid. Only trust Me in My goodness.*

She leaned her head against the wall and a smile parted her lips as she breathed in the presence of Yahweh. She felt Him saturate and warm her soul, infusing her with strength and courage. She felt so rested and at peace that she did not hear the door open. And that is how Sisera found her.

It unnerved him, because he knew men and women. He anticipated that letting them wait increased their fear, for he knew the pictures that flooded their minds as they anticipated what he would do. He expected to see the broken girl he had left in the courtyard, who would submit to him readily. Instead he found her smiling, and surrounded by a sense of power that made his flesh crawl. His nightmares flashed into his mind, and he realised he was succumbing to his own favourite torture: fear. It was an invisible hand that pushed on his larynx, rendering him speechless. The girl was watching him, still in her tranquil state.

He turned and left the room.

Deborah felt confused. Sisera had just come into the room, and walked out. What had he come for? And why had he left?

She closed her eyes and slept. The glare of the winter sun, prodded her awake. She was shivering and her head ached. She pulled the blanket around her, holding it with one arm, and clambered up on the table to look out of the window again. This time she recognised Mount Carmel, lofty and majestic; its peak was crowned in luminous snow, as though to signal its pre-eminence and separation from Canaan.

She recalled Lapidoth's words to her that 'anything that makes me realise how small I am and how great Yahweh is, is always helpful.' She had often found herself drifting back to the memory of that happy evening.

She wondered how he was - was he still alive? Had he turned to Baal, too?

Deborah shivered; the winter breeze that blew through the window opening seemed to have penetrated to the core of her being. In the corner of the window she noticed a silky cocoon. Its transition fascinated and inspired her understanding of Yahweh, and her journey with Him. Words formed in her mind as she felt His hand upon her. Thus she spoke in a hushed whisper:

I'm pushing back the shadows
From the light within
Cocooned – this embryo – my life in Him.

And it seems still and quiet
Emptily so.
A place without utterance;
Only darkness resounds.

And yet I hear the water
It's calling my name
Caressing these bonds: my fear and pain.

I fight the urge to struggle
It hurts less not to move
There love Himself is carrying me
His tenderness is melting me.

Words, still unformed
Shape, undefined.

Surrender!

In Him, I sink
In His arms my healing comes
Wrapped deeply within Your heart
Intertwined.
Inseparable
We are one
Life is birthed
Heaven's mysteries unearthed.

Smiling now, my face You hold.
"Fly butterfly," He whispers,
"You have my wings now."
"Be." He breathes.
"I trust," I say.
"In nothing but Thee."

She turned, the door was open and a soldier stood watching her. Framed in the light of the sun, she looked otherworldly, he thought. He looked uncomfortable; she noted he was the same guard who had taken her into the fortress. He spoke Hebrew with an Egyptian accent.

"You need to follow me." His tone was almost a request.

"Where are you taking me?" she ventured as they left the room.

The guard ignored her and kept walking.

Her heart pounded within her as she ran to keep up with his long strides, wondering what her fate would be. When they reached the courtyard, the guard helped her onto the cart. She sat on one of the benches while he sat opposite. He nodded for the driver to proceed.

17

In the days of Shamgar, son of Anath, in the days of Jael, the highways were deserted. And the travellers walked along the byways.

Judges 5:6

1253 BC – Shamgar and Jael

Shamgar noticed a woman; she shifted her weight from one foot to another as she fiddled with a piece of cord between her fingers. She reminded Shamgar of a wild mountain leopard; though she held herself tall, she had a restless energy that created its own gravity. He watched her talking to customers. It was unusual to see a woman running a market stall, and yet she had a forthrightness that bordered latent aggression. She leant forward when engaging in bartering, with a slight smile that was neither cold, nor friendly. She was stunning rather than classically beautiful - her features were a little too hard and her eyes possessed a piercing shrewdness that most men would find unattractive in a wife. Shamgar couldn't help but wonder if her husband was a fool or a genius to put his wife in such a position. Perhaps both, he mused wryly.

Beside her sat another lady, a shawl covered her head and Shamgar guessed her to be Hebrew. Her plain clothes suggested that she was a slave. She attended to two small children who played in the dust at her feet. He watched the interaction between the two women - they were friends, he observed.

The woman continued to pace, her eyes occasionally scanning the crowd, she looked edgy. Her dark eyes settled on him for a moment, taking in his massive frame, wild hair and hand clasped around an ox-goad. As their eyes met, she didn't look away, whether it was due to defiance or curiosity, he did not know, but he was compelled to meet her stare. Finally, she turned to the other lady, her headdress falling over her face, as she leant down and whispered to her.

Shamgar strode away.

He had just returned from the temple situated on the apex of the *tel*, and could still see the smoke rising from the altar of sacrifice. The entire experience had left him filled with a sense of purpose and power. And yet he was still without any sense of the direction or clarity for which he had come in search. He had naively, and perhaps arrogantly, anticipated that one of the priests would single him out and have some mighty word for him, or that perhaps he would see a vision. He had left, feeling both empowered and frustrated.

With single-minded determination, he reluctantly met the heaving, pulsating market to find presents for the girls and Manoah. He had felt guilty leaving them after what they had been through, and a gift would make them all feel better, himself included. He ruminated briefly on the fact that this raucous, swollen monster was almost as stressful as the Philistine encounter in Gezer, where at least he had an outlet for his frustration. His emotions were still raw.

Different competitors were selling animals for sacrifice at the tabernacle. Other stallholders sold statues of Baal, Asherah and other deities. He picked up a knife with a carved bear on the handle for Manoah, and hastily made an offer to the trader. As he handed over his money, he imagined handing it to his son and his anticipated reaction - it would make him feel empowered as a man, and he needed that after watching his mother die.

He spun around, his senses quickened by the sound of crashing and a voice crying out behind him. A slave was being beaten and had fallen into a vegetable stall. The sight was not unusual, but since Gezer he had found certain things quickened his temper in a visceral, unconscious way he felt neither a desire nor an ability to define, or control. Beside him stood a Canaanite guard wearing the red skirt and bronze breastplate that defined his allegiance. He was flanked by four other guards, who surrounded a petite, elegantly dressed woman. Despite her years, she carried a presence of authority that alluded to her family association. She watched with emotionless superiority as the man before her cringed.

Shamgar felt his heart beat quicken. He had not come to pick a fight with the Canaanites, but to determine Yahweh's will. The guard lifted his whip above his head to deliver another blow to the quivering young man at his feet. The guard jerked backward, his back arching as a projectile slammed into his head and blood poured from the wound. He staggered for a moment before collapsing into the fruit stall.

The guards by his side were hurrying the woman away, their sense of priority clear as they abandoned their fallen comrade.

Shamgar smiled as his eyes noted the tent peg lying some distance away. He instinctively turned to the woman he had seen before. She had covered her mouth with her headscarf, but her eyes flashed with laughter. He walked toward her, drawn by his own curiosity at the woman's foolish bravery.

As he approached the stall her headdress fell and no sign of laughter remained. She had slid behind the face of the trader.

"Can I help you?" She raised an eyebrow. "Our tents are woven from strongest Negev goat's hair."

The woman seemed self-contained, shrewd and assertive, an unusual combination of qualities in a woman, he contemplated.

"Are you alright sir? Are you looking to buy a tent?" she frowned.

He rubbed the back of his neck, suddenly feeling foolish.

She raised her eyebrows and tilted her head. She was expecting an answer.

"Are you looking for something else?"

"Yes...I saw you." he blurted. "You threw a tent peg..." He found himself realising how ridiculous he sounded - this wasn't going well.

"…with great accuracy, may I add. Why did you do it?"

She looked at him coolly, her icy stare was intrusive, he had the feeling she was probing his soul; he met her gaze. "I hate bullies," she stated, leaning forward so that her hands were flat on the table. He couldn't help but wonder if she was reaching for a tent peg.

"Who are you?" she asked finally.

"I'm Shamgar." He frowned. "If the guards find out it was you, they'll kill you."

"I don't believe they will find out," she shrugged nonchalantly.

Shamgar controlled the urge to roll his eyes. "You're either naive or stupid if you believe that. What about your children?"

He knew that his candid reply was impolite, yet the woman evoked it from him. He was fascinated by her reckless faith.

The woman stood tall, her hands on her hips, her face twisted in defiant disdain. "*I* trust in God's protection." He noted the rebuke with wry amusement.

His natural mind wanted to snort in contempt but he was beginning to feel that strange pull in his gut., as though the stars had aligned and the whole market had been set up purely for his benefit. He asked anyway.

"Which God?"

She leant forward, her eyes piercing his with their steely conviction.

"Yahweh."

He began to laugh, he wasn't entirely sure he hadn't gone mad, but it felt like a lifetime since he had laughed, and it felt good.

He turned toward the women and children, who were all looking at him as if he was either completely rude or completely insane.

Shamgar bowed respectfully. "I came to Shiloh looking for answers, and Yahweh has spoken to me. When you hear of Shamgar, who has brought peace to Philistia, you will know it was by Yahweh's strength and your good advice…and aim." He leaned forward as he lowered his voice. "Next time, take out the one in charge." His eyes twinkled as he spoke.

Jael laughed, as he disappeared into the crowd.

"The man's a fool." She shook her head, picking up Levia, her youngest daughter, who had begun to cry. Placing a shawl over her shoulder, she turned her back to the market and began to feed her. Adva knew better than to answer.

"We'll leave early today, "Jael said. "I want to go to the temple tomorrow." The day's events had left her feeling unsettled.

"I'll start packing up," Adva agreed quietly.

"The man was a fool," Jael repeated. Adva sighed inwardly, acknowledging that her silence would not divert her friend's mood: she was looking for an argument, one that would shape or sharpen her thoughts. She pulled Meira close; she was tired and hungry and was beginning to show the warning signs of having an emotional meltdown.

"Perhaps," Adva said with placating impartiality.

Jael turned angrily. "What do you mean 'perhaps?' You say that when you think you have some inside information, and it makes me want to throw something at you."

Adva's lips curved with dark humour. "A good thing that I've packed the tent pegs away then." She kept her eyes downcast.

Jael laughed, her anger dissipating as quickly as it came. She stood, resting eight month-old Levia on her hip, and taking her two year old's hand as her sobs grew louder.

"Tell Jez to pack up the cart. Let's get back to the inn and freshen up before going to the evening sacrifice."

"I still can't believe Heber allowed us to come," Adva said.

Jael snorted. "He would sell his soul for the chance to make more money – if he hasn't already."

Part II

18

When you enter the land the LORD your God is giving you, do not learn to imitate the detestable ways of the nations there. Let no one be found among you who sacrifices their son or daughter in the fire, who practices divination or sorcery, interprets omens, engages in witchcraft, or casts spells, or who is a medium or spiritist or who consults the dead. Anyone who does these things is detestable to the LORD; because of these same detestable practices the LORD your God will drive out those nations before you.
You must be blameless before the LORD your God.
Deuteronomy 18: 9-13

1248 BC - Deborah

As the cart clattered through the bustling streets of the city, people moved out of their way. She met the eyes of a young boy. He was dressed in the Canaanite style of a patterned, striped tunic, with a sash around his waist; he looked about Isaacs's age. He watched her, his young mind spinning a tale as to her possible crime. She met his eyes and smiled sadly.

I need to escape; I need to get out of here. Her eyes flitted to the low entrance of the cart, the road beneath and back to the soldier.

He caught her eyes and shook his head almost imperceptibly, but the message was clear.

She sighed, sinking back against the bench.

As they passed the market place, her senses were hit with the smell of spices, fruit and livestock, reminding her of her rumbling stomach.

She noted that the rounded huts were not in the traditional Canaanite style. Finally, the town opened up, leaving the hectic clutter behind and exposing another, more imposing walled building.

"That's the Governor's House - impressive isn't it?" the soldier said, as though answering her thoughts.

The temple stood separate from the other buildings, signifying its pre-eminence. It rose before her, its mighty stone steps ascending to the open entrance of the temple, which was flanked by basalt pillars and statues of Canaanite deities.

The cart stopped and the soldier stepped off the cart, offering her his hand. He was a few years older than her, a head taller, with thick black hair, a shaved face and skin the colour of honey.

"This is your stop." His eyes flickered with pity for a second, before he slipped behind his role.

Deborah's eyes darted to the temple and back to the soldier as fear began to bubble up within her. Her mind was reeling as she contemplated all the possible reasons she would be taken to a Canaanite temple. She tried to push them down, but it was rising: a silent scream within her, which threatened to suffocate her. She needed to escape. Her eyes flitted down the narrow streets as she considered the possibility.

Following her thoughts and recognising her reluctance to mount the steps, the guard's grip tightened on her arm. There was a steady stream of people, mostly men, ascending and descending the wide stone stairs.

She looked into his eyes and saw her panic reflected, as she acknowledged the military resolution in his.

Inside the temple, the sides were lined with booths meeting at the back where the goddess Asherah stood, arms open wide, to welcome her worshipers. The temple prostitutes, both male and female stood provocatively dressed outside open doors, while others were purposefully closed. She noticed a girl about her own age. She had a familiarity about her. The girl caught her eye, and turned away as she was approached by a worshipper. Deborah noted how the men first approached the temple priest, handing them money, before heading toward one of the booths, choosing either a male or female, as their taste to worship led them.

In the centre of the large hall stood a huge altar stained with the blood of its sacrifices. On one side stood a basalt statue of Anath, Goddess of the Hunt, armed with bow and arrow, while her foot symbolically stood on the contorted remains of Mot. On the other side stood her brother, Baal, whom she had rescued from the underworld, defeating Mot in the process. Their father, El, loomed over the altar. A child, no more than two years of age, was strapped to the altar, the forceful hands of the priest laid on his head, while his arms and legs were tied to the altar. The parents knelt, their hands raised in worship as tears poured down their face, they offered their sacrifice to appease the gods, praying for the fertility of their land and livestock.

Deborah clapped her hand over her mouth, the scream forcing its way out of her body, ripping her open as it merged with the child's. The soldier grabbed her, and she was dragged to the back of the hall where a small door stood ajar. She heard the last scream of the boy as the door closed behind her.

A priest emerged; his ornate robes and headdress distinguished his supremacy over the other priests. He glanced at Deborah, a muscle twitching in the fleshy pouch beneath his left eye. His face was lined into a perpetual grimace that alluded to both superiority, and indifference.

The room offered little space for private conversation. The soldier drew the priest to an alcove, in which stood an altar. She felt faint with nausea and horror, and pressed her back against the stone wall.

Reality seemed to have diminished to a place beyond emotion. She gazed mutely at the backs of the priest and soldier, catching only fragments of the conversation.

"Sisera says she's a Hebrew priestess. He asks that you consult the spirits regarding her."

The priest nodded and moved to an altar situated at the far side of the room. Lighting a bowl of incense he began to chant, breathing in the thick billowing smoke until its sweet aroma filled the room. Deborah felt light-headed and disorientated. She prayed silently as a sense of evil invaded the room. The priest seemed to sway, and as he turned slightly, Deborah could see that he was in a trance, and that he was having a conversation with an unseen figure in the room. She had heard of the Canaanite practice of consulting the spirits for guidance. She wondered who he was speaking to and what was being said. She glanced up at the guard, who was wide-eyed and pale.

As the priest became lucid once again, he turned to Deborah as though to adjust his opinion of her.

"Bring her." He turned abruptly toward the door, his robe swirling in the dissipating cloud, adding to his mystique.

They made their way back through the temple. Deborah purposefully avoided looking at the altar, but the combined effect of inhaling the incense, the heat of the flames from the altar and the smell, all affected their iniquity upon Deborah's frail state. Gagging, she unsuccessfully fought the abhorrence that rose within her. She retched, emitting the bilious contents of her empty stomach onto the legs of the priest and Baal's stone form as she did so.

The soldier rolled his eyes in disbelief as he grabbed her arm and hurried her out of the temple, leaving the curses and outrage of the priests as they muttered superstitiously behind her.

He pushed her into the waiting cart, whether to protect her or punish her, not even he was sure. The priest took his own carriage.

Deborah sat with her head in her hands. The rhythmic bouncing of the cart had both a cathartic and nauseating effect upon her. She allowed her thoughts to drift to her mother and Isaac, to Ephraim. The thought that they were safe nurtured an ember of hope.

She glanced at the guard and saw that he was watching her, his mouth twitched with dark humour.

"Well, you certainly let Baal know what you think of him."

She looked at him with momentary confusion as she replayed the temple incidents, and laughed weakly.

The soldier handed her a skin of water and bread roll.

"Do you know where we are going?" she ventured.

The guard paused before exhaling. "We are returning to Sisera." She noted the pity in his eyes and nodded with resignation.

When they reached the fortress, she was taken through a different entrance. Grand, wooden doors opened onto white, marble floors that were cold on Deborah's bare feet. At the end of the corridor, the guard led her into a room on the left, while the priest veered off to the right.

She sat with her head in her hands, waiting…

Finally, Sisera returned, Talmai with him; she shuddered inwardly. Approaching her, the general grabbed her by the hair. She resisted the urge to flinch as he pulled her face close to his, a cruel smile playing on his lips.

"Prophetess! Tomorrow you will see the power of Canaan."

Deborah shuddered inwardly at Sisera's barbed threat. She tried to imagine *her place*, and her prayer to Yahweh; *I lay my life in Your hand, and in Your mercy I trust.*

Though winter was still upon them, it was a cloudless, mild day that hinted at warmer days to come.

Sisera's army took the highway that bore north-east of Harosheth. The rolling hills of Zebulun could be seen in the distance, verdant with farmland, vineyards and pastures that surrounded the clusters of huts that marked out villages.

Dread rose in Deborah as she saw the small mud and daub huts of a Hebrew village grow closer. Memories of her own village flooded her; these were her people, those she would have made *sukkot* next to at the Feast of Tabernacles, and worshipped next to her at the temple. She watched as mothers, wide-eyed, with terror grabbed their children and ran into their homes, while others tried to flee to the safety of the fields. She fell to her knees, her hands over her ears as arrows flew through the air, and the victims fell.

Deborah gazed in mute horror as Sisera seemed to replay the death of her brother and father before her eyes, swinging his axe into a young man's chest. Talmai had seized an older man and was beating him with his huge fists as his wife and children watched helplessly. When his body finally fell limp, he violated the wife and then ended her life, her face crumpled under the impact of his huge fist.

Deborah tried to look away as deep sobs broke from the deep fissures within her soul. The guard restrained her head in a vice like grip, forcing her to watch. "Sisera commands you to watch. If you try and close your eyes, I will remove your eyelids," he threatened, running his finger over the blade of his curved sword.

As the children were murdered and the women violated, Deborah watched, her helplessness and rage a repressed cauldron of emotion that screamed for the release of righteous vengeance. She listened to their cries as they called out for help; and she stood, helpless as their lives were ended. In all of this Sisera remained calm, only the small smile of cruelty showed on his chiseled features.

By the end of the day, she had witnessed the death and destruction of two more Hebrew villages; the last had been burnt to the ground with the occupants in the houses. Deborah felt that her own soul was a violated wasteland that could never be healed. She grasped to find Yahweh in the midst of it, but she felt that she, too, was burning, and He seemed far away. She cried out for His deliverance, for His mercy, and wondered if He heard.

They set up camp and Deborah was leashed with a rope to a pole outside Sisera's tent. The soldiers leered at her, making obscene comments and gestures. As she sat in the dust, she prayed for protection, for courage, for hope, for herself and for her nation. When she finally fell asleep, her nightmares were filled with screams as her mind replayed the day's events. In her subconscious state, she tried to recall the faces of hope: her family and the memory of Lapidoth as the one who had once saved her.

She was awoken by Sisera who kicked her hard in the back. Panic flooded her senses as she scrambled to stand. Feeling his hands around her throat, she fell into the dirt, choking as the dust filled her lungs, yet unable to escape his grip. And then, when she could bear no more, he seized her hair, forcing her to stand. *Why doesn't he kill me, as he has with the others? Why does he keep me alive? Is it to torment me?*

His voice was level; he gave no indication that he was controlled by anger or any emotion, only that he had a role to perform and would do it well.

"Tell me. What does *your* God say will happen to *your* people today?" he sneered.

She looked up at him, fear and loathing warring within her. *Yahweh let me only speak your words. And give me the courage I need to say them.*

"He says *today*, He will *allow* you to triumph over them."

Sisera's eyes were stony, threatening, as he took in the unspoken message she delivered.

"He will *allow* me?"

"Today, yes," she replied steadily, holding his gaze.

"And tomorrow?"

"I cannot tell what will happen tomorrow," she replied dispassionately.

Sisera weighed her suspiciously and for a moment, she thought she saw uncertainty. His expression, still emotionless, his voice little more than a whisper, he leaned toward her and hissed: "Tomorrow, I will also triumph. Tomorrow, I will be one step closer to my desire to break you...until you no longer have the strength or will to hear from your God, nor to help your people. I will destroy your hope as I will destroy theirs."

The force of his intention slammed into her like a physical blow that rendered her mute. The words reverberated in her mind as they collided with dark and violent images.

True to his word, over the next week, Deborah continued to see the destruction of her people. Sometimes they came upon starving families by the roadside, their clothes hung loosely to their bodies and their faces grey and haunted. Upon seeing the approach of Sisera's army, they would run into the hills, reminding Deborah of frightened rabbits fleeing a fox.

Other times they saw villages already burnt down, bodies unburied, fed on by wild animals and carrion. She knew that Sisera was watching her; she could feel his eyes upon her, his grip of fear suffocating her, as she could feel her own hold on reality ebbing away.

At the beginning of each day he would ask her: "What does your God say today?"

Each day, she would look him in the eye and answer: "Today, *He* will *allow* you to triumph over them."

And he would smile and watch her pain as he crushed them.

As those who forsook their faith in Yahweh fled to the cities, they blamed him for their loss and suffering. They forgot that it was they who had turned from Him when they began to worship the gods of Canaan. Many argued that Yahweh's ways were outdated and restrictive, while the gratification of temple worship momentarily numbed the pain of guilt and loss. When the priests suggested offering their starving children to him, they believed winning his favour would give them a future. Other times, they sold their children into prostitution, in their depraved desire to survive. The more financially astute who had daughters of beauty sold their daughters into marriage with the Canaanites, forming alliances that allowed them privilege and safety. They enjoyed the economic privileges of the Canaanite prominence in trade, consciously allowing their spiritual and cultural foundations to dissipate, and doing what was right in their own eyes. Deborah felt Yahweh's pain for them as their sin destroyed them. And when she pleaded for Him to help them, He answered:

I cannot help them if they will not ask. I will not take choice from them.

After three months, they returned to Harosheth. She tried to remember when she had first come, but it seemed a lifetime ago - and she had been a different girl.

She was once again placed under the guard of the Egyptian soldier.   She read shock and empathy in his eyes as he acknowledged the change in her.

This time she was placed in the slaves' quarters, a large stone room, lined with straw pallets on either side. Each pallet was furnished with a blanket and pillow.

Isis was in charge of the slaves. He was a large man, bare chested and barrel bellied, who wielded his authority by means of a vicious metal-ended whip. Deborah thought his face looked as though someone had trodden on it - it was left in a permanent grimace.

He gripped Deborah's arm and shoved her onto a straw pallet before turning to deal with an argument that had arisen between two slaves. It was solved by way of beating them both until they could not talk. Deborah watched with terror, and then hoping her existence would go unnoticed, she pulled the blanket over her, trembling.

She was awoken the next day with the vicious prod of a stick and Isis' voice booming abuse. None of the slaves looked at each other or spoke, but each evidently lived in a perpetual state of fear and fight for survival. Deborah looked around the room and noted that males and females were separated by a carved wooden screen, each panel containing a graphic scene from Canaanite mythology: Baal being cast into the underworld, Baal as the god of Storm. Asherah rescuing Baal from Mot, god of the Underworld, and Dagon, god of Fertility, in a number of obscene depictions with men, women and animals.

She spent the day shoveling pig manure, while the sun relentlessly assailed them. She watched with numb apathy as others collapsed around her, their lives so cheap, and determined that she would not fall. And so she allowed her mind to wander to the sanctuary of her memories, to *her place*, to Ephraim where the river played her tune and the wind whispered her name as it played in the trees. Her body ached, she felt feverish and alone, and she longed to hear her mother and Isaac's voices. She pulled the blanket over her shoulders, shivering, and drew her knees up to her chest, tears rolling down her face and wetting her hair as she silently cried out to Yahweh.

Deborah noticed that within the slave quarters, there were girls who would be taken during the night. Sometimes they returned the next day and sometimes they were not seen again, and would be replaced.

A numbness crept over Deborah, like a winter frost that protected life beneath; it seemed that the promises of Yahweh, both for herself and her nation, were buried.

The slaves were all busy preparing a banquet in honour of Sisera's mother. Only the most wealthy and powerful in Canaan were invited to attend this exclusive celebration.

When the evening arrived, the sun was beginning to sink beyond the fortress walls and torches lined the courtyard. Conversation and laughter moved like a glittering river of wealth and social ambition into the main building. Everywhere, huge bowls of fire were placed on pedestals that illuminated basalt statues of Sisera's lineage, their shadows purposefully creating a dark army on the marble walls behind them. The floor, made of finest acacia wood, was covered with luxurious imported Turkish rugs. Couches, sumptuously draped with exotic coverings and cushions, were strategically arranged around the room to emphasise the basalt statues. At the far end of the room, centered between two alcoves which held large vases containing lilies and orchids, lay a long table. Deborah felt her hungry stomach growl at the sight of the golden bowls that spilled over with fruit, platters of cakes and delicacies, sliced meats and seafood. The centrepiece was a whole roast pig. She cynically reflected that the unclean animal was a fitting reflection of Canaan's greed and immorality. It angered her as she recalled the starving people she had seen, and remembered how Sisera's carts had taken away the best produce. There was more food here than these people would ever eat.

It was not difficult to spot Sisera's mother; everyone milled around her, desperate for her time and attention. She nodded and smiled at them, poised, controlled and strained, yet despite her petite build, she evidently carried great authority. Deborah had the feeling she was assessing and weighing each person, deciding who her son could use to further his purposes, giving each person her attention whilst shrewd and attentive to the politics in the room. Those deemed worthy of her conversation she would engage, whilst those deemed unimportant were dismissed with a vague smile as she turned away.

Deborah noted how the woman wielded her power; her aloof manner made the sycophants work harder for her approval.

Next to her stood a lady, young and beautiful, composed yet bearing an underlying fragility.

A slave she did not recognise from Sisera's household turned to Deborah. Noticing her observation, she spoke Hebrew. "Her name is Ariya, and the one next to her is Sisera's wife, Jara. Imagine being married to such a monster and having *her* as a mother-in-law."

"It must be dreadful," Deborah replied, relishing hearing the Hebrew language. She looked at the beautiful woman standing next to Ariya, tense, her back straight, her arms loose at her sides. One hand nervously picked on a broken nail, and her eyes flitted from Ariya to the door. Deborah couldn't help but wonder if she was waiting for someone, or perhaps considering escape. Jara listened politely to the conversation, offering little of her own opinion. It was evident that the older lady had very little respect for the younger.

"She's not too bad; a bit lofty and spiteful, seeing where she's from. She used to be kinder when she first came, but over the years…Well, she's married to Sisera, what you can expect? Not that she had much choice in it: her family was poor and the dowry was good."

"Where is she from?" Deborah asked, her curiosity getting the better of her.

"She's from Egypt. Sisera was sent there as a child, to be educated and receive his military training. His step-father was worried he'd become soft if he stayed in Harosheth with his mother; but then Sisera never could do anything right in his step-father's eyes - and nothing wrong in his mother's eyes. A dangerous combination, don't you think?"

"I don't recognise you from Sisera's household?" Deborah queried.

"No, I'm with Jara - have been for five years," she exhaled wearily.

"I'm sorr,." Deborah replied, unsure what to say.

The girl shrugged, her eyes suddenly sad. "It was worse in the beginning – you dream of escape or liberation. You remember who you were. Once you give up, it gets easier." She snorted with cynical apathy and then changed the conversation.

"That lady over there…" she gestured toward a plump lady with an ample bosom, clothed in purple velvet, who seemed wedged into one of the couches, "…that's Pigat, Jabin's mother – the only person here more powerful than Ariya, Sisera's mother. You can watch the dynamics of the two of them together; you'll enjoy it – they hate each other!" she laughed conspiratorially.

"And who is she?" Deborah whispered, motioning to a lady standing next to one of the pillars. She was tall, and wore a dress of scarlet that exposed enough skin to fully accentuate her voluptuous figure. She had long black hair that fell like a silk flag to her waist, high cheekbones and full lips. She was surrounded by servants, and spoke to a lady whose back was turned to Deborah.

"That's Jabin's wife, Padriya." The girl shuddered. "And the woman standing with her back to us is her priestess, but she's practiced in the dark art of Kashapim and even Sisera won't cross her. I've heard it told that nobody escapes her evil eye." As though she heard them, the woman turned around. Her eyes scanned the crowd, as though listening to an inner voice. Finally, her eyes settled on Deborah and stayed there for some time, watching her every move. She turned to Padriya and whispered something to her. Padriya looked up, her kohl painted eyes resembled a cat's.

Isis approached the two of them. He turned to Deborah. "If I see you talk again, I will have you publicly flayed. Take more food to the tables!" He lifted his hand to strike her but Deborah quickly moved away to the kitchens, returning with bowls of oranges and pomegranates.

She listened to the conversations around her, noting how different Canaan was to Israel.

Ariya smiled politely, and Deborah couldn't help but wonder if everything she did was out of a drive to perform and portray perfection and dominance. She listened to their conversation with dark fascination as she wondered: how does one create a person like Sisera?

"And how is Sisera?" The voice held a gentle strength. The woman, in her mid-forties, was still attractive with her dark hair coiled in a plait on her head. She was evidently a woman of some social standing, judging by Ariya's attention to her.

"He's succeeding!" She gave a small laugh that sounded wrong. "His army of chariots will soon ensure our dominance, and rid our country of the Hebrews once and for all."

"Will he not allow them the right to become vassals of Canaan?"

Ariya looked at the woman with undisguised disdain at the suggestion.

"That was never the intention. We will take over their land and distribute its land, spoils and women to those among our people who have been loyal to the cause. It's a soldiers right."

Deborah could feel her ire rising, and was about to walk away when she heard the woman ask a question. She busied herself at the table, her peripheral vision watching for Isis.

"And how are your grandsons, are they here tonight?"

"My grandsons are both in Egypt; they will complete their training within the next year and join my son in his conquest."

"You must miss them," the woman empathised, looking at Jara and smiling.

"Of course, but it's all about children achieving their full potential, isn't it?"

Jara smiled, and she spoke with a gentle yet strained voice. "Potential... it's so open to perspective, based on our own personal values; it means something different to each of us, doesn't it? Performance and domination may be seen as valid goals, but integrity and peace could be argued to be higher ambitions?" She spoke to both women.

The other woman chuckled. "Very much so, integrity and social conscience are as important in defining a man's value, if not more so, than physical ambition or gain. And it is how we wield power that determines our success, not our conquests."

"I couldn't agree more," Jara added, her eyes triumphant.

Ariya scoffed. "You speak as women without nobility or class. You have no understanding of politics and power. Sisera was born to rule. I encouraged his dominance as a child, and I support it now. A man must do what is best for himself." She turned her back on the three of them, turning her attention to another group.

Deborah walked away, her mind reflecting on all that she had heard; for the personal and social dynamics had revealed not only the character and insecurities of each person, but something of the underlying politics of Sisera's court. She had somehow imagined all Canaanites to be evil, selfish people and yet she had seen both courage and kindness in these two women that she could not help but admire.

A year had passed and spring brought with it the season for war. Deborah watched helplessly as her people were crushed in Issachar, Zebulon and Naphtali. She often wondered that Sisera had never killed her, or worse, and yet she knew he took joy in watching her pain as he destroyed her people.

As he had before, each day he would ask: "What does your God say will happen today, Priestess?"

She had not heard from Yahweh for over a year. It seemed as though He, too, had hidden from the atrocities that afflicted His people, and she felt alone. A quiet strength, stubborn resolve and growing hatred gave her the courage to reply: "*Today* he will *allow* you to crush His people."

His eyes narrowed at the double meaning of her words that would add to the violence of his assault.

19

He too saved Israel.
Judges 3:31

1253 BC – Shamgar

Shamgar kept to the byways as he hastened to return to Beit Shemesh. His impatience, anxiety and zeal pushed him into a run for the last few *parasang*. By the time he reached his father's house, the apprehension that he had pushed into the dark recesses of his thoughts had buffeted their way to his consciousness, and he was chiding himself for having left his children with him.

He approached the house with military caution. He knew that the Philistines would not have let the death of one of their lords go unpunished.

As he had anticipated, the flashes of bronze and dots of red signified the gathering of the Philistine army. He noted, too, a smaller gathering of Canaanite soldiers; they appeared to be making preparations to move away.

His father was waiting at the gate, concern and fear lined his face. He seemed to have aged over the week that Shamgar had been gone.

"The children?"

"They're fine. But they can't stay here. Balak's presence has held Philistia's wrath from us as long as he can. But he doesn't have the military power to withhold them much longer."

Nor the desire. Shamgar left his thoughts unspoken. He knew his brother would never jeopardise his position in the Canaanite army by risking war with Philistia to defend his non-conformist brother. He acknowledged too his father's political compromise in helping him, and whilst his mind erred to suspicion, he was grateful for his help in protecting the children.

"How many do you think there are?"

His father shrugged. "I'd say five hundred or more. I've heard that the four Philistine lords have come to witness your defeat - they are gathering in the fields below."

Shamgar sighed; he regretted his father's involvement in his battle, though he knew it was unavoidable now. "You need to leave."

His father nodded - he looked hesitant…"You can't win this battle, son, there are too many. I am leaving you my three best soldiers, and some from Beit Shemesh have said they will stand with you. But there can be no more than fifty against so many." His face, usually impassive and authoritative, was lined with angst.

Shamgar resisted the compulsion of this father's fear. He knew if he yielded to it for even a second, all would be lost.

"My mother's God was with me in Gezer and is with me now."

His father smiled weakly, his lack of conviction evident. "I will take the children to Bethlehem, to your mother's people. It may be there are other Hebrews willing to stand with you," he said with resignation.

Shamgar clasped his father's shoulder.

"I will meet you in Bethlehem…or I will send word to you."

His father looked him in the eye, and Shamgar turned away from the hopelessness and premature grief he saw there, choosing instead to focus on the knowledge that Yahweh was with him, that this was HIS battle.

He watched his father lead the servants, guards and children out of the back entrance of the house and thread their way through the trees that would lead them around the *tel* of Beit Shemesh and on to Bethlehem. In the courtyard, he met those who had assembled to fight with him.

"This battle cannot be won by flesh and blood. There are too many."

He watched the look of uncertainty on the faces of the men, some armed with swords and axes, others like him with ox-goads and plough-shears. They shifted uncomfortably, glancing at each other; this was clearly the worst pre-battle speech ever made.

"But then, I could not defeat two hundred Philistines single-handedly. Yet I did, because I do not fight alone. I fought with Almighty Yahweh - and the battle is His today. The victory is His. We fight for our families, for those who have been killed, those who have been taken and for those who remain. We fight for our self-respect as men. And we fight for Yahweh – for his Kingdom to come and for Philistia and its gods to bow to the Almighty, the only true God.

"Below us sit the four remaining lords of Gaza, Ashkelon, Ashdod and Gath. They have come to gloat over my death and their assured victory. They would not be here if they believed there was any doubt of this victory. But Yahweh will use this day for His name, to wipe their names from the earth, and Israel will rule once again in Philistia."

The men shouted and roared with approval.

"But now, I commend every man here to seek Yahweh. Consecrate your hearts to Him. He is our General, and we await His command to fight."

The men met his suggestion with agreement. Choosing three men to accompany him, including two of his father's soldiers, Shamgar hastened into the house and climbed the stairs to the rooftop. Through the trees that clung to the *tel*, he could see the flicker of the Philistine army on the plain below him, their armour winking in the morning sun, mocking the impossibility of his aspirations.

He knelt, refusing to look at the natural impossibility before him. Instead, he reminded himself of Yahweh's accomplishment and his own inner need for justice.

Yahweh, I trust not in my flesh, nor in the power of my enemy, but in You. Show me, Yahweh, for power and victory belongs to You, Lord of the armies of heaven.

He knew to wait for Yahweh. Though his masculine need for decision and action warred with his knowledge and faith in Him, Shamgar remained with his face pressed to the earth. He felt the heat of the sun on his back and knew that it had reached its apex. He remained prostrated on the ground, acknowledging that unless Yahweh acted, his life and the lives of those who had joined him would be forfeited.

The ground around him took on the warm colours of sunset, swathing him in its rosy wings, while the sun was a fiery orb of judgement that corrupted the clouds. And then he felt the ground around him tremble and strength course through him, and he knew that Yahweh was with him. He sighed with contentment; he would have been happy to remain in this place, even at the forfeit of his life.

The fiery sky had given way to the dark hues of burnt ash and the first stars punched their path into the night sky. He lay prostrate on the ground, noting that his father's guards had resumed the same position. He smiled inwardly, acknowledging that they too, had experienced Yahweh's presence: one man in the hand of Yahweh was worth one hundred!

Within that place, he drifted into a restful slumber. When he awoke with a jolt, he noticed the other men slept too. He peered over the rooftop wall, filled with dread as to what scene he would find. But as his eyes travelled down the hill to where the tents were gathered, he saw that the Philistine camp was also beginning to awaken. He checked the hillside for their advance, but was met with the quiet whisper of the trees. He sighed, taking in the beauty of the scene; the stream that flowed from the top of the tel and wound its way through the Philistine camp, the imposing oak trees, their arms raised to heaven as they sheltered the grazing impala that roamed unknowingly - before the heat of the day poured out its fury in Israel.

And then, in the midst of his thoughts, came the words:
Rise and take what is in your hand. The battle is Mine.

Hastening the men around him, he passed around a jug of water and a bowl of broken bread, saying simply: "Eat quickly, it is time."

Shamgar's fist clenched around the shaft of his ox-goad. His heart pounded and his mouth felt dry. Pictures of his children flashed into his mind as he considered the likelihood of his survival.

He pushed thought and emotion aside and allowed the thought of victory, of what he was fighting for, to drive him forward.

They kept to the shadows of the trees, knowing the obscurity of dawn and the covering of the trees were nature's allies.

One of his father's guards slipped ahead of them, disappearing at a run as he darted in and out of the trees. When he returned moments later, he took gasps of breath and looked unnerved. "They have lookouts all around. We cannot invade unnoticed."

Shamgar nodded, clasping the man's shoulder. "I had expected as much. We must move quickly and attack as one."

Using his ox-goad, he distanced himself mentally from what he knew he had to do. Letting out a battle cry that was echoed by the other men, he ended the life of the first Philistine lookout. Then, using his goad as a spear, he blocked the next soldier's sword, knocking it from his hands before thrusting the pointed shaft into the man's chest. He heard the cries of battle and the clash of steel around him as he fought. Adrenalin flooded his senses as he used the metal blade to stab one man and, in a fluid motion, he used the other end to skewer the next; their death groans curdled the air. Knowledge and experience would have advised him to abandon his ox-goad and take the sword and spear of his fallen victims, but wisdom dictated that he needed to be obedient to Yahweh. He surrendered to this higher thought.

Strength coursed through him as he fought, and it seemed as though his movements were orchestrated by heaven. The sun had once again reached its midday glory, and although the bodies of Philistines mounted around him, a silver wave of their swords and shields pushed forward. He saw one of his father's men fall, surrounded by fifty men as they severed his head from his body and skewered it on a spear. His courage faltered for a second as he imagined his own life ending thus; and he knew that the same thought would be in every man who fought the Philistines.

"Yahweh! Victory belongs to Yahweh!" he bellowed over the sound of battle.

"Yahweh! Victory belongs to Yahweh!" he heard the words repeated, first by one other, and then the cry grew as a victory chant that strengthened their weary arms and souls.

Shamgar noted movement on the grassy slope on the far side of the plain where the four remaining Philistine lords prepared to flee on their chariots. He acknowledged their retreat with both satisfaction and fury; they would not escape their judgement. With renewed battle lust, he tore a path through the Philistine soldiers, dodging their spears as they skillfully sought their target, and destroying the ranks that opposed him until he reached his prize. Throwing himself on the back of a dappled stallion, he charged behind the chariots, ducking low to avoid the arrows of the archers. He was almost upon them when an arrow plunged into his breast and then another brought down his horse. He cried out in agony as he fell to the ground, pulling himself free from the dying beast.

Seeing his fall, the Philistine lords turned from their flight. The archers leapt first from the chariots, their bows pulled back as they warily surrounded him. The Philistine lords secured their chariots, unsheathing their swords as they encircled him. Their faces were twisted with humour, hatred and triumph as they rejoiced in their victory, like wolves that linger around a wounded stag, watching as its life's blood seeps into the ground.

Shamgar's fist tightened around the ox-goad. Pushing back the black shadow that hovered before him, he pulled himself mentally into Yahweh's light. As the four lords raised their swords, he inwardly called upon Almighty Yahweh as his shield and strength and felt the assurance of His victory fortify his blood within. He remained still, groaning as though immobilised, listening to their taunts and intent for his brutal end. His fingers tightened around the wooden shaft and he mentally played his next actions in his mind. When the moment came, he moved with lightning speed. Sweeping his goad in a sinuous arch and knocking three of them from their feet, he kicked the other in the shin toppling him off of his feet as he leapt to his own. The archers had abandoned their bows and taken up their daggers and axes for fear of hitting one of the lords. Before the lords had time to regain their posture, he had sunk his goad into the first lord's chest and swiftly sliced the throat of another. Shamgar forced his mind to focus, repressing the panic that rose up within him and reminded himself that Yahweh's Spirit still sustained him.

The battle is Yours, Yahweh.

He used his ox-goad to disarm the archers before ending their lives, and then, as the last two Philistine lords ran to their chariots, he propelled his goad as a spear, penetrating the first man's body. He sprinted over and pulled it free. The Philistine's eyes bulged with fear, his screams curdling the air as death's painful grip engulfed him.

Shamgar mercifully ended his torment and turned to see that the last lord was now on his chariot and the horses were picking up speed. He acknowledged the gathering distance between himself and his enemy. Lifting his goad, he made a silent plea to Yahweh, and with the strength of heaven he hurled it through the air. The shaft met its target at the base of the man's back. Shamgar watched the man's body crumple and knew that his spine had been broken. His arms were still twisted in the reigns so that he was being dragged behind the chariot as the terrified horses continued to gallop. The lord's agonised screams filled the air and then faded.

Shamgar let out a roar of victory and relief.

It was over!

He looked over the plain before him and saw the last Philistines fleeing up the tel toward his father's house, pursued by his remaining men.

The scene beneath him was violent: butchered bodies lay twisted among those whose lives ebbed into the bloody rivulets of the torn plain. It seemed to Shamgar as though Hades had been inverted.

He thanked Yahweh that victory had been theirs.

As his adrenalin dissipated, the pain from his wound and battle weariness finally threatened to overwhelm him. He hung his head, resting his hands on his thighs as he summoned the strength to stagger back up the tel to his father's house.

He stepped over the bodies of the last Philistines and pushed open the huge oak doors. He was greeted with the weary smiles of twelve of the men who were left; each slumped on benches nursing their own wounds.

"You fought valiantly. Philistia is now Yahweh's. Let Israel rejoice in Yahweh's victory! To Him be the glory." His voice was hoarse with exhaustion and every word felt like an effort.

The men echoed Shamgar's words. He continued, "Tomorrow we will secure our victory; you will be made leaders of cities and of men for your courage and faith.

"But today, we must recover our comrades who fell in battle; are there any among us who have the strength to go to Beit Shemesh?"

One of his father's men stood, along with a younger man. Blood ran from a gash down the side of his face and seeped into the linen of his tunic, yet his youthful vigour remained. Shamgar envied him that. He smiled. "Sir, I am still strong, shall I let your father and children know that the battle is won...and that Shamgar lives?"

Shamgar smiled wearily. "Thank you! You will find them at the home of Ruth and Obed, in Bethlehem."

20

From the end of the earth I call to You when my heart is faint; Lead me to the rock that is higher than I.
Psalm 61:2

1246 BC – Deborah

By the time summer's full heat came upon them and Sisera returned to Harosheth, Deborah felt that her soul had been violated by fear and guilt: that she still lived. The only hope left to her was that her life, too, might end. Her path to Yahweh that had once been so clear was now one she stumbled upon, strewn with lurid blood images that tripped and struck her.

The hills were bleached to shades of gold in the drought of the summer, and the slaves were driven harder to ensure the survival of Canaan. An epidemic hit Harosheth, and Deborah watched as many of the slaves became sick and died. They were promptly replaced, their lives unimportant except for their function. At first she did not care, she did not know them; she had never spoken to them and if anything, she envied them. She watched with the numb detachment that enabled her to survive.

A Hebrew girl from Shechem was moved next to her; her name was Etiya and she carried a child-like faith that reminded Deborah of the person she had once been. She was no older than thirteen. Her father and brother had been in the fields outside of Shechem when Sisera attacked. Her face was pale and oval and her wide, brown eyes had the look of innocence - and horror. Like many, she would often awaken with nightmares and would then sob quietly. Deborah closed her eyes. All suffered here. She could not allow her heart to feel…to reach out to any would be to acknowledge the pain she could do nothing to help. Helplessness and apathy smothered her, drowned her, protected her.

Etiya had no sooner arrived than she caught the epidemic. Deborah watched her young life fade before her eyes, and something within her sparked, like a distant memory from long ago.
I could not save them, I could not save any of them…but could I help this one?

And it warred with another thought: *I cannot bear to hope and see it crushed. To let any tiny seed of hope venture from its fortress, and then to lose it would kill me… and besides, it is better for her to go to Yahweh now than to know this life.*

And His voice answered: *You had no power to save them, but this one, you could…you are only responsible for the gifts I have given you, and then you must trust.*

Deborah sighed, she knew she should remain in her place, that to venture from it would be to risk being beaten; and yet there was no choice if she decided to help the girl.
Yahweh, help me.

Seeing her movement, the Egyptian guard approached her.

"What are you doing?" he hissed, his tone more concerned than aggressive. He looked over his shoulder.

"I may be able to bring the fever down. I have…some knowledge of herbs…could you bring me ginger, in boiling water?"

The guard's eyes were warm, the colour of amber; he gave a small, almost imperceptible smile. "I'll see what I can do. Go back now."

Deborah nodded.

The young girl, whose name she discovered to be Etiya, recovered, and rumour of Deborah's knowledge of herbs spread among the slaves. When Isis was not present, the Egyptian guard, whose name she discovered to be Hur, would bring Deborah herbs and turn a blind eye to their use.

"Tell me of Shechem, I thought it remained Hebrew," Deborah whispered to Etiya, as they wearily collapsed on their pallets.

Etiya paused as she collected her thoughts. "Sisera tried to take Shechem. He killed all those who were outside in the fields, but the walls kept him out and he finally withdrew...for now."

"And so, does Shechem remain faithful to Yahweh?" Deborah frowned, noting Etiya's hesitancy.

"Whilst the Canaanites have not yet been able to physically destroy its walls and mighty gates, its faith and morals have been watered down. A Canaanite temple was opened to accommodate and encourage commerce, and now it is said there are those among the high council that sacrifice at the high places and attend the temple. Hence, our walls of holiness and sanctity have been breached by economic security and the pursuit of natural peace and physical pleasure. But their vulnerability and decay is masked by religious façade and tradition."

Deborah nodded, acknowledging the true weakness of Shechem's defence: she had compromised her defender as sovereign, she had invited the god of their enemy into their midst.

Something began to change within the slave quarters, which was initially imperceptible to the emotionally dead; it was a vein of kindness and its warmth began to resuscitate hope. Though her access to herbs was limited to the assistance and good will of Hur, Deborah had been able to cure several of the slaves. Always, when she gave them medicine, she spoke to them, sensitively asking them questions about their past and sharing some of her own story, and then she would pray. As she reached out to those around her, she felt her own hope grow. Each person had their own story of trauma associated with being taken into slavery, and Deborah was perceptive to the physical healing so often being related to the emotional healing. Those who were healed tentatively reached out to those around them, often nothing more than a smile or a glance that would communicate: 'you are not alone.'

As they worked next to each other in the fields, they whispered of Yahweh's goodness, reminding Him of the promises He had given their ancestors.

Though Deborah's character could not ignore the suffering of those around her - she was driven to help those who were in pain - she felt that her own heart was a desolate wasteland, and she strove to fight the grief that would poison her soul if left untended. Etiya, who slept next to her, was the only one who saw the pain she carried and the silent tears that she hid.

Often, her hand would reach out in the darkness and clasp Deborah's. It was a small act, but its warmth comforted and strengthened her heart.

"Yahweh will console us Deborah, you'll see," Etiya whispered in the darkness.

And so a community began to develop among the slaves who began to find comfort in their shared experiences of grief and hardship, which strengthened them and gave them hope.

Deborah vaguely noted the passing of her twenty-seventh birthday as they laboured from dawn to dusk. She watched those who became weak or sick, labour and fall beside her as they were pushed to bring in the abundant harvest of Canaan.

Sisera had returned from his campaign, hearing his mother was near death. She had just collapsed onto her pallet, her body ached with weariness and her hands were blistered from grinding wheat, when she saw the Egyptian, Hur, hastening toward her. He crouched down beside her, his voice low.

"Sisera's mother, she is sick..."

"With fever?"

"She burns, yes."

Deborah saw the intent behind Hur's words and she felt her heart close: *He wants me to help her and I don't want to. I want him to suffer, as he killed my family, there is nothing in me that wants to make her better.*

"I'm not sure I can help, sorry." She felt her bitterness and pain grow within her, a chasm that threatened to consume her. Hot tears stung her eyes as she acknowledged the state of her soul war with Yahweh's mercy. She stubbornly clung to the icy wall of hatred.

Hur sighed. Bending down, he whispered so that only she could hear.

"I'm actually thinking of you, Deborah. You have a gift that could earn you favour here, and remove you from Sisera's hand. His mother is one of the few people Sisera will listen to."

She turned her head. "Why would you show me kindness?" she asked suspiciously.

His face puckered in a sad half-smile. "I have my own reasons. But I've seen him try to break you – I remember the spark I saw in you the day I first met you – I'd hate to see it go out."

Deborah felt a single tear roll down her cheek, his kind words touched her in a way that Sisera's cruelty could no longer do.

She didn't want to tell him that the spark had gone already; she looked at him and sighed with resignation. "Then take me to her…"

Deborah followed Hur to Ariya's quarters. The walls were lined with basalt, carved with engravings of Asherah and her children in poses of worship; offerings of human sacrifice and sexual obscenities told a story of debasement. Vases filled with fresh flowers on stands carved from acacia wood adorned the space, and a marble table was lined with ointments, oils and burning incense that filled the air. The doors of Ariya's rooms were held open by guards. The matriarch lay on a large bed carved out of Lebanese cedar and a thick mattress. Like a tiny doll, huddled under exquisite oriental throws and propped up with luxurious cushions, lay Ariya, frail and scared, as she was gripped with pain. Her linen robe was soaked with perspiration while her ladies-in-waiting tried to reassure her, wiping her face with wet towels. She turned her head, beginning to cough, and one of the waiting ladies bent, holding a linen cloth to her mouth. When she had finished, she turned weakly to Hur.

"Who is this?" she groaned.

"She is a Hebrew, Mistress. She has knowledge of herbal medicine with which she was able to heal some of the slaves."

Despite her sickness, Ariya maintained her poised loftiness and arrogance; Deborah almost had to admire her strength of character.

"I have the best physicians in Canaan," she answered with disdain, turning her head away.

"I'm sorry my lady, I'll take her away," Hur said, taking Deborah's arm and turning to leave.

"Stop!" she demanded, turning to whisper to one of her attendants.

"My lady asks if you are Sisera's Priestess."

"No, I am Yahweh's Prophetess."

"She bids you to tell her what is wrong with her."

Deborah felt sickened with indignation. "I am no soothsayer. I do not command Yahweh to do as I bid."

"Ask him!" Ariya moaned.

Feeling Yahweh's hand upon her now, for the first time in over a year, she fought with the idea of Him helping her.

Trust.

She nodded, in response to both voices, and slipping to her knees, she pressed her forehead against the floor. After a few moments, she looked up, fixing her eyes on the mother of her enemy with a steady confidence.

"There is blood on the linen."

Ariya's lady-in-waiting's eyes widened slightly, and her head shook, almost imperceptibly. She covered the distance between them and whispered to Hur.

"Master said we are not to mention to her."

"Show me the cloth!" Ariya croaked.

The lady-in-waiting looked hesitant.

"Show me!" She broke into a cough again.

The woman held the cloth to Ariya, who nodded, gesturing to her lady to come to her. She bent down.

"Find the girl what she needs."

Deborah followed Ariya's lady-in-waiting to the kitchen. She smiled sadly as she recalled Miriam explaining how to make the remedy, imagining Tamar's hut with the herbs and ointment lined on the shelf.

She crushed cloves of garlic, mixing it to milk and stirring in honey. She felt the familiar ache of loss in her heart as she allowed her memories to travel to Ephraim, lingering on her mother, Isaac and gentle, wise Tobias. As she returned to Ariya with the mixture, she pushed her memories back to the vault within her heart, and comforted herself with the thought that they were safe.

Isis had grown suspicious, even fearful. The mood amongst the slaves had changed. Their cringing hopelessness had weakened, and in its place there was a quiet peace that was militant in its strength, and it disturbed him. He was astute enough to know that the Hebrew faith was his true enemy. He would need to act quickly if he was to crush their spirits. He would renew their fear and in doing so, quench their faith.

Their workload was doubled and those who could not work were beaten. If they collapsed, they were killed and replaced by others; Hebrew life was cheap.

One night, Etiya was taken by the guards. The look of fear in her eyes as they locked with Deborah's seared her mind, like a red-hot branding iron. When Deborah returned the next evening after work, Etiya lay motionless on her pallet, her body and face were bruised and she would not speak. When Deborah tried to speak to her, Etiya's eyes held Deborah's and then closed, the unspoken words cut the air: "Let me go Deborah. It is enough now." The next morning she passed from this life. Her empty place was taken by another, but the hollow darkness that her loss had created was a chasm of grief and bitterness that hungered for vengeance.

Deborah felt numb, her faith seemed more of a memory than a reality; a mere thread she held onto. Hope had died, the notion of deliverance, a burnt shell, like the villages she had seen destroyed and Etiya's wasted life. *Sisera has won. This is what he wanted. I cannot bear to see my people suffer any more. I feel dead inside, with nothing to offer and no hope to give; I feel only hatred. My desire for revenge, to see him suffer, consumes me. Yahweh, end the life of him who oppresses Your people. I have failed you, Yahweh, take me now, take me from this life.*

She sobbed, wrapping her arms around her body, in a vain attempt to hold herself together. She longed for the security and love of her village. She hungered for freedom. But above all she longed for revenge; to see the man she hated, who had hurt those she loved, who had twisted her soul with bitterness and pain - to see him suffer.

And the words came, like light out of darkness: *let go.*

The words travelled through her, exposing truth: the things that give security in this world also bind us to it.

A divine plumb-line of holiness had been dropped into her soul and it offered a choice: to stay where she was, to seek freedom and revenge in her own strength, or to relinquish all to Him, to lay to death all that she was, her hopes and dreams…even her hatred of Sisera…and trust only in Him.

I relinquish my village, my nation, myself, to You…and my hatred of him. I trust in Your vengeance. Only, take the pain, it hurts so much! End my life as I know it and live in me and through me, and I will be obedient to you.

And then, from within the abyss came the voice: *I am with you. I am your gravity now – your inner horizon. My light will guide you. I am your strength; we fight as one.*

Deborah slept.

When she awoke, something had changed. No great sense of His presence, or overwhelming sense of faith, only the absence of despair. It was as if the world had shifted, so that scene from the window she had been watching it from had not changed, but rather become truly defined.

She recalled the cocoon she had seen in Sisera's fortress and remembered her father's words on that sunny day in Ephraim. Tebah had found a chrysalis and had slit it open, hoping to free a butterfly, and had been upset to find a gloopy, liquid mess. Her father had smiled and explained that in order for a caterpillar to turn into a butterfly, it first needs to digest itself. All of the defining characteristics of the caterpillar cease to be, only the central essence remains and then it is reformed into something beautiful and free.

The words of the prophetic vision she had had came back to her: the spinning darkness that would strip her bare. She had been held in place by so many things: her family and village, her need for others' approval, even her desire for revenge. Now, when everything else was gone, the fragile cords that had kept her secure in this world snapped. She let go in desperation, and He became her gravity. Now, only He mattered and man's hold on her was gone. Fear was replaced with peace.

After three weeks, Ariya's health improved greatly. Deborah was scrubbing the stone floors of the hallway when Hur found her. He seemed anxious.

"Ariya has summoned you. She wishes to visit the temple and offer sacrifice to Baal, to thank him for prolonging her life." Deborah recoiled at the thought, and at the same moment resignedly acknowledged her position and lack of choice.

The queue outside the temple spilled down the steps as the priests took their money and showed them to a booth. Deborah swallowed at the horror that confronted her as she passed the blackened, glowing remains of a small, skeletal form on the altar; a man knelt before it, his head bowed as the priest chanted his blessing.

She recognised the priest that addressed them as the same she had seen on her last visit. He had an elegance that made him appear to glide as his purple robes trailed the floor and his eyes shone with what Deborah first believed to be elation, but the shiver it sent down her soul made her cringe.

He greeted Ariya with a manner that was stiffly pious but laced with a sordid intimacy that made Deborah feel sick. He led her into one of the rooms similar to the one Deborah had been taken to on her last visit.

"We wait here," Hur said, motioning to a stone bench. Deborah sat down next to Ariya's lady-in-waiting, feeling the unsettling nausea that she had felt last time.

She watched the women and men leading their 'worshippers' into the booths and wondered how any person could stoop so low as to be a temple prostitute. She felt the eyes of one of them on her and recognised her as the same girl she had noticed on her last visit. She seemed familiar, so familiar; her long hair framed her beautiful face, falling to her waist, her scant clothing accentuating her feminine curves. She looked away and as she did so, a flood of memories hit Deborah, a wave of understanding that sickened her to her core: it was of *that* day in Ephraim, lying in the forest and the screams, followed by only one memory: Ariel, as she was taken away. That was thirteen years ago. Thirteen years of slavery, of forced service to Canaan. What had they done to her? Ariel's dead, hopeless eyes turned away as she led her next worshipper into the booth. Deborah looked at the other temple prostitutes as anger and pity gripped her.

Once again, she felt the weight of her own powerlessness and pain, and allowed it now to strengthen her anger and resolve.

On the way home, in Ariya's luxurious carriage, Deborah sat silently. Now that her health had returned, Ariya had regained her arrogant air of superiority.

She spoke to her lady-in-waiting who fanned her; the summer heat was upon them. "… We can be thankful that Sisera's irrigation of the Hebrew lands is almost complete. The crops would never survive otherwise."

"You are right, my lady, my lord has the foresight and knowledge to yield the best from our fertile lands."

Ariya glanced at Deborah and a flicker of pity shadowed her eyes.

"War is always painful and distasteful, even if it is necessary. I am sorry for the oppression of your people, even though it is inevitable that I am pleased with the victory of my own."

Deborah nodded. "It is the nature of mankind to seek to prosper, to gain security at the expense of others. But it is the nature of the divine to orchestrate these events, and the nature of a father to defend his children."

Ariya held Deborah's eyes for a moment, weighing the spoken and hidden implication of her words.

"It is said you have the favour of the gods, that you speak their thoughts. Is it true?"

Deborah laughed with dark humour; she tilted her head. "You must have a strange notion of the gods if you find my current position to be one of favour."

Ariya, her lips pursed, cocked a pensive eyebrow. "And yet, here you are."

Deborah quietly acknowledged the woman's probing and carefully considered her response. "I trust in the goodness of Yahweh because I know Him. I have known pain and faced death, yet I trust in His hand, and I speak as *He* gives me utterance."

"He told you what was wrong with me…" the older woman replied thoughtfully.

They sat quietly for the remainder of the journey while Ariya gazed ahead of her. Deborah was unable to get the picture of Ariel's face from her mind. She prayed inwardly as she silently cried out with desperate urgency.

As summer bore down upon them, the workload increased. Within the slaves quarters a silent kinship had evolved from the seed Deborah had unknowingly planted; in saving the girl's life, hope that should never have lived grew wings. Within their pain and hardship, they had begun to look out for each other. At times, with no more than a smile of empathy, a word of encouragement; a hand that reached out to stop another from falling or a glass of water that was given at risk and cost.

Isis was ruthless in his expectations and their lives were cheap, easily replaced by a growing number.

The workday had ended and Deborah, exhausted, her feet and hands blistered, had collapsed on her pallet, the familiar pain of hunger cut into her. She had just drifted off to sleep when Hur came and tapped her.

"Ariya commands you to come."

Deborah frowned. "You seem worried."

"She is not alone."

"Sisera!" Deborah felt the unconscious pound of her heart.

He shook his head. "Hurriya and Keret are there. She used to be a temple priestess and he is a merchant and an Elder in Sisera's council…" The words he left unsaid hung in the air between them: he was worried.

Deborah forced herself to focus on Yahweh: *use me, Yahweh, and I will glorify Your name.*

The door to Ariya's private chambers was open and the sound of voices fluttered down the corridor. Deborah tried to gauge the tone: grave, serious. Her heart picked up a beat as they entered.

Hur bowed before the matriarch. "Madame, as you requested, the Hebrew girl is here."

Deborah felt the two newcomers assess her as she sought Yahweh through the smog of her apprehension. The woman, in her mid-forties, was still beautiful, her dark hair coiled in a thick plait on her head. She recognised her from Ariya's celebrations; she had been the one to challenge the older lady. Deborah's heart had warmed to her then. Her husband was older, his face drawn and fleshy pockets hung under his eyes. Yet he had a stature that alluded to intelligence and strength.

Since the night of her desperation and dream, she often felt Yahweh's spirit on her as she had not before. With it came a level of insight and perception, an instinctive knowledge that came from His spirit upon her. She sighed inwardly. They came for help. Her eyes rested on Ariya, who sat with her back straight, her hands crossed on her lap, her lips thin, set in a straight line. They curved slightly.

"I have spoken of your...gift."

Deborah bowed her head, her heart pounding. She kept her voice low.

"But it is not my gift, Madame. It is Yahweh's gift."

Ariya waved her hand dismissively and picking up a grape, popped it into her mouth. She dismissed herself, nodding to Hur to remain.

Deborah bowed her head. *Yahweh.*

I love all people Deborah, show them who I Am that I might warn them of what will come if they will not stop oppressing My people.

Speak MY words.

Deborah turned to Hurriya and saw the desperate, empty void behind her eyes. Then she knew; a flood of emotion and imagery flooded her own heart as she saw beyond the beauty and dignity to the brokenness. She clasped her hands nervously, her empathy and Yahweh's compassion outweighing her nerves and giving her the courage to speak.

"Fifteen years ago, you were a priestess, ambitious and gifted. You initiated the building of the temple that stands today." She noted Hurriya's intake of breath and continued. "As is Canaan's custom, you suggested that a worship offering be given: the foundation of the temple would be laid with the first born sons of the city. Yours was the first to die, laid at the cornerstone. But you never conceived again. Since then, each night you are tormented by nightmares, the screams of children and the blood that flows from the altar. It covers you until you cannot see, cannot breathe; and then your own screams merge with theirs. Horror grips you and then you wake." She looked up, the sense of Yahweh's power upon her.

Hurriya was pale, her hand clapped over her mouth as the strong, graceful lady that had entered the room dissolved. She gave in to the sobs that travailed her soul as her husband knelt and took her in his arms. It was not difficult to see that he loved her dearly. She knelt too, and lowering her voice so that only they would hear, she added: "What ails your body is the guilt and grief within your soul. For your stomach, use fenugreek seeds, sweetened with honey in tea for two weeks, and drink milk rather than wine." She lay her hand on the woman's. "But this in itself will not cure you. You must know the forgiveness of the one true God, and then you must learn to forgive yourself." Her eyes met Hurriya's and held them before flitting nervously to Ariya.

"Perhaps we could meet again, privately, by your will Ariya?" Keret's tone was polite but commanding. Deborah smiled inwardly as the alpha male and dominant woman silently negotiated. Ariya smiled stiffly.

"Speak to Isis." She motioned to Hur with a wave of her hand.

21

...there was an alliance between Jabin king of Hazor and the family of Heber the Kenite. Judges 4:17
1242 BC - Jael

Jael watched Meira play with her younger sister, Levia, and brother, Uriah. She had heard it said that a mother normally has one willful child and one compliant child, however she had come to the conclusion that this depended very much on who the parents were. Levia had been named 'Lioness', for she had come out of Jael's womb roaring, and had cried every moment she wasn't being fed or held. Uriah had come out with the cord around his neck and his face was blue, and they had thought him to be still born until he smiled. Adva said it was probably wind; newborn babies don't smile. But Jael said he had defied death; that he was a fighter. She called him Uriah, meaning 'my light is Yahweh'.

Meira had just begun her monthly flow at fourteen years old, and Heber had already begun talking about finding her a suitable husband. Meira had poked her tongue out at him behind his back and venomously told her mother that she would not be marrying for some time, and that when she did, she would have a say in it. Jael sighed, for she knew that Heber would use his daughter's beauty to further his own ambition, and there would be little she, or Meria, could do about it. Her heart twisted with protective anger and fear for her child.

Levia was eleven and showed all the symptoms of being a middle child; she skulked around looking for any trouble that she could find. She was tenacious and quick tempered and the only child that Heber showed any interest in. He had found her beating one of the servants because he had not obeyed her – Heber had laughed and commended her character.

Uriah at five years old was still unable to speak. Mary said that she feared he had lacked oxygen when he came from her womb. By his sixth birthday, it was clear that Uriah was slower than his sisters had been, and lacked co-ordination. Heber, who had shown some pride in having a son, now sneered in disdain at the boy's clumsiness and lack of communication.

Following the successful completion of Jabin's chariots, Heber had brought some of the hardest-working slaves home with him. They were to build a wall around their land to protect it from raids, as well as farm it. When the slaves first arrived, Jael had been horrified to see their state; their skin drawn and sallow, their backs were scourged with lash marks, and their eyes desperate and empty.

She had learned over the years to pay lip service to Heber. She had empathy for him, which she did not confuse for love, but she saw the brokenness that had moulded him, and the wrong choices he had made as a result of this.

She knew that, had she told Zimran that she wanted to leave, he would have helped her escape and though her heart longed to be with him, she sensed Yahweh's hand on her life and believed that He would use the difficulties to perform His will. And so, with shrewd judgement and strength of character, she trusted Yahweh to help her navigate the storms. She had the respect and loyalty of the slaves, for they knew she was their advocate.

"I have a caravan coming from Hebron tomorrow. Make sure you are ready for them," Heber grunted.

She nodded, her lips pursed and turned to leave.

She heard him coming behind her and braced herself as he grabbed her arm; he was in a bad mood.

"Yes, Heber, I'll do it," she replied through gritted teeth, gently wrenching herself away from his grip and hastening away.

She sighed heavily, feeling the muscles in her shoulders tighten as they did when Heber was at home.

"Adva, he's back. Keep the children away from him as much as you can, but have them ready and prepared in case he asks for them."

Adva looked up. Uriah was hitting a rock with the head of a wooden doll and repeating Heber's name.

Jael rubbed the back of her neck, her anxiety mounting.

"I'll make sure they are ready, don't worry." She squeezed Jael's arm.

"Thank you."

The next morning the spring air was cool. Jael stood up early, and quietly woke Meira, both picking up their bows and arrows as they left. She loved their early morning hunting trips together. She had asked Zimran to bring her the weapons, and since Heber was on good terms with Jabin, she had not been forbidden them as other Hebrews had been. The bow and arrows were made of ash and worked well. She had learned, over the years, to use it with some precision and then taught Meira.

Wild tulips, purple irises and crocuses dotted the meadow, leading into the forest that bordered Lake Hula. She breathed in the heady smell of the forest, earthy and fresh, and felt her anxiety dissipate.

Seeing movement to her right, she nudged Meira, who reached for an arrow and nocked the string on her bow. She aimed it at the wild impala that tugged unknowingly at a stubborn root. The arrow sped through the air, embedding itself into the animal's neck. Jael gave her a look of approval as the animal twitched, taking its last steps before falling to the ground.

"We can share it with the slaves," Meira stated. "There's enough."

Jael nodded, smiling with pride; she had been thinking the same.

"Make sure your father doesn't find out."

Meira nodded now; she enjoyed their mother-daughter conspiracies.

When they reached the tents, the clearing was hectic with preparations for the imminent arrival of the caravan. Jael rushed out, her heart pounding with the thought of Zimran's arrival. They were early! She was not expecting them until nightfall. She beckoned some of the servants to bring water for the animals and drivers. Then she ordered another to kill a sheep and prepare it to be roasted in the evening.

"Get the men to come and help!" she heard her husband bark.

They were returning to the clearing when she saw him. Even after all the years, her initial reaction was to run to him. She stopped herself, waiting for him to see her. Zimran' s eyes seemed to scan the crowd and then settled on her. She felt herself drawn into their embrace, as his lips curved slightly, and it seemed that the distance between them vanished. He looked the same; his dark skin never seemed to age.

A woman appeared from the caravan, her skin as dark as Zimran' s, and slipped her arms around his waist - and Jael felt her heart constrict. She knew that Zimran had women whose company he enjoyed, though he had never settled with any. She understood, too, that she had no right to claim him for her own. She had been given the decision to be his wife and had turned him down. Yet seeing him with other women was the worst sort of pain; a poison that sickened her spirit. She acknowledged, too, that one day he would take a woman to be his wife and to have his children, and did not know how she would bear it: either the thought of never seeing him again, or seeing him with his own family. And yet she acknowledged her own selfishness in this, too.

Jael organised the servants, handing out bowls for washing and then setting up long tables in the clearing. Platters of bread and fruit were placed next to pitchers of wine. Jez was busy lighting the fire over which the sheep would be roasted, while other servants were setting up temporary tents for the drivers.

Evening came and the camp grew quiet, a few men sat talking quietly around the glowing embers of the fire. Amongst them was Heber. His slurred voice was louder than the others. Most slept, exhausted after the long journey. Zimran and the woman were nowhere to be seen.

Jael felt shattered; it seemed a week had passed since she had awoken with Meira and gone hunting. She made her way to her tent.

"Jael!" Heber's voice hooked beneath her skin, pulling her back, and she felt the familiar surge of adrenalin. She knew what he was like when he was drunk. She forced herself to respond calmly, careful not to awaken the beast she knew was lurking beneath the drunken visage.

"What are you doing?"

"I was going to bed." Her mind raced for the answer he was expecting her to give. "Was there something else you required?"

He grabbed her wrists; his eyes were narrow slits that were looking for offense on which to react. She knew she shouldn't, but she met his scrutiny.

"Next time I bring a caravan, be ready. You embarrassed me today in front of my men and it will not happen again. Do you understand me?" He ran his eyes over her, his mouth twisted with disdain. "You're a mess. You look like the wife of a shepherd, not a man of wealth."

She knew better than to comment on the fact that they had arrived early, but she would not apologise either. His men were there and he would not risk a scene now. "Yes, Heber." She forced the words out.

He released her and she sighed with relief as he walked back to the fire.

While Adva, Mary and the children slept in the front section of the tent, Jael's divan was separated by a large curtain. Mary was still awake. When Jael pulled back the entrance curtain, she sat up groaning in pain.

"I couldn't sleep," she whispered.

"I don't suppose you have eaten." She winced as she stood, pouring
Jael a cup of milk and handing her bread.
She took the cup from her hands, they were shaking and her emotions felt brittle. "I don't know how you can deal with Heber so calmly when he is so rude."

Mary sighed. "When we feel angry with someone there is usually a part of the picture that we don't see. If we understood as Yahweh does, without our own brokenness and sin, we would have mercy."

Her answer annoyed Jael. "Perhaps, but we still have choices to make and there are consequences attached to those decisions. Some of us at least try and make the right decisions," she snapped.

"Yes, but even those right actions can cause pain if they are done with the wrong motive," Mary answered gently.

Jael scowled. It was late and she was in no mind for the 'poor Heber' speech; she had just wanted to rant. She let the conversation drop because she didn't want to take her frustration out on Mary - and she knew she would if she carried on.

Saying goodnight, she lay awake for some time, her mind going over the plight of the slaves, of her love for Zimran and her worries over Miera's future. As she was drifting off to sleep Mary's words echoed in her mind and she began to feel as though there had been something that Mary had been trying to tell her. She told herself she was being neurotic, and forced her thoughts to serve a more productive route.

22

"But I say to you, love your enemies and pray for those who persecute you, so that you may be sons of your Father who is in heaven; for He causes His sun to rise on the evil and the good, and sends rain on the righteous and the unrighteous.
Matthew 5:45

1247 BC – Deborah

Deborah was initially hesitant about sharing her faith with Hurriya; how would this woman, who had served Canaan as a priestess, identify with Yahweh as a Holy, but merciful God?

But Hurriya had long since abandoned her faith in gods that had taken her child from her and was hungry for the forgiveness and goodness of a God who offered mercy.

Keret had returned from a council meeting with the governor and Sisera. Many slaves had died during the heat and epidemic of the summer and more were needed to bring in the bountiful harvest. Sisera was preparing for more raids on villages.

He heard Hurriya's laughter greet him like a missed friend, and when he saw her, her eyes alight and her expression free from the sorrow that had clung to her body and soul - he felt something shift within him. The Hebrew God was powerful, was good, was real and he could not ignore it, for he was grateful beyond words. But this acknowledgement was a double-edged sword that pierced his conscience; Deborah was *His* servant and it was *her* God, *His* children that they oppressed.

He stood in the door, watching the laughter and dialogue between his wife and the Hebrew prophetess, and he allowed the question that bubbled from his unconscious to form in his mind: *What could he do?*

There was a contrast to Deborah's existence, in that while she was still taken to battle and forced to witness Sisera's violence, it now fuelled her relationship to Yahweh with a deeper fervency. In doing so, she felt a strength grow within her that was independent of her own fragility, as though she was being carried or hidden. From that place she grew in both compassion and anointing.

Her relationship with Ariya had changed too. The matriarch had petitioned Sisera for Deborah to be moved to her quarters. Sisera had been initially suspicious, but, convinced of his success in breaking Deborah, he no longer saw her gift as a threat. In his mind, she was now the instrument of Canaan, and he trusted his mother's control and ambition to keep it thus. Ariya reminded Deborah of a loom, all the threads held tightly together with complete control. When she smiled, it was as if the threads were pulled, and if she loosened one for a second, the whole tapestry would fall apart. And yet she had begun to expose the loose threads that had been pulled through to the under-side of the picture and, as Deborah perceived the extent of disarray and fragility that was masked by the outward picture of disdain and militant superiority, she felt pity for the woman.

"You must judge me, but you are ignorant. Generals must be emotionless to do what they have to do. That is why his father was defeated. He was weak, though I loved him," she said, abruptly turning away.

"His father?"

"Yes, he was defeated at Yareah, by *your* people." If the accusation in her tone was unclear, the frosty glare she gave Deborah was not.

Deborah's mind spun as she recalled the stories of Yareah. She recalled her first encounter with Ariya at her party and realised how Ariya had allowed the humiliation and grief of her husband's defeat to shape her parenting of Sisera into a driven, ruthless killer.

Softly, she replied: "Your husband was not defeated because he was weak, but because he defied Yahweh." Tentatively, she added, "The same God was in Yareah as is with me. Joshua was obedient to Yahweh, and He pulled down the walls of Yareah. A man is not weak because he cannot fight and win against Yahweh - he is simply mortal." She swallowed, her mouth felt dry and she could hear her heart pounding in her ears as Yahweh within her warred with her fears and prejudice. She felt an unexpected compassion for Ariya, for she knew now that Yahweh would deliver his people and that it would end with the death of Sisera. Despite her hard and aloof manner, Deborah saw that Ariya was the product of her own pain and ignorance, but she was still a mother who loved her son. Yet how could she tell her that unless her son repented and turned from oppressing her people, he would die?

And she wanted Sisera to die; she hated him and wanted him to pay for what he had done to her people. It was righteous judgement. But knowing these people, she felt pity for them too. They were carnal, sinful and greedy, and many of them were cruel murderers. But some were also kind, generous, compassionate, hungry for truth and terribly broken and misguided.

"Not one Canaanite escaped that city," Ariya smiled sadly.

"One family survived. Their house was built in the wall and when the wall fell down, it alone remained standing."

"The rumours were true? The traitor Rahab was spared?" she reflected bitterly.

Deborah nodded, her heart pounding. "But her and her family's survival was miraculous; only Yahweh could have performed it, as you know. She was promised deliverance for helping Yahweh's people and later married a Hebrew man named Salmon. My father knew their son, Boaz, and his wife Ruth. He died before I was born, but I met Ruth and their son, Obed." She recalled Ehud's summons of the Elders to Bethlehem. Their family relationship with Boaz's went back to the wilderness days, when Salmon and Amos' grandfather had known each other. She felt the dull ache of remorse as she acknowledged how Obed's harmless mention of the Hebrews attacking Canaanite farms had set in place a rolling stone that would eventually have such disastrous consequences. And yet, still it grew in momentum, for she would not be here if he had not.

How Yahweh uses our human frailty and mistakes for His great purpose and glory; surely these are the greater miracles of His sovereignty, she mused.

The following day, Deborah was brought once again to Ariya's quarters. She sat quietly by the window, looking out over the fertile plains of Israel, irrigated with the cultural expertise of Canaan and farmed by Hebrew slaves.

Yahweh deliver your people. Turn their hearts back to You.

"We are all pawns of mighty men and gods," the older lady stated, following Deborah's gaze.

Deborah lifted her eyes for a moment to look into Ariya's. She saw the ghosts of doubt that hid behind alabaster statues, and was aware that Ariya was provoking her for an opinion.

She wondered if a trap was being set for her. "So it seems," she answered tentatively.

Ariya nodded and stood.

"What is your explanation for the persecution of your people?"

Deborah realised that her answer was being weighed and that her life was in Ariya's hand. She turned her eyes inward. *Yahweh what are You saying, what is the reply You would give?*

"As you implied, we are each answerable for our actions. My people have turned from the one, true God and in doing so have placed themselves in the hands of their enemy."

"You do not believe my son's military prowess is due to his own ability, but your people's wayward stupidity?" Ariya provoked, her mouth curved with caustic humour.

Deborah felt sweat bead on her forehead. "You said yourself that we are the pawns of great men and gods, but surely that is hierarchical? Therefore, even Sisera must bow his knee to God."

Ariya smiled, tilting her head by way of conceding to Deborah's argument.

"You are considered a prophetess by your people, are you not?"

"By some."

Ariya motioned dismissively with her hand; she had no time for humility. She smiled and Deborah saw the net laid out before her.

"So what has your God told you regarding my son?"

Deborah swallowed as the ground beneath her feet slipped away and that she had no option but to fall with it and hope she survived. She could withhold the truth, but she knew that her time with Ariya was not by chance; it was Yahweh's mercy to warn them. She took a deep breath. "In Ephraim, I used to go into the mountains to pray, and there, Yahweh would speak to me. He told me that Sisera would come. He showed me the man behind the chariot and the nightmares that assault his sleep."

Ariya paled. "And you told him these?"

"I did." Deborah bowed her head, willing Ariya to stop.

The older woman grew thoughtful, for the question that lingered in the air between them was too great, too dreadful to be uttered. A sense of dark premonition warned her that not to know was better. Deborah watched Ariya's inner conflict and wondered at the nature of mankind: made in God's image, we are ever restless to know the future and then, when presented with the option, we realise that higher wisdom shields our frail humanity from the pain of existing in a fallen world.

Ariya turned away, dismissing Deborah with a wave of her hand. Deborah sighed with relief as she returned to her chores.

When Ariya commanded her presence again the next day, Deborah knew what she would ask. Her heart pounded as she walked the marble corridors to Ariya's apartments, and she pleaded Yahweh for His mercy, for both herself and Ariya.

Dark rings shadowed the older woman's eyes as she clasped her hands in her lap. She twisted a ring nervously on her finger as she bid Deborah to sit by the window once again. Deborah watched the dust cloud the air as a score of iron chariots came into view, then the sound of the wheels as they rattled over the stones, and the hooves of the horses. Finally, voices and the whinnying of tired horses as they entered the mighty gates of Harosheth.

Ariya's ladies-in-waiting attended to her, one rubbing her hands with almond oil, the other brushing and braiding her hair. She sat quietly for some time, her eyes flickering between Deborah and the window. A plate of cakes and a bowl of honeyed almonds were placed before her along with a pitcher of grape juice. One of the ladies poured for her, tasting the wine before handing her the cup. Ariya must have gestured to Deborah, because a cup was passed to her too.

"Eat." It was a command, though gently spoken.

Deborah picked up a honey cake. Her stomach growled. She felt as though she had been hungry for over fifteen years, and yet she felt no appetite. She knew the question that was on Ariya's lips.

"Has Yahweh shown you the future for my son?"

There it was.

"Prophecy is always dependent on our behaviour. Yahweh gives men choice." She felt herself squirm inside.

Ariya stood; her voice was soft, dangerous and anxious. "You are avoiding my question."

Yahweh?

Speak. Warn them. I love all men.

Deborah gazed out of the latticed window, and when she turned to Ariya it was with such compassion that her eyes filled with tears.

"I cannot..." she shook her head.

"Speak!" Ariya demanded.

Deborah's eyes met hers, imploring, not out of fear now, but pity. She was a mother...albeit mother to Sisera.

"I must know." Ariya's voice lost its arrogance as the first trace of fear began to spin their web across her thoughts.

Deborah nodded; the answer was thudding soundlessly in the depth of her soul. She wanted to retreat. As she began to speak, her voice felt distant.

"You sit by the window, watching:

Why is my son's chariot so long coming? You ask.

Why is the clatter of his chariots delayed?

Your ladies, too, are concerned; they talk among themselves.

One of them answers wisely:

Are they not finding and dividing the spoils?

A woman or two for each man

Colourful and embroidered garments for Sisera.

But he does not come."

Deborah closed her eyes, feeling the arms of the guards lift her from her seat and drag her away. Ariya stood, watching from the window, her arms wrapped around her body, her face pale as though death had already touched it. Her ladies-in-waiting tried to console her, to tell her it was not so, that her son would always win, and she tried to believe them.

She did not call for Deborah the next day and Deborah wondered, waiting for her punishment to befall her.

Weeks passed and the days grew shorter. Deborah stood on a stool polishing one of the alabaster statues when Keret found her. If he knew anything of Deborah's prophecy to Ariya, he said nothing. Her conversations with Keret and Hurriya inevitably revolved around Yahweh, and both were hungry to learn more. She learned that, aside from sitting on Sisera's council, Keret was a also a wealthy merchant, trading in murex-dyed linen.

"I have been studying the Law of Moses," he confessed. His eyes shone like a soldier's after a new conquest.

"Hurriya and I would like to offer a sacrifice of thanksgiving at the temple of Yahweh. We would like to take you with us since we have no experience of this."

Shiloh. The tabernacle. The words formed an oasis in her mind.

She smiled, futility clouding her hope. "Nothing would please me more, but have you thought how you will get me past Ariya and Sisera?"

"Sisera will meet us in Ramah, and afterwards we will travel with him to Gezer. He requires my council regarding a delicate political issue, and I have persuaded him that your presence might be...*beneficial*," he smirked.

Deborah frowned.

"And have you told Sisera that we are going to the Temple?" she asked dubiously, wondering if murex fumes had gone to his head.

"No, I have told him I am going on business, and that Hurriya has asked you to accompany her, for health reasons. But I *will* look to establish my business there; I have heard they have a sizeable market. The war between the Greeks and Trojans in the Aegean Sea has made export both dangerous and expensive; I am looking to increase business in Israel."

Deborah felt excitement warm her; it was an alien feeling after three and a half years of darkness.

They travelled with an armed guard to Shiloh and hence the journey was uneventful. Hur accompanied them, by Sisera's order.

Deborah's heart twisted as she once again witnessed the devastation that had been wrought on her people. Entire villages, which would once have been like hers in Ephraim, were laid waste, burnt to the ground. Corpses, impaled to the doorposts of their homes, had been left decomposing, to be feasted on by carrion and wild animals because there were none to bury them.

High places were built on many of the hills, their presence highlighted by swooping crows and vultures. Deborah was also aware during the journey that they were being watched. Robbers that attacked travellers on the roads waited behind rocks and in the trees, kept at bay only by the armed guard that travelled with Keret's caravan.

By the time they reached Shiloh, Deborah began to understand Yahweh's purpose in her capture by Sisera; she had felt the desperate hopelessness of her nation and ached with them. She knew that He was their only hope and she longed to see her nation comforted, strengthened and united in Yahweh, just as He had saved her.

His words to her returned: '*a mother to Israel*'. The promises Yahweh had given to her years before germinated. Tiny seeds that she had felt to be dead, burst open, their roots yet unformed. In the natural, the idea seemed impossible, women did not aspire to greatness; and she had no ambition – only to see her people delivered. However, she acknowledged that her own survival was a miracle, and she knew that Yahweh had kept her alive for a reason.

Deborah remembered the last time she had been in Shiloh: over fifteen years ago, during the Feast of Tabernacles. The streets had been alive with the heady excitement of celebration, spiritual praise, thanksgiving and reunions. She remembered leaving her family to return home with Raisa and Tobias – all to escape the boy who made her feel so nervous. Her thoughts wandered once again to his easy laugh and deep brown eyes, and warmth bubbled up within her. She smiled sadly at how easy, how wonderful, life had been, and how she had taken it all for granted.

The city was busy, but the foothills that had once been surrounded with thousands of tiny booths were bare.

"You seem sad," Hurriya commented, her head tilted with concern.

Feeling ungrateful - she was so thankful to be here - Deborah explained: "I have so many memories here – of my family, of my people. And it's changed so much."

They stayed in an inn not far from the Tabernacle. Leaving Hurriya to rest, Keret took Deborah and Hur to the market with him to buy a lamb for the evening's sacrifice.

"I'm curious to see if Shiloh's market is suitable for the linen trade," Keret said thoughtfully, his business mind scanning the produce and type of customers the town drew.

The lambs were tethered and held in a small, enclosed area. They bleated loudly as they were examined for blemish. Keret raised a critical eyebrow at Deborah's choice.

"It's expensive." He raised a shrewd eyebrow as he perused the gentle creatures. "How about this one?" he asked nodding toward one of the cheaper, thinner lambs.

She smiled at him and shrugged. "It's supposed to be expensive; it has to be without blemish. It's about giving Yahweh our best because He gives us His."

"Like an investment," Keret raised a quizzical eyebrow, his eyes sparkling with humour.

Deborah clicked her lips in mock exasperation.

Keret grinned as he considered the Hebrew girl's logic; whilst his financial reasoning defied her argument, he had come to realise that wealth came in many forms: he had seen Hurriya come to life in recent weeks and had not seen her so well, nor so peaceful in years. He had found himself surprised to conclude that there was no other logical explanation: it was Yahweh. He handed the money over without another word, acknowledging the steely strength and resourcefulness Deborah possessed. She had an integrity born out of compassion, and wisdom that gained her favour with people. They were qualities he could use.

"We could do with buying some more torches while we are here. I saw someone selling them on the way in." He handed her a pouch of money. "I should get back to Hurriya. Can you and Hur fetch some and find your own way back?"

"Of course." She could find her way around Shiloh blindfold. The memories of her people were everywhere; she saw her family in every open window, on the hillside, winding through the market as they laughed and chattered. But she was not that carefree Hebrew girl anymore. She was a slave. She could no more run from this place, as she had once fled to the hills, than she could escape the torment of her memories.

Deborah wound her way through the myriad of stalls, passing the pungent smells of spices, the man selling carved knives, the old lady selling oranges and a Hebrew man who was selling olive oil. She scanned the stalls, looking for the stall selling torches that Keret had seen on the way in.

And then she stopped still, as though the world around her had grown quiet, diminished until only *he* remained. She watched him for a moment, as though he were unreal, belonging to a different lifetime. A memory she had pushed into a locked room, along with so many others. Yet he was different, an unconscious link representing rescue that had travelled with her; he had saved her life once. Her heart lurched and she allowed his name slip from her lips; the sound of it created a warm glow within her.

"Lapidoth."

Hur gave her a strange look but said nothing.

His face had taken on the strong chiseled edge that his youth had alluded to. His deep brown eyes still carried their depth and sensitivity and his mouth was curved into a peaceful smile that seemed to travel inward. Feeling suddenly awkward in the strange encounter of her past and present, she pulled her headscarf around her face and kept her eyes respectfully lowered, maintaining her role as a slave. Her hand trembled as it clasped the moneybag in her hand.

She examined the torches, and then picking several up, held them out.

"How much for these?" She glanced upward, meeting his gaze. He searched her face for a moment and in one fleeting moment she saw recognition, sorrow and something she could not define.

"Six shekels for you," he smiled, holding her gaze as though to find the answers to his questions reflected in her soul. She felt the glow of their warmth fan a glowing ember within her.

Her eyes darted to Hur and she frowned. His eyes flickered with partial understanding and she watched his mind try and make sense of the situation.

"I'll give you two." She knew that Keret was expecting a bargain and that Hur would expect her to barter.

His eyes, those deep forest pools, were lit with the spark of heaven as they smiled back at her. "You have the audacity of one who plays with danger."

She returned his smile. "And you have the calm of one who watches the stars and knows your place among them."

He laughed easily, like Ephraim's stream bubbling over the rocks. He tugged his fingers through his thick wavy hair, and she recalled the habit from their last meeting. It seemed a lifetime ago. "Then, it seems I cannot argue with my destiny." He held out his hand for the money and she saw her own reflection of hope and futility stare back at her from the pools. Her hand touched his as she placed the money in his hand.

Lightning; the impression and sensation was vivid, potent and undefined.

His hand lingered a moment too long and she knew he had felt something too. Reluctantly withdrawing her hand, she forced herself to pick up the torches and walked away. She cast one last look over her shoulder and her heart lurched at the sad smile and deep, brown eyes that followed her as she melted into the crowd.

The memory of her meeting with Lapidoth created both a deep sense of loss, and a longing for a life she could never have. She had often thought of Lapidoth over the years - the handsome, lighthearted boy who had once rescued her - never had she thought to define her feelings for him. But today, both sentiment and thought, which had purposefully been buried behind walls of impossibility and pain, now aligned: she loved him. She had always loved him. Enoch had been right: he was *her* Lapidoth. And yet, there was no hope for their future. There never had been. They had always been separated by distance and circumstance as they were now. The truth gouged a hole within her, and she stepped away from its empty precipice, forcing her hopes to retreat behind the wall of blind faith.

The walls of the tabernacle stood before them and Deborah smiled with a sense of understanding as her eyes took in the quiet messages that Yahweh had given his people. Its boards, made of acacia wood, that gnarled, hardened wood, spoke of man's humanity. The brass sockets and pillars that secured the panels to the ground spoke of our natural judgement. While, in contrast, the linen panels and silver rings spoke of redemption and sacrifice. The silent messages of hope strengthened Deborah, reminding her that she was not alone: *I am part of a big picture, on a journey that is navigated by Sovereign God, and Yahweh is Almighty.*

As they left Shiloh and the tabernacle behind them, Deborah began to feel the pull of destiny strengthen her, and allowed Yahweh's compassion to speak to her as she saw the physical and spiritual poverty of His people in Israel. She interceded, beseeching Yahweh to deliver his people.

And try as she might to force her thoughts of Lapidoth behind the locked vault of her heart, his smile, his words, the memory of his touch, would pop into her thoughts and dreams.

The cart bumped over the uneven road, forming its own kind of cathartic melody. Hurriya was sensitive to Deborah's melancholy, but assumed it related only to Sisera. She leant forward and clasped her arm.

"You are worried about meeting Sisera again?"

Deborah nodded; she wasn't lying, just not sharing the whole picture.

"You know that he's scared of you. He can't kill you, because he fears the gods more; and so his only victory can be to break you." She lowered her voice conspiratorially. "Don't let him."

Deborah smiled affectionately; she had grown fond of Hurriya. "I don't understand why he would be scared of me! I'm just a Hebrew girl in his eyes, surely. In my own village very few people acknowledged my gift at all."

"In Canaanite culture, it is not only normal for women to serve as priestesses, but to make legal contracts, have positions in government and own land. Our government system is hierarchical. Power is held by great men and women to use as they wish, and others will respect and fear those people. Hebrew culture is different, I believe?" Hurriya's intelligent mind enjoyed their conversations about the differences in their culture, even as she also acknowledged Deborah's need for a distraction.

"Yes, but perhaps not as you would imagine; it may seem primitive to you because it has an entirely different foundation. We believe in a Theocracy: Yahweh is our leader, and men of God - chosen by Him for their humility, wisdom and compassion - speak for Him. Our victory is dependent on the obedience of that person to listen to His voice – rather than their charisma or personal strength. Instead of kings, we have Judges in each village and town. They are men who share Yahweh's wisdom and love in matters of disputes, but their role is mostly pastoral. They also create a unity between the tribes and occasionally call people to battle. There is often one Judge who has performed a notable act of courage to whom we look, and they unite the different tribes. But for the large part, we support and guide each other based on our strength of belief and community. Men are physically stronger; their desire to defend and fight is innate, hence they go to war, as they do in Canaan; but when they are completely obedient to Yahweh, even this is an act without fear. Of course, when we turn away from Yahweh, our failure is not only spiritual, but military and social," she sighed sadly.

Hurriya looked unconvinced. "And women, what is their role? How are they esteemed and protected?"

Deborah smiled, understanding how primitive the Hebrew social system must seem compared to sophisticated Canaanite culture. "Hebrew women are respected by Yahweh's law and protected by it; men, as part of a legal covenant made on betrothal, are to love their wives, respect them, to give them children and provide for them. There are different roles, but there is equality in marriage, based on the reality that women are created differently. Nature dictates that we have different priorities to men. We give birth, hence our desire to love and nurture is innate. The men respect women's insight and ability to take care of the emotional, educational and social elements of our village; we women knit the community together. Our relationships are reciprocal and interwoven, based on love and respect for Yahweh and Him for us. They are not governed by fear or control.

"When each of us is knitted to the heart of Yahweh, we do not need autocratic leadership. Equally, we respect and support the men who hunt and protect the village.

"Our oral traditions and written Word commend the courage, prophetic insight and wisdom of many great women."

Hurriya nodded. "I've heard that women are sent outside of the village to be separated from their families during their monthly cycle. Is this true?"

Deborah laughed at the derision on Hurriya's face. "You make it sound dreadful because you are coming at it from the idea of a religious, punitive God rather than a Holy, loving father. Yes we do have a time of separation. We call it Niddah, and in my village the house was called the 'Niddah retreat'. I longed, my whole life to be able to go. It is seen as a time when Yahweh honours women for their work of taking care of a family and home and they were given a rest. It is a time of discomfort and physical uncleanness after all. We would sit together -out of necessity - talking, laughing, and crying. We share what is on our hearts, our wisdom, counsel and dreams. In this place, our differences are sorted out as well as those of our family and village.

"A woman from our village once married a man from the city. He had grown up without the community we know and was selfish and unkind to his wife, beating her and refusing to provide for her. When the wife came to the Niddah and poured out her heart to the other women, they returned to their husbands and spoke to them. They, in turn, took the man aside and spoke sternly, but compassionately to him, explaining Yahweh's ways and those of our kin. He was loved and accepted, but held accountable; and in that way, he changed.

"The word 'Mother' in Hebrew means 'to knit or bond together' and that is what we do – Niddah is a special part of that. In our last days, when our flow stopped, we would bake and tend the garden outside the house. It was such a pretty, well-kept place. I remember as a child, when my mother returned it was always with a bowl of cakes and renewed patience and joy. It is there we find time to meet with Yahweh, understand each other and take time for ourselves, too."

Hurriya looked thoughtful for a moment, as she tried to bend her mind around such a different way of existing. Finally, she sank back onto the couch, a smile playing on her lips.

"I'd been bought up with the impression that the Hebrews were ignorant and backward in their thinking, but your argument makes sense! The loss of my child hit me in a way that it did not upset Keret. Women are different to men. We have different needs, and Yahweh understands that, doesn't He? I am also envious of the community that you have grown up with: true relationship requires love, truthfulness and commitment. Too often we walk away from relationships when they become difficult, rather than allowing it to improve us."

"There is something beautiful and strengthening about weathering life's storms together," smiled Deborah.

23

So shall they fear the name of the LORD from the west, and His glory from the rising of the sun. When the enemy shall come in like a flood, the Spirit of the LORD shall lift up a standard against him.
Isaiah 59:19

1241 BC – Jael

Jael felt herself being shaken awake from the blissful realms of her dreams. She grunted irritably as her oldest daughter whispered in her ear. "Jez has seen a herd of deer by the lake. Dress quickly," she whispered excitedly, throwing her mother's clothes on top of her sleeping form.

Jael groaned. "Give me a moment." She hadn't fallen asleep until the early hours of the morning, and despite being only thirty-one years old, she felt reluctant to embrace the day.

She splashed water in her face and followed Jez and Meira out through the meadow, the beauty of the day reviving her senses. A gentle mist lingered and the air had a dream-like stillness to it. The three of them ran down to the lake and stopped short of the water, where over twenty deer grazed. Their graceful heads could be seen through the long grass. Jael heard Meira next to her as she gripped the bow in her left hand and nocked the arrow into position, focusing on the eye of one of the deer.

"Now!" Meira whispered.

Their three arrows flew through the air, each hitting their mark. Jael's deer ran for a moment before collapsing. They made their way toward their kill.

"We can't make it back with all three. Jez, you go back for help and Meira and I will wait here."

Jez nodded, and broke into a run.

Jael and Meira lay in the long grass, laughing and talking about their victory.

"Have you ever wondered if it would be different, if it were a person, I mean?" Meira asked.

Jael laughed. "It would depend which person and what mood I was in."

An arrow whizzed over their heads, followed by a hoot of victory.

Meira moved to poke her head up to see who it was, but her mother pulled her down. She could hear three voices now. They spoke Canaanite. Jael recognised one of them and tried to place where she had heard it before. The voices were coming closer and another arrow whizzed through the air, landing only feet away from them.

"Stop!" Jael stood, her daughter next to her.

She knew that face, chiseled as though from granite, his cruel, lustful eyes were without conscience or emotion.

She bowed low, suddenly realising the vulnerable predicament they were in.

"Sisera, what an unlikely meeting. What brings you this far east?" She forced herself to sound calm, but she could feel her palms were sticky as they gripped the bow.

"This is my son, Danel and this is Molid, the second son of Jabin. We are escorting him from Sidon to Hazor, and are seeking the hospitality of your husband. We sent the guards ahead of us - I was hoping to show the boys the beauty of the Hula valley." His eyes ran the length of her body.

Jael glanced at the two boys. Danel she guessed to be sixteen, Molid perhaps a year older. Danel was taller and broader. His dark hair and shaved face boasted his good looks, though he carried the same cruel, cold expression of his father. Molid was a slighter build, his face pretty rather than handsome, but he had clearly learned to make up for his lack of physical stature with the arrogance that came from his heritage. He smirked now, as his eyes fixed on Meira. Jael reached instinctively for an arrow as he whispered something to his father, who nodded, smirking with approval.

"Seemingly, they too are quite taken by the beauty of the Hula Valley." He raised his eyebrows with crude implication.

Reaching slowly for her bow she called out to them. "We are honoured to have you here; let us return to the tents where you can enjoy my husband's hospitality."

Jael watched Molid turn to Danel and Sisera and whisper something. Both father and son smirked.

"Thank you for your kind offer, however it has been suggested that we would be better to take advantage of your husband's hospitality now," he called back, moving closer toward them.

Jael gestured to Meira, who nocked her own arrow and matched her mother's target, just below the navel. She hoped that Sisera could not see her hand trembling.

"If you wish to return Molid to his father with the loss of his masculinity, then come closer. If you would like the hospitality of *my husband's* tents, then you are welcome." Jael kept her voice level.

Their smirks slithered from their faces. Finally, Sisera spoke in a low voice to the boys and forced a smile.

"I have told Danel and Molid that there are many ways of enjoying a woman's hospitality and we will wait until we see your husband. Thank you for your kind offer." He nodded by way of taking control of the situation.

There was something in his voice that made Jael's stomach turn.

In the distance she could see the men arriving, but she kept her arrow drawn and pointed at them. Finally, Zimran was there, with another of the caravan drivers and Jez. While the three walked ahead, Zimran dropped back to walk with Meira and Jael.

He laid his hand on her arm, concern creasing his brow. "You're trembling Jael. What's wrong?"

She pressed her fingers into her temple; she didn't want to involve him in a battle that wasn't his. "It's nothing, really, I'll be fine."

"You don't want to talk about it." He sounded hurt.

"I don't want you to get involved."

"I'm already involved, Jael, you know that."

"I don't want you to get more involved," she repeated adamantly, the tremor in her voice giving her away.

"You mean you don't want me to do anything stupid," he laughed sardonically. "That's not *my* way."

Jael grinned reluctantly. Meira was wiping the blood from her arrows; she walked just in front of them.

"How about if I promise to listen and try to persuade you against doing anything stupid?" he grinned, but his eyes were pools of concern.

"That might work," she sighed with resignation. She saw Sisera look back at them and her heart pounded as nauseous anxiety welled up within her.

Keeping her voice low, she narrated to Zimran what had happened.

"I don't trust Heber to honour Meira. That's the short of it. I feel so powerless Zimran."

He listened quietly until she finished. When he looked up, she saw the anger burn in his eyes, and he saw the response of fear in hers.

"We could leave?" he said quietly.

She turned to him and everything in her wanted to say yes.

"There's not a day that passes that I don't think about the choice I made, and if I had my time again, I would have left with you before I went to Heber. But my vow was to Yahweh, not to man, and I must trust Him."

"Then there is your answer." Zimran held her gaze, defeated and yet sincere. True to his word, he had been there for her. He could have used her vulnerability to draw her to himself, but he respected her as much as he loved her. She held his gaze a moment, acknowledging his gift.

They walked silently for some time until the camp was in view.

"I thought you would be interested to know that Philistia has been defeated and is now under Hebrew rule. It is said a single man defeated six hundred Philistines by the strength of Yahweh." She turned to him, he was as restless and constant as the desert sands, unpredictable and yet the feeling of home.

A memory came back to her of a meeting; it was so absurd she was embarrassed to voice it.

"What was his name?"

"Shamgar."

Jael threw back her head and laughed. Sisera turned and looked at her darkly, then his eyes travelled to Zimran and his mouth twitched.

She unravelled the story of her meeting with the hairy man at Shiloh and how she had thought him to be mad.

He laughed. "Your God clearly has you marked for some great purpose."

"What do you mean?" Jael frowned.

"When you travel, you meet many people: fools, visionaries and tyrants. You begin to identify the sense of destiny some carry," he grinned. "All I'm saying is that I find it remarkable that you aren't dead yet. It makes me wonder about this God of yours and His purpose for you."

She sighed; Zimran had a practical understanding and shrewd judgement that she trusted.

They had reached the settlement, and Heber was talking to Sisera and the two young men. Jael felt sick. She knew instinctively that Sisera's forced compliance in the meadow would be paid for.

She took Meira and hurried back to her tent. Adva was preparing goats curds, shaking the milk in a skin while Mary was singing a song to Uriah.

"Meira, I need you, Levia and Uriah to stay out of sight until Sisera and his party leave. Do you understand me?" She felt abnormally anxious.

"Yes Ima. You're scaring me! What's going on?"

"Nothing. Adva and Mary, stay with them…and pray. We've just had a run in with Sisera."

"I don't want to stay here. I'm going to Abba," Levia demanded, willfully asserting her favour with her father.

"Then go!" Jael sparked, too anxious to fight with her fiery daughter. She felt trapped in the rising collision of different forces, like a desert storm, in which heat, wind and sand collided; and she was drowning in the amassing tension around her.

One of Heber's slaves came to the tent; her eyes flicked to Jael's and then fixed on the floor. "Heber tells you to come, mistress."

Jael's heart lurched with dread as she tried to prepare herself for what would be the outcome of this meeting. She pushed aside the goat's skin panel that formed the entrance to Heber's tent.

Sisera was reclining with his son on the camel skin couch. The two were smiling and held goblets of wine. Heber was in his chair and Levia sat cross-legged at his feet. She looked up, smiling in triumph. Then, noting her mother's uncharacteristic angst, she suddenly felt uncomfortable, as though suddenly aware of the tension in the room. Jael noted Zimran's presence and avoided the pull of his dark eyes that shifted between her and Sisera, cold and defiant. Dangerously so.

Heber stood, his eyes flitting to Zimran and then to Jael.

"Sit." She glanced at Zimran. His jaw worked and his knuckles were white, clenched at his sides. "Sisera tells me that there was a *misunderstanding* today in the field. He tells me that you and Meira aimed your arrows at them. Whilst they could have defended themselves, they acted graciously and withdrew in honour of their relationship with me." He raised his chin with self-importance.

The stupid peacock, he has no idea he is being played like a jester's fiddle, Jael thought.

"What do you have to say about this?"

Jael's eyes flickered to Zimran, who shook his head, almost imperceptibly; his eyes seemed to plead with her. She wondered why he was there.

His presence strengthened her resolve and quietened her anger. She bowed low. "I am sorry, my lord, I misread your politeness as a crude intent toward my daughter and myself. We were in the field alone and vulnerable. Forgive me. It is a mother's weakness to be overprotective of her children. I should not have doubted your honour."

Sisera stood and walked toward her, and she felt fear grip her as she stood, her eyes respectfully lowered, though her stance was instinctively defensive.

He smiled, while his cold eyes promised vengeance. "Of course, and to show there are no hard feelings, your family are invited to the 'Festival of Kinship with the Forest', which will begin in Jabin's palace next month. Archery contests are part of the festivities…I look forward to showing you my own skill in this area. And I am sure my son and Molid will enjoy showing Meira some of the other delights of Canaan." Jael shuddered inwardly at his barbed promise.

Heber bowed low to the ground, oblivious to Sisera's implication - any discernment he may have had was clouded by his need for the general's approval and his own ambition.

"My lord, you do us a great honour."

Sisera nodded. "Until then, we take our leave." With that he and his son left the tent.

Jael turned to leave too.

"Not you." Heber waited until the sounds of Sisera's footsteps could no longer be heard. He turned to Zimran. "I hear you kindly escorted my wife through the meadow?"

"She was shaken…Sisera's intent was *not* made clear."

"Yes, Sisera informed me that you were quite *helpful* to her." His eyes were narrow slits.

Zimran swallowed. He was not afraid for himself; nothing would please him more than to end the snake's life.

"Where are you from, Zimran?"

Jael watched as Zimran maintained his calm composure, his eyes held Heber's.

"I am from Midian."

"Did you know my wife before I married her?"

"My caravan would pick up tents that her father sold and deliver them to Timna, as you knew."

Heber turned to Jael and then to Zimran. He picked up the rope and Jael's heart picked up a notch. "Your conduct was questioned today. I would hate to see my wife's reputation tarnished in any way – I would not want to teach her the value of loyalty."

Zimran stepped forward, his fists clenched, but he smiled. "I'm quite certain a man of your reputation and standing knows how to win the respect of his wife without threat or violence."

Heber smiled and Jael silently commended Zimran for his wisdom; he had driven Heber into the corner of his own arena.

"If you assure me that your conduct was pure, then I thank you for your concern for my wife and daughter. You may leave now."

Zimran bowed and left the tent. Heber's eyes followed him; he turned to Jael and poured himself wine. Jael knew Zimran would be waiting outside. He, too, would have felt the unpredictability of Heber's mood.

Heber placed the rope on the table and moved toward her. He took a handful of her hair and pulled her face toward him. He kissed her roughly and then, looking at her with disgust, he shoved her away. She stumbled backward, hitting the central shaft of the tent. Her breathing was ragged with fear as he stepped toward her, his hand hitting her face and then landing in her stomach. She fell to the floor. He grabbed her hair, forcing her to stand and her eyes met his.

"Do not make me look foolish again. I know you never loved me and I know why. If I find out it is him, I will have you both stoned. Do you understand?" he hissed.

Sisera left the next morning and Heber's mood was changed. He was all smiles and laughter as though nothing had happened. He bid Jael to follow him to his tent.

"Sisera has alluded to an alliance between our families; his son is attracted to Meira and this favour would serve us well. We must see to it that she is dressed well for the festival and that she knows the part she must play."

Jael struggled to keep her voice level. "Meira needs to be asked. She is not a piece of meat to be traded."

"Like you were. That's what you are thinking, isn't it?" His words curdled in Jael's mind. "I can have little hope for Uriah providing a future for our family." His voice was barbed with contemptuous disdain and Jael felt his words tear shreds from her heart. She swallowed the retort that longed to push its way from her, wondering if he had any idea how hurtful his words were; he was so locked in his own pain, it blinded him to the suffering he caused others. Everything was about his own protection and gain.

"My daughters, however, have potential. And this marriage will serve Meira well: she will be wealthy and powerful, and will grow to appreciate a life of wealth and social prominence."

Jael fought the urge to throw something at him; she took a deep breath, wondering if he knew his daughter at all. "Please, we cannot do it Heber. The man is a monster and his son too; they would have raped us in the field had I not aimed my arrow at them. You must believe me."

She paused and was pleased to see doubt flicker in his eyes. She continued, defying her pride for the sake of her daughter. Her voice was low and desperate. "Please, please Heber, consider what I am saying."

She looked up at him, her eyes desperate. "Think about it: Sisera would only seek a marriage that would further *his* ambition or hatred. You are a tool Sisera will discard when he is finished with you." She knew as soon as the words left her mouth that she had said too much. She had touched his pain.

He recoiled, like a defensive child. "You are wrong! Sisera respects my work and needs me."

She stood and clasped his hands, allowing tears to fall down her face. They were her final hope. "We are your family and we need you, to protect us and be there for your children."

Heber looked at her, his eyes flickered with fleeting indecision and Jael thought she saw his hard resolve momentarily weaken. He glanced to the door and when he spoke, his voice was stony. "You are a survivor, Jael; do not take me for a fool. I will do what is best for this family, sometimes sacrifices must be made by one person for the good of the whole – but then you know that, don't you?" his lips curved in derision, and he glanced toward the door. "Leave," he barked, turning away.

Jael left, her thoughts jerky and disordered.

When she pushed aside the flap of her tent, Mary was making tea. She smiled, offering a cup to Jael.

Gratefully taking the warm cup, she sat quietly, her mind churning. Mary would look up from time to time; she seemed thoughtful too. Jael knew she should ask her if she was alright, but was in no mind for a deep discussion.

When she eventually went to bed, she spent another night tossing and turning. Finally, she stood up and, lighting the oil lamp, she began to pray.

"Yahweh, I know that You are all powerful. I know that You see everything on earth, and that the suffering of Your children hurts You. Please show us what to do and give us the courage to do it."

24

A gift opens the way and ushers the giver into the presence of the great.
Proverbs 18:16

1246 BC - Deborah

Deborah sat in the luxurious carriage that she shared with Keret, Hurriya and Hur. There was a comfortable silence, each lost in their own thoughts until Ramah loomed ahead of them. Situated in the hill country of the tribe of Benjamin, the road wound around the base of the city before beginning its ascent. The hillside had been cut in the Canaanite style of steep, irrigated slopes that enabled olive and fruit trees and vineyards to grow.

They passed the bustling market and raucous disputes that spilled out of the gates, and found Sisera and his men waiting. Deborah noted Keret taking in the different types of trade, his quick mind assessing the likely access and profitability of the mountain city. The difference between Canaanite oppression here and in the northern tribes was stark. The stories of Canaan's oppression had, of course, reached this city, and thus the presence of the Canaanite army was met with fear and suspicion, but the strength of Hebrew culture and the peace of its people was also evident.

Mounted on horseback, Sisera was accompanied by twenty soldiers. Deborah had heard from Hur that they were on a 'diplomatic' mission to Philistia; she doubted Sisera's ability to engage in diplomacy that did not involve destruction. Yet she was filled with an inner peace; she no longer feared him as she once did. She had let go of her own life and she had trusted Yahweh with the future; his hold on her was gone.

Keret went to meet Sisera and rode next to him for the remainder of the journey. Deborah sat next to Hur.

"Has Keret told you where we are going?"

"No. Do you know?"

He raised his eyebrows. "I believe one of your own has taken control of Philistia."

"A Hebrew?" Deborah sensed Yahweh's purpose go before her.

Hur nodded. "Curious," he muttered.

"Curious?"

Hur smiled. He had a warmth about him that did not fit his role as a soldier. He snorted with disbelief.

"He apparently killed all five of the Philistine lords and six hundred men single-handedly."

Deborah smiled with delight. "I once heard of this man, while I still lived in Ephraim," she said, her eyes shining.

"He has ruled for some time. I think Sisera is only now taking him seriously. Though I doubt he killed so many men alone; such tales are often the product of peoples romantic imaginations."

"You believe such a feat is impossible?" she smiled.

Hur nodded in agreement. "And yet?" he cocked an eyebrow.

"And yet...I think it is probable."

"You think."

"I'm certain."

"How can you be certain?"

"Because I sense Yahweh's hand."

Hur nodded, his common sense silenced by the knowledge that man was not meant to understand all that occurred. Mystery was part of the universe; without it, purpose had no value. And around this average-looking Hebrew girl, the unexplainable hovered...No, loomed - a hushed breath of expectation, a hidden greatness that manifested in humility, strength and compassion, but concealed a yet unborn potency that would bring change.

The retinue of soldiers and Keret's caravan drew up outside the gates of Gezer, moving through the mass that pushed their way into the city under the watchful gaze of the Canaanite guards. They were met inside the city by a soldier who led them to the Canaanite palace.

Balak was aware that Canaan's position in Gezer had been weakened by his brother's conquest. Gezer was a political and economic stronghold that ordered the agricultural calendar and controlled the road to Jerusalem and Hazor, as well as import from the Great Sea. He knew that Sisera would be looking for someone to blame, and his personal and political preference would be that it was Shamgar, rather than himself. Why couldn't his maverick brother just have put his head down and followed the rules? He had always been like that; governed by his own, inner compass - and their mother had favoured him for it. He had done as he was told, and he shouldn't be the one to pay for Shamgar's rebellion! He stepped forward, acknowledging the alpha male strength of Sisera as he bowed before him, despising the sweat he could feel on his palms and brow that betrayed his intimidation.

"When is he arriving?"

"Shortly, sir."

"He is your brother?"

"By blood, not loyalty."

A muscle twitched in Sisera jaw. "Then ally yourself with him, for now…until he can be defeated. My armies will move south. When Philistia is surrounded, we will take it."

"My brother is not a politician. The Hebrews will look to him to judge, but he has no government as such, neither does he have a strong Hebrew foundation. There will be those who will resent his leadership and the fact that his father is a Canaanite. Philistia is weaker now than it was under the five lords, and ripe for the taking." Balak's mind was playing with thought.

Sisera clicked his tongue impatiently. "When Philistia is ours, I will be looking for my own lords to oversee the cities." He rested his cold gaze purposefully on Balak. His implication was not wasted.

"I will not fail you, my lord."

Deborah watched Shamgar's arrival. He would have been intimidating in his own right. His massive form and fiery red hair set him apart from men, but he carried the presence of Yahweh with him, and with it an authority that men yielded to out of respect, rather than fear.

Hur approached her, frowning grimly.

"Sisera bids you to come."

Her heart picked up a notch as she followed him down the marble- floored passageways. Finally, the corridor widened out and imposing oak doors towered before them; their ornate carvings signified the importance of the room they were about to enter. Hur pushed the doors aside, revealing a large, governmental room dominated by a long table. In the centre, wooden fruit bowls were laden with fresh figs and oranges, meats and jugs of wine. Along one side of the room was a simple bench, and it was here that Deborah was bid to sit.

Sisera sat at the head of the table in a carved wooden chair, a golden goblet held in his hand. Keret, Balak and several noblemen sat with him.

The general beckoned Deborah to be brought to him, appraising her countenance. "What does your God say today?" He twisted the goblet in his fingers; he was at ease, like a crocodile lazing on the banks of a river, sure of its kill.

Deborah did not answer immediately. "He shows me an eagle, resting, watchful from its mountain peak. But when the eagle opens its mouth, it has the jaws of a wolf. Seeing the sparrow on the plain below, he leaves his peak, as though to swoop down; but he is deceived about who he is, and he has a misconception of the sparrow. As he draws nearer, he realises that, from his lofty position, he has fatally misjudged his prey – it is a lion.

"He stumbles, he cannot fly; and the lion, being stronger and wiser, devours the eagle."

"Is Shamgar this lion?"

"Shamgar is the sparrow, Yahweh is the Lion. But Yahweh has anointed Shamgar to carry out His will."

Sisera's eyes held hers. He bore the force of his wrath into her eyes, knowing the fear he had previously instilled in her, and was disconcerted that he saw only peace.

She bothered him and he wished nothing more than to break her, body and mind. And yet the words of the priest were a thorn in his side: *she was favoured by the gods and could not be harmed.* His respect for the gods was questionable, but he knew better than to defy the priests who held the favour of the people, of Jabin and his witch. If she could not be killed, then she would be broken; and if she could not be broken, she would be forced into obscurity where her voice could no longer speak curses into his life.

Deborah looked down, recalling Hurriya's words to her, and knowing it was not yet her time.

He turned to Balak who looked like he wanted to slither away. "Ensure he becomes Cannan's ally." He stood, his mouth turned with dismissive disdain as Shamgar and a younger man entered the room.

Balak embraced his brother with uncharacteristic regard, and Shamgar smiled inwardly as he imagined the conversation that Balak had had with Sisera. He had to admit that it felt good that his brother needed his help, for the first time in their lives.

"Brother. It seems congratulations are in order!" Balak gave a strained smile, betrayed by the beads of sweat that dotted his forehead.

He was nervous, thought Shamgar; the stakes must be high.

"You asked to see me." Shamgar returned the smile, his eyes scanning the room before picking up a pomegranate from the bowl.

Balak noted the ox-goad in his hand. He flinched with irritation as Shamgar raised an eyebrow at him. It was the expression they shared as children when they competed; it was a look of confidence.

"Allow me to introduce Sisera of Harosheth-Haggoyim and his Council member, Keret of Nahalal." The men formally acknowledged each other before taking their place at the table.

Deborah remained on the bench, her hands tucked under her legs; she wondered why she still remained in the room.

"Is it true, brother?" Balak asked. He wiped his forehead with the back of his hand, trying to look as nonchalant as possible.

"Is what true, Balak?" Shamgar smiled pleasantly.

"That you killed six hundred men with an ox-goad?" He gestured to Shamgar's hand.

Shamgar grunted. "With Yahweh's help, yes." He scanned the room, noting the guard and the Hebrew woman. She was dressed in slave's attire and yet she did not serve; her presence was clearly deliberate.

She was pretty, in a plain sort of way, with an inner quality that made her seem beautiful, transparent; gentle but strong. Her lips curved and her eyes shone as he spoke and his spirit recognised Yahweh's hand on her life even as his mind acknowledged that he, too, was being assessed.

'Curious,' he mused quietly to himself.

"Canaan acknowledges your rule in Philistia and wishes to ally itself with you." Sisera spoke now, exerting his authority like an invisible net that would envelope those around him. He acknowledged that its metaphoric weight slumped before the man. He stood before an equal.

Shamgar's eyes shifted to the girl as he spoke.

"With pleasure." A hesitant pause filled the air and he noted his brother's jaw relax as he exhaled.

"But first Canaan needs to end its oppression of Yahweh's people in the northern tribes. Free those who have been sold into bondage." His eyes darted to the Hebrew girl and saw that though her expression was unchanged, her eyes shone with bold conviction.

Balak's face went from white to red as he comprehended the implication of Shamgar's ultimatum.

Keret stood then. "Forgive my intrusion and allow me to introduce myself. I am a businessman, and a member of Sisera's government, not a military man. I understand your feelings regarding the oppression of the Hebrews. But you must realise that economic and political unity will give you a voice in Canaan that your opposition or avoidance cannot. You have won the battle to secure Philistia, but now you must rule. You will need to consider Israel's trade with the nations around it if you are to hold your position as an economic stronghold." Shamgar listened to the logic of the man, but his spirit was alert to Yahweh and to His voice, even as his mind assessed the character of the man who spoke to him. He carried an intellectual pride and confidence that came from privileged birth and upbringing, but he carried no malice.

"Your argument is undeniably correct...on both a logical and practical level. Politically and economically, I should ally myself with Canaan to protect Israel. But it is also true that I did not win this battle in my own strength, nor by my own wisdom, but by heeding the voice of Almighty God. And His hand fights against those who persecute His people. Therefore, to ally myself to you would be to sign my own defeat."

Shamgar tried to read what he saw in Keret's expression. At first he thought it was humour, but it was more like curiosity...or understanding.

The politician's eyes darted to the Hebrew girl, as though he would have liked an explanation. By way of silent reply, she raised an eyebrow and her lips curved triumphantly. Shamgar's mind worked as he tried to understand the dynamics of this strange meeting.

Balak had stood, the vein in his neck had risen -that purple viper that had always warned Shamgar as a teenager that he was about to attack. He tried not to allow the memory to influence his behaviour.

"We are blood! Brother, for the sake of our father and his reputation, do not bring this shame on our family."

Shamgar lowered his voice. "For the sake of our mother and her people, for the sake of Yahweh and His kingdom, I will defy all that fight against Him." His eyes shifted to the girl and rested thoughtfully for a moment. It was a guttural act without thought, and one that he later wondered about.

"It is the heart of a father to fight for Israel's children, as it is the heart of a mother to love them and unite them."

Balak broke in, waving his hand dismissively. "And will you not allow us to be united by our mother's blood? Was it not her blood, her name, that caused me to protect your children while you were absent and Philistia's armies stood at our father's door?"

Shamgar paused, what his brother said was true and for a moment he felt his integrity divided. He wrestled with indecision. The girl's eyes bore into his, as fire from a furnace scorches the floor beneath it. "You are my brother, Canaan is not. If Canaan threatens your family, I will offer the same defence."

He allowed his focus to settle on Sisera as he spoke. "But I cannot support Canaan's oppression of Yahweh's people."

He turned, signaling the end of their meeting, and left the room.

Part III

25
...and they were sold into the hand of Jabin...
Judges 4:2
1241 BC- Deborah

As their caravans wound their way out of Harosheth, Deborah sadly observed the slaves bringing in the remainder of the wheat harvest. Passover would be occurring soon. Sorrowfully, she remembered the evening of Passover with her family, the night of her first encounter with Yahweh. It seemed surreal, belonging to a different world. She had been eight then, and twenty-one years had passed. Yet, as painful as the memory was, she had enjoyed those years before the death of her kin and friends.

Keret and Hurriya travelled with the caravan, too, which carried carts loaded with linen to be sold at the market. The festival would draw the custom of wealthy buyers, and whilst the couple would be prominent guests at the festival, their servants would be running the stall. It was not difficult to see how Keret had become successful; he had the ability to make the best of any situation.

The city of Hazor rose to its acropolis on the tel, reminding Deborah of a jewel on a clenched fist: both majestic and threatening. Its ornately decorated walls set it apart as the home of the king. On this day, the city spilled outside the walls. Even the market place seemed to burst with activity and excitement. Families shared food on hillsides, whilst archers prepared for the competitions that would take place the next day.

The caravan paused at the base of the tel, while some of the carts separated to set up camp. Canaanite soldiers shouted commands at the slaves to prepare for Sisera's return.

Deborah watched as the slave-children were off-loaded from the carts. Buckets were placed before them, and they were commanded to strip and wash. They were organised by older women. One young boy broke away, running into the woods. An arrow flew threw the air, and the boy fell to the ground. But he was not dead. His body was dragged back to the other slaves and he was pinned, screaming, against the cart and whipped until his life left him. His body was left as a warning to the others.

"Escape is not an option," the soldier smirked. After that, the others complied. The children were given new clothes and commanded to put them on. As reward for their compliance, they were fed. She recalled the scenes of violence that she had witnessed Sisera inflict on Hebrew villages: after seeing their parents raped and butchered, the children were then loaded onto carts.

"What will happen to them?" Deborah asked Hurriya.

The older woman winced, turning away, as one does from a bad smell. Deborah laid her hand on the woman's arm.

"Please, my cousin is there, I must know."

Hurriya nodded. "They will be prepared for Jabin and his court. Those who are worthy will be trained as temple prostitutes, or offered as sacrifice; some will be put aside for Jabin and his court for their pleasures. Those he does not want will be sold to private buyers. I am sorry, Deborah."

Deborah closed her eyes, sickened by what Hurriya had told her. She watched their frightened, innocent faces and wrestled once again with her own hatred and helplessness.

Hurriya's cart passed the children and Deborah's eyes met with Ariel's, as she handed bread to the children. The eyes stared back at her, all trace of life and hope long gone. Deborah recalled how she had seen her that first day in the temple, and acknowledged the horror her cousin had experienced since that day, fourteen years ago.

Yahweh free me and use me to deliver Your people. I cannot bear to see their suffering.

It was a prestigious troop that marched into the royal city, pushing its way through the buzz and clamour of the crowded streets. Deborah travelled with Keret and Hurriya in their cart. Jara travelled ahead with her daughters and her ladies-in-waiting. Sisera led the procession with Danel and Paebel, his younger son. Behind them, Talmai and the other soldiers travelled, either on chariots or horseback. They drove 'the gifts' - slaves and spoils of war - that would be given to Jabin.

The crowds had parted and stared in awe at Sisera, as he looked ahead; his bronze chain mail and helmet shone in the low evening sun, as did the bronze arm bands that defined his tanned, muscular arms.

Women called out flirtatiously to him, reaching out to touch him as he rode past them and men cheered him for his conquests. To the Canaanites in Hazor, he was god-like, the emissary of Baal, who had brought victory and peace to their cities; he was worthy of their worship.

Deborah watched his two sons. They already carried the cruel, emotionless expression of their father. She glanced at Jara and wondered at the unconditional nature of a mother's love that would always defend her children. She recalled the conversation that Jara had had with Ariya, and did not believe that Jara approved of Sisera's decisions regarding their children.

Her thoughts turned to Yahweh and how Israel had turned away from their maker, their father. What must a parent do to raise their child well? Unconditional love alone was not enough; it must teach consequences too: that wrong choices lead to pain. Children must be taught to learn empathy and compassion. Yahweh's laws had been given with this purpose. She knew that she had learnt empathy because she had suffered. She knew, too, that it broke Yahweh's heart to see His people crushed under the weight of their sin.

They have forgotten Your statutes and they need to be reminded, if I am to be a mother to Your people, I must give them hope, and I cannot do that here, Yahweh.

They crossed the paved outer courtyard. A cultic platform in its centre bore a golden statue of El sitting on his throne, his raised arms indicative of his supremacy and authority over the other Canaanite deities. The priests knelt before him, laying food and gifts at his feet as they chanted. When Sisera passed, he nodded by way of acknowledgement.

Jabin sat, while his cupbearer re-filled his drink. His ornate golden throne had wide legs that were phallic-style representations of Baal. Beside him sat his wife, Padriya. Her eyes were painted with kohl, and her long, dark hair flowed freely like oil on the night water, decorated only by a gold headband. The design was replicated in a thick gold necklace, inlaid with rubies that lay against her chest. Her dress, made of purple linen, was fringed and layered with a woven, elaborately patterned over-garment that was held in place by a toggle pin. Jabin wore a blue and purple robe, elaborately patterned with gold and white embroidery and an imposing headband of thick gold that was of a similar design to Padriya's, but embedded with rubies and sapphires. They were clearly dressed to inspire awe. He smiled as they walked through the hall toward him. Deborah noted that behind Padriya was the woman who had been identified as her priestess. She bent down to say something to Padriya who looked up.

Deborah's gaze shifted towards the mighty statue of Baal that stood behind Jabin. Around her she was aware that all had fallen to their knees and were worshipping; the names of Baal, Asherah, and Jabin's name merged. She had not been prepared for this. She heard Hur next to her.

"Bow!" he hissed.

But she knew that she could not.

Jabin raised a hand and the chanting slowly stopped until the eyes of everyone were on her.

"Donatiya." He lifted his forearm and gestured with his index finger.

The priestess stepped from behind Padriya, her white dress trailing behind her making her movements fluid, like a snake. She stood before Deborah.

"You dare to defy Baal, to dishonour Jabin?" The priestess's voice was malacophonous.

"I fear Yahweh, the Almighty and only God." Deborah matched the woman's volume, her voice level, her eyes steely.

"Sisera, explain why you have brought such blasphemy into my presence. Who is she?" Jabin asked, the arrogance and authority in his voice leaving no doubt as to who wielded the most power; and yet, if Sisera was afraid, he did not show it. His expression was respectful but his tone reflected a bored impatience.

"She is a Hebrew priestess, your highness. The priest in Harosheth, by way of necromancy, divined that she is favoured by the gods."

Jabin nodded with perverse curiosity as a child might over the dissection of a worm. The priestess had walked away. She now returned with a silver bowl filled with thick, dark red fluid.

The woman raised a speculative eyebrow. "I doubt she is favoured by Baal."

"Evidently not. I thought I had broken her. She has been of some use as a healer and diviner to Canaan. Perhaps the games tomorrow will soften her temperament."

Jabin raised a lazy eyebrow. "Perhaps." He waved a casual hand at her, a smile playing at his lips. "So what does the prophetess say of me?" He had the air of one secure in his dominance.

Deborah felt Sisera's and Donitaya's eyes pierce her, even as she felt the Spirit of Yahweh rest upon her and the words filled her mouth.

"You rest secure in your authority, as did your namesake before you. But Yahweh is Almighty God and Baal is a statue without power. Yahweh sees the suffering of His people. He comes to fight for His people. Free His people and liberate this land, for it belongs to Yahweh! If you do not, the day comes when Hazor will be burnt to the ground. He will destroy you, your heirs, your palaces and your leaders of war. The memory of you will be trampled into the ground."

Donatiya hissed, like a viper about to attack. She motioned to Sisera as she stepped forward and Deborah felt her arms pinned violently behind her, forcing her to her knees.

"How dare you blaspheme Baal and insult his anointed!" Her eyes were black slits. She turned and glided to the altar where she poured the contents of a vial into a golden bowl.

Deborah shuddered as the priestess returned, a cruel smile playing on her lips.

"Such faith! It's almost commendable, but faith unchallenged is empty." She motioned to Sisera, who grabbed Deborah's hair in a vice like grip. She felt panic rise up within her, and resisted the urge to struggle; closing her eyes she forced her mind to recede to a place of faith.

"If you are favoured by the gods, you need not fear."

The woman chanted as she forced Deborah's mouth open, pouring the contents into her mouth. She gagged, struggling against Sisera's hold, as she tasted the thick irony-sweetness of blood on her lips. It was mixed with a strong herb. He smiled as he grabbed her hair, forcing her head back and pinching her nose, until she had no choice but to swallow. Falling to the floor, she reeled, gasping as she acknowledged that the herb she had tasted was hemlock; in concentrated form, it caused paralysis leading to suffocation.

I trust in nothing but You Yahweh. Deliver me, and let it be to her as she wished on me. My life is Yours.

She felt Hur's grip on her arm as he helped her up and took her back to where the others stood.

She swayed as 'the child-gifts' were brought in and forced to kneel at Jabin's feet. They were led by Ariel. She looked up; her eyes were haunted, empty shells of a distant memory. They held Deborah's for a moment, sending a shudder through her soul and Deborah reached out to her cousin, feeling desperate for her. She smiled, attempting to bridge the space between them, but it fell flat before them as Ariel turned away.

Jabin stood now and the children had pressed themselves together, a huddle of cringing terror. His expression was one of perverse pleasure as he walked among them dividing them into the worthy and the unworthy.

Deborah stood, waiting for the poison to take effect while her soul, in its own torment at seeing Ariel again, clung helplessly to Yahweh. .A calm spread through her, beginning deep within her stomach and her initial thought was to question if it was the first signs of paralysis, but she knew in the same moment that it was not. She felt God's spirit upon her, heavy and sweet as a morning dew and a smile parted her lips as she bowed her head in exultation: "Yahweh, my deliverer, avenge your people, for I know now that you shall."

Keret and Hurriya were quiet as they made their way out of the city. The road down the tel was lit with lanterns and torches. Light and sordid pleasure spilled out of the gates, a moving river of music, drinking, dancing and orgies, which would continue into the morning and the following day. The forest was the arena for the archery contests in which slaves would be 'set free', only to be hunted down. The evening would bring the sacred full moon, which would be celebrated by mass child-sacrifice; an offering to Baal with prayers for an abundant harvest next year.

Hurriya had long since been disillusioned with the gods of Canaan, and Keret knew he had seen a difference in his wife that could not be explained intellectually – he had tried. But he was a politician and a businessman and as such felt that compromises had to be made, for peace and progress. Yet, for the same reasons, he had to respect the girl, for her conviction and courage. Hurriya was desperately worried, for she knew the reputation of Donatiya. She wrung her hands together.

"I promised Ariya I would watch after you. She was worried about you coming."

Deborah was touched and surprised by Ariya's concern. The woman's aloof and defensive manner gave little away, and after Deborah's prophecy of her son's doom, the matriarch had every reason to hate her. She suddenly had some small understanding of Yahweh's heart for these people.

"You have become dear to a number of us," she frowned. "For that reason, we do wish you would conform, just a little," she sighed.

Deborah leaned forward and squeezed her hand in a genuine act of affection.

How strange, I never anticipated feeling neither such love, nor such loyalty from any in Canaan, and stranger, too, that I reciprocate those feelings.

"Trust, my dear Hurriya. What Donatiya meant for bad, Yahweh will use for good."

Night fell and her heart picked up a notch as she acknowledged that Talmai was leading her to Sisera's tent, and she tried to recall how long it would take for the hemlock to begin its work. The giant ducked to enter the tent. It was not difficult to imagine how these men had gained the reputation of having descended from the Nephilim, fallen angels who had had children with women. His height and frame was a third greater than either Sisera or his other commanders. He bound her hands with rope and attached it to the central tent pole, grabbing her face in his huge hand; his breath was hot against her face.

"We will see how favoured you are by the gods when Sisera is through with you – maybe he will give us a turn too. It seems you angered the gods today – a lesson in humility and obedience would do you good. Pray that the witch's poison works."

Deborah, mute with terror, said nothing.

She waited. She knew it was Sisera's tool to fuel her mind with fear as she played through the revenge he would enact upon her. But it was a game she had learned to survive. For in the face of her great enemy, dread, she had learned to allow it to strengthen her. In utter desperation, she was able to surrender completely to Yahweh. There she found faith that was removed from circumstance or outcome, and that faith neither man, nor demon would conquer. And then she knew she would not die tonight, for Yahweh's word remained unfulfilled.

She moved as far as the rope would allow, gazing out of the open tent so that she could see the moon casting its peaceful shadows through the trees. It brought her comfort. Deborah picked out the constellation of the Great Bear and felt the reminder of Lapidoth's voice warm her heart. "Whatever helps me to remember how big Yahweh is, and how small I am, is infinitely helpful." She wondered where he was, and prayed for his safety. A breeze breathed through the branches. She stood, quietly imagining it weaving its way from her beloved village, wrapping itself around Lapidoth before continuing on its journey. It carried the prayers and love of those she missed, and as it touched her skin, she let its embrace warm her. For a fleeting moment, it seemed real.

She did not notice Sisera arrive, and screamed out in pain as a sharp object hit her in the back of her knees. As she fell to the ground, she instinctively rolled over in an attempt to protect her face with her hands. His feet met her back in blow after blow. She tried to scramble away, and as she did so, her hand knocked against a clay pot. Instinctively, she grabbed it, but she was on her knees and he above her, her hands still tied. She threw it at him, consumed with a feral instinct for survival that momentarily suppressed all fear. He stepped backward, easily avoiding the missile and laughed at her effort. The broken vase lay in pieces on the floor. He bent down and picked up one of the sharper pieces, his own wrath and determination validated by Deborah's audacity. Grabbing her hair, he dragged her away from the open door to the back of the tent. She looked into Sisera's face, fighting the panic that rose within her.

"I have waited so long to teach you submission. How dare you insult Jabin and humiliate me!" He slashed his hand through the air, the sharp edge of the vase smashing into her cheek and knocking her from her feet. She cried out in pain as he pinned her arms to the floor and roughly lifted her dress. His strength was upon her, and she knew she could not fight him and win.

His body suddenly slumped on top of her, a dead weight, and then he was pulled away and a hand reached out to help her to her feet.

"Hur." The Egyptian stood, a wooden club in his hands.

"We're leaving now," he said, untying her hands.

Her mind was spinning. *What was happening? Was Hur rescuing her?*

He sighed impatiently, his eyes darting to the form of Sisera. "This was Keret and Hurriya's idea. You need to trust me. We need to leave now!"

She met his gaze, her eyes steely with determination. "I need to kill him first," she said, eyeing the axe at Sisera's side.

Hur shook his head. "I do not believe it is your destiny to die here tonight. If you kill him now, you will have the whole of Hazor after us. Now, we go to safety." He flung a mantle at her.

"Put this on."

She nodded mechanically, forcing her natural suspicion to surrender to Yahweh's sovereign plan.

26

...there was an alliance between Jabin king of Hazor and the family
of Heber the Kenite.
Judges 4:17

1241 BC –Jael

"You need to hit it harder!" Jael demanded, her anxiety at being in Hazor was knocking holes in the thin walls of her patience.

"It's heavy!" Meira whined, her hands on her hips, her tone indignant.

"Well, give it to me then!" she snapped, snatching the hammer from her daughter's hand and knocking the peg into the hard ground.

She moved to the next peg and relished the force of her strength as the long iron tent peg yielded to her force. The labour intensive task reminded her of Midian; she had discovered it as a vent for her frustration and anxiety long ago. Life had been simpler in those days.

Meira knew her mother was stressed. They had arrived yesterday evening and been invited to Jabin's festivities. He had paraded her beauty like a prize lamb or a temple slave before the king, and her mother had been appalled. Meira understood her mother's concern and was astute enough to see the perverse charade for what it was. Although, she admitted to herself later that night, she had quite enjoyed the compliments and consideration she had received, particularly from her father, who rarely spoke to her unless to bark a command.

At Jabin's request, she and Heber had stayed behind at the palace, while her mother had returned to camp with her younger siblings. Initially, she had felt honoured and grown up, but she quickly realised she was out of her depth and was appalled to see the women of Jabin's court draping themselves over her father, and his provocative response to them. She had watched as men had fondled and kissed each other, and the whole experience had left her feeling dirty. She didn't know whether to mention anything to her mother or not.

Sisera's son, Danel had been overly attentive to her, admiring and praising her beauty, begging her to go on a walk with him; but she knew her mother would have advised against it. She placed her hand over the sapphire necklace he had given her, thinking about how handsome he was, with his mother's raven hair, dark eyes and full lips and his father's physical stature and strong jaw. She wondered what it would be like to kiss him.

"Meira! Please, do something! Arrange the bedding! Where is Levia? Adva! Adva!"

"Jael?" Adva came running.

"Have you got Levia, or is she with Mary?" Her mother had that wild look in her eyes that warned Meira she was at risk of losing her temper.

"I think she's with Mary?"

"Can you check please? She's been sulking all morning!" Jael squeezed the muscles at the back of her neck. Heber had barely acknowledged his 'favoured' daughter yesterday during the feast. Instead, he had acted like the doting father to Meira who, with the blissful naivety of youth, had revelled in his attention rather than seeing it for what it was. Jael was loath to burst her bubble, having watched Heber ignore her for so many years.

Mary appeared from the tent. She was almost doubled over and seemed to have aged rapidly over the last few months. "I thought she was with you," she croaked. "I was playing with Uriah."

"She can't be far," Adva reasoned. She was worried about Jael; she looked like she would snap. She had told her late last night that Sisera had reminded her of their archery contest. She had rarely seen Jael fearful, and yet she knew this time, she was. It was not only her own life that was challenged, but also the survival and future of her children.

"Stay here, Mary and take care of Uriah." Then as an afterthought, she muttered with a hint of impatience. "Meira, take care of Mary."

They began by looking in Heber's tent, but he was gone. Jael continued from tent to tent, calling her name. *She couldn't, wouldn't have gone far, would she?*

By the time the first stars dotted the fading day, both Jael and Adva were frantic. The moon's pitted face frowned down at her, an orb of judgement that signaled its last night of incompletion before the contests the next day.

There were so many tents outside the city gates - Canaanites who had come to enjoy the competition, wealth and depravity of Canaanite worship in the city. She passed tents of mixed-sex orgies and shuddered at the memory of the young girls, not much older than Levia, who had been in Jabin's court. She choked back her tears of impotent fear for her daughter. And then it occurred to her to pray.

Yahweh, please help me, please help me find my little girl.
She staggered on, feeling aimless and weary, yet knew she wouldn't stop until she found her.

It was the sound of music and laughter, the cadence of drums, and tambourines that first alerted her. Then the dancers, who wove their numinous intrigue as they re-enacted the legends of the gods. They inspired a perverse curiosity, and Jael later realised that her young daughter would have been entranced by the same creative impulse as she had been. Men and women, their bodies almost bare, were painted to depict Canaanite gods and goddesses. They moved with a graceful, seductive fluidity as they wound in and out of the scarlet and purple linen fluttering over the tent openings. They twisted their way in and out of the soldiers, provocatively trailing their naked limbs over the leering men as they re-enacted the challenge and defeat of Yam and Baal. The dance continued, portraying Athirat, Anat and Baal persuading El to allow him to have a palace.

Suddenly the beat changed, louder and stronger as Baal, a beautiful muscular man, stood, knife in hand, and that is when she saw her; standing on a tree stump, wearing a skirt of grass and brandishing her own knife.

The soldiers roared with laughter as she approached the man, swaying her hips as the other dancers did, encouraged by the raucous praise of her audience. Jael rushed in, grabbing her petulant daughter by the arm, and marched her away, her rage dissolving with the relief of finding her safe.

When she finally reached the tent, Heber was there. He looked pale and anxious, his clothes askew. Adva was crying, cowering in the corner, but the welts on her arms left no question as to what had happened; only why?

"What's happened?" Jael felt a cold sense of premonition numb her.

"Where is Meira?" she added; she could feel herself shaking.

"Danel has taken her." He seemed morose rather than anxious.

"And why have you beaten Adva?" her teeth were gritted as anxiety and fear resumed their war dance in her soul.

"She should have been looking after her."

"Adva was looking for Levia, who had run away and was dancing for the Canaanite soldiers. Mary was supposed to look after Meira." It annoyed Jael that Heber had favourites and that his favourites were those who adored and obeyed him without question. She was angry with him, and he never responded well to her then.

Heber's face twisted momentarily before he slipped behind his impassive, survival driven composure of spite. "Well then, let's hope she has your disposition; Danel will soon find she is more trouble than she's worth."

Jael's emotions were brittle. She glowered at him, picking up the hammer she had abandoned earlier, grabbing Adva's hand as she helped her stand. With a nod of her head and a threatening glare, she gestured to Levia to walk in front of her. Heber motioned to step toward her, cursing under his breath, but seeing the rage she was in and the hammer in her hand, seemed to think better of it. Swearing at her again, he poured himself wine and slumped onto the cushions. Ordinarily she would have felt smug with his reaction, but she felt like she would splinter if she allowed herself to feel.

Mary was sitting next to the sleeping Uriah on a stool, praying nervously. She opened her eyes, took one look at Adva and gasped with shock, muttering prayers for Yahweh's mercy as she did so.

She was irritating Jael -she hated injustice and cowardice. To just sit there praying while her daughter had been abducted and Adva was wrongfully beaten made her livid. It wasn't holy, it wasn't faithful; it was irresponsible at best and deluded at worst. She was the one person who could have defended Adva, and Heber might have listened.

"Tell me what happened. How did Danel come to take Meira and why was Adva beaten when you were left responsible for our daughter?"

"Well, I could hardly go running after him at my age, could I, dear?"

"No, but you could have used your mouth, the same you use to pray, to defend your sister!" Jael replied curtly.

She felt Adva's gentle hand on her arm. "Meira." She croaked, between her swollen lips. Jael laid her on the cushions, gently placing a cover over her and handing her a glass of water. She sighed, "Tell me what happened."

Mary looked dejected as she spoke. "Danel came with guards. Meira went to greet him; she has your lack of fear, and told him that he must leave, that he broke etiquette entering her tent. He apologised, declaring his ardent love and admiration for her. He ended by saying that her father was at the palace and had bid his family to join him, hence the escort."

"And you believed him!" she spat the words, her face twisted with contempt.

"If Heber bid it, then I would not question it," Mary said with gentle conviction.

Jael wanted to shout: "Do you really think Heber would have ordered his daughter to be brought to the palace by a man who had tried to rape her?" But she acknowledged bitterly that he would have done anything Sisera or Jabin required of him - even the abduction of his daughter - and that Mary would not dare question him.

She sat with Levia and Uriah, half-heartedly helping them build a fortress out of twigs and stones while her mind travelled on a muddied torrent of dangerous emotion. She felt herself struggling to resist the pull of its undercurrent. Her eyes darted to Mary, who looked irritatingly dejected and mumbled prayerfully in the corner of the tent whilst sewing clumsy stitches on a cushion.

Then she looked at Adva, her dear friend who lay quietly in pain on the cushions, and she felt so much pity and compassion for her, but that thought led her to how much she hated Heber for his weakness and his cruelty; which led her to her impossible and unrequited love for Zimran.

But the voice that cried out the loudest was her worry for Meira; it reached out and grabbed her, pulling her deeper and deeper, knocking her on the rocks of her imagination, and she had nothing with which to fight the torrent of fear she felt for her young daughter.

Finally, she was left with the stark realisation that tomorrow she must face Sisera in the archery contest. She imagined him in the forest, waiting for her and knew it was a battle she could not win, only hope he would not make her end too painful.

The totality of her desperation crashed upon her and with it she found that the turbulent river that had coiled around her mind had vomited her onto a large, smooth rock. As she pulled her head above the dark swirling water, gasping for breath, she realised the truth of her situation:

I can do nothing.

Followed by the second truth: *Yahweh is Yahweh and I am not.*

And finally: *I must trust.*

She rested her head on the soft, sun-warmed rock and let the waters subside around her. Mentally, she placed each of her concerns on the rock, and then she stood and walked to Heber's tent. Inside, she found him draped naked around a scantily-clothed woman. He turned and smiled at her, and she smiled impassively back. She mentally placed her husband on the smooth rock of her faith and walked away.

I must trust.

She found Jez, "Come with me to the palace."

There was a surge of excitement around the city walls that Jael initially attributed to her own state and the excitement of the festivities, but voices were tense, and there was a flood of guards hurriedly leaving the city and heading down the tel. She watched their torches merge with the lanterns and fires below her, and caught a man charging toward her. He was fractious.

"What is happening?" she asked.

"You don't want to go into the city; the palace is cursed."

"Cursed?"

"Donatiya, the high priestess has dropped dead – they suspect poisoning - and Sisera has been attacked, he's not come round yet. It's a dreadful disappointment to the festivities. There's talk of them cancelling the contests tomorrow."

Jael concealed the jubilant smile that pushed its way to her lips.

"Dreadful! And does anyone know where his son is?"

"He's gone after the girl."

"The girl?" Jael felt her heart stop, assuming he was referring to Meira.

"The Hebrew prophetess. They say it's all because of her."

"Deborah?" She smiled then.

The man gave her an odd look and shook his head and walked away.

Jael ran back down the hillside, pushing her way through the throngs of people who were returning from their tents for the evening festivities that would be held in the city. She turned and saw Danel, his head above the other men; he, too, was in a hurry to reach the bottom of the tel. She clasped the hammer in her hand, waiting until he was about to overtake her, and then she swung it at him, knocking him from his feet. He stood, blood pouring from his cheekbone as Jael was knocked to her knees by a soldier and then hit across the face. The traffic had divided around them in a river of panic.

"Where is my daughter? What have you done with her?" She lunged at him with feral intensity, shaking off the soldier and tearing her nails down Danel's face. Her voice was ragged, her face wild with fury.

Denel's lips curved as he wiped the blood from his face with the back of his hand.

"I don't have your daughter. Whilst it would have pleased me to have broken that will of hers, I made a deal with Molid and your husband – something about an alliance between your families. She is at the palace, being prepared to become one of Molid's concubines, I believe," he smirked, motioning to the guard to free Jael.

She leapt to her feet, pushing aside the crowds, blind with fury and stress. When she arrived at Heber's tent, the woman who had been there earlier was serving him wine.

"Leave!" she hissed at the woman, who pouted and looked to Heber. He nodded at the woman, who picked up her clothes and left the tent. She cast a last seductive smile at Heber and glowered at Jael. His eyes were narrow slits and his mouth a sneer as Jael approached.

"How could you?" she spat.

"How could I what? Arrange an alliance that will secure business and protection for our family, or arrange for Meira to be taken into the royal retinue?"

"Are you so deceived by your own ego? Do you have any idea what sort of man Molid and his father are? Of their degradation and cruelty? Yahweh will avenge His people, and where will you be when His people burn this city to the ground; will you be there to protect her?"

Heber laughed. "It is precisely because the Hebrews are a dying breed that I have ensured our future. They have neither the strength nor the will to raise their hand against Jabin. I have secured our position amongst the victors." He stepped toward her and she saw the cruelty in his eyes and his violent intent. She backed away, knowing her former anger had dissipated into despair and exhaustion, and with it her strength. His invisible hand of oppression wrapped around her throat long before his fingers pressed into her neck. He sneered, pressing his lips against hers, and she forced herself to recede, even as he forced himself upon her.

When he had finished, she scrambled to her feet, pushing back her tears, and fled to her tent, swallowing her tears of shame and hatred. She once again begged Yahweh for His deliverance; for Meira, for herself and for Israel. She stumbled past Adva, who groaned in her sleep.

When she awoke, the dim light of day cast murky shadows through the opening of her tent. Her body was stiff and her face and neck swollen. Adva was sitting up, her own face swollen and cut. She gave a half-hearted smile. "You too?"

Jael nodded silently, poking her head outside of the tent. The sky was a thick dark grey, like smoke - she imagined Hazor burning.

She saw Heber come out of his tent and walk toward her.

"The festivities have been cancelled, all worship will be conducted at the temple. I'll be back this evening." He looked at her in disgust as though she had deliberately destroyed her face to upset him.

"You'll have to stay here; I can't possibly be seen with you in public. Be ready to leave when I return."

27

Deborah, a prophetess, the wife of Lapidoth.
Judges 4:4

1241 BC – Deborah

They moved quickly, heads lowered until they had cleared the camp of the Canaanite army and then with less caution as they passed the orgies and festivities that spilt out of the camped tents - alcohol, depraved worship and physical pleasure had been flowing for hours, no-one was likely to notice their haste.

Despite her weariness, adrenalin and the desire for freedom pushed Deborah forward. When they were finally swallowed into the covering of the forest, she heaved a sigh of relief. The leafy boughs of the trees filtered shadows of moonlight, its obscurity offering both consolation and disorientation. The noise of the festival gradually faded behind them and the sounds of their freedom filled the air. Save the occasional owl and the chirping of crickets, the night was mercifully soundless. Hur would occasionally stop and look to the moon for direction before leading them on. Finally, the outline of a horse appeared. He untethered it from the tree and helped Deborah mount before grabbing the reigns and joining her. She had never ridden horseback before, and wrapped her arms around Hur's waist, lest she fall off.

As Hur picked up a wider path through the trees, he pushed the horse into a gallop, and for some time the steady cadence of the horse's hooves on the stony path was the only sound they heard.

After some time, Hur looked behind him. He pulled on the reigns, stopping the horse, and dismounted. The tranquility of the forest after their flight seemed ethereal, and the deep smells of mulch and pine were a balm to Deborah's ragged emotions. She closed her eyes, breathing in the earthy scents that represented her freedom. Hur had removed his bronze mail and took a simple tunic out of a saddlebag. He paused for a moment as he acknowledged what he was doing, and then buried his past under the boughs of a fallen tree.

"Where are we going?"

"To Kedesh. It's a Hebrew city of refuge, isn't it? It's less than an hour's ride. You'll be able to find people to help you there. I heard Sisera say that he feared a rebellion was brewing. He grunted with mordant humour. "Seems like your sort of place."

"Hur, thank you. You have shown me such kindness since I was first brought to Harosheth...I cannot understand it. You were always the face of kindness in a world so dark."

Hur looked at her, and she saw the man beneath the soldier, with his own history, pain and hunger and all the complexity of humanity that each person carries.

Smiling dismissively, he sighed, "It's complicated. Let me get you out of here first. Are you hungry?"

"Starving." She realised she was still shaking.

Grinning, he handed her a bag filled with pistachios, figs and almonds. "Loot taken from Jabin's carts," he explained.

She smiled weakly. "Even better."

As they moved further from Sisera, the revelation that she was free swathed her; as the wind hit her face, it was as if the scales of slavery flew from her. They briefly met the Patriarchs Highway, but soldiers were already amassing in number, and so they turned away to a path through the hills and forest.

It was not long before the entrance to Kedesh loomed before them, its imposing gates closed.

Hur sighed, looking up at the high walls and the glow of the guards' watchtower. "It won't be long until morning. Let's find somewhere to get a few hours' sleep."

They found a hollow away from the path, and wrapping her blanket around her, Deborah fell instantly asleep. She had not dreamt vividly for some time, but now the colours, and detail were defined: she saw an almond tree. It grew, surrounded by darkness, its roots pulled the nutrients from the rock on which it was planted, and when the tree was in full flower, she saw first one honey bee, then others pollinate the tree. When the time came to yield its blossom, she saw it was carried in all directions. People began to gather around the almond tree; they were wrapped in chains, their faces grey and drawn and their eyes partially covered in scales. When they saw the gentle white petals, they fell to their knees and wept. As their tears fell to the ground, they were drawn into the sap of the tree. Deborah watched as they travelled up the trunk, through the branches and into the seedpods. The fruit grew, plentiful and healthy, and in its time yielded a harvest. As the people ate from the tree, they grew stronger; colour and life returned to their features. Finally, they turned and saw the darkness that surrounded the tree; the scales fell from their eyes as though they suddenly remembered all they had once had. They stood, and as they did so, light surged from the tree, intense and powerful, pushing back the darkness until the full break of day settled over the land.

Deborah awoke and sighed, feeling the warmth and hope of the dream form a new path of promise before her. The sun pricked its way through the leafy treetops, swathing the forest floor in pools of light. Poppies dotted the ground, their red faces nodding with carefree pleasure in the morning breeze. She smiled, relishing the moment and her liberty. Yahweh was with her, and she felt strengthened with purpose and the knowledge that He had directed her path. Though she did not know *how* His plans and purposes would come to pass, she acknowledged that the road ahead was still long and likely to be difficult. She realised that what she had seen during her years of captivity had fuelled her with resolve and righteous anger to see her nation turn back to their Maker, to see them united. And, to see Canaan crushed.

Hur was awake already. He handed her a skin of water and a handful of almonds. She looked at them and smiled inwardly as she recalled her dream, before popping them in her mouth.

Cautiously, they crept to the road leading to the gates. When they had arrived last night, the entrance to the city had been deserted. Now, there was a file of traffic entering. They noted the watchmen in the tower; their blue skirts and bronze armour defined their Canaanite allegiance.

"Sisera?" Deborah asked, her heart falling into the gallop she had grown accustomed to.

"His men. I imagine that he has sent them to the major cities and roads surrounding Hazor." He sighed with frustration, rubbing the back of his neck as he tried to decide on the best course of action.

Deborah remained silent as she acknowledged their predicament.

He looked down at his blue, Canaanite skirt and Deborah's clothing.

"We are fairly obvious at the moment. I can't risk being recognised. I suggest we try and find a Hebrew settlement in the mountains for the time being. We can get a change of clothes and wait for the dust to settle."

Sticking once again to the cover of the trees, they left behind the fields that would once have been filled with villagers harvesting their crops. Now it was barren, and the air was heavy and sorrowful as the memory of the atrocities it had seen still lingered. Many fields were still darkened with the stubble of their recent destruction, whilst others bore the organised hand of Canaan, with irrigation systems and Hebrew slaves farming the fields.

After some time, steep, grey rock faces, flecked with red basalt that were interspersed with patches of wild heather, framed their journey into the mountains. The Patriarch's Highway, which snaked below them and would once have been bustling with travellers and traders, was now only used by Canaan's troops and guarded caravans. They had walked for the best part of the day, and still saw no sign of any Hebrew settlements.

The air was still and silent, bar the sound of their laboured breathing and infrequent conversation. They had just discussed the need to collect firewood and look for a spring when the first robbers leapt from the rocks above them. It quickly became apparent that fighting would be futile - there were too many. One of the men knocked Hur to the ground, while another placed his foot on his chest and two more held down his arms. She felt her own arms pinned behind her back. Another came forward to examine their prize, and lifted his plough shear into the air as he purposed to bring it down on Hur's neck. Their dialogue defined them as Hebrew.

"Stop! In the name of Yahweh, I beg you stop!" Deborah pleaded in their own tongue.

"Stop!" She heard the command repeated in a male voice. She twisted her neck to see owner of the voice.

It was as though time paused to take in the gravity of the moment as they stood face to face. His deep brown eyes, framed by honey-coloured skin and dark curls. He blinked as though to assure himself that she was real.

It was him – the one who had rescued her on another mountain, a lifetime ago.

"Deborah?" he pushed his hair out of his eyes, pausing with a fistful of hair as he stood staring at her. Finally he broke into a grin.

"Lapidoth!" No other words found a place in her thoughts.

He glanced suspiciously at Hur, and Deborah saw unspoken questions flicker in his eyes. And then he closed the gap, and looked as though he might embrace her, but instead he grabbed her arms, holding her gaze.

She felt her heart pound with the unfamiliar emotion that she had once run from.

"I'm free," she said weakly, for lack of anything better to say.

"Yes, you're free." His eyes seemed to caress her face as the words spiraled like a dream from the depth of his hopes.

They stood for a moment, both discombobulated by their extraordinary meeting, as though their minds and hearts needed to align to the suddenness of reality.

"Shall we kill him?" one of the men broke the silence.

"No! He risked his life to free me. Please, let him live," Deborah pleaded.

Lapidoth looked at Hur, his eyes narrowing with suspicion as he took in Hur's apparel. "He is a Canaanite soldier." He turned to Hur. "Explain yourself."

Hur exhaled. "I saw Sisera attack Deborah and I acted to defend her. But now there is no way back. I would be killed as a traitor." He glanced at Deborah to confirm his story.

Deborah nodded and saw Lapidoth's expression soften. He lay his hand on the Egyptian's shoulder. "Then I am in your debt and you may go on your way, or remain with us, the choice is yours."

"It would be unwise of me to leave now; they are looking for me. I cannot return to Sisera. If I might ask for shelter and a change of clothes until I decide what to do?"

Lapidoth nodded and turned once again to Deborah, as though to reassure himself that he had not imagined her. He smiled, his eyes warm, and beckoned them to follow him. The path led them higher. Wild heather and crocuses contrasted with the red rock and grass. Deborah grabbed fistsful to aid her ascent.

Every now and then she would catch him watching her. His deep brown eyes probed her soul, and the warmth of their intensity made her ache inside. Like a voice that echoes in an empty cavern, Lapidoth's nearness to her reverberated a confusion and clarity that created more questions than gave answers, and she felt instinctively drawn and fearful of its power over her.

He gave her a sideways glance, as though answering her thoughts; his lips curved as he spoke. "We'll talk over food. You're tired now." She recalled the light-hearted boy she had sat with talking about the stars, and wondered if there was still any trace of him behind the man that now led her.

They clambered over rocks, jumping over icy mountain streams that fell from the heights, and still climbing deeper, always going higher and deeper into the mountains, until finally, the warm glow of a settlement came into view. The houses were not mud and daub, but simple shelters made of animal skins that suggested a more transient, nomadic existence, forced upon them by the Canaanite oppression.

There was a flurry of activity when they arrived. The day was fading; lilac-grey clouds illuminated the warm glow of the setting sun as it pierced the mountain heights. After the initial suspicion and guarded looks towards Hur, they were handed bowls of lentil and barley stew, and space was made for them around the fire. Hur was given a change of clothes and his old ones were burned.

Deborah explained to the small company of Hebrews some of her experience, beginning with Sisera's attack on her village and her captivity and terror. She explained that Yahweh had at times spoken to her, telling her what would come. She did not reveal all of what Yahweh had said, but knew to wait for relationships to grow and trust to be established.

Many among the group shared their stories with Deborah. She recalled the destruction of the villages that she had witnessed, and her heart ached with compassion for them and a desire to see the restoration of her nation.

She felt a hand on her shoulder and, turning, saw Lapidoth squatting behind her. "Can we talk?"

"Yes," she smiled, and followed him away from the fire as he held a torch to light her path. They continued only a short way until they reached a ridge, the dark shadow of craggy rocks towered behind them, while a few boulders jutted out on a wide precipice that dropped into the valley below them. Setting the torch between two rocks, Lapidoth sat down as though he was reclining in a familiar chair. His legs stretched out in front of him, his back resting on a rock.

The moon, an iridescent silver orb, solemnly cast its luminous shadows over the mountain range. It averted its gaze from the charred, barren fields and empty houses of the valley, as though allowing the tortured earth its lament.

Lapidoth turned to Deborah, her chin resting on her knees, her dark eyes lost in thought as she struggled to believe that she was free and that she was with Lapidoth. Her broken instincts were still ragged, as though she expected Sisera to appear at any moment; the smallest noise would make her jump. And yet, her soul acknowledged the full and miraculous extent of her deliverance. He watched her silently, aware that the current of change had been swift, and that she must feel disconcerted.

When she finally spoke, it was with startling clarity and strength, yet with the humility and vulnerability that comes from having been broken.

"How quickly everything can change." She stared into the dark chasm beneath them as though it were the dark horror from which she had escaped. "We see only darkness and despair, and yet Yahweh sees that deliverance is within our grasp."

"Do you believe there is hope for our people?"

She turned to him, her tone so emphatic he felt reproached. "There is always hope! We either believe in Yahweh or we don't, it's that simple. If we believe Him, then we believe He is a God of miracles and deliverance; nothing is impossible if we trust!" Silence wrapped itself around the words, cocooning them until their implication pounded the air between them.

"And yet, when one has seen so much hardship, our fragile humanity comes to fear hope. Disappointment and pain are easier to bear without emotion. We survive," he replied with gentle practicality.

She nodded recalling her own plight after the death of Etiya. "We want Yahweh to conform to our expectations. But He is sovereign. When He fails to do as we want, we turn from Him in our pain; we turn from faith, straying further and further from the path until we forget all that He ever did for us."

"And how did you remain on the path, Deborah?"

"I didn't," she admitted. "I faced death, and drowned in despair until I had no choice but to relinquish everything - even my life - and trust Him. It was only when I had no choice that I surrendered; I wonder if that is not the paradox of the human condition."

He nodded with understanding. "Will you tell me what happened?" he asked.

She nodded, taking a deep mental breath before plunging into the tempestuous chasm of her bleak and violent memories. Her tale unravelled, clumsy and emotional, and he listened quietly, his eyes never leaving her. When she spoke of the destruction she had seen in the villages, she felt the hard shell of her resolve splinter, and she shattered. Deep sobs that had been locked away, poured from her, and she wrapped her arms around her body as though the horror of the recollection would tear her apart. Lapidoth said nothing, but took her in his arms, stroking her hair until she finally fell asleep in his arms. He smiled as he carried her back to the settlement, reminded of a distant memory, the first time he had seen her; of when he had first come to love her, and the love he still carried.

When Deborah awoke the next day, she felt cocooned in the embrace of the morning sun. She acknowledged with mixed feeling that Lapidoth must have carried her back down the mountain and was inclined to be embarrassed, but reminded herself with mordant humour that at least she hadn't been dribbling puss over him this time.

Donning her headdress, she stepped outside, where she found Hur poking the embers of last night's fire. He looked up as she approached, and smiled. "Morning."

"I'm sorry for abandoning you last night. Were you alright?" She rubbed her eyes sleepily.

"Yes, once they had established that I wasn't a Canaanite spy, they were mostly very welcoming."

"Mostly?"

"I don't blame them, I'd be the same. I'm actually surprised they let me stay." It was strange to see Hur dressed in Hebrew attire: a simple linen tunic, held in place by a girdle from which hung his curved sword, and a faded, blue mantle that bore several patches.

"Did you discover where they get drinking water from?" Deborah asked.

Hur handed her a skin. "Not yet, but have mine."

A mist hung over the mountain tops, the air cool, still and fresh with Spring's promise. She pulled her mantle over her shoulders and sat in comfortable silence next to Hur, thanking Yahweh for the morning, for her freedom and for Hur's friendship. Aware that she had a tendency not to vocalise her inner thoughts, she turned to him and spoke: "Hur, I cannot believe the sacrifice you made, and continue to make, for my freedom. I am in your debt, and at this time can only offer my heartfelt gratitude."

His lips puckered into a straight line that was something between a smile and a frown. For a moment, he said nothing. "The army was never a life I chose for myself. I hated what I saw Sisera doing. I've worshipped many gods and never been terribly convinced about the authenticity of any of them; I'm not sure that's changed. But from the time that I first met you, your life seemed important and I didn't know why."

She bowed her head, feeling humbled by his admission, and then she gave an embarrassed laugh. "I hope to live up to such expectation."

He pulled a face and smiled with resignation. "It sounds dangerous already."

It was a few days later; Deborah had slept for the first time, uninterrupted by nightmares. When she emerged from her makeshift shelter, the settlement was beginning to come alive; a few of the women were pounding wheat, while another was feeding an infant. An older lady, whose name Deborah had discovered to be Marta, had rekindled last night's fire, adding dry heather and blowing the flames. The men were absent.

"They've gone." The old lady looked up from the fire, giving a toothless grin.

"Where?"

"There were Canaanites on the road, looking for you. Lapidoth and the men will attack them. Any money, food, blankets and clothing they are carrying will be taken and handed out amongst the settlements."

Deborah felt her old panic war within her. *Strange* she thought, *how I was able to surrender my own life to Yahweh, and my fear of Sisera was gone…but to trust Yahweh with Lapidoth's life seems so hard.* And yet, she acknowledged that her feelings for Lapidoth frightened her, because his life had become important to her.

She felt anxious all day, and finally took herself to the mountains to pray. She roughly remembered where Lapidoth had taken her to the night before, and it was not long before the rocks opened out to the ridge. The view was indeed magnificent, dark green hills graduated by vast grey steps of rock, flecked with red basalt. Streams like silver ropes wound their way through the verdant pastures, marred only by the darkened smears, a tribute of Canaan victory of Israel. Where once the landscape would have been thriving with Hebrew villages in which laughter and song would have coiled into the air as families worked vineyards, olive groves, and farmland, the skeletons of homes and the air of tragedy clung now to the earth. Only the Canaanite fields, irrigated and farmed by Hebrew slaves, were visible.

She strained her eyes to the dust road leading to Kedesh from Hazor, hoping and fearing that she might see Lapidoth and the men from the village. A few horses and caravans could be seen, surrounded by billowing dust clouds that concealed unidentifiable forms, but no disturbance or skirmish. To her left lay the city of Tel Kedesh, situated on two hills, and beyond that the Jordan, a brown, pulsing, milky vein that wound its way through Israel. It pooled at Lake Hula, to her right, like a tempered shield that glistened with sapphires. Beyond that lay the outline of Hazor, a dark smudge on the landscape. She breathed in the majesty of Yahweh's creation, allowing the awareness of His power and sovereignty to saturate her thoughts and fears. She breathed His name and felt His breath strengthen her:

Yahweh!
Yahweh!
Yahweh!

A white, voluminous cloud hung low over the hills, having the form of an eagle, powerful and free, its wings spread out. Its shadow covered the road and fields, like the ferocity of her prayers. As it was torn apart by the breeze, it dispersed, settling upon hearts and minds. She stood, her arms out stretched.

Yahweh! Heal this land and deliver Your people. Arise and awaken Your people. Fight on our behalf. Let this nation arise from its slumber. Fight on our behalf!

And then she saw the Angel of the Lord, as He had been all those years before in Ephraim. And in the same way as He had then said, simply 'Wait,' He now said: "The time comes."

Instinct took over as she threw back her head and roared; as a lioness grieves the death of her cubs, or a mother giving birth, she was driven by the anguish and death of all she had seen. It was a spiritual cry that shook the heavens and warned of the vengeance of God - and she was empowered by it.

And that is how Lapidoth found her. It seemed to him that she carried an ethereal beauty and strength, and he was suddenly overwhelmed with a sense of unworthiness. She turned, smiling peacefully, and he stood motionless, uncertain for a moment, as though the ground was holy.

She broke the silence. "I was frightened for you...you were gone."

He stared at her, searching her eyes. *How could she be so strong and so vulnerable at the same time; or was it that her vulnerability makes her strong?*

He sat down tentatively next to her, and she reached out her hand and touched his cheek tenderly. "My Lapidoth, where have you been? Have you never married?" He knew her question was a deeper request than a chronological report, and he allowed the reverberations of its meaning to ripple on the floor of his soul. He turned, kissing her hand, and then wove his fingers between hers, his eyes never leaving hers.

"Not yet..." he said quietly. "I fell in love with a girl many years ago..."

Deborah held her breath, her heart tightening into a knot; of course she was a fool to think he would not have loved, or married. She looked away, not wanting him to see her pain, and he continued. "Her father approached mine: he said his daughter had a gift and he felt she would be used by Yahweh, to deliver Israel, but he feared for her and wished to know that no matter what became of him, his daughter would be provided for and protected by a man from a good family." She frowned, fragments of colour appearing through the nebulous fog of his words.

"Our families agreed on a proposal, but because the girl was not yet of age, it was agreed that nothing would be said until her thirteenth birthday." He paused, his eyes were soft with compassion, as she grasped for understanding.

He swallowed, his face grave. "I only saw the girl one more time. I was fifteen and she was twelve, but I knew that I loved her. Because we were separated by distance, and the instability of the time we were in, with the consent of my father, I asked that the covenant be signed. This was agreed, with the understanding that the girl would be asked when she came of age; it was less than a year after all. I longed for the day when our betrothal would be public. Unfortunately, and unknowing, before her thirteenth birthday, her father was murdered by Sisera and her mother, overcome with grief, never spoke of the proposal, nor the arranged betrothal.

"Feasts were never attended after that. Mother and Rebecca were murdered, and I never saw the girl again...I lost hope, fearing that she too was dead.

"And then, a couple of years ago, I saw her - she was a slave at my stall..." he smiled, as Deborah realised who he was talking about, she clapped her hand over her mouth and tears ran down her face as she talked through her sobs.

"Me...my father arranged our betrothal...to you?"

Lapidoth smiled, his eyes solemn as he searched her face, saddened to see she was crying.

"You waited for me, though you did not know I would ever be yours."

"It is covenant, and I was unable to love another." He paused, and he recognised that he was fearful to speak further. Finally, he looked up, his eyes probing hers. "Of course, you are in no way bound to honour that betrothal."

She reached out and touched his face. "No! I love you too, Lapidoth...I cry only because of my father's presence in all of this...his gift to me and Yahweh's hand...that He knew all of this...I am overwhelmed by His goodness. And that you love me, when I have carried you in my heart for so long."

He nodded, cupping her face in his hand as he wiped away her tears with his thumb. Then, leaning forward, his lips touched hers, remaining for a moment before he pulled away. His eyes searched hers and she wondered: how could a kiss make her feel so whole, and yet somehow like she was also falling apart? She placed her hand on his chest, and felt the gallop of his heart match her own.

"Will you consent, then, to our betrothal?"

She leant forward and kissed the creases between his eyes. "With all my heart. Yes!"

His lips curved peacefully and he remained silent for a moment, as though allowing his mind to catch up with this long-awaited and almost abandoned dream. Finally, he spoke. "Then I will travel to Kedesh tomorrow and ask my father for the signed papers; then before him and our people, we will be husband and wife."

How can one perfect day chase away so much sadness? Deborah mused the following day, as she watched Lapidoth and his friends slip over the rock fortress of the hillside.

She felt a hand take hers, and turned to see Sen, the wife of Maor, one of Lapidoth's friends.

"I have something for you," she said shyly. "It was mine," she explained, holding up the lilac dress embroidered with white and blue flowers, complete with a matching veil.

Sen took her to the pool which the ladies used as a *mikveh*. It collected at the bottom of a waterfall and then disappeared back into the ground further down the mountain. When she had finished bathing, Ruth brushed her hair and rubbed her skin with olive oil.

She returned then to the ridge, and there she waited, her stomach churning with excitement and nerves.

Finally, Maor arrived; he had run ahead of the rest.

"The groom arrives!" he grinned.

Deborah stood, her head spinning as Lapidoth came into view. Beside him walked Abinoam, aged and slow on his feet; he was breathless with exertion, and yet he beamed when he saw Deborah. Seeing him now reminded her of her own father and his absence among them, creating a flood of bittersweet memories.

Ruth, Lapidoth's sister, was there, too, with her husband. Next to her was Josiah, with his wife and a priest. She embraced them, aware of the pain they had each experienced since their last meeting.

"I am so sorry to hear of Hannah and Rebecca." Her words caught in her throat.

Abinoam embraced her. "I, too, am grieved to hear of the loss of your father and Enoch. He was a good man, and a good friend. This is a day of joy that has been long awaited by both of our families. Come, my daughter, with your permission, I wondered if you might allow me the honour of giving you away today."

Deborah nodded through tear-glazed eyes. It was as her father would have wished. He had loved Abinoam.

She stood before Lapidoth as the priest read the betrothal papers and blessed their marriage.

"Two souls are birthed as one, the old has passed away," the priest announced. When she saw the *Kettubah*, signed by Lapidoth and her father, her eyes filled with tears. It was as though he was with her.

The bright sun smiled down upon them, and a single white cloud looped like a ribbon through the sky while the ground was carpeted in spring poppies and heather.

Lapidoth handed her a wooden box. Engraved on the lid were the words, 'Yahweh Shammeh'.

"The Lord is there," Deborah whispered, opening the box. Inside was a necklace, made of twisted gold. It dropped to a pendant that was embedded with three gems: a ruby, an emerald and a sapphire. She smiled up at Lapidoth. "It's so beautiful. Thank you."

"It was my grandmother, Yemina's, my mother's, and is now yours. The gems speak of Yahweh's complete work in our lives, formed under intense heat and pressure, and the gold is a symbol of His sovereignty over our trials." He placed it around her neck, and together they drank wine from the marriage cup, symbolising their unity as husband and wife.

Amidst the singing and congratulations of the settlement, Lapidoth silently took her hand, smiling as he drew her away from the crowd.

"Where are you taking me?" she laughed.

He turned, taking her face in his hands and kissed her. "It's a secret," he smiled, leading her through a narrow passage of rock. It towered above them on either side for some time, and whilst she had no idea in what direction they were heading, she was aware that they were walking upward and deeper into the mountains. Occasionally, he would turn and smile, his eyes dancing with joy. And then the path opened out, and Deborah saw that in the side of the mountain there was a cave. The opening was large, and at its side fell a waterfall. It gathered into a pool before continuing its journey down the mountain. The floor of the cave was lined with lichen and smelled of the earth, of Ephraim, of home; it was like a wedding present from Yahweh. She noticed a rock ledge that had been lined with food and wine, and in the back, cushions and covers.

"It's our hiding place. If there is a raid, we would come here." He looked around nervously and then added: "Do you like it?"

"I love it," she whispered in awe.

He went to the ledge and poured them both a cup of wine.

"You are so beautiful, my Deborah. I have dreamt of this moment for so long, I struggle to accept it is real. I cannot believe that you are finally mine, " he whispered.

She slipped her fingers into his hair. "I am yours and you are mine." She whispered, drawing his face down to meet hers. He nodded, bending to kiss her.

During their week of *Sheva Brechot*, it seemed that they had been cocooned in a heavenly shelter that was outside of time and reality. At times, she would awake thinking she was in *her place*, before darkness had rolled over their land. And then she would feel Lapidoth's arms around her, and her heart would sing that he was hers. They walked in the mountains, sharing their experiences and growing to understand each other.

When their time came to leave, they reluctantly left the warm embrace of the cave behind them, and were received as husband and wife into the arms of the settlement. She made her home in Lapidoth's shelter. Sen, Ruth and Marta had been working to make their bed linen, and Dan and Joseph had carved wooden bowls for them.

28

...the sons of Israel made for themselves the dens which were in the mountains and the caves and the strongholds.

Judges 6:2

1240 BC – Deborah and Lapidoth

Eight moons passed, and Deborah grew to love the people and the rhythm of life in the mountains. She had become good friends with Ruth and Sen and together they would take the children collecting herbs and other wild food. Whilst she loved their children and enjoyed playing with them, she found herself longing for the day she would have children of her own and felt somehow alienated in their bond of motherhood.

Hur came and sat next to her while she was preparing chickpea stew. She often thanked Yahweh for him: an Egyptian guard, risking his life and leaving his post to rescue a slave girl, and now living in a Hebrew village.

"How is it on the other side?" she grinned.

He sighed. "I feel freer here than I ever did in Harosheth. It's strange how we build walls around our perception of reality and persuade ourselves that everything outside of it is wrong," Hur laughed.

Deborah sighed. "I know. I feel the same about Canaan. Despite the evil I saw and the idolatry, there were good people too, people I came to love and respect." She kneaded the bread and rolled it into balls, placing them on the griddle over the fire. She looked up from her crouched position, her hair falling across her face. "Tell me Hur, how is it you came to work for Sisera?"

Hur sighed. "I was brought up with Jara, in Egypt. Our parents were friends; we were in love and spoke of the day when we would marry. When Sisera came and offered her father more wealth than I could ever hope to raise, her father could not refuse. Sisera needed guards to escort him back to Israel..."

"And you offered?"

"I wasn't ready to see her disappear...I knew what sort of man Sisera was, and was misguided that I could protect her," he smiled sadly.

"Do you still love her?"

Hur smiled weakly. "We cannot choose the matters of the heart," he sighed. "But when I saw Sisera with you that night...it triggered something in me. Hitting him over the head...it felt good. Stopping was the hard part," he added, grinning.

"But now you do not see Jara."

"No, not now. But it was for the best; she became like a drug to me, I needed her even though it was killing me."

She nodded. "I liked Jara...I did not expect to like the wife of Sisera."

"You met her?"

"I didn't meet her, I was a slave," she reminded him, smirking. "But I observed her standing up to Ariya and noted that she had a quiet integrity and courage that I respected."

Hur nodded thoughtfully.

Deborah loved the evenings, when work abated and the settlement drew around the fire. There, as they shared food, the flow of conversation and laughter merged into prayers and worship as stories of Yahweh's faithfulness strengthened their hearts and eased the hardships of their lives.

She valued Marta's company; the old lady had such wisdom and love for Yahweh. Her husband had died several years after they were married and after their village was raided, her daughter had gone with her husband and children to Kedesh.

"Why did you not go with them?" Deborah asked.

The old lady's face creased into a sad smile. "When you are young you love change, and are ready to take on the world. When you are older you hunger for what is familiar. My home is in the mountains, my memories are here. But we do not control our own destiny...I have prayed for Yahweh to turn the hearts of His children back to Him." She paused to stoke the fire. "You bring Yahweh into our midst. I am glad to be here at this time."

Deborah often retreated to the precipice where Lapidoth had proposed to her. It caught the first rays of the morning sun, when the day was not yet birthed and a hushed mist would rest over the barren plains that had once teemed with village life. There she would pray. Sometimes Lapidoth would find her clothed in an ethereal peace; she would turn and smile and he would feel Yahweh's presence envelope him. Other times, she would be reminded of the hour only by her thirst that found her in the midday sun.

Winter was upon them again; a layer of snow covered the mountaintops. The mountain stream was a trickle of icy water and food was scarce.

Feeling the cramps in her abdomen, she sadly acknowledged the passing of another month in which she had failed to conceive. She stood shivering as she stepped away from the fire, and made her monthly visit to the Niddah shelter. It was set back from the camp, hidden around a mound of rock and grass and inaccessible other than the path from the camp, thus making it safe. But, it also meant that they had a level of privacy. The shelter was neither as large, nor as comfortable as they would previously have enjoyed in established village life, and so as often as they were able they would sit outside.

Deborah arrived first and was pleased when Ruth arrived the next day. She seemed troubled. "The men have been talking about resuming their raids on Canaanite caravans, now that winter is almost upon us. They fear that food will grow scarce again."

Deborah shuddered. She hated the thought of Lapidoth encountering the cruelty of the Canaanites, and had persuaded him that he should not go to war for the first year of marriage, as the Torah prescribed. He had dutifully agreed.

But without crops from the harvest, inadequate provision was made for winter. For this reason, many in the mountains had fled to the cities where they could find work.

She looked up, struggling to find words of comfort. "And Saul, how does he feel about it?"

Ruth snorted; she was a tall, well-built woman and her responses had a straightforward brusqueness to them. "He's a man – they love the thought of battle as a dog likes to roll in its own faeces."

Deborah grinned at Ruth's analogy and the woman laughed conspiratorially.

"It's hardest to trust when you are still raw from pain," Deborah acknowledged.

"And yet you make faith look so easy," Ruth accused playfully.

Deborah laughed. "I found faith in weakness, grief and pain. Had I not clung to Yahweh, I would have been washed onto the shore of insanity."

Ruth nodded in agreement, looking up as the first drops of rain hit her face. "We should go inside, it's started raining."

When Sen arrived the next day, she was spent. Having sorted out her sanitary requirements, she came and threw herself down on the bench.

A small fire burnt in the opening of the shelter, though it seemed to be battling for its life against the rain and wind outside.

"Elijah threw a stone at Samuel this morning and cut his head. They've been inside since yesterday and are fighting non-stop. I was so pleased to leave them with Maor and come here, " she admitted, massaging her temples.

Deborah squeezed her hand and offered her a blanket and bowl of pigeon soup. She smiled gratefully, clutching the soup in her hands and watching the steam disappear into the cool air.

They sat chatting into the night, the moon a silver sliver that the stars danced around. They asked Deborah about Ephraim and as she began to describe her village and family to them, she was aware how much she missed her people. Sen and Ruth spoke of Kedesh, and how abundant the harvests had been due to the fertility of the land. They spoke of how people, in their comfort, had turned away from Yahweh to the pleasures of Canaan, and how everything had fallen apart. Deborah noted the way of the women as they spoke, listened and prayed with each other. It was not merely an exchange of information, but a spiritual connection with the heart of Yahweh in its compassion, perception and intuition. It was where empathy and encouragement of the other was married with self-reflection and personal growth. By truly understanding the events, feelings and perceptions of the other, we make ourselves vulnerable to our own fragility and imperfection, thus enabling us to accept the failings of others. In prayer and communion, they were joined in heart and purpose. This was the strength of women, and this was the foundation of a nation that would be victorious.

The night sky was starless and thick grey, voluminous clouds were beginning to lower ominously.

Ruth nodded to the glow of a fire that spiraled from one of the upper peaks. "So many attend the high places now. There are few of us that remain faithful."

"The dreadful irony of it is that they are starving. They sacrifice their children and believe Baal will provide a harvest they cannot sow nor reap," Sen added.

Deborah said nothing. Her thoughts lingered, spiraling to heaven as the smoke from the fire. *How would her nation ever be turned from their path of destruction, when they were blind to their deception and their need?* The magnitude of the spiritual and physical battle that rose before them seemed insurmountable.

It was a week later when she returned from the precipice to see Lapidoth deep in a heated discussion with Joel, Dan and Saul. Hur was whittling a stick as he watched with indifferent curiosity from the shelter he shared with Dan. When Lapidoth saw her coming, he stood up and walked toward her.

"I need to go for a walk and clear my head." His tone was strained, a frown etched on his handsome features as his fingers caught in his tangled hair.

She waited for him to speak, walking silently next to him; she had a fairly good idea what he had argued about.

"The men want to begin raiding Canaanite caravans again."

"And how do you feel about that?"

"I promised you a year." He looked torn, and she felt it was only his love for her that held him back rather than a feeling of genuine conviction in Yahweh's purposes.

She pressed her lips against his. "I love you no matter what you choose. Yahweh makes laws for our good and those laws protect us. But make no choice based on your love for me."

He took her face in his hands and lowered his head to meet hers. "I love you," he whispered, and she felt the strength of her frustration melt in the urgency of his kisses.

They returned to the village after midday to find that the men were gone, and Sen and Ruth arguing amongst themselves.

"They should have waited," Lapidoth grumbled, pacing the area in front of the fire. He picked up his sword and bow. "Where are they?"

"They heard word of a troop returning to Hazor and are waiting for them at the crossroads."

"There's no cover there. What are they thinking of?!" His expression was panicked, if not defeated. He turned to Deborah and she realised he had no choice now. "I need to go. I'm sorry. Please pray."

And then he broke into a run and was gone, and it seemed that the air was filled with a silent vacuous void as the women and children waited.

"I will pray. I can do nothing else, would anyone like to join me?" Deborah sighed. Ruth, Sen and Marta nodded silently and together they began their vigil.

The first muffled voices pricked the silence, even as the stars poked their way into the black sky. The women strained to hear the voices of their loved ones, and then the sounds of groans and screams grew louder. Dread lurched in the women's minds as they scrambled to meet them.

Deborah saw Hur and Lapidoth first. Their expressions were grim. Between them, they supported Saul, his face was grey and one arm hung limp at his side, while the other held a wound on his stomach, blood pumped beneath his fingers. Deborah heard Ruth's desperate groan as she ran to her husband. Deborah grabbed her medicine chest from their shelter and ran to help him, but already she sensed death hovering over him. She looked at Lapidoth as he leaned over his friend, and saw his own resignation and remorse, even as it registered within her own mind: *his wounds are too deep, the damage to great.* She shook her head silently. "Stay with him and Ruth," she said quietly, her heart knotting at the pain that had pooled around the dying man.

She moved on to Maor next. A spear had skewered his shoulder, and removing it had caused considerable loss of blood, and he wandered in and out of consciousness. She took some of the myrrh resin, dissolving a small part in water and mixing it with honey. As she applied it to his wound she prayed for his healing. She was aware that her myrrh would be difficult to replace once it was gone; it had been brought from Egypt. Joseph's wounds were more superficial and so, on these, she placed only honey, binding the cuts to prevent infection.

As she stood and looked around her, before moving on to treat a deep gash in Joel's thigh, she felt Lapidoth's eyes upon her. He smiled sadly; the crease between his eyes seemed to have shattered momentarily, twisting his face with grief. And then he composed himself. Squatting next to Saul, he gently gripped his friend's shoulder while his wife, Ruth, held his hand, tears rolling down her face as her husband drew his last breaths.

"They will be taken care of my friend...rest with your fathers in Abraham's bosom, until we meet again. Know they will be taken care of." He wiped his eyes with the back of his hand.

When she had finished, Deborah walked wearily to the spring and washed her hands. The old lady, Marta, had rekindled the fire and was hunched over it making a lentil stew.

"Shall I make bread? Do you have wheat?" Deborah asked, wearily.

"Not wheat. Barley." Her sad eyes gestured to one of the shelters.

Despite her tiredness, grinding the barley felt cathartic, reminding her of Ephraim. In the diminished light, she felt the smoothness of the flour before mixing it with water and oil, forming it into small balls and laying them in a scorched black pan.

Hur came and sat next to her.

She turned and smiled. "Are you alright, Hur?"

"Tired…but whole," he replied, quietly gazing into the blazing fire.

"You fought against Canaan today, Hur, my friend. It must have been hard for you?"

Hur shook his head. "I have seen that sometimes in life we carve out our destiny, and other times destiny finds us. I have learnt to be content travelling either road."

He pushed another log into the fire. "It's good to see you happy; it's been a long time coming," he added, cocking his head as he smiled.

Deborah nodded. "It's a strange feeling."

"Happiness?"

She exhaled. "Yes, it scares me if I'm honest."

"In case you lose it?"

She nodded, unable to admit the battle of faith she faced: how she had learnt to trust Yahweh in her suffering, yet now acknowledged her fear in the midst of happiness and security.

She shook the thought. "You must miss the luxuries of Canaan?"

"It's better to eat bread with peace in the company of righteous men, than meat with distrust."

"It would seem that your destiny has embraced you," Deborah laughed. "You even speak like a Hebrew."

Hur raised an eyebrow. "Your ways make sense to me. I feel more at home here than I ever did in Harosheth, and probably in Egypt, too."

"I'm glad, Hur." The flames flickered in her eyes and she sat back, allowing their ancient dance, bright and hungry, to sear the wounds that the day had brought. She felt arms wrapped around her waist and Lapidoth's beard tickled her face. She sighed as she once again recalled how he had carried her to safety nearly twenty years ago.

That night, she lay with her head on his chest as she listened to the steady rhythm of his life.

"You did well today," he whispered, kissing her hair.

"So did you. It must have been awful…"

"Saul came with me from Kedesh; our families grew up together." She felt his chest rise and fall as a deep sigh escaped his soul. "Maor took a blow that was meant for me – he saved my life. Do you think he'll make it?"

"I think he will." She felt the quiet tension of his grief and remained silent, knowing that words were futile and the morning unknown.

When she awoke the next morning, Lapidoth was already busy. The sun lay dutifully in its mountain cradle, surrounded in a haze of mist, as though it, too, was reluctant to face the day.

Deborah splashed her face with water and sat with Marta, who was once again stoking the fire. Sen and Maor's children, Abram and Eli, played with rocks, making them into a wall, while Jakeyla toddled over to her and gave her a flower. Deborah smiled, placing it to her nose and then tickling the child's nose, making her giggle.

"That's Jakeyla, she's one of Saul's, poor little thing. Lapidoth is preparing his body for burial. We'll bury him this morning." Her lined face was a map of grief and reconciled weariness.

Deborah nodded, and went to check on the other men.

"Can I come in?" she whispered outside Sen and Maor's shelter.

"Yes, come," she heard Sen answer. She pushed aside the deerskin that covered the opening and entered into the shelter. Sen sat next to Maor. His eyes were glazed with pain, but he was awake. She smiled gratefully at Deborah as she knelt next to him, feeling his head and lifting the bandages on his wound.

"He's not burning, which is good. Make sure you keep the wound clean." Then speaking to Maor she added, "I need to put some more salve on the wound."

The man nodded, wincing as Deborah applied the precious myrrh to the area and applied new bandages.

Leaving them alone, she saw Joel emerging from his shelter. She remembered treating a deep gash across his thigh the previous evening.

"You shouldn't be walking, you'll reopen the wound," Deborah admonished, smiling.

He glowered at her, opened his mouth as though he was going to speak, exhaled sharply and strode away.

"Pain makes some men crabby," Marta sighed, taking a handful of barley and gently crushed it between the two stones.

"Can I help?" Deborah asked. She felt Joel's behaviour claw at the old scar: *I will always be on the outside.* She recognised it for what it was, shaking her head to dislodge the thought; *I am where You want me, Yahweh. My life and times are in Your hand and man's opinion has no hold on me.*

Following the burial of Saul, Lapidoth seemed to collapse inside of himself with grief. The diminished group ate silently together, and then each went about the business of survival with a numb gratitude for anything that would take their minds off of the missing spaces and their own mortality.

"I need to walk, will you come with me?" Lapidoth asked.

She slipped her hand into his as he led her on an unworn path that clung to the side of the mountain. He didn't speak. Neither did she. She liked that about him. Finally, the path ended and they needed to climb a rocky slope. She smiled, suddenly reminded of *her place*.

"Do you need me to help?" he asked, holding out his hand.

She shook her head, easily reaching for the foot and handholds and pulling herself up. When they reached the top of the rock, the path continued and then sloped downward, continuing its journey around the side of the mountain, winding down in a zigzag to the enclosed valley below. A silver ribbon of twisting water sparkled at its base.

Lapidoth sat on a large, flat rock, reaching for his water skin and handing it to Deborah.

"It clears the mind, the vastness, the majesty, the purity of Yahweh's creation. I find perspective again."

"Anything that helps me to realise how small I am and how big Yahweh is, is infinitely helpful," she smiled, taking in the detail of his handsome features.

"Gibeah," Lapidoth sighed. "It seems a lifetime ago." His eyes bore deep into Deborah's soul.

She returned the intensity of his gaze. "It does. I've often recalled those words. When I looked at the stars, you were there." She handed the water to Lapidoth.

He smiled, his boyish eyes twinkling. "So you thought of me?"

"Often." She smiled at his childlike openness; he had the same attributes that she had always admired in Hadas.

He paused for a moment, a smile playing on his lips. She knew he wanted her to continue, but she had never found it easy to talk about her inward journey.

He sighed. "The heat is picking up. We ought to keep moving." They kept on in their descent of the mountain. Wild grass, blue lupins and yellow corn marigolds coloured the landscape, stirred only by the occasional impala or gazelle lazing in the tall grass. A pigeon swooped down, settling on a rock by the stream. They were near enough now to hear its noisy babble, a fluid, joyful melody that bounded with naïve optimism, effervescent and glistening without knowledge or care for the death it would later witness.

Let us steal this perfect moment, let us enjoy it for what it is, it whispered.

Lapidoth strung his bow, and the arrow flew through the air, settling in the body of the pigeon. He whooped with childlike joy and raced down to it, removing the arrow and placing it in his bag. Deborah joined him, laughing as he stripped off his top and tunic and leapt into the stream.

Suddenly, his head disappeared beneath the water and Deborah feared he had been swept away. She raced over, peering into the white, frothing water. A hand shot out, grabbed her and pulled her in. She screamed, laughing.

"It's cold!" she gasped.

He gestured to the mountains tops. "It comes from up there," he grinned, wiping the grime and blood from his hair.

"A bath was long overdue," he sighed, smirking.

"No argument there," she agreed, pulling herself out of the icy water.

She ran her fingers through his wet hair, and he turned and kissed her hand.

"I needed to get away...otherwise it gets too much." His face twisted as though he were struggling to justify his actions.

"It's important to remember what we are fighting for," she agreed leaning to kiss him.

"It is," he whispered in agreement, pulling himself out of the water and returning her kisses.

The sun was a blood red orb that rested on the mountaintops, leaking into the sky and colouring the landscape with its amber and pink rays. It heralded their need to return home.

"Tell me again about the dreams you had," Lapidoth asked as they walked.

"Of finding you again? Or the ones from Yahweh?" she laughed, offering him a small token of her inward journey.

He grinned, his eyes shining. "Of course the ones of me!"

She laughed. "After I saw you at the market, I thought of you often. I would sometimes wonder what you were doing, whether you were safe. I would remember your smile, your words to me and I would feel happy and wish that I could see you again...because I knew that I loved you." She stopped, suddenly feeling embarrassed.

He stopped, taking her in his arms. "Thank you for telling me. I know it must be difficult talking about that time."

As they continued, she began to tell him about the dreams Yahweh had given her, first when she was eight, then the one she had had the previous year.

"A mother to Israel...How does that work?"

Deborah shrugged. "Your guess is as good as mine. I rest in the hand of Yahweh, waiting for Him to show me."

"So, what is it you would like to do?" he frowned.

She sighed; it was a good question and one she had never consciously considered. Finally, she said, "I would like to gather Israel into my arms, and remind her of who she is and Yahweh's promises for her. And I would fight for her as a young lion does her cubs."

He stopped, running his fingers through his hair. "Well, you've explained the what...so the question is how?"

He kept walking and they both grew silent. They slid down the rock they had clambered up earlier that day and began the last stretch of the path. Suddenly he stopped, holding his finger to his lips as he withdrew his bow again, slowly and quietly stringing the arrow. It whizzed through the air. Deborah struggled to see what he was aiming for. He exhaled with exasperation, stringing again. When he turned, his eyes shone in the waning light.

"Gazelle for dinner tonight." He flashed her a satisfied smile before running to collect his prize. She watched with pride as he tied the deer's legs together, his muscular arms effortlessly hoisting the animal onto his back.

There was a riotous welcome as they returned to the village.

"I can't help wondering if you are more pleased to see the gazelle than you are me," Lapidoth smiled with wry humour, dumping the deer and pigeon next to the fire.

Dan stepped forward. He was tall and thick set, with pale brown thinning hair, green eyes and his front tooth missing. He slapped Lapidoth on the back and pulled a knife from his belt.

"There's no doubt in my mind!" he winked. "If I prepare it, though, I get the first cut," he grinned, grabbing the prize and slitting its throat as he lifted it.

Deborah bent down, picking up Saul and Ruth's smallest child, Jakeyla; at three years old, she had a simple understanding of her loss that was endearing. "Abba has gone to stay with his fathers." She had no comprehension as yet that she would not see him again this side of eternity. Her brother, Raphael, was four years her senior, and his features were a painful reminder to Ruth of her loss. He took Deborah's hand and begged her to play. Her heart ached for him; he was too young to be burdened with so much pain. She smiled.

"Of course, what shall we play?"

"Let's play fight." He handed her a carved wooden doll, a piece of wood had been tied to its hand that represented a sword. He held a similar version in his own hand.

Deborah felt a nudge in her heart, and she smiled, "Of course. Tell me about your warrior, Raphael?"

Raphael puffed out his chest. "He is a mighty warrior. He has never been defeated!"

"Hmmm, and who is he fighting?"

Raphael looked at her as if he was stupid. "Canaanite soldiers, of course."

"Would you like my doll to play the Canaanite soldier?"

He nodded, his dark eyes solemn.

Deborah acted out that she was a fearsome Canaanite, while Raphael re-enacted the mental imagery of his father's death. This time, the Canaanite was killed. Deborah watched as the boy poured out his anger and grief in his play. It culminated in the expression of his grief, and Deborah held him as his feelings of loss spilled from his dark eyes. Jakeyla, seeing her brother cry, wept too and she held both of them in her arms. When his tears were spent, he wiped his face with the back of his hand. She stroked his hair, and looking into his eyes she said, "It's alright to be angry and sad – I lost my father when I was young. Only remember that Yahweh is there and you can always talk to Him, because He understands. And remember, too, that if you need a hug or someone to talk to and Ima is busy, you can always come to me."

Each day, Deborah would escape to the precipice where she had first spoken to Lapidoth, and from that place she would pray. From here, it was as though she could see all of Israel. Sometimes he would join her, but he was restless, preferring to wield a sword or axe to the battle she engaged in. She knew Yahweh must act, but that she could do nothing until He led.

29

As one whom his mother comforts, so I will comfort you;
Isaiah 66:13

1239 BC – Deborah and Lapidoth

Deborah sat with Ruth in the Niddah shelter. It was not far from the rest of the settlement, due to safety, but it was a place that was theirs. As she sat next to the grieving woman, she was reminded of her mother after her father and Enoch had died. She existed. Her eyes stared blankly into space, varied only by the huge silent tears that would often streak her face. Deborah remembered her own prison of grief, and knew it was too early to ask her to open the doors to the pain in her soul. Instead, she prayed for her when she was alone, or sat next to her, chatting about simple occurrences in the village and those she visited.

Whenever she had time, she would play with her children. She had been married to Lapidoth for over a year now, and her thirtieth birthday had passed and still she had not fallen pregnant. She felt the ache within her to hold her own children, even as her longing to see her own mother and brother was constant.

The sun blazed down from a cloudless sky, intense and unyielding, the mountains had turned yellow for lack of water and the streams were shallow. Lapidoth and his men had attacked a large Canaanite caravan and secured enough food to last until summer abated; of that they would distribute to the other clans hidden in the mountains. Joel continued to regard her with disdain, but Deborah purposed to show no offense.

She sat with Lapidoth, lazily enjoying the shadow of their shelter. He was sharpening his sword and she was grinding hyssop ready for use as a poultice. Then, shrill panic pierced the smoggy haze that the noon heat buried them in.

"Help!! Please!! Our settlement has been attacked, please come quickly!" Lapidoth leapt up.

"Josiah!" he embraced the man and then handed him a water bottle.

"We were attacked....Please help. They came on foot to our village. There was hardly any warning. They've taken some, killed others and still more are wounded. Please, can you help us?"

Lapidoth spun around to see Deborah standing, her medicine box already in her hand. He nodded and called for a few others.

"Micah, take the women and children to the hideout. Make sure you don't leave any tracks. Dan, Joel, Hur and Joseph come with us."

Joel took Lapidoth to the side; he cast a dismissive frown toward Deborah. "Is it wise to bring your woman?"

"Imperative. She will tend to the sick."

Having witnessed Sisera's destruction of villages until her mind became numb, she was able to deal with the sight that befell her. It was as though her grief and frustration had been fused with a lifetime of prayer and desperate hope so that now, faced with the horror before her, Yahweh poured Himself through her as though they worked as one.

Something occurred in the settlement that was not the work of a woman with a medicine kit, but of Yahweh drawing His people to Himself. Deborah spoke as she worked, encouraging them of Yahweh's love and deliverance. She spoke as she perceived Yahweh's heart and thoughts.

Some were too grief stricken and traumatised to listen, and the words would take time to sink through the desiccated layers of their hardship. For others, hearing Yahweh's name again was like a balm that they desperately clung to.

Yahweh's name had become a historic culture that defined them; they lived in the mountains because they would not turn to Canaan's ways. But their true faith and passion had been diluted by suffering and the base need to survive. Yahweh's mighty deliverances of their nation were historic stories they told their children; but they had no anticipation of His aid to them personally because their relationship with Him had become a memory. But as Deborah spoke, her faith created a ripple of hope in the midst of despair that was undefined and yet potent. She prayed simply, taking the hand of those who reached out to Him and placing it in the hands of the loving Father she had come to know. She tended them as a mother tends to a hurt child, and they hungered for what they saw in her.

They began to remember. By the time she left the village, Deborah felt as though she, too, had grown. Something had been birthed within her, and she knew that she had seen His heart in her own.

As she sat with Lapidoth in their shelter that night, the dim light of the oil lamp flickered on the makeshift table, swathing the room in a pool of light.

"Something happened today. It was awful, we know those people, they are our friends, some our family…and yet in the midst of it, something shifted, it was tangible, but unexplainable." Lapidoth rubbed the back of his neck.

Deborah nodded, looking up at her husband. The light cast shadows on Lapidoth's olive skin, so that half of him seemed to glow, the other half was cast in shadows; she shuddered inwardly as a dark sense of premonition pricked her thoughts.

"It has begun," she agreed. "Light travels outward, and draws men to it." She gently pushed his hands away and massaged his shoulders. When he finally relaxed, she wrapped her arms around his neck and murmured into his ear.

"You're good for me Lapidoth."

He smiled sleepily and answered, "I know."

Ten days later another man arrived, the same story came from another settlement. They sadly made the journey through the mountains to where the small community dwelt. Lapidoth and Joel tended to the dead while Deborah cared for the wounded: it was a pitiful scene, women holding their children, or grieving those who had been taken. No family had been left untouched. When evening finally settled its shadowy cloak over the gathering, a fire burnt, but neither its warmth nor its light could dissipate the heaviness that hung over the community.

"We came to the mountains because they were deemed safe. The chariots couldn't come into the mountains, we believed. Now nowhere is safe." The woman clutched her two children close to her, her eldest daughter had been taken.

There were murmurs of agreement.

"There's nowhere left to hide." It was a statement of finality, its speaker's gaze fell despondently into the fire as though watching his remaining hopes turn to ash. A still, empty silence settled on the gathering.

"Lapidoth, tell us about your woman," Sheduer, cut through the gloom, gesturing to Deborah. He was a well-built man in his fifties, with dark, shoulder length hair and a cut that ran from his right ear to his top lip.

"Anyone who has fought Sisera and survived can tell her own story. Her name is Deborah," Lapidoth asserted, throwing Sheduer a skin of wine.

Sheduer raised his eyebrows and gave a smirk of respect and agreement.

"So, will you tell us then? What are you? Healer or Warrior?" he grinned.

Deborah smiled weakly. "In these times, it pays to be both, and yet the courage I have belongs to Yahweh. My father and brother were murdered by Sisera when I was twelve. Later, I was Sisera's slave for nearly five years. I was taken because I stood up to him; I told him his past and future as Yahweh had shown me, and in doing so, I was able to keep him from destroying my village. He wished to make me a priestess of Canaan, but I would not submit to him. His own priests warned him to respect me, for they believed the hands of the gods were upon me, but it was Yahweh who preserved my life." She looked around the shadowy faces of those around her, faintly lit by the roaring fire. "You must not think I did not fear. At first, I lived in fear and horror, dragged with Sisera on his war parties, in his attempt to break me. And he did. But as Joseph said to his brothers 'what they intended for bad, Yahweh used for good.' My pain and grief caused me to cleave to Him, to become knitted to the fabric of His being, and from necessity I found my life and strength in Him. Then, I feared no more, and that Sisera could not fathom. One day I defied and humiliated him in front of Jabin; I failed to bow down to Baal. He attacked me, but Hur risked his life, attacking Sisera and rescuing me." She paused, looking around at the intent expressions on their faces as they flickered in the firelight.

She continued, "While I was in captivity, I travelled to Philistia, where I met a man called Shamgar. He single-handedly killed six hundred Philistines with an ox-goad, including the five lords. He has taken Philistia for Yahweh. Yahweh awakens His people and desires to draw them to Himself and heal this land, if they will turn to Him."

Sheduer was the first to stand.

"Something more than a healer then…a prophet?" He was thoughtful for a moment and Deborah allowed the silence to linger; she knew Yahweh spoke in silence as much as in words. Finally, he exhaled deeply before continuing. "We used to live on the outskirts of Kedesh, a village of about fifty people," Sheduer explained.

"It was attacked fifteen years ago," another added.

"Initially we tried to keep up with Sisera's demands, but then he began to take the children and violate our women." Sheduer grimaced at the memories. "I lost my wife and daughter.

"Many fled to the cities, but the corruption there is too great, and we didn't want to raise our children to accept the ways of the Canaanites. And so we came to the mountains, because Jabin's chariots cannot come here. We have held our belief in Yahweh, but hope is weak."

Deborah felt Yahweh's hand upon her, and she spoke as Yahweh put the words in her mouth, His boldness strengthening her: "Sheduer, son of

Gad, you who were born at sunrise with a cry so loud that your father proudly declared you were born to fight with Israel's armies. He spoke truly; you will see victory over your enemies. Yahweh will avenge your loss." There were a few surprised whispers and she knew she had their attention now.

She continued. "A new day dawns and Yahweh's light breaks forth. He calls us back to Him. Let us humble ourselves and fast and pray; let us seek His face, for the God of Jacob, of Abraham, of Moses and Joshua fights with us; salvation is at hand."

The man looked up and held Deborah's eyes, and she saw him war with the fear and desire that hope and trust evoked in him and she felt compassion, for she, too, had wrestled with the same fear. She knew that only Yahweh could reach through the pain and defence that this man and his village had built around themselves to survive the years of wilderness. Finally he spoke, his head bowed.

"I know Yahweh is the true God. I want to hope."

Several others stood too.

"It is brave to hope when you have seen so much pain. Yahweh will not disappoint, for hope nurtured, becomes faith and faith in Yahweh will bring deliverance and victory over enemies."

She continued, her voice was authoritative as she was driven by both her compassion and zeal for Yahweh's kingdom. "Tell those in neighbouring clans what you have heard. At the next full moon let us meet, those of us who are willing, that we might pray and seek Yahweh."

Joel spoke now, and she felt her stomach tighten. "And who will lead Yahweh's army?" She sensed a hidden motive in his question.

"Yahweh will lead His army...any men worthy to fight with Him will know to give Him the glory; for salvation belongs to Him." She turned away.

An old man came forward; stooped over a stick, in his other hand he held a cloth. He trembled as he proceeded to unwrap the string that bound it and finally held up a ram's horn.

"I did not expect to hear it blown again. This was my father's before me; it was used at Jericho on the day they brought down its mighty walls. We are Levites. When the time comes, it will be my honour to call Yahweh's people to battle."

Deborah nodded; standing to her feet she felt Yahweh's spirit upon her as she raised her voice. "The time will come and it will not tarry. But first Yahweh must awaken His people. Let us go into the neighbouring villages and tell them that His deliverance draws near. Let His people turn back to Him, let them consecrate their hearts and seek His face. For He is holy. He is worthy. He is sovereign and He comes to fight for His people!" Her words were echoed by the prayers and declarations of allegiance from the village. More had gathered now, drawn by His presence. It was unspoken, unfathomable, but they were no longer two settlements that had come together under grave conditions, but God's children - Israel. A unity had formed, of hearts and minds knitted in spirit and purpose to Yahweh's. Thus, they already carried a power that was greater than the sum total of the individuals present.

As they said their goodbyes and wearily made their way back to their own settlement, Deborah felt a single shaft of light had pierced the clouds that ensconced her nation. She saw, too, that within those clouds a vulture hovered.

Lapidoth walked ahead with Joel, while Hur walked next to Deborah.

"I see the spark has turned to flame," Hur smiled, an almost fatherly pride in his expression, though he could not be more than five years her senior.

She turned to him and smiled, "You were obedient to Yahweh, even though you did not know Him, Hur. You saw something in me, when no one else did. He had purposed that you might be one of His people. But that is for you to decide."

"You honour me more than I deserve. I admit, I am curious about the ways of your people…" He let his words hang in the air. Lapidoth was walking ahead next to Joel some distance ahead of them. They kept their voices lowered, but in the flickering torchlight, it was evident that they were arguing vehemently. Dan walked behind them and was clearly trying to play the role of diplomat.

When they reached the dip in the hills that marked their territory, they were pleased to see the glow of the fire. Each person wearily made their way to their own shelter. Hur was sharing with Dan, who had lost his wife to sickness the previous year.

Lapidoth was still agitated when he sat on the pallet. He gave a heavy sigh, his head bent and his curly hair poking out between the fingers of his clenched fist.

She sat up and put her arms around him. "Do you want to talk about it?"

"No, I don't," he answered abruptly.

Deborah lay awake; mentally discussing the disquiet that had risen within her, with Yahweh. *Perhaps there is a part of me that will always feel on the outside. Is it that that keeps me close to You?* she brooded.

When she woke the next morning, Lapidoth was already awake. He lay next to her, watching her. He looked so sad, as though his frown had burrowed into his mind.

"I'm sorry about last night. You spoke well…It's wonderful to see Yahweh's plans for you coming to pass." His tone lacked its usual warmth.

Perhaps he is struggling with the death and loss of those he knows and loves, she wondered.

She smiled and kissed him; he didn't want to speak about what was bothering him and so she decided to let it pass.

Word began to travel in the mountains of Kedesh about the wife of Lapidoth, who had defied Sisera and spoke the words of Yahweh.

Lapidoth was already known and respected as a warrior, who attacked the Canaanites and brought food and provision to the villages. Over the next few months, men were sent from their settlements to hear Deborah's story, to judge the truth of it and take it back to their clans.

Whilst she would tell her story to each settlement they visited, she was shrewdly aware that this would not be enough to turn the hearts of Israel's men. But she spoke Yahweh's prophetic words as He gave her utterance, encouraging them in their faith for Him and assuring them of His deliverance.

"Fast, pray and wait," she told them.

Joel kept his distance from Deborah, but his allegiance and friendship with Lapidoth was seemingly restored and Deborah had accepted his distrust of her, whilst feeling no need to change it. She, in turn, treated him as she did any of the other men, and pretended to ignore his disdain. Maor had made a complete recovery from his wound, as had the other men, and the spiritual awakening that touched the other settlements burned brightly within their own. They often sat around the fire in the evenings telling stories of Yahweh's acts and His great deliverances of old; they once again reminded the children of His laws. On the Sabbath they sung and prayed along with those who had travelled to visit them and at the full moon, they gathered with other settlements in the mountains in unity. It was at these times that the spiritual awakening was most felt, and the increasing number of those who had turned back to Yahweh was most evident.

She and Lapidoth had gone to the precipice to pray. She sat on the warm grey stone looking out over the hills and rolling plains below her, Lapidoth held his hand in hers. "How can we reach the other tribes, the cities? How can I do this?"

"You can't. You can only pray and wait for Yahweh. He will bring them," he answered with his usual confidence.

Lapidoth was right; within the space of a few months, men had come from as far as Zebulon, Asher and Issachar. Word had travelled from village to village and with it the message: 'Yahweh awakens His people. Deborah the wife of Lapidoth, the prophetess, exposes the truth of men's hearts and is residing in the hill country outside Kedesh. The question on the hearts and minds of Israel was: *has Yahweh raised her up as judge. But, would He choose a woman?* On this they were divided.

The men had decreased their attacks on Canaanite caravans; their time now was taken watching for, and directing, those who came. Many came to judge for themselves if what they heard was true: *what manner of woman was this?* Some initially tested her with the private disputes of their village: *would her answer reflect Yahweh's wisdom; the word of the Torah?* She would rarely answer them immediately, but wait for Yahweh to speak; in the silence she weighed their hearts. When they left, convinced of Yahweh's hand on Deborah's life, those who had wealth left gifts. Deborah distributed these among the settlements, as well as within her own. With Lapidoth's agreement, they kept only a small portion for themselves.

She sat with Lapidoth on the precipice. He seemed distant, and she didn't know how to bridge the gap; she had watched the creases in his brow deepen, and for all her insight, had no idea how to reach him. He was the one to talk about his feelings, and his silence made her nervous.

"Everything has been…overwhelming. How are you in the midst of it all?" she asked tentatively.

He didn't answer immediately, and when he finally spoke a deep sigh escaped his lips. His eyes shifted from hers to the expanse before them.

"You've done so well. Everything Yahweh promised you is coming to pass…I'm so proud of you." She knew that he was sparing her feelings, that there was a world of thought he had fenced from her.

She reached out and held the face she loved in her hands, her eyes boring into his soul. He closed his eyes.

"Please don't look at me like I'm wounded."

"And yet, you are struggling…I don't know how…why won't you talk to me?"

He rested his head in his hand, a handful of black curls poking out between his fingers.

"I love you…This is my battle and you don't need to be thinking of me in the midst of everything else you're doing." He looked wretched as he stood, and Deborah didn't know if she should run after him or not. She couldn't help feeling she had done something to upset him.

Lapidoth climbed to the summit of the mountain, he enjoyed the physical effort. It helped him order his thoughts. He felt as though he was falling, and he needed to do it alone.

Sitting down, he sighed, frustrated by his emotions. He had known all along that Deborah had the call of Yahweh on her life and he had loved that about her. But more than that: he loved her. He had loved her since he first saw her lying crumpled and broken in the mountains. He remembered his mother smiling when he had brought wounded birds and animals back from his walks: *'you always fall in love with anything wounded and broken. You were made to rescue people, my Lapidoth,'* she had said with pride.

He had grown to be satisfied with his life in the mountains. He was acknowledged as being a warrior and leader among his men, and felt a sense of purpose and achievement for the provisions he handed out to the other settlements.

When Deborah had first arrived in the mountains, he had loved her more than he had anticipated. That she had loved him too had been more than he had hoped for. He recalled the day he had found her on the precipice, she had radiated the glory of Yahweh and he had thought: *I am not good enough for you.*

But their love for each other had been enough. When Deborah suggested that he stopped raiding the caravans until the year of their marriage was over, he had been fine with that, because he loved her. So, what was wrong? He was proud of her, wasn't he? He wanted her to be who Yahweh had called her to be and he wanted to see his nation liberated, didn't he? So why did he feel like he was dying inside? He didn't know who he was anymore. Deborah's husband. Was that all he would ever be now? Was that his great destiny? Why couldn't he just be pleased about the fact that those he loved accepted his wife and her calling? It was like two rivers converging, each with their own powerful course, but as they journeyed, the stronger swallowed the weaker until it was no longer recognisable in its own right. Was that Yahweh's will?

And then, the ugly truth presented itself: he resented what Yahweh was doing in her life; he resented feeling overshadowed and no longer the one people needed or respected, and equally, he resented that she did not need him anymore. Ultimately, he didn't know who he was anymore, or what his future held - and that made him feel a failure and unworthy to stand by her side. But the shame and frustration he felt regarding these revelations superseded the pain of their actual sting.

It was a week later. They had escaped to the valley again, and it seemed to Deborah that Lapidoth had left his troubles behind him.

They were on their return home when Lapidoth looked up to the pink streaks that patterned the horizon. He sighed as though a message had been painted in the clouds. "I need to travel to Kedesh...I need to tell Saul's family."

Deborah nodded. "When must we leave?"

Lapidoth looked hesitant. He bowed his head, aware that Yahweh was probably calling his wife to the city. And yet, his flesh warred with the idea. He told himself that he feared for her safety, but he acknowledged with shame that it was more than that. Kedesh was his home, where he was still known and respected for who he was.

She sadly acknowledged his reticence without understanding why, and laid a hand on his arm. "Or I can stay here if you'd prefer."

He despised himself almost as much as he loved her. He reached out and touched her face tenderly. "Of course you must come." The words sunk into his chest with a dull ache.

Three days later, as the party prepared to leave the settlement, a gentle mist covered the mountains. They agreed that they would return before the next Sabbath, giving them five days to complete their journey. Dan and Hur travelled with them.

As they neared the north road, a Canaanite chariot charged past them, as though fleeing for its life.

Hur ran ahead of them, returning minutes later. "There's trouble on the road. Do you want to turn around?"

"What sort of trouble?"

The Egyptian's face twisted. "It's a blood bath. The Canaanite we passed must have been fleeing. There are two other Canaanites dead and twenty or so Hebrews. It looks as though they must have tried attacking the chariots, but came off worse."

"Is the way clear now?" Dan asked.

"We can pass, if that's what you mean."

Lapidoth sighed. "It's nothing we haven't seen before, maybe we can help."

Deborah's stomach churned at the sight of the mutilated bodies. "Can you tell if any escaped?"

Hur and Lapidoth searched the area, and for a moment Deborah wondered what was keeping them. They appeared to have disappeared into the rocky hills. "A few of them escaped into the mountains." Lapidoth raked his fingers through his hair and Deborah knew then he was worried and that he would follow them.

"It won't be long and the area will be covered in Canaanite chariots and they will show no mercy," Dan pointed out.

Hur nodded. "That is my fear."

Lapidoth shook his head, his exasperation clear. "Their tracks are plain to see. They might as well have sign-posted their route. We should follow them. They acted foolishly, but they do not deserve to watch their families die. We need to warn them to escape."

"If we are caught with them, we too will be killed," Hur argued. He knew the death of the Canaanite warriors would be paid for.

"We need to warn them. Surely we have a little time until the chariot reaches help and then returns." She turned to Lapidoth, united in their mutual compassion and desire to help those in need.

"We need to reach Kedesh by twilight, so we still have six hours of daylight," Hur sighed. "We could probably afford a couple of hours."

They walked for some time, following the trail through the hills. The ground was flatter here, and for some time they were following a stream. Lapidoth was just beginning to question how much further the camp was and whether they should turn back, when the sound of raised voices and the wail of mourning cut through the stillness of the countryside.

Conversation ended abruptly and even the wails diminished to gentle sobs as the group's presence was acknowledged. A man pushed his way through the crowd; his tunic was torn and smudged with fresh blood. He gripped in his hand a plough shear and his expression was ripe with territorial suspicion.

"Who are you?" he growled.

"We are Hebrews on our way to Kedesh; we met the Canaanite massacre on the road..."

"Why did you follow us, to commend us?" the man sneered.

"No, to warn you." Panicked whispers of speculation travelled between the villagers.

"One of the chariots escaped. They will be on their way for reinforcements now and your attack will be paid for with the blood of your families. If we were able to follow your tracks, so too will the Canaanites."

"Their chariots cannot travel in the mountains," The man sneered, as though they were stupid.

"They have new, stronger chariots and they are well able to travel on horseback or on foot." Hur spoke now, his accent causing murmurs of concern.

Deborah noted that whilst the settlement looked at the man with the plough-shear, they remained mute, neither to question, nor to defend him. She allowed their response, their faces, and the atmosphere to rest as a question before Yahweh while she remained silent, only watching. And then she knew - a memory, a feeling and an awareness of the forceful hand of control under which men cowered, afraid to speak or question authority. She recognised, too, the character of those who suffocated beneath it.

Lapidoth stepped forward, introducing himself and those with him. "My wife, Deborah, escaped from Sisera's army, and knows from bitter experience that they will exact their vengeance upon you and your children if you are still here," he pleaded. "If you leave now, we will help you cover your tracks."

An older man, silver haired, with pale watery eyes stepped forward. "I told you not to go. Elizaphan, we told you you shouldn't fight."

"We must fight, we must show them that we are not afraid," Elizaphan spat, the unspoken message he threw at the old man was clear: *you will pay for questioning my authority.*

Lapidoth stepped forward; he placed his hand on the man's shoulder. "I understand your frustration, it is mine, too, and you show great courage. We share your pain. But Yahweh calls us to wait."

Elizaphan shook Lapidoth's hand away. "Yahweh! Yahweh doesn't care about us! Why do you speak of the old way! Baal provides our harvest; we owe our allegiance to him. I lead this village! We do not need your help here and we do not need Yahweh!"

Deborah stepped forward and her eyes bore into Elizaphan's, for she saw now that the iron will of this man stood between Yahweh and *His* children.

"Baal is made of stone; he does not answer your prayers. His priests demand your children as sacrifice and you allow it because he offers you temple prostitutes in return. Your heart is exalted against Yahweh and you do only what it right in your own eyes. You have led your village astray and the cries of grieving mothers touch the heart of Yahweh."

Elizaphan's face twisted in disdain. "You should keep your woman in line," he sneered at Lapidoth. "The day I listen to a woman I will breathe my last."

"By your own mouth you have ordained it." Deborah yielded her fear and insecurity to Yahweh, and as she did, she felt the words of Yahweh flood her mind, even as His strength saturated her soul.

"You lead this people, but not with the compassion, humility and the wisdom of Yahweh, but by your own selfish need to rule. And though you would have attained greatness, you will not listen either to Yahweh, nor to the people he has placed around you. Though you claim to be Hebrew, you lead as a Canaanite. How then will you defeat Canaan when you are a god in your own eyes, and it is your own kingdom you wish to establish?"

"You speak as one who does not understand battle, but as a woman of limited intelligence and strength." He looked at Hur, as though he was expecting him to agree with him.

Hur rested his hand on his sword and turned to Deborah.

She continued, her eyes moving between Elizaphan and the people. "Not by your might, nor by your power, but by Yahweh's power will we see victory in this land. But first, people's hearts must be ready, submitted to His sovereign will. Then He will call those who are humble, those who love Him and listen to Him, who have allowed themselves to be conformed into His image. *They* will lead this nation into victory."

Elizaphan's face twisted in disdain. "We stay here and we fight!"

"You have determined your own destiny. So let it be." Deborah turned away, and as she did so, the man fell to the ground, clutching his chest. There he died.

Deborah looked at the people, her heart aching with compassion.

"One alone is your leader, One alone cares for you, and He is Yahweh, your deliverer. Will you turn to Him today, with all your heart, soul and strength and be obedient to His voice?"

The people fell to their knees. "We will."

Deborah scanned the crowd. *Who has the courage, humility and compassion to listen to those around him and the conviction to ultimately be answerable to You alone; to be obedient and show integrity?*

And He answered: *Ask them.*

"Moses commanded you to pick a person amongst you, one who will not lord it over you. They should be chosen not because of their natural charisma, nor physical strength but their love for Yahweh. One who has shown compassion, humility, courage and integrity. Who will you choose?"

The people spoke among themselves. Deborah noted that already freedom had spread its roots.

"We choose Abraham."

A man, in his forties, stood unmoving. She caught the surprise that flickered in his eyes before he looked downward. When he looked up, his eyes glistened.

"Is this man married?"

A woman stepped forward. She carried a quiet grace, the strength of a mother. She smiled and her eyes shone with transparency and warmth as they met Deborah's. There was the connection of two similar souls in which an unspoken trust was formed.

"He is," she replied.

"Your name?"

"Naomi."

"And do you, Abraham and Naomi, accept this role?"

"I am not worthy," the man shook his head.

"Do you care for the people?"

"They are my family."

"Then you are the right person to lead your village. For none are worthy, only the wisest and strongest have the wisdom to know their dependency on Him and the courage to walk in vulnerability before others. You will recognise your need for Yahweh and for others. Yahweh blesses you to lead this village to physical and spiritual safety."

Lapidoth added, "First, you must lead your people to a place away from here. Move quickly, and we will do our best to cover your tracks."

Abraham nodded and calmly gathered the people together.

30

"My heart goes out to the commanders of Israel,
The volunteers among the people.
Bless the LORD!
Judges 5:9

1239 BC – Deborah and Lapidoth

The grey stone towers of Kedesh rose like giants of old to meet them. Set on two hills, with a spring running between them, the city had once been designated a safe city by Joshua. But in recent years it had been won back by the Canaanites. As such, it seemed charged as though it balanced on the edge of several realities: twenty years ago, it had drawn a questionable crowd of villains, fugitives, the misjudged and discontented, as well as the usual number of settled families and tradesmen, creating a buzz of energy and possibility. Many of these still lived in the city, of those most had turned to Baal, or their faith was so watered down it was a shadowy sentiment of their past, in the same way as one keeps an old rug for its attached memories. The modern belief, that El was Yahweh, combined with the fact that the Law was no longer spoken of, meant that truth could be twisted.

Wasn't Abraham told to sacrifice his child? Wasn't it Yahweh, known as El, who demanded it of him? How then can it be wrong? There was no one to remind them that Yahweh had tested his heart; that He had been the one to stop him, or that Yahweh commanded Abraham to leave behind the ways of idolatry that his father had followed.

However, the Canaanite military and religious culture of Kedesh that was reinforced by the infrastructure of its settled population was by far the most dominant force. Intermarraige, homosexuality, and temple prostitution were normal, as was child sacrifice.

Deborah's heart beat wildly as they passed through the sea of market booths, a rolling, churning body of people and noise that seemed to move with its own current before pushing them out the other side. She heard the political clamour of the city elders as they aired their own importance, none listening to the other's opinions, and each destined to leave both discouraged in their aims and reaffirmed in their own importance. They would once have used the Torah as their plumb line to determine Yahweh's will, but now they stood as gods in their own eyes, arguing for their own rights and best interest.

They passed beneath the towers and Deborah felt as though the scrutiny of the guards would burn holes in her back. She recalled the first time she had been there with Hur the night of her escape; it seemed a lifetime ago. The openness of people's carnality made Deborah feel nauseous with disgust. She slipped her fingers between Lapidoth's.

"Not difficult to see why I left, is it?" he grimaced.

"No," she said, feeling a surge of pride in her husband's strength of character.

Lapidoth led them down the narrow streets, houses of the same grey stone that were typical of Naphtali, each with a small courtyard that divided into an area for livestock and an outside cooking area.

"I have so many memories of Saul and me running around these streets as children," he sighed sadly. A moment later, he stopped in front of a wooden door.

"This is my father's home. He will be pleased to see you. You, Hur and Dan can stay here and wait. It's better that I go alone to Saul's family."

"Of course," Deborah replied.

Lapidoth knocked on the door. Shortly after, a boy answered, no older than seven years. He shrieked when he saw Lapidoth and threw himself into his arms. He had the same dark curls as Lapidoth and Abinoam, and the sight of him in Lapidoth's arms created an ache in Deborah. His father was followed by Ruth, her husband Micah and their other two children, who raced across the courtyard, each in turn throwing themselves at Lapidoth. He picked them up, spinning them in circles and kissing them. Deborah watched, feeling both love and fascination for him, and wondering again at how much she didn't know about her husband's life.

He laughed, turning to Deborah, his eyes alight with joy.

"My nieces and nephews." He ruffled the boy's hair affectionately and turned to Ruth, who had just arrived. "Did you tell them the story of the girl who fought the snake?"

The boy gasped, "It's you!"

Deborah grinned, rolling her eyes. "And your uncle, my hero, rescued me." The children looked at Lapidoth and their pride and affection for him warmed her heart.

They crossed the courtyard and entered the house, which consisted of a large living area and three smaller sleeping rooms.

As they sat around the table eating chickpea stew with bread, they discussed all that had happened since the wedding.

Abinoam nodded. "There has been word of it in the city; a murmur, no more than an undercurrent, that many do not want to hear, and yet more are afraid to hear. Since Lapidoth came last time and spoke to us of your journey with Yahweh, I have spoken with those who will listen. Amongst the elders who talk at the city gates, there are those who remember and hold onto Yahweh's deliverance. But many have lived without Yahweh for so long they are trapped in their own sin and blinded by deception."

Deborah listened. "Do you think they would come and meet with us?"

"By Yahweh's will they might. Some out of hope and others out of curiosity."

"And yet more to criticise,," Micah warned.

Lapidoth raised an eyebrow.

Abinoam held up his hands. "Micah is right, there is always opposition to change. We must expect it. There are those who are skeptical that Yahweh would raise up a woman to speak to His people," he added with grim candour.

"There are women, too, who would like to hear you speak," Ruth grinned. "You will find less opposition amongst them."

"When do you leave?" Abinoam stroked his beard thoughtfully.

"We must return before the Sabbath. There have been raids on the settlements in the mountains. I don't want to leave our people alone too long," Lapidoth replied.

The following morning, Lapidoth left to speak with Saul's family. When he returned he seemed spent. He smiled sadly from the doorway and Deborah hurried across the courtyard to meet him. She wrapped her arms around his neck and held him.

"How has it been here?"

"Lovely, I've been playing 'markets' with the girls and made honey cakes with Ruth."

He smiled, wrapping his arms around her waist and kissing her hair. "Hmm honey cakes, Ima's recipe? I hope you saved me some." She loved that about him; his ability to be deeply emotional and then the next minute resume his child-like optimism.

That night, Abinoam announced that he had been able to organise for the elders and other influential men to come and listen to Deborah the following evening. Ruth had asked some of the women to come in the morning.

Interesting, Deborah mused. *The women come first; He will use the hearts of mothers to turn His nation back to Him, for are we not the heart of this nation: the ones who unite and heal our own families, our communities, knitting the fragments into one cover.*

The women arrived before noon the following day. They brought their children with them. It was a delightful medley of noise, chatter and laughter that reminded Deborah of Raisa's home in Ephraim. She smiled and handed out honey cakes that she and Ruth had made the previous day. As the clamour died down and faces turned to her, she was introduced by Ruth. She began by telling them her journey thus far, beginning with her first encounter with Yahweh and her first meeting with Lapidoth. Many of the older women had known Lapidoth as a child and had heard about the betrothal. With all the responsiveness that women do so well, she knew she would gain their trust if they came to feel they knew her and so she spoke freely about her life. She told them about defending her village and being taken by Sisera, and related her crippling fear and despair and how Yahweh had given her hope.

"And how did you come to be here now?" one of them asked, bouncing a small child on her knee.

"I was taken to Jabin's palace during the 'Festival of Kinship with the forest', and was ordered to worship Baal. But I would not. Instead I told them what would come if they did not stop oppressing Yahweh's people. His priestess tried to poison me, and Sisera attacked me for humiliating him, but I was saved by Yahweh and the courage of my guard. He is with us here today, having turned away from Sisera."

"Did you know that Jabin's priestess, Donitaya, died during the festival – of poisoning - they say?" the woman asked, feeding cake to her child.

"I did not know." She paused as she absorbed the news. "Yahweh brought her own judgement upon her."

"Has Yahweh told you that you will deliver Israel?" Another woman asked. Her eyes were skeptical and Deborah had the impression she was looking for attention, to bring discord.

"He told me I would be a mother to Israel," she replied simply.

"Where are your children today?" the woman asked.

"I have no children of my own...yet." Deborah winced inwardly as she spoke the words.

"Then how can you be a mother to Israel if you are not a mother?"

"Rebecca!! You are under my roof and Deborah is my guest! Please!" Ruth admonished.

Deborah felt the full force of the words as they attacked her calling, her womanhood and her deepest desire in one blow.

She remained silent for longer than was publicly acceptable, and felt the eyes of the other women weighing her, pitying her. She fought the urge to answer in her own strength, knowing that her reply would be barbed. She resisted, allowing the silence to remain until it would either cripple her or redeem her. And yet she chose to trust.

Yahweh, help me.

She looked at the woman, whose mouth was curved in smug disdain, and suddenly, as though a window had been opened to the woman's soul, Deborah perceived the pain that this woman had suffered and not spoken of that had scarred her innermost being.

"I will not defend myself before you," Deborah answered, meeting the woman's eyes. Her voice was gentle yet self-assured. "For, to do so would be to fight for my own kingdom. My heart grieves that Yahweh has not given me a child *yet*. But I have long since stopped needing to answer to man, nor to make Yahweh conform to my expectations: He is God and I am not."

She approached the woman and knelt before her, her hand rested on the woman's arm as she leaned forward. When the woman turned her face away, she continued, whispering into her ear, so that only she could hear. "Yahweh sees all that you have lost, how your child was taken and sacrificed to Baal by your husband, who visits the temple prostitutes. He says to let you know how proud of you He is, that you still love Him, that you still love your children and that you stand. He wants you to know, your deliverance will come and that He takes care of your little boy." The woman broke down, her body racked with deep sobs that shuddered through her and tore out of the walls she had constructed. Deborah held her in her arms. When she finally stood, there was silence.

"My sisters, tell me what you see? Speak openly about your plight, it will go no further." Deborah spoke with the gentle voice of authority.

The woman who sat next to Ruth answered first. "We see the weight of Canaan, bearing down on our children and our husbands. They work every hour Yahweh gives them for the Canaanites and there is never enough, they turn to temple prostitutes and drunkenness because it is relief from this world."

An older woman spoke next. "Our children have forgotten the truth and it fades in our own minds, so we mix it with Canaan's values. They lie with men and women without thought, and their unwanted children are offered to Baal."

"It feels as though the only way we can endure is to take on Canaan's values. It does our children no good to have their heads filled with the old ways; they need to be able to make their way in this world," another argued.

"I see merit in teaching them the old ways. It was a moral code that kept them safe, and grounded us, but its truth is faded in my own mind and I am too busy trying to survive to have the time or the strength to find my way back."

Another nodded her agreement. "Our children are drawn by Canaan's pull and we are helpless to stop it."

Deborah listened to the women as they talked among themselves.

Finally, Rebecca stood. She looked weary, as though she had just done battle, but a peaceful smile lit her face.

"What do you say Deborah?"

Deborah held her gaze for a moment and she smiled with compassion at the woman before her. *How Yahweh knits souls through vulnerability and compassion,* she acknowledged.

"It is because we have forgotten the old ways that we suffer Sisera's oppression. But it was never a moral code that united us. It was our Maker: Yahweh! He did not give us the Law to bind us but to free us and to keep us in that liberty. I believe that Yahweh will use spiritual mothers to restore hope and to knit the fractures in our land together. Are we not life-givers? Is it not in our natures to encourage, to lay down our lives for those we love? To love unconditionally and to offer hospitality to those who are in need? In this way our nation will be restored. Let us speak Yahweh's laws and stories to our children, let us pray for our husbands, our children and for our land. Let us consecrate our own hearts to the Father of Fathers, to the Sovereign over all powers and then, let us watch as He delivers this nation."

There was a holy calm that settled over the women in Abinoam's courtyard. Rebecca was the first to fall to her knees, drawing her children with her. Then Ruth, until every woman and child in the room had their heads bowed to the ground.

It always amazed Deborah when Yahweh spoke through her, for she knew in her own strength she could never have moved people's hearts.

That evening, Abinoam's courtyard was filled with a sense of strained anticipation and wariness. These were the men who prided themselves on their positions, their reputations, their knowledge of Hebrew history and the Law, even where they had chosen to compromise it. Their faces glowed in the torchlight as they waited to listen and give their judgement on the woman before them. It was the first time Deborah had felt nervous. She had always been able to hide behind her role of helping those who were sick and wounded. What would she say to these men, leaders in the city? She knew that many had heard from their wives what she had said earlier. For some of the men, it had softened their hearts, for others it was further evidence of her unsuitability as a woman: speak to women, yes, but not to men, and certainly not to a nation. She thought of Jared and the disdain he had shown her, and hoped they would not be similar.

Abinoam began by welcoming his friends and praying. Deborah had never seen him in his own environment before, and was fascinated to see how respected he was in the city. She realised, once again, that despite her love for Lapidoth, there was so much she did not know about him.

He introduced Lapidoth, explaining proudly to the people how his son had gathered men around him in the mountains; how they had been attacking Canaanite caravans and taking their food and provisions to the neediest Hebrews.

"Men of Israel, for so long now we have lived under Jabin's oppression. Our lives have not been our own and we have been crushed, no longer having the will, nor the strength to fight for what was once ours. We have been divided and weakened by individualism and poisoned by compromise and carnality. These are our true enemies and the battle begins within our own hearts. But now, Yahweh has spoken that if we turn back to Him with our whole hearts, He will deliver us. The time for apathy is over," Lapidoth urged.

There was a strained, reflective silence, while the men considered his words. Finally, one man stood. He was in his fifties, broad in stature, both physically and in influence. "Lapidoth, we all admire your youthful enthusiasm and passion, but clearly you have not lived in the city for some time and no longer understand the dynamics we are faced with. We have a peace here, albeit fragile, and we are reluctant to give hope to people that will lead to their families unrest and possible death. Passion is a volatile beast."

"That may be true, Abraham, but the peace you speak of deceives you. For in truth, it is apathy and fear, born out of subjugation and compromise. If you will not have faith, you will never be free. I do not offer a hope based on man's empty words. Twenty years ago, Deborah, my wife, was given a dream. Ehud confirmed that she spoke of what would come. There is hope. Canaan can be crushed," Lapidoth replied.

The men began to mutter amongst themselves. Amos, Deborah and Lapidoth watched as the men constructed a wall of cynicism around themselves to protect them from the fear of change. Finally, one of them spoke.

"What you are suggesting is impossible. Israel is divided and no longer has weapons. Even if we were to stand against Sisera, how can we fight his chariots armed only with plough-shears and ox-goads?

And Lapidoth answered, "Quite simply, I do not know. But then I do not know how an eighteen-year-old girl can save her village by prophesying to Sisera about his end. I do not know how it is that she can defy Sisera and Jabin in his own palace, and yet escape unharmed. Nor do I know how she can kill a man with her words alone or bring hope to people who have none. The answer is simply that *she* cannot. But Yahweh *can* and *will* use her, use those who are obedient to Him as He used Shamgar of Philistia to defeat six hundred men with an ox-goad and bring peace to Israel. The question is: do we have the courage to believe?"

Many of the men began to talk among themselves, their conversations dividing in opinion, united in passion. Finally, the voices quietened and Deborah was aware that another man had stood, no older than his mid-thirties, yet he evidently carried a status and authority that was recognised by the other men. She had noticed him earlier, though surrounded by people he seemed set apart as he sat on the stone bench; Yahweh's hand was upon him. His voice was low, yet every ear strained to hear him, and when he spoke it was like an engravers knife on silver. His eyes bore into hers, and as she returned his scrutiny she was aware that a mutual respect had silently been formed.

"Tell us Deborah…tell us how you came to be here today…and pray, tell us the end of Sisera that you see."

One of the men, well dressed, with a nose that reminded Deborah of a beak stood, "Hillel, she's a woman, since when do the elders listen to women?"

The man held up his hand, his eyebrow cocked. "Remember the story of Balaam? If Yahweh can speak through a donkey, he can surely use a woman. Perhaps He wants to teach us men a lesson in humility and His sovereignty." His mouth twitched with humour as he looked to Deborah. Deborah felt herself rest in Yahweh's arms and, from that place of peace, she spoke, her eyes looking at each face before her.

"Men of Israel. You are right to ask such questions; I have asked the same of myself – and I have no answers for you. I do not deserve the favour Yahweh has shown me.

"As a young girl, I met Yahweh and He showed me that Israel would wander away from Him. Later, the Angel of the Lord appeared and told me I would be a mother to Israel. He showed me Sisera, the nightmares he has and the wild mountain goat that he fears. The one who will trample him to the dust. His own priest warned him that I was feared by the gods – we know that this was Yahweh's hand. When Sisera took me captive, I was forced to witness the atrocities he inflicted on our people until I was numb with fear and dead inside. I called out to Yahweh and He saved me from my despair and empowered me. Then I met Shamgar, a farmer in Philistia who defeated the Philistines.

"On the same night as I was liberated, Yahweh spoke to me again in a dream. He told me that He would awaken His people. A few months ago, the Angel of the Lord appeared again and said: 'it is time'. In the mountains, many are filled with hope and the anticipation that Yahweh's deliverance is near."

She paused, sensing the skepticism of these religious men and knowing that their report would impact the families of Yahweh's people.

She had known that her words alone would not change their minds. Only Yahweh could. And she felt His righteous anger burn against their narrow-minded, religious skepticism and cowardice as they fought to keep life without challenge, without war or pain, but at the expense of holiness and Yahweh's kingdom and of life.

She sighed, her eyes flitting to Hillel, to Lapidoth and then to Abinoam. "I could go around this room. I could prove to you that I hear Yahweh. I could ask you..." she looked at the beak man, "Why do you despise a woman's voice when you find no problem visiting them in Baal's temples?" Her eyes rested on another. "Or, I could point out that your problem is not with me, but your trust in Yahweh, for your heart grieves for all that you have seen." She moved to the next man. "I could beg you to remember who you are; that your wife will receive her healing on the day that you speak Yahweh's hope and laws to your people again." She smiled. "But, you are men of God, you don't need me to prove to you what Yahweh has spoken to your hearts, do you? And so I will only remind you that Yahweh promised Moses that He would drive out the seven nations before him, if he was obedient to *all* that Yahweh had called him to do. I will tell you that Yahweh sees your faithfulness and how you have persevered under hardship and that I have seen Sisera's end – if Israel returns to Him." She noted Hillel. He had leaned back, his lips curved into a peaceful smile and his arms folded loosely across his chest. He looked to Abinoam and nodded, standing in the silence that surrounded them.

"This dream you had, in which Yahweh told you He awakens His people. Tell us if you would the detail of this dream?"

Deborah nodded. "I saw an almond tree...." She heard the sharp intake of breaths and muttering around her and smiled inwardly; Yahweh had gone before her. She stepped back into the vivid memory of that dream. "...It grew, surrounded by darkness, its roots pulled the nutrients from the rock on which it was planted and when the tree was in full flower, I saw first one honey bee, then others pollinate the tree. When the time came to yield its blossom, I saw it was carried in all directions. People began to gather around the almond tree; they were wrapped in chains and their eyes were partially covered in scales. When they saw the gentle white petals, they fell to their knees and wept. As their tears fell to the ground, they were drawn into the sap of the tree. I watched as they travelled up the trunk, through the branches and into the seedpods. The fruit grew, plentiful and healthy, and in its time yielded fruit. As the people ate from the tree, they in turn grew strong. Finally, they turned, and saw the darkness that surrounded the tree; the scales fell from their eyes as though they suddenly remembered all they had once had. They stood, and as they did so, light surged from the tree, intense and powerful, pushing back the darkness until the full break of day settled over the land." She looked around at the open mouths and stunned silence. "But you already know about the dream, don't you? Many of you have also seen what I have seen."

Hillel stroked his beard. "Remind us, what does Deborah mean?"

Deborah bowed her head, when she raised it, her voice was malacophonous as the wind and her eyes glistened with humility and awe in Yahweh's goodness. "It means honey bee."

There was an excited clamour of voices and Deborah sighed with relief; Kedesh would stand with them.

"And who will lead Israel's armies?" the beak man asked.

"Yahweh has not shown me yet, but when Israel is ready, He will arise. Men of Kedesh, I beseech you, remember who you are. Remember your true names, for it is the banner under which you will know victory once again, and it is the call to Kedesh."

There was a silent reflection as the implication of Deborah's words dispersed within their hearts. For 'Kedesh' in Hebrew meant 'consecrated and sanctified'. Its true name had been forgotten, and now it called them back. They bowed their heads and Deborah motioned to Hillel to pray, for she acknowledged the men were humbled, and that in their vulnerability they would welcome one of their own. She asked too, by way of acknowledging his leadership in Kedesh, for after she left, he would lead the men forward. She thanked Yahweh silently for His mercy and victory in men's hearts.

Hillel finally ended the meeting by adding that his brother was an elder in Issachar, and that they too would be told about tonight's meeting.

Others agreed that those in Zebulun and Reuben that were known, should also be readied.

Deborah looked around for Lapidoth, but he was gone. She spoke to the men for a while and then excused herself and went to look for Lapidoth. She found him in their room, sitting on the pallet. She could see his handsome features framed in the glow of the lamp; he was sitting on the bench, his headdress removed and his head rested in his hands. He looked up when he saw her enter, but said nothing. She sensed the same heaviness over him that she had seen before. She went and knelt before him, wrapping her arms around his neck.

"What is it, my Lapidoth?"

"It's nothing," he sighed, kissing her hair. "You should sleep, it's been a long night."

Deborah felt her heart constrict. She felt so helpless and couldn't help but feel it was something she had done. She lay awake taking it to Yahweh and asking him for wisdom, but the only thing He said to her was: "Trust Me."

Their return home was mercifully uneventful, and they took care to avoid Canaanite land. Initially, their journey took them through the forested area, where they were hidden by the oak, pine and tamarind trees that grew prolifically. Deborah found wild coriander, mustard and onion, which she collected for use in poultices and medicines.

As they began their climb up the mountains, the summer heat bore its full vengeance; the grass was bleached golden and the air moist and heavy. The silence was broken only by the effort of their exertion and the crooning of kestrels and honey buzzards.

Once they knew that they were out of the range of Canaanite chariots, they relaxed, singing songs as they walked and speaking with excitement of Yahweh's anticipated deliverance.

They stopped midday by a stream, and Hur impressed them by catching fish using a method he had learnt from his father as a child. He stood in the stream and stabbed them with a spear, grinning triumphantly as he threw his prize upon the bank. Lapidoth tried, too, and Deborah tried not to laugh as she watched his face, twisted with concentration and determination as he stabbed the rocky bed of the stream without success. Finally, he lost his footing and fell. Hur laughed and offered his hand to his fallen comrade. Deborah laughed, remembering how Lapidoth had tricked her. She saw the look of surprise on the Egyptian's face as Lapidoth jerked his arm, pulling him into the frothy, cool water. Seeing them both sitting there, everyone laughed, the two sodden fishermen not least. It was the first time she had seen any camaraderie between the two and it pleased her.

As they crossed the road leading to Kedesh, a convoy plodded past them, their riders attired in purple robes decorated with gold embroidery; the luxurious blankets upon which they sat defined them as noblemen.

"Their guards are domestic, not military." Hur raised an eyebrow.

Lapidoth nodded, noting the loaded saddlebags. "They look as if they carry wealth."

If the noblemen were wary, they hid their emotion behind unyielding expressions of disdain. The Hebrews nodded, pretending to pass them and then, signaling to Hur and Dan, Lapidoth turned and quick as lightning skillfully fired two arrows consecutively, bringing down the guards. They caught up with the noblemen, relieving them of their donkeys, their cloaks and blankets and the goods they carried, but leaving them unharmed.

When they reached the settlement, they celebrated their return with the wine and food taken from the noblemen. They told the others what had happened in Kedesh and an excited optimism fuelled their conversations. Dan suggested they make a journey to Shiloh for the Feast of Tabernacles at the next full moon and there was an excited agreement from everyone. Lapidoth would lead the pilgrimage, travelling the byways, through the hill land and forests so as to avoid Sisera's armies. Deborah found it strange that the prospect of danger seemed to bring Lapidoth alive; he regained his former passion and peace with life.

31

I would have lost heart, unless I had believed
that I would see the goodness of the LORD
In the land of the living.
Wait on the LORD;
Be of good courage,
And He shall strengthen your heart;
Wait, I say, on the LORD!
Psalm 27 : 13-14

1238 BC - Deborah

Deborah acknowledged that the next full moon would mark three years of her time in Naphtali. Rain, cold and relentless, fell in sheets, flooding the streams and running in rivulets off the hills and through the camp.

Lapidoth had decided to move the women and children to the cave where it was drier and making a fire was possible. The higher mountains were peaked with white snow and food was scarce.

Deborah broke off a piece of bread, her teeth jarring against each other as she handed it to Ruth's little boy, Raphael. Her stomach growled and she had felt weak and nauseous for the last week. He snuggled up to her and she tucked him under her blanket as they watched the rain run in rivers from the cave mouth.

The men continued to patrol the hills, looking for caravans that could be stopped and hunting for food. When Lapidoth and the other men arrived in the evening, they were cold and wet through, with no fruit from their labours. They wrapped blankets around themselves and were ushered before the fire. Deborah and Sen handed out hot stew made from wild nettles and barley. When night dropped its inky black cloak over the mountains, they curled up in family groups in an attempt to keep warm.

Lapidoth was awake when he heard the shouts. He leapt to his feet, adrenalin meeting his weariness and causing him to stagger shakily for a moment. He shook his head and ran to the cave mouth. He could see an oil-lamp waving in the darkness, and grabbing his sword, he ran out to meet them.

"Naddav! Pardes?"

"There's been a landslide. Please help!" Their tone was distraught.

Behind him, others were waking, grabbing their cloaks and lighting lamps as they headed out into the moonless night.

Deborah woke, too, and fumbled in the darkness to find her herbs.

"Are you sure you're well enough?" Lapidoth asked with concern.

"Of course, it's just a stomach upset, I'll be fine," she reassured him, drawing her blanket around her shoulders.

They arrived at the settlement to find the devastating extent of the disaster. Their ramshackle homes, made of wood and animal skins, looked as though they had never existed. The cries of those in pain, blurred with the sobs of grief and loss as the dark canopy of the firmament had lowered, crushing life and hope. Lapidoth's men rushed to help the villagers as they wildly struggled to pull back the fallen rocks and debris - but they were aware that the chance of finding anyone surviving under so much rock and sediment was unlikely.

Deborah treated those who were hurt, setting broken limbs in splints, applying honey or myrrh to wounds and offering words of comfort to the relatives of those who had not been found.

One man's leg had been completely crushed by a rock; his screams of agony merged with the anguished groans of his family. The sound ripped through Deborah's heart, and she fell to her knees beside him and prayed, her heart crying out to Yahweh in desperation as she saw his family struggle with the thought of losing him.

They toiled until morning, when the rain finally abated and a feathery mist lay over the mountains. One family was still missing, including the elder of the village.

Lapidoth came and knelt next to her, resting his hand on her arm. Dark circles shadowed his eyes, but she saw that concern, not tiredness, motivated his thoughts. "We need to get back and check on the others."

She looked around her and sighed, her own weariness a heavy mantle she longed to concede to – and yet compassion drove her.

"I can't leave them here like this Lapidoth." She looked around at the suffering. "You go, Lapidoth, check on the others and I'll stay until you return."

He exhaled with frustration and rose to stand. "You've done all you can here, Deborah, you need to return. You're not well!"

"Lapidoth," she asserted, "You're not listening to me! Look around you!" One of the shelters, bowing under the weight of sediment, collapsed as though to emphasise her point. Though no longer occupied, it caused the wife of the deceased occupant to sob with renewed grief.

She looked into his eyes, resolute. "I cannot go," she repeated with gentle resolve.

Irritation flickered in his brown eyes and then his expression hardened. "You've clearly decided and my concerns are not important." He paused angrily and the silence filled the air between them. Turning as though to leave, he motioned to Joel who was watching, his arms folded. He spun around. "I try to defend you, but you're so head-strong and self-sufficient; could you not conform just a little for my sake?" he blurted angrily.

"You knew who I was called to be before you married me, Lapidoth!" she replied curtly. She was bristling with indignation, his words had left a sting; he had found her when she was weak, he had rescued her in her brokenness, twice. Had he wanted her to stay that way, so that he could always be the hero? He had always known that she had been called by God to His people. Had he expected her to be a woman without unction, without strength of character, that he would be her god, the only one she would obey? And yet he, of all people, spent his life helping others – why would he condemn her for doing the same? It was as though he was in competition. His attitude diminished her respect for him, and whilst she knew she should stop, her weariness undermined her self-control. "You cannot choose which parts of my character and calling you like and which do not suit your purposes. I come as a whole," she challenged.

The hurt she saw quickly vanished, as his own battle for value before her was lost. He retreated behind the battlements of his pride and frustration, and from there he let loose the arrows he knew would be most likely to gain him victory. His voice was quiet, his expression icy. "Don't condescend to me, Deborah. I am not a child! Must I remind you that it was before God you agreed to be my wife and to accept my authority, not only when it suits you. I am making this decision because I believe it is in your best interest, and yet you treat me as though I was a tyrant. Will you forge your destiny alone? You have given me no indication that I have any part in your great plans. Must I wait at home grinding wheat and brushing the floor, waiting for you to report the great victories you have accomplished?" His lip curled in disdain, and she realised now that a great river drove the rudder of his emotion.

On another occasion, she would have been wise and compassionate in her response, perceiving and responding to his real concerns with wisdom and gentleness. But as with any great storm, it is the amassing of conflicting pressures that creates such great destruction. Now, weary and riled, she felt that he wished to control her because of his own insecurity and legalism, and that she could not respect, nor yield to. Furthermore, she could not help but wonder if his outburst was what lay behind his recent silences and withdrawal from her. She felt her frustration spark to fire and she spoke from her own fury, ignoring the voice within. Her tone was icy with condescension. "I had not thought you to be a child! Though your comments disappoint me greatly. I would not have thought you to stoop so low as to wield your position and my faith as a weapon. You *are* my husband, and I would hope that you would respect my heart for these people's plight, not see it as a threat to *your* position."

But the resolve she saw in his eyes frightened her, and she wished she could take back the words. When he spoke, his voice was quiet and detached, as though he had stepped over a wall in his thoughts:

"Clearly you desire neither my counsel, nor my aid." He glanced over her shoulder to where Joel waited, and the pain she saw in his eyes caused both sadness and resentment. "I had once believed we would fight this battle together, Deborah, but I see now that there was never room for another in your great plan." He slung his bow across his shoulder. "Shalom, Deborah." And then he was gone.

Hur had remained, and spent the day helping rebuild shelters and looking for remaining victims. When they finally found their broken, crumpled bodies there was a sense of grief, as well as closure.

Deborah had spent the morning tending to those who were wounded, driven by compassion and her desire to drown out Lapidoth's words. She felt lightheaded and nauseous due to lack of sleep and food, and had not felt so emotionally spent since her early days of travelling with Sisera.

The sting of Lapidoth's words now burrowed within the catacombs of her mind and, as she recalled the times he had seemed quiet and dismissive of late, she was forced to acknowledge that there was more to what he had said today than her refusal to go with him. She longed to see him again, to speak to him and bring darkness to light. Perhaps she should have gone with him. Now that she had had time to reflect, she wondered if he had been struggling with the change of dynamics in their relationship, something she had been too busy and occupied to realise. Her anger must have been the final point for him, and she now wished she had spoken with greater wisdom and understanding. She hated to see a rift form between them, and knew how easily it could happen.

Her thoughts were interrupted by a little girl tugging her sleeve, her dark brown eyes peered out of thick eyelashes, her face smeared with tears and dirt, and a smile that seemed so out of place in the midst of such sorrow that it pierced the fog of Deborah's fatigue. Beside her stood a man; she recognised his face from last night and now sought to identify him. His eyes shone with a joy that made Deborah wonder about his sanity and then he pulled up the hem of his tunic, revealing a normal, if somewhat hairy, lower leg.

Deborah looked at him, wondering if she had treated him for a blow to the head and laughed awkwardly. "Why are you showing me your leg?"

The girl spoke first. "Thank you for making Abba better."

Suddenly, she recognised the man; devoid of his pain induced grimace he looked completely different. He had been the man she had prayed for last night, whose leg had been crushed. Nothing she had been able to offer would have saved the man's life, bar amputation. She recalled the desperate prayers that they had uttered.

"I had not thought I would see my daughter again..." He blinked back the tears that brimmed in his eyes, as he squeezed the tiny hand that held his. Deborah felt a smile of exultation part her lips as though it had escaped from the depths of her being. She knelt down before the girl, her eyes shifting to the father as she spoke. "Yahweh made your Abba better, so you'd better be thanking Him."

As word spread, there was a surge of excitement in the village; Yahweh had performed a miracle, and despite their loss, there was hope for the future.

The sky was icy blue, and white luminous clouds were being blown in the cool wind over the hilltops. Deborah watched for Lapidoth's return, eager to see him again, to make her peace with him and tell him what had happened.

His last words punched holes in her thoughts: *'Everybody needs you...you are everyone's answer. But you don't need anyone, do you?'* Did he really believe that? Had he felt overshadowed by what Yahweh was doing through her? Did he not know how much she needed him, how much respect she had for him? Had she not told him how proud of him she was? She sighed with frustration at her lack of communication; perhaps he did not know because she had never said as much. How could she communicate Yahweh's thoughts and will so effectively, and her own so poorly?

Dusk was almost upon them, and neither Lapidoth, nor any of the other men had returned. She began to wonder if he was too angry with her, and worse still that he no longer loved her. She recalled the cool anger she had seen in his eyes. Why had he not come back? It was so unlike him. She felt anxiety grow within her.

When Hur approached her, his expression mirrored her own weary concern. "We ought to return. We cannot spend another night here, they have little enough food. We can check what is holding the men up and return tomorrow."

Deborah agreed and packed up her things. She left the remainder of her vial of myrrh and strips of white willow bark for those in pain.

By the time they were nearing the settlement, she struggled to put one foot in front of the next.

Hur noticed first: the black smoke carried the stench of death as it coiled into the air. He turned and the panic she saw in his eyes fuelled her own. She looked up at the carrion that were gathering over the hills.

"No! No! No!" Her eyes were wild as they gripped Hur's arms. He tried to hold her back, but she pushed him aside and ran forward, and he arrived a few steps behind her.

She stopped, bile rising in her throat, as horror gripped her. The settlement was no more. The shelters had been burnt to the ground and the donkeys slaughtered. The charred remains of Marta's body were slumped into the burning embers of the fire along with the dismembered remains of at least two others. Hur looked up and watched as Deborah slipped to her knees, and then the world slipped away beneath her as darkness covered her.

When she came around, Hur held her in his arms. He gripped her face in his hands and looked into her eyes. "Trust," he said. "We don't know that he was killed – we've only found three bodies; they may have taken him."

His words were a spear that pierced the thick smog of fear, both torturing her and offering hope. The idea of Lapidoth in Sisera's cruel hands poisoned her mind. But to think of a life without him was more than she could bear. Her body turned by sheer force of will, but her mind cowered behind the precipice beyond her; *no more pain, please, no more.* She looked up at Hur with a wild desperation in her eyes.

"I should have gone with him; he wanted me to go with him… if I hadn't been so stubborn. I should have gone with him," she repeated, refusing the tears that brimmed her eyes.

He shook her, for he saw she was slipping into the chasm of guilt and grief. His voice was harsh. "Do you think you could have saved him if you had been here?"

She stood and paced, taking deep breaths, because she was scared at the emotion within her; as her grief ebbed her anger rose. Finally, she fell to her knees, her palms on the floor.

"Yahweh!" She roared as a woman giving birth.

"Yahweh!" She cried as a warrior delivering his last blows before death takes him.

Hur put his hand on her shoulder. She turned to look up at him, her eyes were wild and her hair, loose of it's mantle, hung around her shoulders.

"We need to leave Deborah," he said gently, and she saw the old pity in his eyes.

She shook her head. "I will not, I cannot leave until I have heard from Him: from Yahweh. If I leave now, my faith and my vision will fail me."

Hur sighed, and said with gentle resignation as he sat down, "Then we will wait."

Deborah nodded, and picking herself up, she stumbled to the precipice, her memories of Lapidoth's proposal assaulting her as she laid herself flat on the ground, her cheek flat against the dust, and the desolate wasteland of her soul open only to heaven.

She prayed and she wept, for Lapidoth and for the violence to end. The sun went down and still she prayed. She heard footsteps come, and then go. She waited and prayed. For three days, she refused to accept either food or drink. After one week, Hur pleaded with her to take some sustenance. She looked up, dark rings haloing her eyes and an ethereal presence emanating from her body.

"Not until I see hope. Not until I see light break forth in this nation. Not until I know *His* will."

On the evening of the twelfth day, it rained. Mud and water washed down the mountain in rivulets that pooled around her. She drew her knees up to her body, and closed her eyes as she mouthed her silent plea to Yahweh. And then, as darkness wrapped her wings over the mountain, the thunder came, distant at first, like the marching of an invisible army that drew always closer. She stood, her clothes drenched, and lifted her voice to heaven. Her arms rose into fists that punched the sky, as the thunder and lightning seemed to battle above her - a simultaneous explosion of sound and light that charged the air. It continued crash after crash, fork-lightning that divided the sky and gave her a momentary glimpse into the spiritual realm. In that moment, she saw Michael, the angel of war, as he fought the darkness that wrestled with Israel. Angels, like stars that fought from the heavenlies, exacting their judgement on the earth. Fuelled by the words that Yahweh placed in her mouth, she spoke:

Apathy and desolation,
Buffeted the walls of my conviction.
Yet Your sovereign hand,
Granted me the strength to stand.
Your spirit bestows the courage to fight,
The wisdom to know which path is right

I see the war that must be waged

With faith, fortitude and holy rage.
And so my prayer resounds
From this peak, this hallowed ground:
Let dark and light divide!
And into this battle, I will ride!
My face striped with the colours you give!
(This shell laid forfeit, for by grace I live).

A battle cry that divides the heavens
Ushering in Your angelic presence.

All earthly treasures I surrender
As heaven's armies march in splendour.

"Rest," He breathes.

Awakened by Your breath of life
I am clothed in armour, dressed in white

And from this mountain fortress,
He trains my hands for war
His eyes, his voice a whispered promise:
"You are mine, and I am yours."

I find 'my place', that hallowed cave,
Where love himself keeps me safe,
Within His kingdom I now abide,
Your words, Your love, my sacred guide

This battle now is easy,
(I am Yours and You are mine)
My love, my life, my peace.

The rain had stopped and the dark clouds that were being blown across the horizon were illuminated by the sun, glorious in victory. The air smelled fresh, whispering of a new day.

Deborah walked back to where the settlement had been. She noted the piles of rocks over fresh graves and saw Hur, his back to her, as he sought to make a fire. He turned, hearing her approach, and shuddered with reverence for the God he saw within her. He had feared for her sanity when he last saw her. Whilst she still carried the brokenness, it was now with a strength that bore compassion, wisdom, and the authority of one who has embraced their deepest fears and found God as sovereign in the midst of it. This was the woman who would defeat Sisera.

"Food?" he asked. The question seemed a little flat, yet he felt not to press her for detail.

"I am hungry," she smiled weakly, sitting on a rock next to him.

"Unfortunately, I can only offer nettle soup and bread. I managed to find a bag of barley flour in the cave. I'm afraid I ate the hedgehog yesterday." He wrinkled his face in disgust.

"Prickly?" she laughed, wrinkling her nose in mock horror.

He frowned, but his tired eyes were playful. "I had the good sense to skin it before I ate it." He handed her the food and she dropped a bag at his feet.

"It's our share of the gifts we were given. Lapidoth hid them on the precipice. I've left half there...in case he returns. We might need it."

"I found Sen and the children in the cave," he smiled. "They escaped in time."

Deborah's heart lurched with relief. "And Ruth?"

He smiled warmly, pleased to be the source of good information.

"She ran to Sheduer's clan for help. She was too late to save the men, but he came and took Sen and the children with him. They are safe...as safe as one is, in these times," he added grimly.

Hur gestured to the ridge. "What happened up there?"

She paused, and for a moment she seemed lost to another world.

"When I left you, I was desperate and I couldn't go on – I could not imagine life without Lapidoth - it all seemed a terrible mistake and I doubted Yahweh's sovereignty as I never have before. Fear prevented me from seeing a future.

"But, in the midst of it all, I knew He was my only hope." She paused as she assembled her thoughts. "In Ephraim, I found Yahweh as my father. In Harosheth, I found Him as my fortress and deliverer. And now, He is my husband; He is everything, and this knowledge is my strength. I will not be crushed by adversity, but in Him I will grow stronger. I will allow the pain to sharpen me into a sword that will silence my enemy."

Hur nodded, acknowledging the authority he had seen in a few great men. Yet he noted that in Deborah, her authority grounded, her roots were steeped in righteousness and compassion, rather than personal ambition. He handed her a skin of water and waited for her to continue.

"Yahweh showed me the battle in which we fight, and that which we *must* fight. I saw Heaven fighting with us and the victory we are promised: the stars fought from their courses in heaven, they fought against Sisera." Her eyes shone with anticipated victory. "But first Israel must repent."

Hur sighed. "And so, what will you do now?"

"I will pray as never before, and I will speak as Yahweh gives me utterance, urging them to return to their Maker. We must journey south, to Ephraim, for it is in my heart to do so. I trust Yahweh to direct our steps, that He will lead me to those He needs to speak to." She looked down as she tried to formulate the words she needed to say. When she looked up, her eyes glistened with tears, and he again marveled at both the steely strength and humility that this woman was able to carry. "Hur, Thank you for all you have done, for waiting for me these twelve days, for being my friend and protector. I cannot assume that you will make this journey with me."

He smiled. "And where should I go? It would seem that Yahweh has placed you under my protection for a while longer. Allow me to take you to Ephraim."

Deborah cocked an eyebrow at his choice of words. "Yahweh? Since when did you pledge your allegiance to Yahweh?"

He gave a low chuckle. "I cannot say. You have whittled me down since the first day I met you with your unyielding faith and resilience. But, I think the day Elizaphan dropped dead settled things in my mind. What I see in you cannot be explained with my mind…but more than that, it…He… demands my respect and my allegiance."

32

*"I the Lord search the heart and test the mind, to give every man
according to his ways, according to the fruit of his deeds."*
Jeremiah 17:10

1238 BC – Deborah

Deborah and Hur wound their way through the mountains and forest,
keeping clear of the main roads.

The Sea of Chinnereth lay below them, like a silver platter that cradled
the winter sun. They ate fish that Hur had caught, along with wild
coriander and barley bread. Deborah forced the food down, still nauseous
despite her hunger. Though only thirty-two years old, she felt like she was
eighty.

"Spring will come soon," Hur commented, noting the tiny, closed buds
on an almond tree.

"It will." Deborah pulled her mantle around her shoulders and lent
toward the fire.

There was a quiet peace between them, a friendship that had been
forged in fire and was almost familial, and completely platonic. He had
seen her at her worst, and his loyalty was absurd, yet treasured.

"Tell me again about Joshua and Jericho," he asked.

"There are other stories of Yahweh's deliverance," Deborah laughed.

"That may be. But I'm a soldier; my natural mind struggles to
understand how you plan to defeat Sisera with ox-goads and plough-shears.
Yet my gut tells me you will."

She smiled, grateful for Hur's faith in her that she often lacked in
herself. She trusted Yahweh implicitly, but she struggled to see how *He*

would use *her*, a woman, and a normal one at that, to defeat an entire army and a military tyrant.

When she reached the end of the story, Hur shook his head. "I don't understand. Why on the seventh time did the walls fall down? Surely Yahweh could have done it on the first time? It makes no sense."

"Yahweh is a God of detail. Numbers, colours and detail have special meaning for us - they bear their own message. The number seven speaks of perfection. Yahweh told Joshua he would fight seven armies when he entered Israel. He was telling Joshua the physical impossibility of defeating the perfect enemy, yet He added: '*I* will go before you, and you *will* defeat them.' It is also the number of rest. Yahweh told Israel that the land must rest every seven years, and that man must rest every seven days. It is the time when we give up our labours, our ability to make things happen, and trust Yahweh."

Hur nodded thoughtfully. "Like Shamgar."

"Yes, like Shamgar."

"So, do you think there was a reason that you waited twelve days before Yahweh spoke?"

Deborah tilted her head, a smile playing on her lips. "Yes, I do." She paused as she formulated her thoughts. "When I was a child, I remember a conversation with a wise man in our village. I had said that I wished I were a man, for had I been a man, I would have killed Sisera for what he did to my family and to my people. He replied that, had Yahweh wanted for me to be a man, I would have been. What Israel needed was a mother.

"It was the first time I heard it mentioned, but not the last. In Harosheth, Yahweh confirmed to me that I would be a mother to Israel," Deborah sighed, poking the fire with a stick.

"I realise now that Israel's problem is not Sisera. It is that she has become divided; our society has become sick, fragmented by each man living for himself. She has forgotten who her Father is, and who she is. It needs a mother before it needs a warrior. For it is a mother who knits her family together, who nurtures, admonishes and teaches a child who they are.

"The number twelve symbolises brotherhood and community; there were twelve patriarchs in Israel who later became the twelve tribes. I have no idea how Yahweh will unite Israel; but I believe it has already begun."

"And do you have any idea why you are being called back to Ephraim?"

"Not really, other than that is where my family, my community are. You can only birth what you have within you. Geographically, it makes sense because Ephraim is central. But I have learnt not to attempt to understand Yahweh's ways; His ways are so far above ours and rarely conform to our logic."

Their journey was slow and they stopped frequently to rest along the way. Deborah picked wild mint and chewed it in an attempt to curb her nausea. Their path took them around the side of Mount Ebal, a towering, grey, limestone peak that offered very little opportunity for foraging. They came to a pile of stones that formed an altar. They were made from uncut stones. When Deborah saw them she knelt down and worshipped Yahweh. Hur watched with interest; Deborah's faith was infectious and he found himself drawn to know more of her God. He sat down to wait, his own reflections turning heavenward.

When she eventually stood, her eyes alight with an ethereal peace, she explained, "This was built by Joshua after he defeated Ai."

They slept near the altar, finding no natural shelter and cooking the remaining barley bread they had been able to rescue from the settlement.

The next day, hungry and stiff, they began their descent. As they rounded the side of the mountain, Mount Gerizim could be seen and cradled between the two mountains was the great city of Shechem. Deborah gazed in awe at the city she had grown up hearing so much about, and revelation flooded her.

Her voice was low as though she was speaking inwardly. "I grew up hearing about Ebal. It is strange to finally sit here, and yet it is easier now to understand why it was from *this* mountain that Joshua was told to speak of Yahweh's curses towards Israel should they turn from Him."

"I don't understand," Hur admitted.

"It is so lofty, so majestic and yet barren, bearing so little fruit and offering so little consolation to those who sojourn here."

"The symbolism is significant?" the Egyptian questioned. "So did Yahweh command His blessings to be pronounced too?"

Deborah nodded thoughtfully, and pointed to Mount Gerizim, lush and clad with forest, the silver line of a stream could be seen descending from it. It was from that mountain that Moses and Levi, Judah, Issachar, Joseph and Benjamin were called to pronounce the blessings over Israel.

Hur nodded. "An underground spring from Gerizim supplies Shechem with water – another reason Sisera has been unable to defeat the city. It can sustain itself."

"Is that true?"

Hur laughed. "Yes, Canaanites are a little arrogant about their intellect and knowledge, I'm afraid."

"Mount Gerizim, a source of life and protection. Water is a symbol for Yahweh's spirit that sustains His people. Everything is significant. He is so mighty, His creative inspiration and desire to communicate with us is knit into everything, particularly the work of His hands."

Hur considered what Deborah said. "A beautiful relationship of harmony between Yahweh, Man and His creation. And yet, what a travesty that suffering is so great. What is the answer?"

She gazed silently up at the summit of the mountain behind her. "Where the root problem is spiritual: where man is his own god and each does what is right in their own eyes, our best weapons are integrity, humility, the wisdom found in Yahweh's holy laws and the faith to fight."

Hur nodded, but his thoughts were distracted and a frown marked his expression.

"And yet?" Deborah asked, responding to his doubt.

He sighed. "And yet it seems a little unfair. How did He decide that six of the tribes would pronounce the blessings while the others were doomed to declare curses? I know which mountain I would rather be on."

Deborah nodded. "When we entered the land, Yahweh told us He would go before us, giving us victory. And He did. Our part was to drive out the inhabitants and tear down their altars, because Yahweh saw that we would be influenced by them to make wrong decisions, which would ultimately draw us away from Him and our destiny. Of those, Ephraim, Manasseh, Zebulon, Asher and Naphtali and Dan failed to do so. They dwelt among them, either forcing them to pay tribute or forced labour."

"And so?"

"And so, Yahweh said that He would not drive their enemies before them any more, but would allow them to be thorns in their side; that their gods would be a snare to His people. Judah on the other hand, defeated Kiriath Arba."

"The city of four, the sons of Anak. That's no minor feat. How did they do it?" Hur mused, thinking of Talmai with a shudder.

"Yahweh went before them. But they believed, they trusted in Him, in the victory that He promised despite the logical impossibility."

"And yet the same promise was given to all?"

"It was, and Yahweh knew that if they failed to obey, what would come." She waved her hand emphatically. "And here we are," she sighed.

"So He punished them?"

"It's less about punishment and more about Yahweh, in His wisdom, weaving our poor choices for the ultimate good; it's the longer route in which lessons must be learnt."

"But there have been times when your people have been at peace and have ruled the Canaanites."

"Yahweh, realising mankind's natural inclination to get themselves in trouble, raised up judges to remind them and guide them in His ways. As long as these judges lived, they stuck to the path and things went well."

"Why didn't Yahweh just ensure a succession to each judge?"

She shrugged as she looked him in the eye. "Because He gave us choice, and He sometimes allows our hearts to be tested."

Her eyes searched his expression, and she acknowledged with pleasure that Hur's questions carried their own hunger, and that Yahweh was responding to his longing.

She paused, reluctant to move on as she pondered on the rich heritage of the land before her. "It was here that Abraham received the covenant from Yahweh that his descendants would inherit the land," she added.

She silently took in the cherished city, its solid grey walls wrapped around her, like defensive arms. Deborah felt herself longing for that place of security.

Hur broke the silence. "It's imposing isn't it? It's still under Israelite rule; we can find shelter here tonight."

"I've never seen walls so commanding, nor so intimidating." Deborah stared in awe.

"They are meant to be, Shechem is a prize." He pointed to the grey cross that split the verdant plains in two. "From those roads, all of Israel can be accessed. The pass between Mount Gerizim to the south and Ebal to the North offers some strategic protection, but other than that, it has no natural fortifications; most cities of this importance are located on hills. Without these walls, the city would be very vulnerable to attack."

"Does Shechem still remain Hebrew then?" Deborah asked, recalling her conversation with Etiya in Harosheth.

The air around them was still, the warmth of spring a cloak of possibility. They passed the farmers bringing in carts laden with barley and tending to their fledgling crops. Their heads were lowered, expressions grim, they did not look up as they passed, but their attire and bearded faces defined them as Hebrew.

Hur paused as though deliberating on his next words. Finally he gave a weighted sigh, and pointed to the edge of the field. Deborah squinted and could see the charred remains of trees, like dark spectres that stood memorial to the atrocities they had witnessed. "A few years ago I was here with Sisera. He hoped to defeat it. You had been taken under Ariya's wing by then, thankfully. We were unable to breach her walls, but burned the fields and took away their livestock. We had done it before. Those we captured were murdered before the city gates, but we were not able to take the city. Sisera will return though, before long."

Deborah nodded, noting the images that played before his eyes and the guilt he carried. She laid her hand on Hur's arm. "Thank you for taking me to Ariya that day, Hur. Yahweh is merciful. Remember you were a soldier under orders."

Hur shrugged thoughtfully. "It was a strange thing that I was commanded to guard you and yet I found myself driven to protect you."

He paused, gazing at Mount Gerizim. "And here we are. I wonder now if it was not you who was saving me."

"Such is the interwoven miracle of friendship: we sow freely and find a harvest we did not anticipate. I cannot imagine how I would be here today were it not for your obedience to a God you did not know." Deborah acknowledged the hand of Yahweh in both of their lives; how He had used such an extraordinary and unlikely relationship to accomplish His will.

Hur nodded, his gaze focusing on a point below him. "It takes some reckoning, doesn't it?"

They descended the mountain and coming to a deep man-made well, Hur lowered the bucket to refill their water-skins.

"I was told this is Jacob's well," Hur pointed out, chuckling at Deborah's excitement. She lowered the bucket into the depths of the ancient shaft and found herself wondering if her namesake had drawn water from this place, too. She told Hur the story of Jacob, and how Deborah, his nurse, had been her distant ancestor and her namesake.

"You have such a sense of history, of belonging. I envy that," Hur said wistfully.

"It's part of the fabric of my being. We grow up hearing the stories, singing songs and learning Yahweh's Law, it is the joy and responsibility of a parent to pass these treasures on to their children. To fight for my belief and culture is instinctive.

"Shechem has *such* history. It was here that Joseph's body, brought back from Egypt was buried." She looked around her, feeling the power of Yahweh's thread that ran through the ages and had brought her here today. A shiver ran through her, empowering her with a sense of shared destiny, of Yahweh's covenant to establish Israel, and the victory that they could have, even as He had spoken to those before her.

"It appears to still be under Israelite command; we can find lodging here tonight," Hur said.

"Yes, it's a Levitical city, a city of refuge," she mused. "The idea of sleeping in a bed and eating proper food does sound good." But her inner thoughts turned to Yahweh: *What are Your purposes here, for this Holy City, my Lord?*

The words formed within her mind, with a clarity that pierced her natural thoughts: *Find the home of Eliav, son of Gersham;* with it came the impression of a fountain, and a grey, brick governmental-looking building. Without understanding, they continued through the green wheat fields.

The market traders were packing up as they entered the mighty gates of the city, its last wily customers heckling in hope of a good price at the close of a day with weary stall holders.

The watchman looked down from the enormous stone towers, relieved at another day without trouble and looking forward to closing the gates.

The stone streets of the great city pulsated with the hustle and bustle of folk returning home, pulling carts, hurrying children, while the chatter of families, sharing their evening meal, fluttered over walled courtyards competing with the bleating of sheep, goats and the squawking of chickens. The sound of her own language warmed Deborah's soul, though some were clearly Canaanite. She caught the eye of a woman climbing down the steps of her rooftop and they exchanged a conspiratorial smile, in the way that women do. Deborah noted with disappointed consciousness the household gods that stood in many open windows and adorned walls, as well as those that had none.

They walked without real direction, but rather following an inner gravity that drew them into the city centre. When finally, the narrow street opened onto a large public square, and she was relieved to find in the centre a natural fountain enclosed by a shallow stone wall.

She looked around. "Yahweh showed me this fountain – to come here."

"What now?"

"I have no idea. I need to find the home of Eliav, son of Gersham," she shrugged and stared around her.

A large governmental looking building dominated the square; there was a steady flow of traffic heading up and down the stone steps. At the base stood a phallic-looking depiction of Baal opposite Asherah.

Around the perimeter of the square were a few less ostentatious, but equally formal, buildings that were separated only by a narrow alleyway.

Deborah wandered into the alleyway, followed by Hur. The smell of cooking made her empty stomach growl. They opened the gate to the first courtyard, and covered the short distance to a patched wooden door. Drawing her headdress around her face, Deborah knocked. It took some time before the shuffle of footsteps preceded a wizened face eyeing them suspiciously through the narrow opening.

"Shalom," he said, though his expression was anything but contented.

"Shalom," Deborah bowed her head. "We search for the home of Eliav, son of Gersham."

The man recoiled slightly, a frown consuming his countenance, before replying, "Well, you won't find him here." The door closed.

Deborah turned to Hur, a bemused look on her face.

"Odd."

"Hmmm. And yet his tone implies a story. I don't think we are far." He closed the gate behind him and moved on to the next house.

It was the fifth house, and Deborah, feeling exhausted, was wondering if they should find an inn and resume their search in the morning. The house before them was larger, having a high wall with its own door and a large iron fixture which groaned with neglect as Hur pounded the knocker. Finally, the sound of footsteps could be heard crossing the courtyard. A woman answered, opening the door only a fraction and thereby concealing the house behind her. Her hair was hidden under a pale blue mantle, but her tired eyes bore a hidden profundity. Deborah reckoned the woman to be in her sixties.

"I am searching for Eliav, son of Gersham. Does he live here?"

The woman's face grew distant, drawn with the shades of grief. She stepped back as though she would close the door and Deborah shifted uncomfortably in acknowledgment of her response, respectfully widening the gap between them. "I am sorry, I meant no harm."

The woman sighed, and the door opened a little further as she seemed to waver between curiosity and suspicion. "I *knew* him," she ventured tentatively. "Eliav was my husband. He was killed three years ago…by Sisera's men."

Deborah acknowledged, with some confusion, the alignment of events, which as yet had no clarity or purpose. She felt Hur shift uncomfortably behind her and wondered what part he had played in the attack.

Why have you brought me to a dead man's home, Yahweh?

She gently held the woman's scrutiny. "I am sorry for your loss, my own father and brother were killed by Sisera and my husband taken. I know the pain you must feel."

The woman's eyes darted enquiringly to Hur. "This is my friend, Hur. We escaped from a Hebrew village after it was attacked by Sisera's men," Deborah explained.

She gave slight nod of empathy, by way of response and opened the door wide.

Following her across the stone courtyard, they were led into the house. The room they were in showed signs of worn comfort, as though life had once been easier. A small wooden table and bench with an oil lamp stood in one corner and in the other corner, a rudimentary couch draped in a patched covering. A younger lady sat here, with two small children. She looked up and smiled cautiously, her eyes darting to the older woman for explanation of their guest.

The boy, Deborah reckoned to be around ten years of age, reminded her of Tebah; a deep frown was etched onto his young face. He stood, boldly approaching them while the older woman disappeared through arched door opening.

"Who are you?" he asked abruptly.

"Jacob!" The mother blushed crimson with embarrassment. "I am so sorry, we don't entertain str…people very often."

Deborah smiled with understanding and a strange sense of nostalgia for her old friend. "It's fine, really. In these times, it's right for the man of the house to show caution when strangers enter. My name is Deborah, and this is my friend, Hur. Our story is a little unusual, somewhat of a riddle, and I am hoping you will be able to help us."

The older woman returned with a tray bearing hot bowls of stew, bread and a pitcher of water. She instructed Jacob to bring bowls and cups as the younger woman helped her to set the table. "My name is Rebecca and this is my daughter-in-law, Maya, and the children, Miriam and Jacob. My son was with my husband on the day…" She brushed her grief behind a wall of stoicism.

"Please, wash, sit and let me serve you food and drink. We were about to eat and I'm sure you must be hungry. Then we will talk."

Gratefully, they ate lentil stew with fresh barley bread while Deborah told her story, leading to Yahweh giving her the name of this house.

Rebecca listened silently, her eyes glazed with tears.

"Should we not call for the Elders?" Maya suggested, handing her young daughter a doll carved out of wood. The child sat at her feet 'feeding' it crumbs of her bread.

Rebecca laid a hand on the younger woman's arm. "That may well come, but first let us hear what Deborah says." The woman carried a quiet authority that came from having lived, seen and lost so much that she cared little for the opinion of others, but was guided only by her own inner integrity to God.

"Eliav had been one of the Elders. He had seen the moral and spiritual decline of our nation and prayed. He saw how we had been weakened and divided by our degeneration and prayed for Yahweh to raise up another Judge - one who would rule with compassion, wisdom and humility. He said our nation did not need a warrior as much as it needed a parent to draw His children together and back into His arms."

She smiled wistfully. "Eliav said that Israel was like a wayward child that needed admonishing, guiding and nurturing. She needed to be reminded of who She was and the promises She had been given. Only then would we find the vision and courage to fight for what Yahweh had promised us."

The two women silently exchanged their thoughts. While Deborah acknowledged that Yahweh had used this woman to confirm her calling to her, Rebecca felt the tragedy she had experienced take on meaning; she knew that Yahweh loved her personally and had heard her prayers.

Maya broke the silence. "The women have prayed for this day, since… *that* day," she pondered reverently.

"Yahweh saw his prayers. That He gave you my husband's name; it is as if He is letting me know that none of it was in vain." She clasped her hands over her mouth, as though to push back the emotion that welled up within her.

"Their lives seemed so wasted," Maya agreed, pulling Miriam onto her lap.

Deborah touched the gems that hung around her neck. "He used your prayer and suffering and turned them into jewels that His kingdom might be built upon."

"Should we not call for the Elders?" Maya repeated, twisting a strand of her daughter's hair between her fingers.

Rebecca placed a hand on Maya's arm, but her eyes held Deborah's. The sun had begun its descent and the walls of the courtyard were bathed in soft rosy hues. "Not tonight. First our guests must sleep. Tomorrow, with Deborah's consent, we will speak to Ephraim. He will know what to do."

Maya nodded compliantly and stood to prepare beds in the shelter of the courtyard.

The following morning, Deborah was led to an impressive stone building, which she immediately recognised from the vision that Yahweh had shown her. It was not a place of worship, which was only to be carried out at Shiloh, but it was a governmental place where the Elders met to discuss disputes and pray. The pillars were inscribed with the laws of Moses and Deborah paused, tracing her finger over the words, the sight of them nourishing her soul.

The men were already assembled on wooden benches around a long trestle table. They had clearly been discussing the reason for a woman being invited to their counsel meetings, and were divided about its reason and the use of their time. She smiled circumspectly, allowing her natural perception of people to filter and weigh the men sat before her. She had long since abandoned the notion that these men would be righteous, or even friendly, just because they held position.

Conversation had stopped abruptly upon Deborah's entrance. She was equally aware of their scrutiny of her; they were clearly expecting her to be of some stature and wealth, and she was dressed as a farmer's wife, her head covered in a simple linen mantle. Their disappointment was evident, and an obstacle that she knew would shade her message.

Yahweh, I am here - an empty vessel to be used by You. Not my will, nor my reputation, but Your Holiness, Your power, Your words be manifest, I pray.

The men stood, and one, an elderly man, tall and thin with watery eyes that were warm with compassion and wisdom, smiled now, clasping Rebecca's arms. Deborah acknowledged the respect and affection that Rebecca was regarded with. Despite their prejudices, they would listen to her message out of loyalty to her and the memory of Eliav.

"It is good to see you my dear." He turned to Deborah, his expression still warm, if curious. "I am Ephraim, a Levite and Elder among the counsel, please come and take a seat among us, both of you."

Ephraim remained standing. "If we understand correctly, you believe that Yahweh has brought you here to speak with us?" He turned to the other men now, and ignoring the skepticism and disdain that was apparent in their expressions, he spoke. "For the sake of Eliav and his wife, I ask that we listen and that we cast aside judgements until Deborah has stated her case."

He nodded solemnly to Deborah. "Please tell us what you feel Yahweh has shown you." Deborah noted that the tone of his voice was not unkind, but rather as someone might speak to a child. She knew she had already been weighed and that she must trust Yahweh to address the balance. For herself, she would treat these men as though they were men of God. She would not allow their judgements to change her integrity. If Yahweh showed her otherwise, she would speak with the authority, wisdom and courage He gave her.

"Elders of Shechem, Israel's Jewel, I thank you for listening to me today." She kept her hands tucked under the folds of her robe. "Yahweh, I ask that my words might reflect Your heart and that Your great will might be established today."

She looked up at the stony faces and reminded herself that neither her future, nor the future of Israel, was dependent on their approval of her, nor their belief in what she said. Yahweh's will would be done regardless – though Shechem's journey would be dependent on their response. And so, she told them of how the Elders in Kedesh had responded to Yahweh's call; she told them the dream He had given her, for she hoped that one among them might also have been shown what she had seen.

When she had finished, she looked around the room. She did not observe open hostility, but tolerance, and its response shook her, for she acknowledged that they were trapped within their comfort, safety and religious mindsets. It was a stronghold that would not weaken easily. And yet she would try to take an axe to the foundations of the walls that hemmed them in from the revelation of truth of their complacency, their tolerance and mediocrity. For she perceived that if she did not, if she failed, Shechem would fall and its slaughter would be brutal. Her memories of such destruction filled her with compassion and furious determination.

Ephraim cleared his throat, pulling his robe straight. "Your story is an incredible one, and though there are those among us who may find it difficult to relate to, it is obvious that your courage and conviction are to be commended and aspired to."

Deborah smiled as the old man sought to appease her and those around him. *Lest you offend, you will compromise the holiness of Yahweh.*

Another stood, his greying hair exposed a lofty forehead so that when he raised his eyebrow as he spoke, Deborah suddenly had the oddest memory of the gecko that had frequented *her place,* sitting upon the rounded rock, as it watched her. The memory seemed so out of place, so entirely removed from her present situation that she fought the urge to laugh. When his eyebrow wiggled up and down, she smiled, hoping to appear friendly rather than distracted, or worse still, mentally unstable. "You must know Deborah, that Shechem has maintained its Hebrew roots. We have not forsaken Yahweh as other cities have."

The man next to him nodded. "Zachariah is right, we are tolerant to other religions for the sake of peace and commerce, but we have not bowed our knee to Baal, nor to Sisera. We teach the Torah and observe the Sabbath. For this reason we remain undefeated," he asserted, his expression bristling with the pride he held in his city.

Her eyes travelled around the room, resting on different men as she spoke. Her voice was compassionate, insistent and commanding; for the authority of heaven rested upon her words. "I perceive that there are those among you who have maintained your passion for Yahweh and await His deliverance. I perceive, too, that for many, your confidence is in walls made by men. Still others have forsaken the Laws of Yahweh and you hide your secret sin behind your religious façade."

"I speak to those of you who have not bowed your knee to Baal, for you congratulate yourself in this, but your hearts are hardened to Yahweh because of your pride and your security, thus your faith and relationship is compromised." She smiled. "Yahweh commends your faithfulness and calls you to return to Him with your whole heart."

There was a sharp intake of breath, as though the air had been sucked from the room. Silence floundered in its density. Finally, Zachariah leapt to his feet. "Such arrogance! How dare you question Yahweh's servants?" His face had turned crimson. "You are a woman and have no right to speak with such disrespect to Yahweh's anointed!" There were a few grunts of agreement, while others avoided eye contact.

Rather than answer Zachariah from her own indignation, she ignored him. Her eyes burned with fire-like intensity that seared the souls of those they rested upon, even as her voice shook with fury.

"Yet there are others among you, who maintain your positions as Elders, for you love the prominence. But you are hypocrites, who judge others for sins that you commit. In your religious pride, you take your sin outside of the city and seek Canaan's delights from the villages outside the walls. There you visit the high places and watch while others sacrifice your illegitimate children to Baal. Thus, your faith is a veneer that you cling to. It has the depth and health of a stagnant pool within which you will perish. Repent from your secret sins and rid the city of Canaan's gods." She watched the men's faces pale as they shifted uncomfortably. Her eyes finally settled on Zachariah.

"And you, sir, are one of those men." There was a deadly silence as though the unthinkable had been said. The man's eyes were narrow, icy slits that defied judgement though his complexion looked ready to combust with indignation. He opened his mouth to speak, but Deborah continued, her tone quiet and measured. "You...who sit on the counsel of Elders, while the blood of innocent children is on your hands - what is done in secret shall be exposed." Zachariah's eyes widened as he looked down at his hands and a strangled garbled sound escaped from his chest. He stood, pushing away the bench, his hands outstretched and his expression one of horror as blood oozed from the pores in his hands. He staggered as he hastened from the room.

The strained silence was now acute, a drawn breath, in which the curtain had been pulled back...but she had their attention. Eyes shifted uncomfortably to the floor as their consciences writhed within them, pricking some with rage and others with repentance. But those who wished to criticise her said nothing, for they knew their hearts had been weighed and were fearful of exposure.

A young man stood, a mop of straight black hair, fell over his deep brown eyes that turned down at the corners, giving him a solemn sincerity. He stroked his beard, a gesture that seemed to belong to someone older than his years. He looked questioningly to Ephraim as though requesting permission to speak and Deborah perceived both the purity of his heart and conviction. The Elder nodded, his expression warm with pride and affection. "Speak, Yoseph, my son."

The young man, in his early thirties spoke falteringly though, he did not seem to lack courage. "Deborah, some time ago..." he looked around the room awkwardly, "I, too, had a dream which I shared with my father." He motioned to Ephraim, who looked embarrassed. Yoseph quickly added, "I did not acknowledge its significance at the time, and so I am sure that nobody else would have thought it relevant. It was shortly after Shechem had been surrounded by Sisera's army and fear was ripe - his threats and violence filled all of our nightmares. It was at this time, that I, too, dreamt of a tree. Around the tree was a wall, it was built of many treasures, it was strong and the words of the Torah were inscribed within it. I saw an axe being laid to the foot of the tree. As the axe hit the tree, the violence cracked the earth and weakened the wall. Blow after blow was delivered and I lamented the destruction of the wall, until my tears pooled at the base of the tree. While the tree was yet dead to the natural eye, the honey bee began to pollinate the tree and life emerged where it should not have. I awoke, believing that the dream held a message, but did not understand until I heard you spoke. I now I believe that it was a warning to Shechem, to repent from its religious pride, its material security and false spirituality. I believe that you, Deborah, are the honey bee that will bring life to our nation while it is yet barren." He looked around the room when he had finished, and Deborah acknowledged that the tension was beginning to crack and splinter. Yoseph had altered the balance. None spoke.

Ephraim sighed, wishing he had had some warning when he awoke this morning what a difficult day it would be. He realised now that he must accept the unthinkable: that Yahweh would raise up a woman to judge Israel and not only a judge, but a prophetess. He winced at the mess she had created among his Elders, recognising that he would be left to sort it out after she moved on. The solution to his predicament was obvious, and he congratulated himself on the brilliance of his idea - she must remain among them, where she could be helped, watched and most importantly sort out the mess she had begun.

He cleared his throat. "Deborah...I...clearly we must acknowledge Yahweh's hand on your life, and that you call Israel back to her Father. But, I fear, in all honesty, that without a husband to stand with you, the men of Israel will not listen to you. Certainly, there is a need for repentance among Yahweh's people and we will spend time fasting and searching our hearts. We will seek Yahweh in who might stand with you... As I am sure you know, rightly or wrongly, people have 'expectations' for those who lead us. As Levites, as Men called by Yahweh, we could support you, stand with you." Beads of sweat pricked the old man's brow and he felt as though he was rapidly aging, even as he spoke.

Deborah smiled inwardly at Ephraim's predicament and his obvious discomfort. "I thank you for your kind offer, and I see that your heart is without personal ambition. I am aware that many will find my choices..." she smirked wryly, her eyebrow raised, "...as poor as Yahweh's election. However, I was once asked by Him to lay down my need for worldly security and hope; I will not take it back. I do not believe any man (or woman) has it in their ability to turn a nation back to Yahweh. Yet, perhaps it is my natural vulnerability that has woven me and made me dependent on Him. In this way, He will show His glory, His might, and His love so that His people can never put their trust in the salvation of men. Thus it is my great delight to acknowledge my weakness and the natural absurdity of my hope. And yet..." she paused, her eyes focusing on each man in the room, "I do not need to remind you that no woman was found worshipping the golden calf in the wilderness when Moses returned to the mountain, and it is the prayers of women that brought me here today. Yahweh has not called me to lead Israel into battle; He has called me to be a mother, to bind His children together. To restore the unity of Israel and to cause His people to cleave to their heavenly Father. I call Israel to hope in Him who is greater than their own ability and strength, for He has called me to love, admonish and heal. He has called me to be a mother to Israel. How can I call Israel to unity, to humility and courage when I sit behind walls? How can I accept importance and security when my people are starving and afraid? I fully acknowledge that people will have expectations of who will lead them. I take no such yoke upon myself, nor is it an aspiration I would attain to. But…" she kept eye contact with the men in the room as she spoke, "I will be obedient to all that He calls me to and by His grace and power I will both defy and exceed expectation.

"Yahweh would warn you: the day will come when Canaan will surround this city. Pray that your hearts will be ready. For our safety lies not in walls made by man, but in obedience and in faith. Ready His people."

The tension in the air had grown so that it was as a physical pressure that became heavier as Deborah spoke. Ephraim nervously cleared his throat. The sound was like iron on stone, and cut the nervous silence, demanding a response that would sever the cords of the comfortable cradle they had hitherto rested in.

Finally, one of the Elders stood up. "I take my leave of you. I will have no more part in this meeting." Four others stood with him and hurriedly departed, leaving five remaining.

Deborah sensed Yahweh's peace rest upon those who remained. "Moses stood before the congregation of Israel. He offered them two options, to choose life or death. I believe you remain here because you have chosen life, to follow Yahweh's path and His purposes. There is no middle road of mediocrity. Therefore, I urge you to repent of anything that has held you back from living militantly, and pledge your allegiance to serve Him, with all your heart, soul and strength. We serve a merciful and loving God, a mighty deliverer, who calls us to courage to stand against Canaan and its influence and put your trust in Him."

Yoseph was the first to stand, followed by his father. The remaining five men joined them.

"Then let us pray, men of God."

Yahweh's presence had filled the room, and as they lifted their voices to their Sovereign King, the deception of material and religious comfort was replaced by the invincible truth of His holiness and faithfulness.

Finally, Deborah pulled her mantle around her and bidding farewell, she left the counsel.

The next morning, Deborah and Hur prepared to leave. She embraced Maya and Rebecca. As she clasped their hands in her own, she felt the bond of sisterhood that had knitted their hearts, defying the length of time she had actually known them. "Do not underestimate the importance of who you are and what you do, my sisters. Yahweh calls mothers to pray, to knit together the hearts of His people. You have served him so faithfully in your compassion, your devotion and your kindness. You know that He hears your prayers. Continue in all that you are and do. He is proud to call you His daughters."

At Deborah's request, they stopped at Shiloh because she was desirous to visit the Tabernacle. As the city walls came into view, she was taken back to the day she had first come with her father.

She took a handful of gold and silver from the pouch of gifts to purchase a lamb. Her heart leapt with anticipation as she saw the pale walls of the tabernacle raised against the green hills of Ephraim.

She sighed, *'I am home.'*

Deborah waited for the man before her to offer his sacrifice and then stepped up to the altar.

The high-priest's eyes bore into hers and Deborah respectfully lowered her eyes. He was identified by his attire: the golden breastplate, inlaid with the twelve stones that represented the twelve tribes, the linen turban with the gold plate upon which was ascribed: holiness to the Lord.

"You are the one we have waited for: the Mother of Israel, are you not?"

Her eyes flickered with surprise before meeting his. "I am who Yahweh says I am," she replied with humility.

The priest nodded with thoughtful approval. "Yahweh has spoken to us concerning you. You will judge His people and you will unite them once again."

Deborah nodded, tears stinging her eyes.

"But you know this already," he stated.

"I am the wife of Lapidoth, the son of Abinoam of Naphtali, and I am as you have spoken."

The old man smiled. "I knew Abinoam; his father provided the tabernacle with torches. Does he still live?"

"He does."

Remembrance flickered on the old man's face and he smiled. "You are the girl who was bitten by a snake."

She laughed. "Yes, Yahweh works His purposes in mysterious ways. I was taken a slave by Sisera. When I escaped, I ran into Lapidoth in the mountains of Kedesh. Yahweh has begun to awaken the northern tribes."

The priest's eyes burned with long awaited anticipation. "We will blow the shofar call of awakening, even as it resounds in the heavens." He frowned. "And where is Lapidoth now?"

"I believe he was taken by Canaan, though I cannot be sure. I trust Yahweh that he still lives." She unconsciously clasped the necklace he had given her.

The priest followed her action. "The necklace of Yemina."

Deborah was taken aback. "You know it?"

He smiled. "It was given to Josiah for his service to the temple; each gem represents a part of Yahweh: the red, the sacrifice; the blue the colour of the heavenlies and the spirit of Yahweh, and the green, Yahweh, creator and giver of life. All held in place by the gold of His sovereignty."

His old eyes sharpened and Deborah felt the weight of his words penetrate her soul. "Each of these precious gems began as a worthless rock, but through intense pressure and heat, it became something of immense value."

Deborah nodded, recalling the day Lapidoth had said the same words to her, and her conversation with Rebecca in Shechem.

She laid her hands on the head of the lamb and allowed the solemnity of the moment to weigh upon her as the throat of the lamb was slit, its life seeping into the bowl held out by the priest. When the sacrifice was made, she went and knelt, worshipping Yahweh and felt the gentle reassurance of His presence with her.

As she made to leave, a different priest came after her; he laid his hand on her arm. "Do not return to your village. Sisera came looking for you eight moons ago; your people wait for you by the place of your namesake."

Anxiety mounted in Deborah's heart as she considered the obvious truth that Sisera, angry and vengeful, had assumed she would return to Ephraim.

She met Hur and left Shiloh behind her, feeling as though an emotional cauldron was swirling within her. She was elated that the priest had confirmed her calling and alluded at her ability to serve as judge. But overriding all other thought was her concern for her beloved village.

33

Until I, Deborah, arose, until I arose, a mother in Israel.
Judges 5:7

1238 BC - Deborah

They reached the famous terebinth tree the following day and found the place deserted. She leaned against 'the tree of weeping,' feeling a deep affiliation with the tree; its ancient roots had long since found their stability in the rocky earth, and its branches, raised to heaven despite the storms they had weathered, brought consolation and hope to Deborah's soul. The gnarled, rutted trunk dug into her back while the sun, flickering through the leafy roof, warmed her countenance. She acknowledged that she had inadvertently imagined Tobias to be waiting for her, his warm wrinkled smile and outstretched arms would have embraced her and she would have known she was home. Now she felt the disappointment as a wave of anxiety.

Her mind travelled to the time of her namesake's burial. She had been the kinswoman of Abraham. When Isaac went to find a wife from his father's people, he had chosen Rebecca. The young girl left home, taking her nurse, Deborah with her. After her mistress died she had then, possibly at Rebecca's request, travelled many miles back to her homeland, to look after Jacob and his children.

She imagined Jacob, surrounded by his wives, his sons and poor Dinah, burying the woman who had helped bring his children into the world, who had nursed them when they were sick, their sorrow feeding the roots of the tree.

Hur roamed the area, looking for signs of recent activity. When he returned he crouched next to her and exhaled deeply, scratching his newly grown beard. "There is a track leading into the forest, it's frequently used…It's as well Sisera didn't know to look here, they might as well have sent a welcoming party." He rolled his eyes with humourless incredulity and Deborah laughed.

"It's my guess they have made their homes in the covering of the forest, but they come here hoping to find you. Shall we surprise them?" he grinned, offering Deborah his hand.

Deborah laughed, allowing Hur to pull her up. Her eyes lit with anticipation at the prospect of seeing her mother and Isaac again. She swallowed as a wave of nausea hit her.

"I'm going to try and cover the tracks behind us, though – call it self preservation," he smirked.

They wandered through the forest, silently admiring the ancient oaks, pines and myrtle trees that whispered above them creating a symphony with the birds' chorus.

At last, through the trees, appeared the form of a man sitting on a tree stump talking to two others. It looked like Tobias, but as she came nearer, she realised it was Gershon, and the other she recognised as Menachem. Behind him was a younger man with a woman and child. They were sitting under a goatskin canopy. Menachem squinted, grabbing the ram's horn by his waist, clearly unsure of who it was.

There was a flurry of activity, in which the village hesitantly poured out of the trees and homes armed with plough-shears and anxiety. A man her own age stood with a bow and arrow which he raised, and Hur reached for his own.

"Stop where you are," the man commanded. She recognised his voice, his face.

"Isaac?"

The man who sat with his wife and child turned, dropping the bowl in his hand as he stood. "Deborah?"

"Isaac?" she laughed, running toward him and sobbing as she embraced him. He picked her up and crushed her against his body until she squealed. She looked into his kind brown eyes.

"It's so good to see you, Deborah! When we heard that you had escaped, we hoped. I've missed you so much." He embraced her again.

"You remind me of Abba," she smiled, her eyes welling up with tears.

"So I'm told, though I'm afraid I remember so little of him," he smiled sadly.

The rest of the village had crowded around her now and she was suddenly swamped in a huge embrace of tears, laughter and questions.

She was hugged by a woman while her other hand held Isaac's. Recognition and joy flooded Deborah: it was Gabriella. She remembered the wistful discussions her mother and Orpah had had in the Niddah retreat; so many betrothals had begun in this way.

And then, in the middle of warmth, a cold shiver ran down Deborah's spine. Her eyes scanned the crowd, as the frantic realisation of who was missing struck her. She gripped Isaac's arms.

"Mama? Where's Mama?" she said looking around.

Isaac simply shook his head; his own eyes brimming with tears.

Deborah collapsed to her knees and wept; she had not been prepared for this. In all she had been through she had believed it was for the sake of her village, yes, but her mother, who had brought her into the world, had loved her and had suffered so much. The idea that she was still alive had made it worth something.

Gershon and Isaac were kneeling beside her now. Gershon's arm was around her, as it had been all those years ago when her brother had been killed. "She's with your father and Enoch, Deborah. It was what she wanted in the end; she died of fever the winter after you left... She didn't have to see the destruction of the village." His eyes clouded with grief. He looked so much like Tobias, she ached in her heart to see the old man and yet she realised, he must be gone too.

She looked around her, suddenly feeling nauseous and dazed.

"The village, what happened?"

Gershon nodded. "Please come into our home. Is this your husband?" he said, smiling at Hur.

"No, my husband was taken. Hur is my friend and my protector." Her words tumbled out of her, for she felt a wild grief as loss avalanched within her.

"Where are Hadas and Miriam?" she asked with panic.

Deborah saw deep emotion stir in Gershon's eyes, and her heart lurched with dread. "Please, come." He motioned to Isaac. "Let's find you some food and talk." Deborah felt an icy ripple hit her midriff and spread its fingers through her.

Gershon pushed aside the deer hide door and invited them to sit down on the rudimentary bench. He handed Hur a skin of goats' milk.

"Tell me what happened...who is left?" the question formed in her mind and fell, writhing, begging to be left unasked.

Gershon hunched his shoulders as though the words had hit him with a physical blow. He looked up, his face one of personal agony, and empathy for the added pain he would shortly inflict on one who had already suffered too much. He inhaled. "Sisera came eight months ago...we had some warning...Dan had been on the hills with the sheep when Sisera's men were sighted. Isaac took the children, and many of the women to the hills...to the place you used to pray... and they hid there. Dan, Menachem and I went too. Tobias and Raisa insisted on staying behind.

Deborah thought of dear, selfless, brave Tobias trembling alone as he awaited Sisera's arrival. She swallowed the sob as it caught in her throat.

"And?"

He stared vacantly ahead of him and then bowed his head, pressing his palms into his eyes. "We forgot to check the Niddah retreat. Miriam was there with Uriel and Netanya." He looked up with haunted eyes.

Deborah said nothing, the mental images of Sisera's cruelty played involuntarily in her mind; she knew Sisera would have made those left behind pay for her and the rest of the village's escape. She felt numbed to her core.

"And Hadas?"

"Hadas is with child and expected to give birth any day. I am sure she is longing to see you," Gershon smiled, pleased to be able to impart some good news.

It was after midday by the time she stepped outside. A tall, wiry man was leaning up against a tree waiting for her. His arms were crossed and he wore an angry frown that seemed to leak from within.

It was the frown that caused her to recognise him. It was Tebah; the selfish boy was gone, and before her stood a man, his former strength hardened by pain. She remembered the last time she had seen him, his body thrown on top of his parents as he tried to protect them with his own body. She strode up to him and embraced him. He looked haunted as though the image played continually before him.

"Tebah, how are you?"

"I need vengeance Deborah; I cannot rest until I see them pay."

She nodded. "You will. Yahweh raises His army."

She turned, noting a lady walking toward her, two small children at her side, while another woman, older, walked next to her also with two small children. Deborah squinted, trying to recognise who it was.

"Tamar!" She rushed over to the two women embracing both.

"Nissa! Are these yours?"

Nissa smiled. "Anna and Job are our adopted children. Their mother came to the village the winter you were taken; she had the same fever that took your mother."

Deborah smiled weakly. "I am so happy for you Nissa; they are so fortunate to have you as a mother."

"Thank you. I love them as though they were my own." She squeezed the tiny hands that held hers.

"Where is Hadas?"

"She has been unwell, she will have her third child any day but she has taken to bed. I have pumped her with so many herbs, I am sure the baby will come out green, with leaves instead of hair; but there is nothing else she can do, bar rest. She insists you must come immediately or she will drag herself to you. Please go!" Tamar begged, laughing.

"I need to see her, I have missed her so much…and Miriam," she added sadly.

Tamar put her arm around her shoulder. "So much pain to return to. But we are glad to see you. Come."

Deborah turned to Hur, who grinned. "Go, I can look after myself."

Hadas was lying on a straw pallet; her legs raised above her and her stomach a massive swollen mound. She had propped herself up on one arm and Deborah stifled a giggle.

Hadas laughed too. "If you are going to laugh at me at least hug me while you do it."

"Hello Tel Hadas. Will you birth a city I wonder?" she laughed, embracing her friend.

Hadas chuckled, giving an exaggerated groan. "That better not be prophetic, or we are going to have words, my friend." She patted the stool beside her bed. "Laugh at me while I'm comfortable at least," she said, flopping backward.

"Tell me; tell me everything that has happened since you left!"

Deborah smiled, thanking Yahweh that she was once again among her people.

She narrated to Hadas her last five years, telling her how her knowledge of the use of herbs had brought her favour with Sisera's mother, and also how she had seen the man in Kedesh healed supernaturally. She ended the story with Lapidoth's capture.

"And what does Yahweh say?"

"He says I must trust that he is in His hands. And I try, but I wish I could have a few more specifics: does that mean he rests in Abraham's bosom, is he in pain?"

Hadas smiled. "It must be frustrating for you…You usually get more of the details of this life than most of us…"

Deborah nodded thoughtfully.

"I have not seen Adiel yet. How is he? Did he and Miriam have children?" Deborah's heart ached.

Hadas's eyes brimmed. "They have three." There was a heavy silence between them and she did not speak for a few moments. "He lives in the forest with his children. Of course, he blames us for leaving Miriam. He rarely comes in…only if one of the children are ill, then he seeks out Ima."

Deborah nodded, the tears she swallowed knotted in her chest as she acknowledged the pain this man must carry – pain she understood - and the guilt the village felt, like poison running through its veins. They sat quietly as though the horror of all that happened lingered, demanding remembrance, restitution and justice. Deborah's spirit assented to its soundless scream.

Finally, she broke the silence. "And Aaliya, Reuben and Hannah?"

She could not bring herself to utter the words: *do they still live?*

Hadas smiled. "Aaliya still lives; she shares her home with Hillel. Her daughter, Hannah, is married to Gershon and Raisa's son, Edom." She laughed. "You have a lot of catching up to do, my friend."

Deborah laughed. "I'm looking forward to it, but first, tell me about your life: I know only that you have two children, and can only imagine how Miriam's death must have affected you?"

Hadas grimaced. "Not nearly as traumatic, nor as eventful as your experience. I have had Dan and the children, and my immediate family have been thankfully untouched. But, it has been painful to see those you love taken from you, and Adiel of course, worries me and Ima. Enoch and the others who followed Baal left for the city after Sisera came. In many ways life was easier…but their loss is felt by us all. Can you pass me the water please?" she asked, motioning to the skin on the table.

Handing her the water, another wave of nausea hit her. She sighed.

"Hadas, I've been feeling sick lately. I've tried peppermint and ginger, but they have honestly done little to help. Any suggestions?"

Hadas pursed her lips thoughtfully for a moment, and then raised an eyebrow. "When did you last see Lapidoth? When did you last visit Niddah?"

The question hit Deborah with force, and she felt herself disperse with the impact of the question. She had longed for this moment…to have Lapidoth's child…but he was not here.

She leapt up, stumbled out of the hut and vomited behind a tree, finally giving in to her malaise.

Resting her hands on her legs, she gulped in deep breaths, her eyes squeezed shut as she endeavoured to adjust to her the reality of her situation.

Yahweh, bring him back to me. He must live, please. It was a groan from her spirit. She wandered into the forest, seeking solitude and peace amongst the ancient oak trees and bird song. When the trees thinned out, she found herself in an open clearing, the ground was dotted with the round, dainty faces of red anemones. The sight was so unexpected and so perfect it made her glad. She sat quietly, the sun warm on her face and felt consolation in the glory of creation, of Yahweh's provision and care. When she was ready to return to the settlement, she first pulled up some of the herb, wrapping it in the folds of her robe. She had seen its properties aid cramps, nervous conditions and would also help Isaac's cough.

When the first shelters came into view, she saw Isaac, arms laden with firewood returning from the forest.

He grinned. "It seems a feast will be given in your honour tonight. But I warn you, people are hungry to hear what you have to say."

Deborah sighed mentally; the day had been full and she felt tired, but she needed to share her burden.

"Do you have a moment Isaac?"

He noted the pensive look on his sister's face, and thought again how thankful he was for her return. Setting the wood onto the floor, he took her hands. "Of course, what is it?"

"I just need to let you know...I don't want you to make a big thing of it, I'm still trying to adjust to it myself." She paused, forming the words in her mind. "I'm pregnant Isaac; I'm having Lapidoth's child."

"Deborah." He took her into his arms. It was just a word, but it carried with it the sentiment of shared grief, anxiety and joy.

After a moment, he drew away from her so that he could look in her eyes and added by way of clarifying the thought. "It's wonderful news! You won't be alone, you know that." She knew the pity in his eyes was meant to make her feel comforted, but instead it warred with her faith and made her want to sob.

As the sun slipped behind the trees, the village drew around the warmth of the fire. A sheep was slaughtered and a barrel of wine opened. As people surrounded her, she noted Hur sitting by himself; occasionally people would glance his way. Whilst she appreciated that her journey had been different to theirs, their prejudice upset her sense of loyalty and fairness.

Gershon invited her to come and share what had happened since they last saw her. Despite her weariness, as she looked out at the smiling faces that reflected their affection for her, she felt such gratitude to be amongst her people. And so she told them of her capture, her despair, Yahweh's subsequent redemption and how she had met Shamgar.

When she shared with them about finding Lapidoth, her father's betrothal and how Yahweh had sent men from the tribes in Northern Israel to hear of Yahweh's call to repentance and his deliverance, she felt hope stir among them. She did not linger on Lapidoth's disappearance but rather on Yahweh's promises to her on the mountain ledge. And yet, the pity and doubt that their expressions conveyed, irked her.

"Yahweh's beloved and my own people. We have seen so much pain and lost so much. Our grief makes us weary before it makes us strong. In our pain, we learn desolation, and in desolation, we must surrender our will, our hopes and our values to Him. Moses spoke of two paths: one leading to faith and life, the other to moral compromise and death. The question I ask today is simple: do we trust Yahweh? We either do, or we don't! There is no middle ground. We either obey him and live for him, or we live for ourselves. It is not simply what we do, but the motive and intent of our hearts that Yahweh weighs. Will you stand in faith with me, to trust

Yahweh's promises?" Her eyes blazed, and the air bristled with both indignation and humble reflection. Isaac, Gershon and Tamar stood first, followed by Menachem and Nissa. Hur joined the number that stood, and she watched sadly as sideways glances and muttered comments were cast toward him. Her spirit challenged them, because they were rooted in fear and pride, the true enemies of both faith and community. She felt her sense of loyalty and righteousness blaze a path before her.

"My friends, you know it is my nature to speak candidly, to bring into the light that which hides in the shadows so that it can be judged right or wrong. And so I ask, as I embrace my community, that you help me in a matter. Should Hur be allowed to stand with us?" She cast a look toward her friend, and he knew her well enough to trust her motive. He stepped back, his head lowered and arms folded across his chest.

"By whom were the Israelites helped when they first entered the promised land?"

There was a silence, as the truth pricked consciences. Finally Gershon spoke, his eyes warm, his tone affirming. "It was Rahab, the Canaanite prostitute, Deborah."

"Hmmm. That's true. And why does our history commend this woman?"

Isaac spoke next. He darted a look of gratitude to Hur as he spoke. "We commend her courage and faith, and Deborah would not be with us now were it not for Hur's courage and obedience to a God he did not know."

One of the Levites among them stood next. "Our battle is one of faith, Deborah. I think we both agree that it is Hur's faith that must be questioned."

Deborah was surprised when Tebah walked out of the covering of the trees. He still wore the shadowy cloak of his anger, his arms folded under his robe, but as he spoke, Deborah saw that beneath his bitterness he bore a flame of righteous anger. He nodded toward Hur. "Is faith not measured in action over words? I will fight with the Egyptian."

Joshua stepped forward; his tone was of malice, borne out of his own loss. "Have you shed Hebrew blood?"

There were mutters of agreement as to the appropriateness of the question and Deborah watched as Hur lifted his head. "I have," he replied simply, offering neither apology, nor explanation.

The voices rose as they spoke over each other, many insisting that this was the conclusion of his judgement.

Nobody had known that Adiel had been there, for he, too, had remained in the shadows. She recalled Hadas telling her how her brother had separated himself from the others, and prayed now that the veil of unspoken words that stifled her people might come down.

"And death that is the result of negligence, cowardice and self-preservation? Are we to judge that tonight, too?" Adiel spat, his hands clenched, as his voice shook with emotion. "Who of you stood to defy Sisera so that Miriam and the others might live?"

There it was, the river of grief and guilt they had built walls to hold back, now engulfed them, like liquid thunder in their midst, and her heart broke as she watched them crumble. Silence was thick, barbed with shards that assaulted their mindsets and exposed the wound for what it was.

"I choose to seek life and mercy, for under judgement I must perish. Hur?" The Egyptian met his eyes. "Shalom, brother." Menachem walked up to Hur and embraced him. For some it took longer, but over the next few days, many others followed.

When Deborah had time, she had taken to visiting Adiel. She wondered if he would blame her; Sisera's return to the village had, after all, been to find her and for this she carried her own guilt. But he did not. When he first saw her they sobbed together – the fact that she had not been there that day he had lost Miriam, and that she had loved her too, united them. He was lonely and broken, but too locked behind his pain to receive help. Deborah understood that. She said nothing of her triumph in Yahweh, only shared in her own pain and loss and listened as he began to talk about his anger and resentment. It was not until six months later that he asked her how she had come through her darkness. She told him how she had come to the point of wanting only to die and end the pain, but in her desperation and surrender she had thrown herself into Yahweh and He had saved her. He nodded, and as she left, she heard his choked sobs follow her down the path. She knew his journey with Yahweh was personal and that she could only pray for him at this moment.

Hur had begun to make patrols of the road nearest to the forest, and it was here that he discovered two Hebrew men searching for Deborah. After questioning them, he told them to wait by the Terebinth tree of weeping, fearing they could be Sisera's spies. He relayed to Deborah what they had said and she agreed to meet them. Isaac and Tebah went with Hur, carrying their bows and plough shears.

"Shalom," she said nodding at them.

They bowed before her. "Shalom. We have come from Bethel. We have heard you are judging Israel."

"Who told you this?"

"An Elder from Shechem."

She nodded, wondering who the Elder was, and what had come to pass in the city since she left. "Please, speak."

"A man in our town was married. He owned some considerable estate. He had two younger brothers. When he died without having produced an heir, the older of the two brothers demanded rights to marry the woman. But the younger loves her and she him. Legally, the older brother has rights to her, though he has no love for her."

"Tell me, when a woman has never married and her family wish to betroth her to a man, is her opinion asked?"

"Yes."

"Why, do you think?"

"Because of Yahweh's love and mercy for all mankind," the man replied.

Deborah nodded. "And was the law made to imprison men, or to guide them and lead them?"

"To guide and lead?"

"Why then was the law made, that the brother of the deceased should marry the widow?"

"To protect her and provide her with children, that she may be honoured."

"That is Yahweh's grace; though the covenant between the man and his wife can no longer be fulfilled, the covenant of Yahweh with his people continues. Allow the woman to choose."

Deborah's baby grew within her, as did her concerns for Lapidoth. His absence was a constant ache within her, and the memories of her last moments with him a sadness that would not abate. In the midnight hour she would awake, imagining him in Sisera's hands, and her faith would battle with her anxiety.

More people had begun to arrive at the terebinth tree. It had informally become the place she judged from, and she would often remain there in the daylight hours, talking to Yahweh when nobody was with her. Tebah, Isaac and Hur patrolled the roads, watching out for Canaanite raiding parties and also directing those who came searching.

Her decision to set up her seat of counsel under the tree was both sentimental and practical: for whilst close enough to the settlement to be accessible, it was far enough away to keep its position and existence safe. It was near to the cross roads, set between the cities of Ramah and Bethel and central to the twelve tribes and Shiloh, yet set back so that it was not immediately visible to Canaanite soldiers. Her natural inclinations would have placed her nearer to Zebulun and Naphtali where Sisera's hold was the greatest and the oppression the worst; where she could better help her people. Yet Yahweh had spoken clearly: her strength was as a mother, her wisdom as a judge and her power as a prophetess. The tree spoke of her history, her affiliation and her heart, for all came to her here. There was no ostentatious building or seat that must be approached; she was one of the people, their advocate and friend. Whilst some questioned her lack of propriety, others commended her for her humility.

It was Sabbath, summer was upon them, hot and unyielding, and even the shade of the trees offered little respite. Deborah felt the baby kick inside her and smiled, placing her hand on her growing stomach.

"Is he kicking?" Gabriella asked. She was sitting cross-legged with her and Isaac's son, Amos, telling him the story of Noah as she drew pictures in the dirt. She had recently announced that she was pregnant with their second child.

"Hmmm," Deborah nodded, smiling lazily as she nibbled on yesterday's bread.

"So!" Gabriella laughed, "Does being a prophetess mean you know what sex the child will be?"

Deborah chuckled. "No! I'm rather inclined to believe Yahweh likes to surprise us with such things."

Hagar and Tamar came and joined them.

"Some of the men have been asking Gershon about building huts of wattle and daub, something more permanent," Hagar stated.

Deborah sighed, sitting up. "I don't think we should. We need to be ready to leave in an instant. Just because Sisera hasn't found us yet, we can't grow complacent. Moreover, if we set up home here, I'm inclined to question whether we will grow comfortable. We are meant to be dissatisfied with our existence at the moment; it's what will drive us to change it."

Hagar nodded. "You're right," she sighed. "Will you speak to Gershon and the others?"

Deborah nodded, yawning. "Remind me if I forget," she grinned.

It was a few weeks later that Deborah arrived back at the settlement to discover that an argument had broken out between Tebah and Adiel. The summer air was dense, moist and still, the grass bleached to shades of gold. Most of the village had taken cover under the leafy canopy of the trees where they languished lazily, sipping water, chatting and cowering from the midday sun. But where repressed temperament and grief had been seething under the surface, it now came to the boil. Both men carried their grief and guilt for not having been able to save the ones they loved, like iron mantles that might have protected them, but in reality it burned red hot, crushing them under its weight.

Tebah's hopes were for revenge, and were displayed in anger with the world at large; but he found relief through hard work and protecting the village. In this way, people mostly accepted him. Adiel had withdrawn behind a wall of bitter apathy and would have nothing to do with the village, neither to help them, nor to receive help, other than his immediate family. Tebah found Adiel's response to grief weak, and lacking responsibility. Adiel thought Tebah was aggressive and egotistic, lacking moral depth: had he been so intent on protecting the village, he would have remembered his wife! Deborah sighed when she saw the two. Her robe clung to her body, and though the baby was still two moons from arriving, she felt weary. She cared deeply for both men and, whilst unsurprised that they had finally come to blows, she was saddened and frustrated. Aaliya, tiny and frail herself, was unsuccessfully trying to part the two men. Deborah stepped in, planting one hand on each of the men's chest. She could feel their anger seething like a pulsating beast crouched beneath each palm.

"Will you tear each other apart? Why do you judge each other because you sin differently? There is one judge. Will you stand before Him and have your actions and hearts laid bare? Are you blameless; shall I cast my judgement, for I have been anointed to do so? Or will you let go of your anger, your judgements and bitterness, and embrace the victory that Yahweh would give you. You cannot move forward if you are anchored in the past. Choose!" Her fists were clenched now, like mallets over their hearts and her eyes blazed with ethereal intensity as she bore into their souls. The furious strength of both men was triumphed in that moment. For what they encountered was not a woman, but a sovereign, holy and righteous God and the reflection of their own souls, dark and tarnished through pain and resentment. God pierced the membrane of their self-righteous disdain for each other. Tebah was the first to lower his eyes and then step back, Adiel after him.

From that time on Adiel rejoined the rest of the settlement, and he and Tebah finally made their peace.

34

Awake, Awake Deborah.
Judges 5:12

1237 BC - Deborah

When her time came to give birth, Deborah called Tamar and Hadas to her. She sat on the birthing stool, listening to Hadas' words of comfort and encouragement while she sipped a chamomile infusion to relax her. As the first contractions came upon her, her friend held her hand and wiped her forehead, while Tamar applied warm compresses and used olive oil to aid a smooth delivery.

"This is our moment of glory. Our greatest feat, as Yahweh birthed creation, so we bring forth life. There is no higher honour."

Deborah nodded, closing her eyes as she focused on what she must do. She imagined the child within her, pushing it's way through the birthing canal, and in the same way, she thought of the triumph of Yahweh's people as they claimed their inheritance. Her teeth clenched, the sweat rolling from her brow as she chose to focus, not on the pain, but on the victory that would come.

When she at last pushed her child into the world, she felt a sense of weary elation.

"It's a boy!" Tamar smiled, handing the pink bundle to Deborah.

She tenderly stroked the tiny, downy curls that clung in wet spirals to his head, and as he opened his brown eyes and took in his first glance of the world around him, she choked back a sob as a rush of emotion overcame her. Hadas silently held her, clasping her friend for she understood the sorrow she felt.

"He should be here. He should be here," she repeated, clutching their son to her with a desperate, possessive embrace.

Over the next few days, Deborah struggled with the well of emotion that her little boy had unleashed within her. Emotion and thought married into a storm that tore through her, faster than words could be spoken, while cords of deepest tenderness wove around her heart, pushing open every cavity and resolve, because nothing could contain the fierceness of her love and need to protect this tiny life.

What type of world have I brought you into? What if you are taken from me, like Lapidoth was? What if you are killed, as my father was? I could not bear to lose you — I would die.

And the climax to her emotional tumult was silenced by the revelation: *Is this how You feel, Yahweh, about Your children?* With that knowledge, she wept, for His children, for their redemption and their peace. And then, strengthened once again, she stood.

"Let him be named Othniel: the strength of God," Deborah said, placing the baby to her breast.

35

Do not withhold good from those to whom it is due,
when it is in your power to do it.
Proverbs 3:27

1237 BC – Jael

Jael watched the two Canaanite guards. They were overseeing the building of the walls, which was carried out by the slaves. One of the slaves had dropped his tool. As he bent down to pick it up, one of guards stepped forward, cursing him as he brought his whip down on the man's back. The man cried out, dropping the tool he had been holding, and jerked as the whip cracked again. This time, the guards laughed, telling him to pick it up and then bringing the whip on his hand as he reached out for it.

Another slave turned, his own back covered in lash marks. Dirty sweat ran from his face as he used the back of his hand to wipe the hair from his eyes. Jael watched his face twist with anger as he watched the guard and then impulsively ran, blocking the blow before it met its mark.

The whip left a red welt on the underside of his arm, and as he picked up the tool, the whip again came down on his back, reopening the fresh wounds. He handed the tool to the other slave and looked darkly at the guard.

The guard sneered, advancing towards the man as he brought the whip down across his face. The man stood his ground, his eyes hard as he ignored the blood that pumped from his split lip.

"You insolent, Hebrew pig, you dare to challenge me, we will see." He lifted the whip again.

"Stop!" Jael marched over to them, noting their indignation and careful to know how far she could assert the little authority she had as a woman.

"Take care not to damage my husband's property." She kept her voice level, then added, her eyes shifting to the slave, "Heber requires help unloading one of the caravans."

The guard's lips curved as he took in the fiery woman that stood before him, his thoughts momentarily distracted by her feminine curves.

"You want slaves?" he asked pleasantly.

"I'll get them myself, thank you." She ignored his leering and, holding her head high, motioned to the two slaves.

"Come with me, both of you," she directed.

The man with the split lip wiped it now, as he kept pace with her. He had a sense of resolute strength to him, as one who has been forged in fire – a sense of destiny that was indefinable and raw.

"What is your name?" she asked.

He paused, as though deliberating whether to tell her. "Barak," he answered, looking back at the guard and slave.

He ran his fingers through his curly dark hair, a deep frown on his otherwise handsome features.

"What is it you want us to do?"

"A caravan has come with acacia wood, it needs unloading."

The man nodded. He stood, and Jael winced at the welts from lashes on his back, yet he held himself tall.

"Would you like me to ask the others?"

Jael nodded, acknowledging the authority of the man and the other men's respect for him.

"I, too, am Hebrew," she whispered. "I am a Kenite from Arad."

"Like your husband?" Barak's eyes reflected his cold derision.

"I follow Yahweh. My husband does not," she answered defensively, annoyed by the man's attitude.

"And yet you keep Hebrew slaves," the man provoked, with cool disdain. "If you truly follow Yahweh, then ask your true master what you should do with the leader of His army." His eyes bore into hers, searing into her conscience, and then he strode away to help unload the carts.

His words hung in the air and seemed to grow until they filled her mind, disturbing her peace. She strode outside, her eyes scanning the camels and men until she found who she was looking for: Zimran. Her heart quickened and she resisted the urge to run to him. She had never felt so lonely since Meira was taken nearly two years ago. Her anxiety for her daughter made her feel sick and haunted her dreams. His eyes found and held hers, and she felt strengthened by his presence in the camp. He nodded to one of the men and pulled himself away from her gaze as he lifted acacia wood from one of the carts.

Jael returned to the tent and sat down with Urriah and Adva. Urriah had begun to speak the week after Meira was taken. He was now able to manage small, two word sentences, but it brought joy to Jael's heart.

"Ima sad," he said, taking Jael's face in his hands with an expression of such deep profundity and empathy that it brought tears to Jael's eyes. She embraced him, thanking Yahweh for his affectionate, uncomplicated character.

"Is he here?" Adva asked, looking up from her sewing.

Jael nodded, smiling at her friend, to whom she had confided regarding Zimran. After Hazor, she would never question her loyalty again.

Adva laughed. "The vacant expression on your face gave you away."

"Yes...he is..." she sighed. "We should set up tables for this evening, before the sun is high and we can rest."

As they worked together setting up tables and putting out pitchers for wine, Jael and Adva talked, their conversations easy, half-finished and forming their own path.

"And what about you my dear Adva, have you ever known love?" Jael asked, half whimsically.

"I love you and your children...and I am a slave," Jael replied with finality.

"That's a curious response. Why is it I have never asked you this before?"

Adva smiled. "I am a slave and you have had your own burden of slavery to bear, my friend."

Jael felt suddenly ashamed; Barak's words to her had provoked her thoughts. "And if you weren't a slave?"

She was silent for a moment as though staring at an invisible wall of impossibility. Finally, she replied, "Then Jez and I would have married years ago," she smiled sadly.

Jael felt Adva's words hit the core of her empathy; they had both been separated by slavery in different ways. "Oh, Adva, I'm so sorry..." She chided herself for never having asked before. *How had she never noticed? Was she so selfish not to have noticed the love that two of her slaves shared for each other?*

She lay down, while the sun was at its apex, knowing that food and wine would need to be prepared for the guards and caravan drivers who had arrived that morning. She drifted into a half-hearted slumber with Barak's words and Adva's confession echoing in the inner sanctum of her mind.

Emerging a short time later, Jael still felt tired and restless. She walked the short distance under the leafy canopy of the trees to the well where she found Zimran. She realised he must have been waiting for her and smiled inwardly, her heart skipping a beat.

He returned her smile wordlessly and, taking the bucket from her hands, lowered the bucket into the water.

"How are you, Zimran?" His name slipped from her lips like the sweetest honey.

"You mean other than desperate with unrequited love?" he grinned, his eyes shining playfully.

She laughed. "You are wrong," she admonished.

"I am?" He tilted his head to one side.

"Yes." She laughed and then sadly replied, "For your love is returned, just not gratified."

His gaze was hungry and desperate, and she held it until the pain and longing was too much and it reminded her of the empty cavern of her soul.

"Meira was taken by Jabin." She said it plainly.

His eyes reached out and embraced her. "I heard. I'm so sorry..." He paused as though unsure of whether to continue, for he acknowledged that nothing he could say would ease her pain. "She has your strength, she will survive."

Jael snorted irately. "That's what Heber said. You know nothing of what it is to have a child!"

"Perhaps not, but I do know what it is to have someone you care about in the hands of a brute...to worry about them every day of your life and to be helpless to save them."

Her eyes brimmed with tears and she reached out and clasped his hand.

And then she pulled away, forcing the gravity between them to abate.

36

*The villagers in Israel would not fight; they held back until I,
Deborah, arose, until I arose, a mother in Israel.*
Judges 5:7

1236 BC - Deborah

Dark fingers punctured the cool, blue sky, shrouding Mount Ephraim
and stroking its lesser peaks. *It will rain later,* Deborah acknowledged,
drawing the blanket over her shoulders as she stoked the fire.

She had been here two years and three moons now, and her thirty forth
birthday would arrive with the grape harvest. Othniel was eighteen months
old, and his black ringlets, deep, brown eyes and easy going nature were a
constant reminder to her of Lapidoth. Watching him would create
bittersweet memories of her husband that would dance across her mind,
leaving their heavy footprints imprinted in her heart. Aaliya had told her
she needed to move on and realise he would not return, and that she was
still young enough to remarry. But there was no space in her heart for
another and she could not, would not, entertain the thought that Lapidoth
did not live.

Her trips to 'The tree of Deborah' had become more frequent. Isaac,
Tebah and Hur had set up a fire pit, with a stone shelf and a rudimentary
shelter that provided some protection from the elements. It was set back
from the road so that it was not immediately obvious; yet close enough to
see a new arrival.

She often took Othniel with her; he would play with Hur while she met
those who came. She loved to tell him stories of Yahweh and watch his
chubby little face, wide-eyed as it wrinkled into laughter. He toddled
about, running with a sense of urgency that made Deborah laugh.

Of those who came to her, some came to settle private disputes over land and property. Many enquired over issues related to moral sin and the Law, whilst others came for wisdom regarding their personal walk. A few came skeptically, to determine if Yahweh would really choose a woman to lead His people. Upon discovering that He would indeed, they then wished to know when she would deliver Israel.

Regardless of who came, and what their motive was, she revealed the secrets of men's hearts and led them to the Father - to the Author of light. In this light they saw themselves as they truly were. She called all to holiness and zeal.

Gershon and Dan, protective of her time, had argued that she should only speak regarding traditional judgements related to the Law, but Deborah responded: "I have been called as a mother, to remind our nation who she is and how to live, that she might be healed. Only then can she know what and who she fights for."

In this way, Israel began to unite under the hope of one woman and her relationship with Yahweh. They dared to hope for a future that had long retreated to the recesses of their hearts, shrouded in cobwebs and dust where it was protected and hidden.

Sisera's campaign, which had previously been at its worst in the northern tribes of Israel, with smaller raids being carried out in central Israel, was now threatening the villages and towns of Ephraim.

Shechem had been attacked again, and Sisera had positioned his troops around the city. Though its walls had held, without access to the fields, it was questionable how long they could survive.

Whilst Sisera's ambition had grown, so had his fear. He knew that Shamgar's success in Philistia would fuel the other tribes of Israel. He had spoken to Balak, who seemed no happier with his brother's success than Sisera was. Taking Philistia back from the Hebrews was a political move that would crush the Hebrews and unite Canaan. He knew that the Philistines would rather have Canaan rule, than Israel - who pulled down the high places and forbade the worship of Baal. He would take Ephraim and use Gezer as his stronghold to take the rest of Philistia.

Many who had lost their homes and loved ones came looking for hope and protection, and were embraced into the forest community where they were cared for. Together, they waited prayerfully for Yahweh to vindicate and liberate their nation.

Hur, too, had chosen to stay. Deborah laughed as she recalled his decision to become a Hebrew. Crouched, stoking the fire, they were sitting in comfortable silence when he had turned to her.

"It could be I will stay here with you…When the time comes I will fight with you…"

She raised an eyebrow. "Are you saying you would like to become a Hebrew? You know what that entails?"

He winced, "I do."

Deborah smiled warmly, squeezing his arm. He was like another brother to her, and she was pleased that he had chosen to remain with them. "We have one among us who can perform the task."

The winter trees were bare, making it easy to see the arrival of the two men who approached. She ground the wheat, pounding it with the smooth rock until it was fine enough to mix with water. Then she placed an iron pot over the fire to warm the water and stepped into the crisp morning air.

"Shalom," she smiled.

"Are you Deborah?" the older man asked, eyeing her uncertainly.

"I am." She sat on the bench under the deerskin covering of her shelter and stared steadily at the two men, silently seeking Yahweh's wisdom.

Finally, handing them bowls of water to wash their hands, she offered them bread, and goats' cheese and water to drink.

"And you are Eglon and Seth from the tribe of Manasseh." Her eyes stared through them as though her focus was elsewhere.

They exchanged uneasy gazes; they had not yet introduced themselves. "We had heard that Yahweh speaks to you, and that you have said Yahweh will restore Israel?"

"I am who Yahweh says I am," she smiled casually, her head tilted. "Who does Yahweh say you are?"

The men looked at each other, disconcerted.

"As you said, I am Eglon and this is my brother-in-law Seth."

She smiled warmly, tilting her head. "That has been made clear… But, who does Yahweh, your creator, say you are?"

Seth, the younger of the two, coughed nervously.

"I am married, I have six children and I help decide judicial matters in our settlement with Eglon."

"You have told me your functions and your family status. Who does Yahweh say you are?"

The man sighed with confusion and defeat. "I have no idea."

"No, but Yahweh does…You have overcome. When those around you have fallen, and though you grow weary of the fight, Yahweh sees your faithfulness and love for Him, to your family and your village. Your youngest child has been unwell and Yahweh will heal her now, as we speak. And you will fight with Israel's men, you will lead those around you to hope, and He will restore to you all that you have lost."

Seth fell to one knee, tears welling in his eyes. "It is true that you are a prophetess. Yahweh be praised, I know, now, that Israel will be restored."

Eglon stepped forward now. "And I?"

Deborah fixed her gaze on him; her eyes were both warm and steely as she spoke.

"You, too, have stood through the storms that have afflicted our nation, and Yahweh sees how you have taken those into your home who have been orphaned and widowed. But you have grown weary and Yahweh would strengthen you and warn you: do not allow your compassion to water down His holiness. The man regarding whom you have come to seek me, murdered his brother's wife and must be stoned." The shock on the men's faces was evident.

Deborah sighed sadly, "If our nation is to see deliverance, we must turn with our whole hearts to Yahweh and to his Law; we must establish righteousness and justice as our foundation. We must make holiness our fortress: get rid of the high places and consecrate our hearts to Him."

37

Most blessed of women is Jael,
The wife of Heber the Kenite;
Most blessed is she of women in the tent.
Judges 5:24

1935 BC - Jael

"There's a man, one of the slaves; he was with me yesterday when you unloaded the wood." Jael looked nervously over her shoulder.

"Barak?" Zimran asked, watching Jael adeptly shearing a protesting goat.

"He is Hebrew. Have you spoken to him?" She released the animal, wiping her brow with the back of her hand.

Zimran nodded, and was thoughtful for a moment. "He has the character of one who has suffered and allowed it to make him stronger, yet he carries the pain with him so that he wields his strength with compassion and wisdom," Zimran concluded.

"He told me he has been called to lead Israel's armies," Jael confided.

"Then he's either a fool or Israel's deliverer."

"That's what I called Shamgar."

"A deliverer?"

"A fool."

"Oh…Does he seem a fool to you?" Zimran laughed. "Not that you have proven to be a very good judge of character so far."

She elbowed him, laughing too. "Well, you're evidence of that! But no, no he doesn't. Can you talk to him? If he is genuine and Yahweh is with him, we must help him."

Zimran frowned. "Maybe it's nothing, but when I stopped in Bethel there was talk of a woman, Deborah. She is in Ephraim, but I have heard rumour that she is drawing people to her. She is a prophetess."

Jael felt a smile part her lips and travel through her soul. Day was dawning in Israel, and she was ready to fight.

She lay in bed that night, feeling the warmth of Zimran's words nourish the emptiness of her heart and prayed.

Yahweh, show me my part in what You are doing. How I can help the slaves? Help me know the truth behind Barak's words and show me what I can do. Protect my daughter and...Heber and Zimran I lay in Your hands...I trust You Yahweh.

And a thought returned to her. It carried a pain that she recognized, and a love that stung her eyes with tears even as it brought comfort: *I know your pain, My children too have been taken by Jabin, oppressed by the hand of Sisera. I hear their cries and the time comes when I will fight on their behalf.* The promise wove through the dark passages of her mind, bringing hope and light, until she felt embraced by the warmth and began to drift into a peaceful sleep.

"Jael!"

Hearing the shout, she wrapped a blanket around herself, her heart pounding as she climbed past the sleeping forms of her children. The moon was full, a bright orb that dominated the sky, illuminating the encampment.

Some of the men had fallen asleep around the fire, which had now died down to glowing embers, while others had gone to their tents. She instinctively walked around the back of the tent, wandering into the dark covering of the forest.

Zimran's dark form was concealed in the shadows of the trees. He touched her arm, bidding her not to be alarmed, and then drew her into the darkness of the forest. He spoke in a hushed tone. "I have spoken with Barak and the other slaves, as you asked. The man's stories line up with those I have heard from others."

"And do you think he is who he says he is?" Jael quizzed.

Zimran sighed. "Even if he is misguided about what he believes, he has the confidence of the men, the strength of character and conviction to shake Canaan. He knows of the woman, Deborah, and will join her. If you decide to go through with this, Jez and I have come up with a plan to get him and the other men out without raising suspicion."

"Go on." Jael realised she was stepping into dangerous territory.

A fire will begin at sunrise. The guards' wine was drugged and they should sleep through the escape. It will need to look as though the slaves made a run for it, so that your help is not implied in this. But there will be a cart waiting for them in the forest. We will take Barak and the others as far as Kedesh, where he has men who will stand with him. He seems to think it will be easy to raise an army in Naphtali, where the people know him."

"And their chains?"

"We have already undone their chains and put the keys back with the sleeping guard. The chains will not be found and the guards will never be sure what happened."

"You and Jez organised this?" Her heart constricted as she recalled her conversation with Adva earlier and remembered what Heber had done to her friend in Hazor.

"Yes," he frowned.

She sighed. "Can you arrange for two more to go with them? Tell Barak to take care of them."

"Who are you thinking of?" he asked.

"Jez and Adva. They are in love and Heber will never allow them to be together. He beat Adva so badly last time, I feared for her life."

He exhaled and looked to the ground; when he looked up his voice was hoarse with emotion. "And who will rescue you, Jael?"

"Yahweh will. When the time is right, He will liberate me. For now I know I need to be here." She looked away from the intensity of his eyes.

He hesitated, reaching out to touch her face and his eyes met hers. She saw the carefully guarded pain he buried…and his love for her, and giving in to impulse, she kissed him once on the lips.

Once, for all the times Heber has beat me and been unfaithful, she said to herself and pulled away.

He took her face in his trembling hands, his eyes drinking her in.

"It will only ever be you," he whispered.

"It will only ever be you," she agreed.

He drew her into his arms, kissing her hair, and in that moment, she felt safe as she had not felt since that last fateful day in Midian.

"Yahweh goes with you, Zimran. Stay safe." And then she returned to the tent, shutting out the painful pull of her heart that she had grown accustomed to whenever she walked away from him.

Entering her tent, she gently shook Adva and bid her come into her quarters.

"You are leaving. I have secured a way for you and Jez to be free."

Adva looked at her bleary eyed and blinked. "What?!"

"Barak is a leader among the Hebrews. He will take you with him."

"What?!" she repeated. "Are you out of your mind? Heber will kill you. No, I won't go!"

"Dearest Adva, dearest friend, you are still thinking of me. Zimran has organised it so that Heber won't know I had any part to play."

Adva felt unexpected hope war with her loyalty. She shook her head, as though to dislodge the hope that was begging to take root. "I can't do it my friend…"

"You have been a slave so long the idea of freedom terrifies you, I understand that. But I am ordering you to choose freedom. Now go and pack your things. Now!" She grabbed Adva's arm, almost forcefully, before adding, "Barak will find Deborah. When you meet her, tell her I am her servant, the servant of Yahweh and that I fight with Israel."

Adva threw her arms around her friend, tears of sadness and joy streaking her face. "I will…Thank you, my friend."

Jael then slept fitfully. Her mind was waiting, ready, so that when the first voices filled the air, adrenalin pounded through her veins and her heart raced with panic. It was time. *Yahweh, let them escape, please let them escape.* She felt sick with anxiety, if they failed to escape, the consequences would be dire. She had risked everything: Zimran's life, Barak's, Adva and Jez's, not to mention her own. And if they succeeded, if they escaped, Heber would be furious. Furious and powerless to do anything about it – the thought brought her a certain satisfaction.

She looked out as wild flames thrashed the slaves' tent, burning the oily goatskin covering as though it were made of papyrus. Adva was gone, as were the slaves.

One of the guards was now alerted, but his reactions were so slow. By the time he had strung his bow and arrow, the forms of Barak and the men had vanished. He collapsed next to the fire and began cursing his comrades, who groaned sleepily.

By the time Heber emerged from his tent, bleary-eyed and hungover, the air was still, bar the crackling of the fire. Jael wrestled not to look jubilant and defiant as her husband wielded his own fiery fury. "What is this?" he eyed her suspiciously, his fingers digging painfully into her arm.

She acted shocked as she stared wide-eyed, innocently back at him. "I… I don't know. I was sleeping…there was a fire and now they are gone. Even Adva has deserted me." She burst into tears; they were genuine tears for her loss and fear. She was truly alone now. She would ordinarily never let him see her weakness but she knew it would disarm him. She felt smug in her victory over him, even as she feared his wrath.

He looked at her with suspicious disdain, but released his grip and turned on the guards.

38

And what more shall I say? For time will fail me if I tell of Gideon, Barak, Samson, Jephthah of David and Samuel and the prophets, who by faith conquered kingdoms, performed acts of righteousness, obtained promises, shut the mouths of lions, quenched the power of fire, escaped from the edge of the sword, from weakness were made strong, became mighty in war, put foreign armies to flight.

Hebrews 11:32

1235 BC – Deborah and Barak

Seeing Gabriella, Deborah stood and embraced her.

"Sister, your expression tells me that you come with good news."

"The family that arrived yesterday from Naphtali; they have spoken of a man named Barak. He recently escaped from slavery and men are gathering around him to fight for Israel. He has asked where you might be found."

Deborah's eyes flashed with excitement as Yahweh's spirit met with hers. "Ask Malachi and Tebah to come to me."

Gabriella nodded, striding away and Deborah turned to the men.

"You are welcome to stay the night and eat with us. When you return to your village, tell those you meet on the byways that Yahweh's deliverance draws near. When they hear the ram's horn, let them come."

Malachi and Tebah had arrived, and she drew them aside. "I need you to take men to Kedesh and bring Barak to me – tell him he will lead Israel's armies into victory, and that the time for Israel's deliverance draws near."

Deborah was left alone; she ran her fingers over the necklace that Lapidoth had given her at their betrothal, clasping the hard stone into her palm until its chiseled surface indented her flesh.

His words came back to her, *'Formed in the darkness, under the pressure of force and heat'*. She sighed resting her head in her hands. When she took her eyes off of Yahweh for even a moment she felt the twist in her heart, and the hole that Lapidoth had left, grow until it was a chasm that threatened to consume her.

She pulled herself away from the chasm of her own thoughts and fears and, taking the outstretched arms of Yahweh, forced her thoughts into the quiet waters of her faith.

The following day, Deborah's monthly cycle took her to the Niddah retreat, where she met Gabriella and several of the other women. She wondered again at the way women in community came to synchronise; at the mysterious rhythm of life, where lives and hearts were knitted. She wondered if Yahweh understood what happened in this place and had designed it to be so. Moses had said: the life of the flesh is in the blood. It was a curious, unrelated thought, since they were, of course, physically unclean, and yet another life emerged, the heart of the village that pumped with its love, its prayers, its proposals. Its pain was discussed along with those who needed help, and how best to meet it.

Gabriella hugged her, handing her a cup of warm milk and Bara, the wife of a Levite, handed her bread. Food was scarce in the forest and they no longer enjoyed the treats they had once remembered in the seclusion when they had been able to farm the land. They sat silently for a while.

Bara smiled. "I think apathy is what I have struggled with the most. When I was younger I wanted to change the world, now I want only to be safe and find happiness."

Deborah stoked the fire, staring into its embers.

"I, too, feel battle-weary. I know Yahweh's presence and yet I want to grow old in it. I can't bear to see any more that I love being taken from me." She paused. "And yet happiness is a complicated friend, found in the least expected places. I have known it in chaos and lack, where I have not seen it in comfort. It is found in following one's destiny, despite the difficulty of circumstances. In Canaan, people had so much and yet they were not happy; and here, with hunger and the knowledge that we could be invaded at any moment but surrounded by love, acceptance, integrity and faith, I am at peace." She closed her eyes, a weary sigh shuddering its way from the depths of her soul. "That said, I do long for it to be over, for the battle to pass."

Gabriella drew next to her and put her arm around her sister-in-law's shoulders. "I feel a little inadequate to ask, but could I, we, pray for you?"

Deborah smiled. "You of all people should know how frail and human I really am. I would truly welcome your prayers."

Gabriella smiled. "I, of all people, have seen your incredible ability to turn weakness to strength by surrendering to Yahweh. It is a lesson I try to emulate." She clasped Deborah's hands in her own.

"Yahweh, You see the hopelessness that grips our nation, our villages destroyed and our unity broken. Each man lives for himself and we are weakened by it. My youngest memories of Deborah are teaching us Your Laws, tending to us when we were upset, or sick and fighting for us when we were bullied. She is the mother to this nation. It is who she is. Strengthen her, I pray, to carry the mantle you have placed upon her: to unite us, to awaken us and to lead us into battle, that You might deliver us through Your power. Amen."

Bara squeezed Deborah's arm. "You are judge and prophetess but as a mother, you have awakened and united this nation that Yahweh might deliver it."

Deborah's eyes held Gabriella's fondly as she too recalled their shared childhood. "I saw a young girl, many years ago, timid but with the fire of indignation at her strong brother's taunts." She laughed. "Now, I see a woman of God that burns with the righteousness and strength of Yahweh. You have blessed me, sisters, and revived my heart, and I thank you for it." She paused in thoughtful reflection, before adding: "On my journey throughout Israel, the thing that has surprised me the most is the power of women's prayers, and the strength of their compassion for those around them that creates both a wall of security and a foundation of integrity. It makes me think of the pillars around the tent of meeting: their bronze settings, made of copper and iron embrace both heaven and earth. Made of acacia wood, that is gnarled and grows in the desert, we as women give out selflessly, though we often have little control over our circumstances. Their silver tops represent our suffering yielded to heaven, and the walls they support that protect those within, yet yearn for the presence of our Maker."

On the third day of her separation, they were joined by Ornat, a lady in her forties, with four children. Her husband had been killed two years ago, and coming to the retreat marked a rest from parenting. She looked weary.

"Come and sit down, let us tend to you," Gabriella said. Handing her warm milk and picking up the spice-infused olive oil, she began to massage Ornat's chapped hands. Deborah began to sing a song of worship, and before long they all joined in. Afterward, she picked up a brush and began to gently brush Ornat's hair.

There was a gentle knock on the door, and a girl they had not seen before, entered. She was in her early twenties. She had long dark hair and almond shaped eyes that were downcast. Her lips parted in a nervous smile.

"Hello, my name is Rina."

Deborah stood introducing herself and the others. "Welcome! You must have arrived in the last few days. You will find all that you need in the room behind. Then come and join us for bread and wine."

"Thank you. I have come with Barak. He found the remains of our village along the way and a few of us hiding in the mountains. But we had no food, we were starving."

"You are welcome to stay with us…You say, Barak is here?"

"Yes…he waits for you," Rina's eyes shifted to the floor as she spoke.

On the seventh day, Deborah visited the mikveh, ending her period of confinement, before going to meet Barak.

She felt a surge of excitement and curiosity at the thought of meeting Barak, for she knew Yahweh's hand was upon this man; that he was called to lead Israel's armies into battle, and that his presence among them marked Yahweh's call. This was the time they had waited for.

She met Isaac first. "Where is Barak? I must speak with him."

"He awaits you in your home." His mouth twitched with humour that seemed out of place, but then Isaac always had been light-hearted.

Deborah frowned. *What was it with men and their desire to battle that turned them into boys? And how entirely inappropriate that Barak should wait for me in my home; I do hope he isn't going to be arrogant and difficult.*

She stepped through the door, ready to confront the commander of Israel's army on his lack of etiquette. He crouched, talking to Othniel, with his back to her, silhouetted in the light of the fire. Othniel giggled and pointed to his mother.

"Ima's here," he explained. Barak turned, his hand sweeping through his dark curly hair, his dark eyes drinking her in as he stepped into the light.

They stood for a moment, Deborah taking in the lash mark that ran across his face: *his* face. He seemed to have grown since she had last seen him: physically broader, but in stature too, he carried a chiseled depth and strength that set him apart.

She stood, her previous thoughts evaporated as she allowed the truth to saturate her soul, awakening the wilderness of her heart. He was alive. Her Lapidoth, perfect and strong and beautiful, was here, and she loved him!

"You're here, Lapidoth. You're alive," she whispered, as tears of relief and unbelief rolled quietly down her face. She covered her face with her hands and wept with joy as the years of repressed longing flooded from her.

He stepped toward her, taking her in his arms and wiping the tears from her face. "I am here. And I have a son," he whispered.

She looked up, nodding through her tears. "I was weeks with child when you were taken." Then, confused, she asked, "Are you here with

Barak? They told me he was here?" Her eyes scanned the room as though he might be hiding in a corner.

He kissed her forehead, laughing quietly. "No, I am Barak." He handed her a cup of wine and drew her to sit with him before the fire. Othniel clambered onto his lap.

His familiar frown marked his features, and for a moment she shared in his anguish as she watched his memories rip through his soul. He took her face in his hands and kissed her. "I'm sorry for all I have put you through."

She smiled, feeling confused. "You didn't mean to get captured."

"No, I didn't, but I needed to find myself and find Yahweh...I wish there had been an easier way...that I had been less pig-headed."

He exhaled deeply. "When I left you at the settlement, and even before, I felt so inadequate to be your husband...I had been respected as a leader and fighter in the hills of Kedesh before we were married, and I loved you so much - I love you so much. And then everyone looked to you and I felt so unimportant; it bothered me that you didn't need me; that you had no fear. People would ask who will lead Israel's armies, and you would say that Yahweh would raise someone.

"When we arrived back at the settlement that day, it was already being attacked. We were badly outnumbered, tired and unprepared. We didn't stand a chance." He paused, and she saw the emotion gather in his expression.

"I watched them kill Joseph and Joel. When I tried to defend them, they set on me. By the time I and the other men were loaded onto the cart, I was barely conscious, Maor and Dan didn't think I would make the journey; but Yahweh kept me alive. We were sent to the mines at Gerasha. It was like Hades in those mines. Days of not seeing the light of day and guards who flay you if you don't work fast enough. Those who fell were killed and replaced." He closed his eyes to wipe out the memory.

"What were you mining?"

"Iron, for weapons, armour and chariots."

"Sisera is using Hebrew slaves to build his army?"

Lapidoth nodded grimly. He continued. "Tunnel collapses were common, nobody bothered trying to rescue those who were trapped, they were just left. I had been told to dig; I could see that the roof was weak, but I had to go in, or be killed anyway. When the tunnel did collapse, I believed that was where I would die. I had faced death every day in the tunnels and got to a place of...maybe it was resignation...Or perhaps surrender of my life completely to Yahweh's will."

Deborah nodded, remembering that night in Sisera's house when she had come to the end of herself.

"I cried out to Yahweh...I didn't want to die there...but in many ways, I did...my own dreams, my ability to bring about change, to protect those I loved, died – I let go, by forced necessity. And then, I knew that He was there with me…" Lapidoth turned to Deborah.

"I felt His presence and suddenly I understood in that moment, His heart for us…His love and His power to redeem us…but He needs to work with us, and so often we are trying to do it in our own strength. It's only in the place of surrender that we become dependent on Him.

"And then He spoke and it seemed that light flooded the darkness that I was in, whether it was spiritual or physical I do not know, only that there was a clarity and holiness which made everything visible and filled me with reverence and awe."

Deborah smiled, and tears of joy and thanks ran down her face as she thought of the anxiety she had had for Lapidoth, and now she saw how he had been held in Yahweh's hand, even as she had been held in the other.

Lapidoth leaned toward her, his voice now lowered as though the memory of the moment was hallowed. "He said to me: 'Your name is Lapidoth, now you shall be called Barak. I will go before you and give you victory.'" His own eyes glistened with tears and he swallowed, gathering himself, before he continued. "I sat in His presence until I felt strengthened. When I knew that it was time to leave, I was aware of light entering the cavern. I am certain it had not been there before: it came from an opening in the rocks which I was able to widen and escape through."

She paused, piecing together the events. "And so, after that how did you come to be with Heber in Zaanannim?"

"After the tunnel collapse and my miraculous survival, I was sent to forge the metal. There I learnt the art of smelting iron and shaping it into weapons." He grinned. "In that was Yahweh's hand and favour. I worked hard and was strong. When the work was complete, Heber requested the release of men to help build his personal estate; I was chosen, along with Maor."

Deborah thought of her night on the mountaintop in Kedesh, in which she had seen the lightning split the sky and Michael warring with demons of Baal.

"Baal, god of storm will be defeated by Yahweh's lightning." She felt Yahweh's presence upon her as she spoke and recounted her own experience on the mountaintop in Kedesh and all that had happened since.

"Deborah, like a honey bee, you are a mother, and you have pollinated the branches of our nation, with your courage, truth and grace; but your sting will be Yahweh's righteous judgement upon Baal and Jabin. Spring has come, when armies go to war and life springs forth upon the land. The honey that flows forth is His righteous judgement, spoken by you, which will restore and unite our nation. Your sting will be Yahweh's holy vengeance upon Baal and his cohorts."

She looked at him, her heart overwhelmed with love and respect for this man. Not only what he had been through, but how he had allowed Yahweh to work His will in the midst of pain. "I laid a man that I loved in the palm of Yahweh's hand…I trusted my life to His protection, and out of Yahweh's hand arises the leader of Yahweh's army, who will defeat the Canaanites." She ran her hand tenderly through his curly hair, and across his strong, tanned jaw, tracing the line of the whip mark to his lip. He took her hand and kissed it.

"Tell me, how did you escape, Barak?" she smiled as she tested his name. It seemed natural, as though it had always been there, like a set of clothes that one wears beneath an outer cloak.

"I was brought to the home of Heber, the tyrant who ran the mines. When our work was slowed, he took us to his home north of Hazor to be his slaves. Dan and Maor were brought with me and are here now. Heber's wife was a Hebrew." He smiled. "She showed both shrewdness and courage – a quality I find in few men. She opposed her husband to free us - I hope she still lives. Her servant travels with us." He looked down to Othniel, who had fallen asleep in his arms.

"And you returned to Kedesh?"

"I was taken to Kedesh and there I found that hearts have turned to Yahweh since I was gone. In Zebulun, too, where the desperation was greatest, they have turned to Him. Men gathered to me when they discovered I was free; Dan and others are preparing Israel's armies for war." He grew quiet.

"I am so sorry I left you alone that day," he whispered.

"I'm sorry I didn't listen to you," she responded. "I should have gone with you."

As tears rolled down her face, he wiped them away with his thumb, then, taking her face in his hands, he kissed her tenderly; he had never thought to hold her again.

When Deborah awoke the next day, Lapidoth lay beside her watching her. She smiled sleepily, wrapping her arms around him.

As they stepped outside, it was as though the air outside was charged with anticipation. She looked around her. In the centre of the village grew an almond tree, its blossom fluttered in the early spring breeze, dotting the ground with its white petals. Its beauty touched her, though its sign was a portent she wanted to turn from. For her heart was finally at peace, and it heralded the time for war.

Men and women put down what they were doing and turned to them.

Deborah smiled, a happy sigh escaping her lips. "My husband has returned: As Yahweh changed Abram's name to Abraham and Jacob's name to Israel, Lapidoth, man of torches, becomes Barak, Yahweh's lightning that will bring victory in battle upon Baal, god of storm and war.

He will lead Israel's armies to victory. It is not long now and Israel will see her deliverance."

She saw Maor and ran to him. "Did you find Sen and the children?"

"We did," he smiled, embracing her. "They send their love."

Deborah returned his smile. Her two worlds had collided and it warmed her heart. "Who else escaped?"

"Sen and Dan remain in Naphtali; he and others are smelting and forging plough shears into swords. What Sisera intended for evil, Yahweh uses to His advantage," he grinned, referring to the skills they had been taught in Sisera's mines.

She felt Barak's arms around her waist. "Can I introduce you to Jez and Adva? Adva is the friend of Jael; she wished to speak to you."

"Jael?"

"Yes."

Deborah felt a nudge in her spirit. She took his hand.

"Take me to her."

She noted the unfamiliar man and woman sitting on a log. They clasped each other's hands, and everything about them seemed as though they had woken up in heaven and had no idea how to behave. *They were slaves,* Deborah acknowledged, as she sat before them.

"I am Deborah, welcome to our village, it is your home. Please, I am interested to hear of your mistress who set my husband free."

Adva smiled, and Deborah read more in Adva's eyes about the character of Jael than a lengthy description could have told her.

"Jael told me to say that she is your servant and fights for Israel with you."

"Jael means wild mountain goat, doesn't it?" Deborah asked, her mind travelling back to a time when she had told Sisera of his dreams.

Adva chuckled. It was a low, warm sound that rippled with affection and affirmed the aptness of her mistress's name.

"I look forward to meeting her," Deborah smiled. "I like her already."

The man leaned forward, loyalty and love lined his expression. "Her daughter was taken as Jabin's concubine. When you take Hazor, I beg you to find her."

"You have my word." Deborah's eyes met his. "Come now, the village gathers to worship and pray. Let us pray too, for Jael and her children. And then we will find you a place to stay."

A deer that had been trapped earlier that day was roasting over the fire, and the women had been busy making bread. That evening marked the beginning of the Sabbath. As they gathered around the fire, Deborah watched the excited faith that rippled among the people as they discussed Yahweh's liberation. They lifted their voices to heaven, crying out for the deliverance of Israel. Deborah knew that Yahweh was with them and that the battle would be His.

She noticed that Adiel had joined them. He stood with his mother at the back of the crowd, next to Jael and Adva. Deborah felt a surge of emotion, and she knew Yahweh's heart was glad at the unity and the hunger of His people.

As darkness wrapped them in its starry blanket and the embers of the fire glowed, they made their way to their homes, hearts fanned to flame and spirits awakened with faith and anticipation. She noticed that Adva and Jez were being led towards his home by Adiel, while Tamar took his children back to her own home.

My world is well, Yahweh, thank you. When, Yahweh? When will You summon Your people to war?

Wait.

She closed the door of her shelter behind her and was enveloped into Barak's arms. He sighed, "I feel torn at this moment. I am restless for battle; I feel it burning within me, like a steed that pushes to drive forward. Yet my heart longs for the day I can hold you in my arms and know that we will never be parted."

She laughed. "The torch and the lightning."

He grinned. "Has Yahweh told you when we must go?"

She shook her head. "He says: wait."

The green scent of April permeated the air, filling Deborah's heart with optimism. Spring, vibrant, warm and colourful, was upon them and Deborah was aware that, in former years, they would have been busy with the barley harvest.

Barak would travel to the cities and towns of the south telling them that the time for Israel's liberation drew near, and that they should come when they heard the ram's horn blown.

Deborah sat under the mighty oak, judging Israel with the wisdom and insight that Yahweh had given her. The early morning sun speared the leafy shafts of the boughs above her, caressing her face with its warmth. Red poppies and blue lupins danced in the gentle breeze as Deborah lifted her voice to Yahweh, seeking His face for what the day would bring.

Some came with simple matters such as land disputes, and others with more complicated matters. Always, she referred to the Law and to Yahweh's spirit within her. When they left she would tell them: 'Prepare for war, for Yahweh will deliver His people soon. Return to your cities and villages and tell those you know, the time draws near.'

One morning, she noted a large group approaching with much agitation and debate. A man, bound in shackles, was pushed roughly to Deborah's feet and when he looked up, she felt compassion for him. She stood from her seat and helped him to his feet before offering him a seat, water to wash his hands, and water and bread to eat. Then she turned to those waiting and offered them the same hospitality. Their faces were set like flint, and she noted the outrage and the hardness in their hearts towards herself and the man.

Gently she spoke. "This man is a Hebrew, and will be treated with mercy and compassion until his guilt - or innocence - is established."

"This man killed my son. The law of Moses says he must die."

Deborah saw the grief in the man's eyes. "I am sorry for your loss. Be assured that justice will be administered today. But that it will not take away your pain. Only Yahweh will bring comfort to your heart. Now tell me your story."

Deborah listened as the man told how his seventeen-year old son, who had been betrothed, was killed by the axe of the man in shackles.

Deborah nodded with deep empathy for his loss. She turned to the man accused. Gently, she spoke. "And tell me *your* story. Is this accusation true?"

The man bowed his head. When he looked up, he looked her in the eyes. "It is true that my axe killed his son, though not by my intent. We were both collecting firewood. As I swung my axe, the axe head flew from its handle and hit Isaac, his son. I tried to save him." His eyes were filled with anguish as he recalled the incident. "When I returned, my hands and clothes were covered in blood and the body of his was son in my arms...I am aware that my guilt seemed apparent, but my heart is innocent of this crime."

The father and his friends erupted in a chorus of furious contention. Deborah listened to their arguments for a moment, as she sought to perceive their hearts on the matter. As she listened, it became apparent that one man was most vehement, most passionate regarding the guilt of the accused, while the grief-struck father was a ship without a rudder, guided by the strongest will. Finally, she held up her hand to speak.

"This matter is not easily decided. I wish to speak to each man individually. I will also call upon the help of a Levite priest from our village, for his discernment and knowledge of the Torah.

"I invite you all to the hospitality of our settlement while we find the truth and establish justice in this matter. Hur, Tebah, please assure that the accused is given the same welcome as our other guests." Assenting, they led the party through the forest.

Over the next few days, Aaron and Deborah spoke to each man in turn, seeking to ascertain the motive of each man's heart as they sought to determine guilt. Aaron advised her both on his perception and the detail of the Law. Upon asking to see the axe head, it was apparent that it had broken from the shaft and that it had not been done by force, but rather wear.

After two days, Deborah came to a place of understanding. The accused was a man of both wealth and land. Of the father's friends, two felt grief for him and acknowledged that justice was necessary, but were undecided on how this should be administered. It became evident that the land of the accused bordered the land of the man who had pushed for the death of the accused, and one of the father's friends had let slip that he had been hoping to purchase the land for a reduced price from the widow. When Deborah spoke to the man, she noted that he did not make eye contact with her, but instead spoke to Aaron. She perceived the hardness and selfishness of the man's heart, and that his greed superseded his fear of Yahweh.

Finally, she called the group forward. "Aaron and I have listened to each man in turn. We have both prayed and consulted the Law, and have reached a conclusion." She looked at the men and saw the accused, his face grey, but resigned. "This man's son was indeed killed by the axe head of the accused. However, it was not murder; it was not deliberate. It is as he said. Nonetheless, he is a manslayer, and since men require retribution, he must flee to a safe-city." Her eyes were on the father's friend that had sought the man's land. She watched his rage at the decision turn to calculated satisfaction. "His lands may be sold for a good price so that he may live in comfort when he settles. Of this amount he must give one fifth of his wealth to the father of the deceased as compensation for his loss, and one fifth to the betrothed.

"However, it has also become apparent that there is one among you that acted with malicious motivation and selfish ambition, who would have allowed this man to be killed for a crime he knew he had not wittingly committed, for his own personal gain." She turned to the man in question. "You would have condemned him so that you could take his land. This, Yahweh judges. The law decrees that the punishment you would have exacted on the man should be done to you, that all will know Yahweh's justice and holiness. An eye for an eye, a tooth for a tooth. Does not the Law state: you shall not bear false witness?"

Her gaze rested on her beloved community. "We cannot live under the yoke of each man doing what is right in his own eyes. Life cannot be sustained unless we look to the good of each other and for the holiness that is above all. In selfishness and isolation no army can stand, for they are the enemies of unity. Yahweh's standard of righteousness must be raised over this nation if we will live under its victory." She turned to Hur and Tebah and nodded. "Let him be stoned to death."

The formerly accused and owner of the axe requested that, after settling the sale of his land, he might be allowed to bring his family to the forest to live. Deborah willingly accepted his suggestion.

The stoning was a sombre affair; none enjoyed ending a man's life. And yet, it reminded each person to weigh not only their actions, but also the intents of their heart. It was a memorial of Yahweh's holiness and justice that assured them He could be trusted.

Deborah went into her shelter and sank onto the pallet that had been made of wild ferns and heather. She felt drained. Othniel threw his arms around her. "Ima, cuddle," he demanded, climbing onto her lap. She found comfort in his joyful simplicity and held him close to her. Noting her seriousness, he pulled a face and she laughed, kissing his curly hair.

There was a knock on the door and Deborah groaned. She felt in no mood to deal with judicial or political matters.

"It's only me." Aaliya's head poked through the door.

Deborah sighed with relief. Aaliya was the last remaining thread from her parents' generation, and a welcome guest. As she stepped into the old lady's embrace, she felt weary tears sting her eyes.

"Oh honey bee, I knew today would have been hard for you. Mercy is a two edged sword, isn't it?" she stated simply.

Deborah nodded, her throat tight, as sorrow pressed against her chest. Aaliya said nothing, but held her as she acknowledged the pain that her decision had cost her.

She pulled herself away. She had walked in her integrity before Yahweh; she would not succumb to tears, nor bear the weight of guilt or regret. And yet, did Yahweh, Himself, not mourn at the consequences of men's poor choices?

Deborah spoke as though to clarify Aaliya's statement. "It is not enough for them to know Yahweh's love. They must also understand that His holiness requires justice."

Aaliya nodded. "It is as it was in the early days of Ehud."

"Thank you, Aaliya. I feel so surrounded by the love and support of those around me, and yet, at times so alone. If I stop to think of what must be accomplished, I feel overwhelmed."

"It's who Yahweh has made you to be that draws men and women to follow you, Deborah. Your unconditional love and acceptance for them is married with your strength and unyielding expectation of their victory in Yahweh. They trust you because you are both just and merciful, even as He is. They follow you because you set a standard that you live by, and offer them hope that you have found in the midst of darkness; they know His hand is upon you."

Deborah smiled weakly, squeezing the hands that held hers. "Thank you, dear Aaliya. You have been His arms of love and encouragement to me today, as always. How grateful I am for your continued friendship."

Word spread of Deborah's judgements, and Yahweh's standard of righteousness began to filter into the bloodstream of the nation. Its purity was cleansing, strengthening and life-giving; it became a rock of stability that united them. But it flowed from the Father of righteousness and mercy, pumped by the heart of a mother whose breath uttered:

Live passionately. For your Maker calls you to make your stand.

The almond tree had budded, its proliferous green shells promising an abundant harvest. She stood to watch the cheerful warbling of a sparrow as she fed her young, marveling at Yahweh's ability to instill the mother-heart in such a tiny creature. The song was interrupted by the long, extended screech of a buzzard that grew louder and louder until its giant wings blocked out the family huddled under the mother's wings, and Deborah felt her heart lurch with concern for their survival. When their death seemed inevitable, the sparrow, driven by a motivation greater than her own need to survive, fluttered up to meet the buzzard. Confident in its pre-eminence the buzzard hovered, watching its prey and then - the least expected thing possible occurred; the sparrow darted at the buzzard, her tiny beak stabbing the larger bird in the eye. The buzzard squawked and flew away.

Deborah felt a sense of exultant triumph at the sparrow's courage and victory. But greater than that was the peace and inner destiny, for she had learnt to listen to the lessons Yahweh taught her through nature.

Is it time? she asked.

It is time. He answered.

She called Barak to her. Her voice trembled as she spoke. "Barak, The LORD, the God of Israel, commands you: 'Go, take with you ten thousand men of Naphtali and Zebulun and lead them up to Mount Tabor.' He says, 'I will lead Sisera, the commander of Jabin's army, with his chariots and his troops to the Kishon River and give him into your hands.'"

Barak grew silent. His mind journeyed back to the mines of Gerasha and his own battle that, by the grace of God, he had fought and won. But now, as with all battles, the ground he had won was being challenged: Yahweh was offering him personal glory, and yet he knew it was not his to take.

He felt his ego rise. A year ago he would have jumped at the chance to prove to himself worthy to be leader of Israel's army; to prove to Deborah that he was good enough to be her equal. And Yahweh was offering him this double-edged sword. But was it his to take? And what if he made the wrong decision and failed? Was it not together that they had found their strength? Was it not she that Yahweh had chosen to be a mother to Israel; her wisdom, compassion and prophetic judgements that had awakened the nation?

He recalled the question that he had once asked Deborah: *What is it you want?* He asked himself the same question now and realised: he had neither the will, nor the ability, to awaken faith in men. That, Deborah did well. He could inspire men, motivate them, encourage them and instill courage in them. He knew men would follow him into battle and that, by Yahweh's grace, he would lead them to victory. His blood thirsted for war, to fight and defend his nation, and that was enough. He acknowledged that men would question his decision to allow his wife to come with him, but Yahweh had placed them together, and he had long since stopped answering to men. His marriage would be forged on equality and trust, and that would be his answer to those who criticised him.

He looked up at her, his eyes warm, like deepest amber. "If you go with me, I will go; but if you don't go with me, I won't go. We lead this army together, or not at all."

She considered his reply silently, weighing her indignation at his reply: *Was it cowardice that motivated him?* Her dark eyes pierced his and he knew that she was weighing him. He remained passive; he would not defend himself. She saw his personal journey written out like a scroll, and she understood the integrity of her husband: he no longer cared for his own reputation, but Yahweh's glory. She smiled inwardly, her heart expanding with pride and love for him. She knew the challenge Yahweh had set for him and the battle that he had fought. She looked at him steadfastly. "You share with me the authority that Yahweh has given you, and I will not reject it. Certainly, I will go with you, but because of the course you are taking, the honour will not be yours, for the LORD will deliver Sisera into the hands of a woman." It was a statement of fact, not a judgement; he was choosing to share the glory Yahweh was offering him, and she wanted him to acknowledge now the price he would pay. And yet, equally, she recognised, it was as it was meant to be.

His heart melted at the respect that flickered in his wife's eyes. "It is as it should be; many have suffered and all should glory in the victory Yahweh gives us. For myself, I have yielded my will to His."

She wrapped her arms around his neck and pressed her lips to his.

"Men will write and speak of your victory and character a thousand years from now. Your name will be heard of until the end of time, for you lead with a humility and true courage that is not afraid to share its glory."

The settlement drew together for morning prayers, and afterward Barak lifted his voice. "Long ago, Yahweh promised this land to His servant, Abraham. He reinforced this promise, first to Jacob and then to Moses. Through our disobedience, it was taken from us and we found ourselves oppressed by those around us. But now, we turn our hearts to Him, we repent of falling away from Him, from abandoning His Laws and He promises to crush our enemies and restore our peace. Yahweh has said that it is time to take back our inheritance; to seize that which He has given us.

Let us consecrate our hearts to Him, for He goes before us to destroy the name of Sisera and to break the power of Jabin. The battle belongs to Yahweh." There were roars of approval and shouts of praise as men pledged their allegiance.

He called Tebah, Isaac, Hur, Maor and some of the other men to him, asking them to gather those who were willing to go to battle. They went out to Reuben, to Ephraim and to Benjamin. But those of Rueben, despite much thought and deliberation among their pastures and sheepfolds, decided that the atrocities their brothers west of the river had experienced were not their problem, and that they therefore did not need to come.

It was agreed that those in Judah and Simeon were to stand with Shamgar, to defend Philistia.

At the next new moon they arrived: the leaders of each village with those whose hearts were willing. They came armed only with plough-shears, ox-goads and faith. They had no armour, but wore linen tunics and repentant hearts. Instead of shields, they carried raw courage born out of desperation for their existence and zeal for Yahweh's kingdom. Shepherds, vinedressers, farmers, and boys joined them, drawn by the blare of the ram's horn as it resounded in the hills and across the plains.

They came as warriors.

As darkness draped its starry mantle over the congregation, the flames of their conviction lit the night sky. They cried out to Yahweh with one voice, thanking Him for the promises He had given them, for His love, His Law and pledging their lives to Him.

The next morning Deborah reluctantly handed Othniel over to Tamar. She kissed his tiny mouth and closed her eyes to fight back the tears that threatened to disempower her. He wrapped his little arms around her neck, and when Barak came and hugged his son, Othniel cried. She pulled herself away from him and felt the tear of separation as a physical pain.

Tamar, her eyes deep with empathy, laid her hand on Deborah's. "Yahweh is with you. Have no fear for your son; he will be loved and cared for."

Deborah swallowed; hot tears burning her throat - Tamar knew her secret fear. It would not control her, it did not torment her. It was a seed she would not nurture. It was the fear that she might never see her son again; the fear that, if they failed, he would be taken slave or murdered, that he may never know Yahweh.

"Tell the women to pray, for our victory lies not in flesh but in faith, in spirit and in prayer." Taking one last look at Othniel, she walked away.

39

Then down marched the survivors to the nobles;
The people of the LORD *marched down for Me against the mighty.*
"From Ephraim those whose root is in Amalek came down,
After you, Benjamin, with your relatives;
From Machir came down commanders and rulers,
And from Zebulun those who handle the scepter of the [office of] scribe.
"And the heads of Issachar came with Deborah;
As Issachar, so was Barak;
Into the valley they rushed at his heels;
Among the divisions of Reuben
There were great searchings of heart.
Judges 5 13-15.

1234 BC – The Armies of God

The settlement closed behind them, its leafy gates concealing its existence. Barak walked next to her and slipped his fingers between hers. "We fight for an Israel that will be free for our son and for our children, where Yahweh is the only name he will grow up hearing - where fear will have no power to map his destiny."

Deborah nodded, her resolve strengthened.

They marched north, meeting the Patriarchs' highway and boldly stating their claim, knowing that word would reach Sisera. As they marched, they sang the old songs; their hearts stirred as they remembered the mighty men who had gone before them. Yahweh's anticipated victory stirred their blood and reminded them of who they were: Yahweh's chosen - *His* army.

Word spread across the plains and mountains, like a summer fire that forges its own path. From Manasseh, leaders left of the Jordan joined them - those from Machir, west of the Jordan.

Maor and some of the other men had travelled east of the Jordan, to gather men to fight. When he returned, his jaw was set in resolute fury.

"Those from East Manasseh and Gad will not come. They say it is not their battle to fight – it does not affect their boundaries because the river protects them from Canaan's threat." He seethed, pacing as he spoke. "Are they blind or stupid that they put their trust in a river, rather than Yahweh, and turn their back on their people?!"

"And Dan? Would they not come to our aid?" Barak asked, his tone cautious.

"Dan have remained independent because of their excellence in commerce. They are secure in their shipping with the Greeks and Trojans. For this reason, their land remains unconquered, respected and protected by both Philistines and Canaan."

"And Asher?"

Maor scoffed with disdain. "Dan is a wealthy old woman, too fat on her greed and comfort to want to move."

Barak noted his friend's sense of frustration and failure. He embraced him. "You did what you were meant to, my friend. Sometimes Yahweh uses us only to test others' hearts. Isolation and self-preservation bear their own fruits. If you live alone, you will die alone. Do not allow their failure to weigh on you. You were obedient to what Yahweh commanded you to do."

As they passed Garasha, Barak was aware of the caravan that followed behind them. He grimly acknowledged the dark, Midianite features of its leader and memories of Heber's cruelty brought a sudden carnal desire for revenge. He contemplated, with pleasure, the idea of sending a well-aimed arrow and ending the tyrant's life. But, as the thought began to grow, he sensed Yahweh's gentle authority, a white hot brand of righteous anger that seared his conscience with the knowledge that he must wait for His judgement, His timing. To act now, in his own strength, would risk all. He turned away.

In Zebulun, Issachar and Naphtali, the story and hope of Barak and Deborah had travelled, and men were waiting. Many had met Lapidoth and Deborah, and still more had heard of them. When the low drone of the ram's horn echoed in the hills, sounding from place to place, men were ready. They kissed their wives and children, promising of Yahweh's deliverance, and left their homes, plough shears and ox-goads in their hands, to where they were joined by their friends and family. Their blood stirred with the ancient sound of the horn that called them to war, to faith, to liberty. As they passed villages, others joined them, like brooks that grow into streams, until they finally merged with the river of men that surged toward Kedesh. Thousands poured out of the hills and cities of

Zebulun and Naphtali, and there they met on the raised plateau of Kedesh. Barak stood looking down from the elevated slope with Deborah beside him.

He raised his voice and it seemed as though even the wind held its breath, for the authority Barak carried was not his own.

"Men of Israel, many of us only remember the rule and oppression of Sisera, we have only known death and fear. For our nation turned aside from Yahweh, from the truth that leads us and protects us. We allowed apathy to drug us and deceive us, and then we accepted the beliefs of Canaan because our flesh ruled our souls. And so we turned against Yahweh and enjoyed the pleasures of Canaan. But its delights poisoned us and blinded us until we could no longer see the road back. Yahweh heard our cries and He raised up a mother, a mother who awoke our nation and draws us with compassion back to the Father. A prophetess who speaks Yahweh's words and a judge who will restore truth and justice as the plumb line of our nation. We go now to fight for those we have lost, for those who live, for our freedom and dignity as men, and above all for the Name of Yahweh, the Name above all names, for He rides before us. He commands us to march to Mount Tabor, where He will deliver Sisera into our hands. He will go before us as a consuming fire, not because of our righteousness, but His great mercy." The men roared their agreement.

He continued, as the Levite, Aaron had instructed him, reading from the Torah. "But, I call you now, according to the words of Moses, that if there is any man among you who has built a house and not dedicated it, let him return to his house, in case he dies in battle and another should dedicate it.

If there is any man who has planted a vineyard and not eaten of it, let him return to it, in case he dies in battle and another eat of it.

If there is any man that is betrothed to a wife and has not taken her, let him return to his house, in case he dies in battle and another take her.

If there is any here that is faint-hearted, let him return to his house, in case his fear spread to those around him."

The crowd parted to allow men to leave; some held their heads high, others hung their heads in shame. When the number had re-gathered, there were ten thousand men left. Barak set captains over the armies. Of these, Maor, Hur, Tebah, Isaac and Dan were numbered.

Deborah stepped forward then. She pushed back the mantle that covered her hair so that they might see her countenance, for her eyes blazed with the fire of heaven and her voice was as a sharp sword that cut the air as she spoke. "Yahweh promised our ancestors, Abraham and Jacob, that He would give them this land. When Moses and Joshua entered Canaan, He reiterated that promise, setting before them a choice: to choose life, or death. For blessing and life flow from obedience, but curses and death are the consequences of disobedience. Our hearts forsook our heavenly

Father, and for many years Israel wandered from her Maker. She fled to the arms of gods who cannot help her, who do not love her, but enslaved her and oppressed her. In her despair, she remembered her first love; Yahweh heard her cries and had compassion on her. He called her back to Himself. If you will turn to Him with your whole heart, turn away from your own ways and listen to His voice, He will deliver us. I have seen the battle that can be won. I have seen Michael, angel of war, destroy Canaan and her gods. He will fight on our behalf. He will bless this land and its fruit and bring peace once again to our people.

"I call each of you to account today, humble yourselves before Yahweh. I pronounce a seven-day fast, and as we pray, we must examine our hearts and seek Yahweh's face. Then we march to victory." The army once again roared its agreement; its praise to Yahweh ascending to the heavens like a holy sacrifice.

Maor approached Barak, his eyes on the caravan that had pulled up in the trees. "Heber watches. He listens."

Barak smiled, following his gaze. "He does. I have noted his presence since Gerasha, but he does so only by Yahweh's will. He judges the heart and allows men to choose their own destiny. Let him be our adversary's pawn, and let him claim his own righteous judgement." He nodded to his men who came with weapons: axes, daggers, arrows and spears with metal tips and newly forged swords that were handed out to Israel's leaders and strongest men. Hur chose a Canaanite sword, with a curved blade, while Maor and Tebab took an axe and spear. Sen took arrows and a dagger and Dan had already made his own axe and dagger.

Barak ran his finger down the length of the sharpened edge of his sword, noting with satisfaction the hardened edge of the blade. His eyes met with Heber's, and the Kenite's face paled as he perceived Barak's awareness of his presence; he swiftly departed. One man from Heber's caravan remained, his face dark as the night with long black tendrils of hair that reached his waist. Barak strode down to meet him, a grateful smile parting his lips as he embraced the man to whom he owed his freedom.

"Zimran, it is good to see you, though I cannot say the same for the man you serve. I feared for you after we parted company."

It was Zimran's turn to grin now. His gaze fell on the multitude before him; they were farmers, vinedressers and shepherds. He wondered if they were aware of the probability of their defeat. Still, Barak had done what he said he would do: he had raised an army.

"It would seem you have honoured our trust. We were right to have believed you."

Barak nodded, clasping the man's shoulder. "I owe you my life, friend. I do not know where your faith lies, nor your loyalty. We fight for Yahweh, for Israel. Will you be on your way, or will you fight with us?"

The thought had crossed Zimran's mind when he chose to remain. He knew he had chosen loyalties when he refused to continue with Heber. It had been a conviction without deliberate consideration. He rested his hand unconsciously on the long curved sword at his waist, wondering why he had chosen to remain. "I admit your God intrigues me. The courage and the character I see in those who follow Him force me to question either their sanity, or His sovereignty. I believe in your fight to end tyranny and oppression, and I have some of my own reasons for wishing Sisera and his supporters defeated." Zimran clasped Barak's arm, his right hand still symbolically upon his sword. "I will fight with Israel's armies, for Yahweh's victory."

"We are honoured to have you among our number."

As the company marched to Mount Tabor, Heber sent his caravan driver on alone to Zaanannim, while he himself took his horse and rode with haste to Harosheth. As he rode, he congratulated himself on the approval he would receive from Sisera. He imagined the General's disdain slipping from his face, as respect and gratitude took their place. He imagined the elevation his name would receive for having personally saved Canaan.

Mount Tabor rose before the army, a symbol of majesty, arising from the level plains. They ascended its summit, and there they waited. A warm breeze fluttered in the late spring air. The ground was dry and hard; the spring rains had not arrived and summer would soon be upon them. The birds and crickets hummed their melody from the heights of the forested slopes.

Sisera's lips curved as Heber spoke. He welcomed him in, offering him a seat of honour at his table and the finest of his food. He recognised Heber for what he was; he could be trusted because his sycophantic nature hungered for approval. However, the Kenite's assessment was marred by weakness, and that was to be despised. The idea of Israel uniting and forming an army were two suggestions ludicrous enough to be humorous. 'Yet, they had done it before', a small voice warned. He would not march into battle until this word had been confirmed. But he would seek confirmation. He called Danel to him; it would be a safe mission, without risk, that would bolster his son's confidence.

When he returned late that evening with his company of soldiers, his son's face was dark.

"It is true; more than ten thousand wait on Mount Tabor."

"Do not look so worried, my son, they are vinedressers and farmers; their spirits crushed by the might of Canaan. They are armed only with plough-shears and ox-goads, not chariots or swords. This man, Barak, has offered them false hope and they have believed him. Herein lies our opportunity to be rid of the Hebrews for good."

Danel nodded. He knew better than to suggest to his father that they seemed anything but downtrodden, nor to remind him that his grandfather had no doubt thought the same.

"Send out soldiers, tell the kings of Canaan to arise and gather their warriors. We will meet in Taanach near the waters of Megiddo, where the waters are shallow, and from there we will march on Tabor." He turned to Heber. The man irritated him, like a fly that buzzes around your head, begging to be swatted; he smiled stiffly. "Won't you come with us; fight with the kings of Canaan." He knew the bait he offered him, this Hebrew Kenite who had wormed his way into Jabin's favour by offering his daughter. He knew, too, that she had favoured Danel and that his son had wanted her for himself. But, it wasn't his greed or his deviousness that he despised, but his cringing cowardice and personal weakness.

"I am no warrior," Heber swallowed, suddenly wishing he had not come.

"It's your choice; to stand with the kings of Canaan as we crush the Hebrews would perhaps cut across your loyalties?" He turned away and shoved a fig cake into his mouth.

Heber's expression darkened. "I would not be here if my loyalties were not certain," he spluttered.

Sisera nodded, drawing him in. "Of course when Israel is crushed, her land and wealth will be divided among those who stood with Canaan in battle."

Heber straightened in his chair, the hook firmly embedded, as he was reeled in. "Of course, it would give me the greatest honour to pledge my loyalty and to stand with the Kings of Canaan."

Barak's army set up camp on the hillside of Mount Tabor. The morning was airless and laden with heat. Anticipation hovered in the air and a nervous energy fuelled their prayers and worship. As they waited, each man felt their spirits strengthened as they stripped themselves of the yoke of bondage and clothed themselves in the knowledge of who Yahweh said they were: His warriors, in whom victory was assured. They positioned themselves on the wooded slopes, cloaked by the trees. Deborah and Barak watched from their rocky lookout. The late spring sun was cooler on the mountain top, a welcome relief after the dry heat they had marched in.

The Esdraelon plains looked yellow and withered and the Kishon River was a polished bronze thread, shallow enough to paddle through.

"Our visibility is clear. We can see for miles in all directions," Barak acknowledged.

Hur nodded. "Sisera's chariots would not make it up the rocky slopes."

"The tactical advantage is ours...As long as Sisera comes to us."

"He will. He does not consider you a threat; he is assured that victory will be easy."

Barak nodded now, but his thoughts were distracted as he fought the urge to pre-empt Yahweh's plan.

On the evening of the third day, the air cooled and the sky lowered; dark brooding shadows, hovered over the mountain, sweeping in from the east. It was a canopy of gloom that divided dark and light and threatened their zeal. A cold wind hit the mountain, whistling through the trees and blocking out the stars. Deborah held her head back and a smile parted her lips as the first raindrops splashed on her face.

"This wind comes from the east and yet it is cold," she smiled.

Barak nodded. "Unusual. It would normally be driven in from the Great Sea."

"This wind is driven by heaven." She raised her hands to heaven as lightning charged the air, drawing the water into vats that opened in mighty torrents upon both mountain and plain.

"It is as you said it would be." Barak's voice was steady, solid as the rock beneath their feet; his eyes set like flint as they stared ahead.

"It is as Yahweh showed me," she agreed.

"Has He shown you how?"

"No." She turned; her eyes alight with love and pride. "I saw only lightning, rain...and victory."

He took in the fine details of her face and shuddered inwardly with reverent awe at Yahweh's power.

The sun was hidden as though to conceal the long hours of waiting.

Finally, it was reported that Sisera's nine hundred chariots and warlords were crossing the rising waters of Meggido.

The men's faith now warred with the reality of their unequal skill and weapons.

Deborah stood on the mountain summit, looking at the river Kishon snaking its way to the great sea, and the Esdraelon plains where Sisera's chariots could be seen. Like the dull, leaden scales of a dragon, the monsters of destruction moved toward them as one body, churning up the mud and spitting it toward heaven. Thunder and lightning crashed simultaneously, assaulting the plains before them, and the dragon winked menacingly at them. But for Deborah, what had once been the herald of fear, now promised victory.

Maor appeared, his own countenance uncharacteristically perturbed. "The men grow fearful; Sisera's army is great. It will not be long until they are upon us." He hesitated. "They say this battle cannot be won."

Even Barak looked uneasy at the growing tide of chariots and warriors, for he had not seen the spiritual battle, thus his sight was on the natural. He looked to Deborah, acknowledging the wisdom of her presence among them.

"Take me to them." Deborah's voice cut the air with calm authority.

As she stood before Israel's men, she sensed fear among them as a tangible shadow that had infiltrated their pores and was poisoning their faith.

"Men of Israel, do not give in to the reality of the natural realm, for you are children of a greater kingdom. Yahweh urges you to remember who you are. You are a people who have sworn allegiance to the Most High God. You are His people. He swore to Abraham, to Jacob, to Moses and Joshua that He would drive out the inhabitants of the land before them, if they were obedient to Him. He drowned the Egyptians who sought to defeat His people. He tore down the mighty walls of Jericho by His great power. I have seen the battle that must be fought. I have seen the stars that will fight from heaven on our behalf. From their courses they will fight Sisera. Our enemy will know Yahweh's vengeance for the murder and oppression of our people. And we shall be free!! No longer will we live in fear and poverty! We will once again harvest the fruit of the land and eat from it. We will live in peace, watching our children grow, knowing Yahweh's goodness. The battle is yours Israel! Gird yourself with courage and take what is yours!"

Barak raised his voice as a war cry that rose, piercing the gloom and others joined him until the army was strengthened, united in their vision, and fear had retreated.

The east wind had intensified, and icy daggers of hail the size of pomegranates rained down upon the mountain. It was as though the ceiling of Yahweh's patience had shattered and His vengeance was spewed to earth; a holy reply to hell's force.

Deborah moved her cloak aside. "Look," she pointed. "There awaits our triumph." The river Kishon had become a writhing, pulsating beast that had swollen as though it would birth Leviathan. The horses, two abreast, pulled the chariots, driven by their relentless masters.

Lightning split the sky, its golden shafts spearing both land and water.

"We must wait only a little longer." Her hair, wet with rain, stuck to her face.

"I will go and reassure the men," Barak said, drawing his cloak around him.

She laid her hand on his arm. "He comes," she whispered, her eyes focused on an unseen realm. "The Captain of the host rides before you.

"Go!" The fire of heaven lit her eyes, and her voice seemed to resound with an unearthly authority. "Go now and take what is yours, for Yahweh has delivered them into your hand." She watched as heaven's armies, descended from heaven: angels, mighty and glorious, armed with swords and bows stood, unseen yet resplendent, among Barak's armies.

Barak stood before the army, his hand rested on his sword: *His sword*, that had been forged by his own strength, yielded to Yahweh, tested by fire and tempered by Yahweh's words to him. He stood with assurance and men looked to him, knowing that they would follow him, whether to life or death, for they knew that he fought not for his own glory, but for Israel and for freedom. They trusted him.

With one voice the Israelite army raced down the mountain, their weapons raised high. Israel's archers and heaven's stars released a cloud of arrows.

The Canaanites took their bows and aimed their slings, but the wind and hail drove into their faces, impeding their vision and forming a wall that caused their missiles to thud ineffectually in the sodden ground before them. Conversely, the arrows of the Israelites were empowered by nature's force, guided by heaven, and finding their mark.

The Canaanites watched their comrades fall under the blows of heaven's wrath. As Sisera watched his men retreat, their shields held above their heads, he questioned for the first time if victory was inevitable.

Those at the front heard the exclamations and shouts of panic that travelled as a tremor beneath the canopy of Canaanite shields. Behind them the river Kishon had flooded, making their retreat across the waters impossible. It caught the young saplings and seized the chariots in its forceful grip as they attempted to cross. The horses beat their hooves, rearing with fright as they struggled to free themselves of their iron bondage. They thrashed wildly, throwing their drivers and archers into the churning waters of debris and panic, where their heavy bronze armour aided their demise.

Those who escaped the flood tried to clamber to the muddied banks, their swords drawn as they grasped clumsily for their shields.

Barak's voice thundered loud as a trumpet blast: "Victory belongs to Yahweh!!" He led his men, charging to meet them in the valley of Jezreel. The two armies faced one another and cast their spears into the air. Canaan's spears were met with the wild onslaught, the chilly breath of Yahweh's judgement as it prevailed against His enemies.

Deborah watched, her prayers potent and unyielding, as she waged her battle within the spirit realm. She saw Barak and his leaders lead the men into the fray, slashing and stabbing with the force of heaven upon them.

Hur watched his enemies fall around him like the saplings on the riverside; he felt the righteous thrill of battle pulse through him as he skillfully wielded his familiar blade.

Victory seemed inevitable.

Talmai stood towering over Barak, his upper arms the breadth of Barak's waist; he seemed to Israel's leader to be more like a grotesque mythical creature than a human. The Israelite's eyes narrowed as he took in his enemy, but he stood his ground, legs planted firmly apart.

The brutal face, the thunderous voice, the violent fury of Talmai sliced the air between them. "Barak, leader of Israel's armies, they have placed their hope in you in vain. You have no training, no skill, only misguided passion. By nightfall your head will decorate Harosheth's gates and your prophetess will know the might of Canaan as she is passed among our men. And then, she will join you. Israel's hope will be subdued. We will wipe you and your people's name from this land."

Barak kept his voice steady, forcing courage to command his words. "Talmai, the might of Canaan is no match for the sovereign Lord! I fight for Yahweh and victory is His!" Barak swung his sword in the air and it met Talmai's as a blade of grass might blow against a mighty oak.

The face of Baal's warrior twisted in a hideous grimace as he slashed sideways. One direct hit and Barak knew he would not survive. He acknowledged that speed and agility were his greatest natural strengths in this fight. Ducking Talmai's sword and heavy swings, his body arched as the blade slashed the air where his head had been. Barak's blows were deft and quick, but blocked by the heavy blade of the seasoned warrior. The rain and hail drove down, and the ground beneath them became a bloody quagmire, slowing their movements. Barak found himself slowly backing away, his strength failing as his efforts were consumed by blocking the barrage of attack. The force of each blow was debilitating and Barak knew his strength could not hold out indefinitely. For the first time, the fear of failure threatened to overwhelm him, and he faltered. Talmai swept his sword downwards and Barak felt the blade pierce his tunic, slicing into his arm. He cried out, forcing the pain and fear to focus him, to remind him what he was fighting for.

"YAHWEH!" His voice splintered in the unseen realm, delivering shards of militant resolve that silenced the voice of defeat and strengthened his arm. He swept his sword sideways, slashing with wild desperation as he considered the consequences of failure.

Thunder exploded around them and lightning devoured the sky behind him. Talmai blinked for a flickering of a moment as the light hit his eyes, and in that moment, Barak leapt into the air. It was an action that would bring victory or defeat. He brought his sword down, slicing through the giant's collarbone and cutting into his chest. The monster fell, his gurgled rasping swallowed by the muddy banks of the Kishon, and there Barak ended his life, separating his head from his body. He held it in the air and hollered with feral jubilation.

Gathering his breath now, his eyes frantically searched for Sisera. But without their chariots, covered in mud, every man looked the same. He spotted Maor as he ducked a Canaanite sword and then swung his axe sinking it into his assailant's ribs. Pulling it free, he turned to face the next man. Beside him fought Zimran, his years as a caravan driver fighting off raiding parties had taught him well. He held his axe in one hand and dagger in the other, and wielded them with a fluidity of movement that suggested they were one weapon.

The Canaanite army was turning to the defence; the river had rivaled itself as their greater enemy, a frenzied monster that no man would master. The icy wind coiled around the soldiers' bare legs, tugging and pulling; invisible hands that sought their destruction, stabbing with clawed fingers against their armoured chests. They swung their swords blindly, slashing the air in panic and blinking as heaven's onslaught bore daggers to their senses.

Barak saw him then; Sisera was leading the retreat. Realising that their path was blocked, he led them towards Harosheth: to his fortress.

The Israelites pursued them, their fatigue subdued by the faith and victory that pumped through their weary limbs. The archers pulled back their bows, and their arrows, carried by the east wind, found their targets, taking down those in the rear.

Meroz arose before them, and Barak's heart leapt, for it was a Hebrew town that would come to their defence. They, who had known Sisera's cruelty, would certainly be desperate to exact Yahweh's vengeance and end the battle. Israel's general pursued them into the town, and a smile curved on his lips as he tasted the anticipated exultation of victory.

But Meroz, poisoned by fear and apathy, listened to the voice of the tyrant rather than that of their Maker. Sisera offered leniency for obedience; mercy and provision for allegiance. The Elders considered his offer: it was improbable that Israel could win this battle after all. They were simply looking after their own, protecting their families, weren't they? *(Although at what cost?)* And so, it was agreed: as the Canaanite army approached, they opened their gates. Remorsefully then, they watched as the soldiers turned their barns and homes into fortresses and battlements where they lay in wait. Now, the realisation of what they had done crept toward them, like a winter mist that clung to their conscience. They began to wonder if they had made the right decision, but the time for regret was past.

When the Israelites came through the gates they followed Sisera's orders; they had no choice now. They joined their enemy as they hurled spears from open windows; their arrows flew from roof tops and they watched in dismay as their people were slain. Dan was among those who was murdered by the apathy and cowardice of Meroz.

Another was killed, too; he rode on a Canaanite chariot and was killed by a spear that was meant for the Israelites. The Kenite fell, his thin lips parted in a grimace of horror as the spear protruded from his stomach. Heber was killed by his own narcissism, cowardice and betrayal; his selfish ambition and disloyalty had reaped their own consequence.

Deborah, her eyes set on the heavenly battle, saw the spiritual failure of Meroz to stand for righteousness. And she saw the Angel of the Lord, His staff raised in judgement as He cried: "Curse Meroz. Utterly curse its inhabitants, because it did not come to the help of the Lord, to the help of the Lord against the warriors." As co-general of Israel's armies, she waged her own war from the mountaintop, a spiritual battle that commanded the natural. And she did not cease to pray, to intercede, for victory, freedom and righteousness to be restored to her nation; to Yahweh's people.

The rain had stopped.

Still Israel's armies pressed forward, until the gates of Harosheth rose before them. Hur looked up and saw the faintly distinguishable form of Sisera's mother standing in the latticed window of the fortress, her aged hands clasped with anxiety as she watched the bodies of her son's army carried toward the sea. Behind her stood another, and her face spurred him on: *'Let Harosheth fall and her life be spared,'* his silent plea called out to Yahweh.

He turned to see Danel, her son. "Traitor!! You are a traitor, Hur!" the young man screamed, his face smeared with the blood of battle and twisted with rage.

He thrust his curved blade downward with the speed of youth and the skill of his military training in Egypt.

Hur's body arched with lightning reflex as he blocked the blow with his shield. But the strike had come from nowhere, catching him off balance. Noting the Egyptian's vulnerability, the boy's sword stabbed downwards, piercing the shield and penetrating Hur's thigh. He cried out in pain – he was trapped and his reaction must be swift. Bracing himself for the searing pain, he pulled and twisted the shield, wrenching the sword from the wound and out of Danel's grasp. The action caused the young man to stagger backward, but he did not fall. The tyrant's son took his axe from his belt - he wielded it with skill. Blood pumped from Hur's leg and his head spun with agony and loss of blood. He knew he needed to finish this fight soon if he were to survive.

Through a haze of searing pain, he fought with automatic instinct, driven by his desire to survive. He saw the battle raging around him, and Harosheth's walls somberly towering over them. A chariot had been carried down the river, not far from where they fought. It had reached a shallow patch and picked up branches, bodies and the corpse of a horse along the way; a dam was forming behind it.

Danel's sword clashed with Hur's axe as they studied each other for weakness. They clumsily contested the heavy mire in a hesitant, stumbling, lurching war dance.

They were evenly matched: Danel's youth and training and Hur's experience. Yet one was wounded; one would need cunning if he were to win. He silently prayed for help.

Hur pushed Danel back, closer to the river, and still the waters rose.

A week ago their horses would have crossed the river here, and now it was a mangled dam of bodies, trees, horses and chariots.

But Danel was no fool. He pushed against the tide of the Egyptian's attack. Now they were both only a short distance from the amassing, defiled waters. Lightning shattered the sky around them, and both looked cautious as they continued to deliver blow after blow.

The sediment and water had gathered at their knees and movement was laboured; yet to clamber to safety would expose them to a vulnerability neither could afford. Still another chariot lurched toward them, its lifeless horse carried behind it. In a few short moments, it would collide with them. Fear flickered on Danel's face and his decision was made; he pulled his legs free, but as he did so, he fell, his heavy armour pulling him under the current toward the carnage ahead.

Hur watched with quiet victory as the muddied waters covered the boy's fear contorted visage. And then, at the last moment, Jara's face pierced Hur's conscience and he grunted begrudgingly at its irony. Wrenching himself free of the sludge he groaned as his muscles pulled his torn flesh. He had to move deeper into the river now and he knew that his own life was greatly at risk. He stared through the cloudy waters at Danel's grimace; reconciled to death as the last bubbles of life escaped through his mouth. Reaching down, he grabbed his arm, hauling him to the safety of land. If the young man would die, it would not be by his hand, for the sake of his mother.

As the battle cries travelled further away, Deborah gazed down on the bloodied banks of the river and plains. She acknowledged, now, the magnitude of Yahweh's deliverance: that which had seemed a dream was reality. She felt overwhelmed by the glory she had witnessed, and in response to her wonder, the question formed in her mind: *Why Yahweh? Why did you choose me, a woman?*

The distant rumble of thunder rolled across the plains before her, and shafts of light pierced the dark clouds as though to push back their territory. In that moment, she saw a momentary glimpse of a battle that would not be fought for over three thousand millennia; this battle would end all battles, would end time.

She shuddered. It was a battle that would be won by the spiritual tenacity and humility of spiritual mothers and fathers. Those who did not conform to the pattern of this world, with its ambition and pursuit of self, but had learnt to be sons and daughters of the highest God. Those who sought not their own glory, but Yahweh's kingdom, who had been tested by fire and were yielded to the Master's hand. These were the people who had found Him in brokenness and adversity and knew Him, trusted Him and had allowed His character to be formed in their lives. They were those who loved not their own lives to the death.

That no man might glory and all might know My power and My love.

By evening not one man in Sisera's army lived. Harosheth was surrounded and its unarmed walls would be easily taken.

But Sisera was not among the number. Seeing the defeat of his army, he ran. He knew better than to flee to Hazor, for to face Jabin with defeat would be worse than to die by Barak's hand.

Barak returned. His linen clothing, bloodied and wet, clung to his body and as he frowned, the rain ran down the furrows in his brow, and off his beard.

"There are tracks leading north-east. Maor saw Sisera flee on foot," Hur added, wincing. Now that the adrenalin of battle waned, he felt the pain in his leg and loss of blood.

Barak's jaw tightened, his fists clenched and white with restrained fury. "Let us follow him and pray he does not reach Hazor before we find him."

Deborah nodded, casting her husband an anxious glance. Once again, she felt her faith war within her; she had no desire to think of Barak, injured, facing Sisera alone. Had Yahweh not said that a woman would have the victory?

"I will attend to those who are wounded and address the men," she said, by way of relinquishing control and handing his fate to Yahweh.

The sky had cleared and the sun's jubilant smile reflected on the receding waters of the Kishon as it washed away the stains of battle.

Tebah returned from following Sisera's tracks. Deborah noted that, although weary, her old childhood friend had found peace on the battlefield today. "He is on foot. His direction bears northeast. He does not flee to Hazor."

"Kedesh?" Barak asked.

Zimran's stomach twisted with sudden knowledge. "I believe he will make for Zaanannim. It is the last place you would ever think to search for him. He had an alliance with Heber and knows that Jael will be alone.

"Jael!" The blood drained from Zimran's face as he and Barak hastily mounted the Canaanite horses that had survived the torrents. Tebah, already mounted, joined them.

Casting a grim look toward Hur, Maor and Deborah, Barak grabbed the reigns. "Lead the men until I return."

40

Sisera asked for water and she gave him milk;
She brought him curds in a magnificent bowl.
"She reached out her [left] hand for the tent peg,
And her right hand for the workmen's hammer.
Then she struck Sisera, she smashed his head;
And she shattered and pierced his temple.
"He bowed, he fell, he lay [still] at her feet;
At her feet he bowed, he fell;
Where he bowed, there he fell dead.
Judges 5: 25-27

1234 BC – Jael

"Where is my husband?" Jael demanded. The air was hot, tense and clammy, as though nature held its breath in anticipation.

The driver squirmed. "The Hebrew armies gather for battle at Kedesh."

Jael felt adrenalin rush through her. She wished she had been a man that could fight; to have been given some righteous release to her passion.

"And where is Heber now?" she repeated, thankful that he hadn't returned, but a dark sense of intuition broke fissures in her relief.

The driver bit his lip, and he looked to the ground nervously. "He has gone to Harosheth to tell Sisera of their plans."

Jael felt the blood drain from her face. She turned away, closing her eyes against the truth of her husband's betrayal: He would bring the judgement of Yahweh upon her family. The man was a fool. And what if they sought vengeance? She told Mary to take Uriah to her tent and sent several of the slaves and servants to watch in the fields for approach.

A feeling of nausea hit her: Heber normally brought two drivers with a caravan this size.

"Did you travel alone?"

"No, I travelled with Zimran."

She swallowed. "And where is he now?"

"He has pledged his allegiance to Israel. He fights with their armies." Jael felt a surge of pride for the man she loved, and yet it warred with the consternation that besieged her ragged emotions - another of those she loved was now at the mercy of Sisera's violence.

Jael had never felt more alone than she did in the next few days. The lives of those whom she loved, and her daughter's freedom, lay in the success of Israel in battle.

She began pacing the fields, waiting for a report, but by the end of the first day, it brought her more frustration than comfort. The air was hot, the pressure thick, clogging her skull and fuelling her temperament.

She would previously have gone hunting when she felt this anxious, but since Miera's capture she had lost the desire.

She found that Levia was more compliant when Heber wasn't there and she persuaded her, with some effort, to help her finish weaving goats' hair into panels and patching holes in their tent. The reward of her labour was that when she finally lay down at night, she slept.

The next morning she awoke early, adrenalin jolting her awake. Frustration gnawed on her thoughts; if she hadn't had the children to watch, she would have leapt onto a horse and rode to Mount Tabor. She thought of Zimran, fighting against the force of Sisera's mighty army, and helpless anxiety built in her chest.

The weather mirrored her mood: restless and agitated - the warm air prickled with tension that demanded a tempestuous conclusion. She fed the animals, checked on the livestock and then, against her better judgement, set about the labour intensive process of washing the heavy bed coverings. While they were drying, she beat out the rugs and sleeping mats, airing them over branches. After that, she and Levia set about tidying inside the tents: piling the grain around the tent poles and cleaning out the mill and mortar. She straightened out the low, wooden table and plumped up the cushions - anything that diverted her thoughts of Zimran and Israel's battle. She worked without speaking, and Levia knew not to try and pierce the tense canopy her mother had drawn around herself. The young girl silently refilled the lamp with olive oil, her eyes only occasionally flitting to her mother. Finally, Jael rearranged the skin bags and leather bucket from hooks on the poles, along with the pots and pans. There was nothing left to do.

She stood back, without satisfaction, as she appraised the work they had done. It was as though she was preparing for an important guest, but she knew her work was born out of frustration and lack of control over her circumstances.

On the third day, she awoke with a headache, and the dark density of the air told her that the storm would break soon. A sense of foreboding had travelled before the caravan; even as the storm clouds could be seen raining down their fury in the south for the last few days. Dry lightning flickered in the sky, turning the clouds to a shade of milky purple.

She told Levia to milk the goats, handing her a wooden bowl and she went about the task of securing the tent. She pulled out the cords until they were taut and secured the tent pegs as the first drops of rain hit the roof of the tent. It seemed to Jael that a thick, black canopy crept towards her, blocking out light and heralding death.

Jael drew inside with Levia, Uriah and Mary, feeling a sense of completion about their work. Though the hour was not yet late, the sky was the colour of charcoal and they had lit the oil lamps. They made a small fire around the hearth that was rarely used inside the tent. The smoke filled the tent, and before long, the smell of bread and courgette soup made their mouths water. The rain pounded loudly on the tent like the approach of a mighty army.

"Our generations have done this since the beginning of time," Jael said, skillfully dotting patterns of henna on the back of Levia's hand. She found herself longing for home, for Midian.

"Tell us a s…s…story," Uriah stuttered.

Jael nodded, smiling, pleased that Uriah's language was improving.

"Well, there was once a man of God, called Abraham," she began to recount the familiar story. "His first wife, Sarai, died and he remarried to a woman called Ketur…" She paused as thunder crashed overhead, like a hammer striking stone and drew Uriah into her arms, sending up a silent prayer for mercy. "Now Keturah had six sons. One of whom was Zimran and one of whom was Midian. Now, because he favoured Isaac, the son of his first wife, he sent the others away with gifts. Midian eventually settled in the place of our fathers and became the father of the Midianites and of our ancestor Jeth…"

The flap of the tent was pulled aside, and the caravan driver stood in the door, his face grey and water pouring from his face. "Sisera has been seen, and he makes haste towards us."

Jael felt bile rise in her throat, and panic momentarily immobilised her.

"Sisera?" she uttered, her eyes meeting the driver's, as she sought consolation or at least a helpful suggestion. Her silent request fell flat, filling the space between them. Her anger at the man's cowardice aroused her from her fear.

"Take the children to the slaves' tent and watch over them. Levia, stay in your tent and do *not* come out or I will beat you within an inch of your life. Do you understand?" Levia swallowed. Her mother had never made such a threat before, and she knew she feared for her. She nodded, hastily grabbing her brother's hand.

Turning to the driver, her hands planted on her hips, her eyes narrowed, she spoke. "If I fail, protect my children with your life. Die a man."

He nodded grimly. "What will you do?"

"I will do what a mother does: whatever I need to, to protect my children. Now go!!"

Jael had learnt to be grateful for the speed and clarity of thought that formulated in her mind during times of stress. It was one of her better attributes that, when pressed, she knew she would do whatever she had to survive and to protect those she loved.

The memory of her wedding day flooded her mind, and her vow: 'that she would overcome and that she would not compromise who she was.'

Now came her final test.

Yahweh. Do not let my fury oust my integrity to You. Let my actions not be my own, but be driven by Your perfect judgement.

She tugged a tent peg out of the wet ground, wiping it with the inside of her skirt, and placed it next to the bag of flour, along with the hammer, to conceal it.

Slipping into her own section of the tent, she hastily tore off her dress and put on the one she had made for the festivities in Hazor. Made of red linen and decorated with delicate gold and purple embroidery, she knew that it accentuated her feminine curves and dark colouring.

She muttered impatiently under her breath, willing her hands to steady as she outlined her eyes with kohl. Finally, she bit her lips, forcing colour into them.

The rain had lost its intensity when Jael went outside to meet Sisera. She trembled with fear, now, as the practicalities of her plan seemed impossible. But as she took him in she acknowledged, with some small relief, the state of his physical exhaustion.

Running to meet him, she feigned concern, her hand clasped to her mouth. "My lord, what fortune brings you to us?"

Surprise flickered in his eyes, but his normal intuition was marred with fatigue. As she held out her arms, he staggered into them, gasping, for he was near to collapse, and the death of his son played before his eyes.

"The Hebrews. We were defeated at Tabor. Hide me!" She hid both her elation and trepidation.

"Turn aside, my master, turn aside to me, do not be afraid," she whispered in his ear.

He looked up at her, and she saw suspicion flicker in his eyes.

She answered his unspoken question. "My husband is not here. I do not know where he is, but he bids me to show you our hospitality." She lowered her eyes.

She saw lust glimmer in his tired eyes and she reached out to brush his blood and sweat-matted hair.

"You are exhausted. Come into my tent," she coaxed, looking at him through her dark eyelashes. She knew that she broke all appropriate etiquette inviting this man into her tent, but he had once done so without invitation, and so she knew he would not question it now.

"Lie down, lie down my master, and I will cover you." She knelt next to the cushioned bed, her eyes meeting his. Taking his calloused hand, she drew him down to the cushions and he collapsed upon them without hesitation. She swallowed nervously.

"Please give me a little water to drink. I have thirst," Sisera gasped.

Standing, she took the bowl that had been given to Heber by Jabin. It was an ornate silver bowl, decorated with jewels, and she poured into it the goats' milk, sweetened with honey, as she would make for her children to send them to sleep. Kneeling next to him, she held it to his lips, looking with feigned concern into his eyes as he drank.

"Sleep now," she spoke softly, her voice a balm to his ragged emotion as she gently stroked his hair. It was the action of a mother, or a lover, that quenched both suspicion and caution.

He grabbed her arm, an act of desperation rather than violence.

"Stand in the doorway of the tent, and if anyone comes and inquires of you and says, 'Is there anyone here?' you shall say, 'no'."

She took one of the coverings that she had washed the previous day and lay it carefully over him.

"They will never expect to find you in my tent. You did well to come to me. Rest now."

Sisera nodded in agreement. Weariness darkened his eyes and his judgement, for he had not anticipated Jael's welcome. His eyes took in Jael's curves as she stood with her back to him in the tent door. If he were twenty years younger, he wouldn't have needed to renew his strength, but war had taken its toll on his body. Nonetheless, when he awoke, he would enjoy taking Heber's beautiful and hospitable wife.

The images of his intent slowed in his weary mind until they slipped into the habitation of his unconscious world.

Jael waited until she heard Sisera's gentle snores. Her heart pounded at what she must do, and for a moment the magnitude of her intent disabled her thoughts. She forced her fear into submission and stared at him, playing over in her mind what she must do, reminding herself that she had no choice, and that Israel's deliverance lay in her grasp.

His eyelids did not flicker. Summoning her courage, she picked up the long tent peg, designed to drive deep into the shifting sands of the desert. The hammer lay next to it, both where she had placed them earlier.

Stepping toward him, she checked the tent opening, once again considering the gravity of what she intended to do: to end a man's life.

Her heart pounded in her ears.

Yahweh? It was a single utterance that juddered through her as a question, a plea that sought justification.

The answer pierced her thoughts with passionate conviction: *let us free our children from the hand of the oppressor. I am with you.*

The weight of this man's cruelty and violence hit Jael, and left no doubt in her mind as to the righteous deed she was called to do.

She would not wait. Waiting was for cowards. She placed the iron peg over his temple and lifted the hammer with her right hand. Imagining that she was driving it into dry stony ground, she brought down the hammer. In one blow, it pierced Sisera's skull, shattering his temple so that the peg went into the ground. His body spasmed violently and his face twisted into a hellish grimace. Jael recoiled, still clutching the hammer as Sisera's blood spurted from the wound and pooled around his head. A strangled gurgle escaped his mouth as death gathered around him.

She watched with a mixture of exultation, disgust and fear. Logic told her that no man could survive such a blow. And yet, this was Sisera - and if he did survive, his revenge would be terrible.

Sisera's legs twitched one last time, before his eyes took on the misty glaze of death.

And then silence.

She looked unmoving at the man who had inflicted pain and death on so many. He was dead, by her hand. Rocking back on her heels, the reality of what she had done hit her: Sisera, leader of Jabin's armies, the subject of men's nightmares, was humbled, was brought low, was subdued beneath her. A tremor of relief and exultation was exhaled from her soul at the irony of what she had done: Sisera, the terrorizer of women, had been defeated by her, a woman.

And then, acknowledging her inner triumph, her relief and her hope, she prayed: *...I have killed the man who has murdered and enslaved Your children. I pray, let Hazor fall and my daughter be returned to me Yahweh...it is done.*

Her senses were quickened once again by the sound of a horse drawing near. She froze, as she anticipated the arrival of one of Sisera's men; she must keep him from discovering Sisera's body.

She hastened out of the tent as the faint form of a lone rider emerged from the shadows of the trees. Barak's steed had been faster than the other animals, and so he was minutes ahead of them.

His form, clothed in twilight's obscurity, drew into the tented enclosure. She strode out to meet him as he dismounted from his horse and tied it to a tree. Now that he was close, she sighed inwardly with relief as she identified the form of the slave she had freed: Barak.

"Sisera. Is he here?" he asked. The initial relief at finding Jael alive was replaced by concern that they had lost his trail. Jael acknowledged both the military zeal and physical exhaustion on his visage.

She took in the blood on his clothing and the fresh blood that seeped from a wound on his arm, and she surmised the events that had come to pass. "He is. Come, I will show you the man you are seeking."

She held her chin high with her usual defiance, and Barak saw the pride of a lioness, the resilience of a mountain goat.

He entered the tent with her and beheld Sisera. He noted the blood that had had pooled around his head, like a red flag; his face was contorted as though he had seen the demons that came for him in his death. Then his gaze fell on Jael, the fresh blood not yet dry on her dress and he pieced together what had occurred. Deborah's prophetic words returned to him: *a woman will receive the glory.* He smiled inwardly: *it is as it was meant to be.*

He turned to her. "By your courage and wisdom you have ended tyranny." It was simply stated and he felt no sense of failure, or envy, in her success.

She answered with a solitary nod, but her eyes reflected a desperation that seemed out of place in this woman of strength and fury. "Hazor must fall now…my daughter is captive."

He acknowledged her expression as the vulnerability that every mother carries for the safety of their children. "Hazor *will* fall – Jabin cannot stand without Sisera and his war lords."

She raised an eyebrow. "It would seem my faith in you was not unwarranted."

He smiled with weary gratitude as she handed him wine and bread. "Tell me what came to pass at Tabor."

It was then that he remembered Heber, and the arrow of Morez that had pierced and ended his life. He had found no sorrow in his heart for the man's demise; he had died as he had lived, in compromise and selfish-ambition. But he would spare this woman, who had shown the courage of ten men, any more sorrow. He found himself wondering about the woman's affection for her husband, the man whose loyalties she had now betrayed twice. He had shown kindness to neither man nor beast, and yet, he was aware that love was a strange master.

"Jael, I am sorry to be the bearer of such news in your hour of victory. But, Heber was found among the dead. He fought with Sisera."

She looked at him while a flood of muddled, weary emotion lapped at the rocky shores of her thoughts. As she tried to separate and identify them: shock, betrayal, anger, vindication, loss, the one that bore the most clarity was relief, followed by a mild, nagging guilt at that relief. She bowed her head as the truth trickled into her thoughts: *It was over. Both men, who had caused her such pain, were gone.*

Then, emerging powerfully, the words she was scared to bring form to - the thought that had barraged the tender walls of her inner sanctum for the last few days. *And what of Zimran; what of him? Does he live?* She could not face the possibility that he lived no more.

Her thoughts were broken by the gentle thud of hooves on the soft mud – accompanied by the final song of birds as they bid the day farewell. They seemed like a dirge. She lifted her head as the two men dismounted, tying their horses to the branch of a tree. A sliver of grey split the black sky, cloaking the identity of the new arrivals, while the gentle light that spilled from the tent silhouetted Jael and Barak. He stepped into the light and she beheld his form, that she had watched for so many years, the hair that fell to his waist, the strength of his walk – he held himself like a prince, she thought. He was here.

He closed the gap between them and she stepped into his embrace; she was free!

Epilogue

*So may all your enemies perish, LORD! But may all who love you be
like the sun when it rises in its strength."
Then the land had peace forty years.
Judges 5:31*

1208 BC - Shiloh

Deborah and Barak looked out over the congregation of Israelites. A
strand of grey hair had escaped from the hood of her mantle and fluttered
in the gentle spring breeze. She turned her head and looked at the man she
had loved for so long. His tanned face now lined with courage and
compassion, he was still handsome and strong, and he still commanded the
respect and loyalty of his men for his humility and selflessness.

They had journeyed to Shiloh via the Patriarchs' Highway, their carts
laden with the first fruits of wheat and barley. Shepherds walked behind
herding lambs, oxen and goats. Most of the village had come with them,
joining in with the other pilgrims as they talked and sang. Those on white
donkeys rode next to those on foot – rich and poor sang the old songs of
Israel's victory, and the song of Deborah.

The spring sun was warm on their backs and the fields and vineyards
hummed with the laughter and chatter of families as they worked together.
An entire generation had grown up never knowing the tyranny of
oppression, yet their parents' memories of the horrors they had experienced
reminded them of Yahweh's mercy and deliverance and the importance of
keeping His Laws – fear was gone and peace reigned. Tobias' words to her
as a child pricked her thoughts and she wondered: *for how much longer will they
remember?*

Deborah saw the faces of those she loved, and as she did, she recalled
her journey from that night at Passover, so many years ago, when she had
first met Yahweh.

The first moment of my beautiful friendship with Yahweh: Creator, Redeemer and Friend.

Then to that fateful day when she had first met Lapidoth, when he had rescued her physically, and again so many years later, when his love had reached out to her in her desperation; it was then she had first realised that she loved him.

Now, here she was again in beloved Shiloh, as mother to Israel – the culmination of her journey.

She raised her voice, her eyes warm with compassion as they rested on those she loved. She saw her natural children, and their children with them; they had grown up never knowing fear or oppression, never having compromised their faith in Yahweh. Beside them were Isaac and Gabriella, Hadas and Dan with their children's children.

"Beloved of Yahweh, and of my own heart, let us thank HIM, Creator and Redeemer that we stand here today. It is my prayer that our children might never know the pain of slavery and oppression. Therefore, let us remember to live deliberately, with holy reverence for Yahweh as our staff and our lamp.

"It is my prayer that each of us might act as though our choices determined those of us all. We do not live alone, but we are knitted to the heart of Yahweh, we take care of each other, no longer each man doing what is right in his own eyes, but caring for his neighbour as the Law dictates.

"Let us do good as we have received, knowing that each of us is a vital part of a whole. Therefore, let us live deliberately and militantly.

"Let us treat each other as we desire to be treated ourselves.

"But most importantly, let us love Yahweh, with all our hearts, souls and strength."

Her eyes rested on the man who stood beside Barak, his stature and authority still apparent, and his eyes sharpened by wisdom and compassion. Beside him stood his son Manoah. "Let us thank Him, for the victory of Shamgar and for the peace of Judah and Simeon. May it long continue.

"Let us thank Him for the courage and tenacity of Jael." She looked out at the woman and her eyes twinkled with affection for the woman who had become her friend, that holy firebrand that spoke before she thought and knew no fear. She saw Jael's steely eyes fix on hers, and their unspoken memories of *that* day bridged the gap between them. They had pulled down the gates and Yahweh's armies had marched triumphantly into the city. Barak, Zimran and Tebah had led the storming of the palace and Barak had slain Jabin on his throne. Maor and Isaac had found Ariel and liberated her, along with the other slaves, while Zimran, Tebah and Jael found Meira with Molid. The latter had been taken and publicly executed with the remainder of his family. The high places had been pulled down and the city burned to the ground. The smoke had turned the sky black as though the sin and death they had reaped for so long hovered, demanding vengeance.

Beside Jael stood Zimran and the children they had had together.

Meira, Levia and Uriah were there too, with their spouses and children and Adva and Jez's family. They had returned to Zaanannim after Hazor fell and worked making tents for their own profit.

She smiled. "Let us thank Yahweh, for the fall of Hazor and the death of Jabin. For the victory and peace that He has brought to His people."

Though Sisera's children had been executed, Hur had pleaded with Barak for Jara's life and his request had been granted: she was, after all, little more than a slave. They had married not long after, and stood now with their children and grandchildren.

"Beloved, we come together to celebrate the year of Jubilee, and in doing so, we not only enter into our rest, but allow others to enter theirs: for those who are in bondage, and land that was taken is returned. We celebrate the liberty Yahweh has given us and our beloved nation.

"I have judged, by Yahweh's grace and wisdom for over thirty years. But, there will come a time when I will rest with my fathers. Let us remember the lessons that our history has taught us.

"For though physical Canaan is subdued, spiritual Canaan is our true enemy. It is a serpent that lures us with promises of wealth and physical pleasure. It offers peace by suggesting there are many ways to one god and offers liberation from our moral code, but its venom condemns us and binds, taking our children from us and breaching our relationship with our Creator and each other.

"Let us remember the lesson of Meroz, where the compromise and cowardice led to the needless death of Israel's men and was cursed by Yahweh. While its buildings and inhabitants are no more, its spiritual threat remains: in cowardice, disloyalty and apathy, its poison weakens our faith and ultimately leads to our destruction. Let us stand against it: to defend the weak and oppressed, let us not ignore the cries of those who suffer. Like East-Mannaseh, Reuben, Gad and Asher who turned their head from their brothers' suffering because it did not affect them, because they could not see, they could not hear the cries that Yahweh heard. We are connected, by one Father and one Spirit, and we must stand and fight as one. We fight for righteousness and Yahweh's kingdom, not because it benefits us, but because He is worthy!!

"Therefore, protect yourselves with the truth; arm yourself with Yahweh's promises. Moses commanded you to write the Laws on your doorposts, to tell your children and your children's children. Remember the Sabbath and the Sabbath year, as the land needs rest, so do we. This rest is *in* Him; it is trust in His provision, His sovereignty. It declares that we are His children. He has warned, if we neglect the Sabbath, He will allow us to be taken captive by other nations, that the land might receive its rest. For in rest comes restoration, and in the breaking of the ground, the weeds that suffocate life are removed. Was that not what we saw: the villages ceased, the land lay barren for twenty years? Sabbath year is about recognising our rest in Yahweh, our dependency on Him in all things. It is in realising that our greatest weapons are not sword, nor hammer – they are evidence that we have strayed from the truth, and that He calls us back. Our great force and defence is in His word and prayer.

"But Yahweh had mercy on us. For He is a loving God and a faithful father." She paused to allow her words sink in.

"Find Yahweh for yourselves, each of you. Find strength not in a woman, nor in a man, but in Yahweh and His word. We are slaves no longer, but children of the most high God and our souls yearn for His kingdom to come on earth!"

Her eyes settled on a man. He was younger than her. She recognised him from her childhood – he had once sat with them in Bethlehem and had told her brother about the uprising of Israelites against Canaan. His name was Obed, the great grandson of the prostitute Rahab, and she saw the hand of Yahweh's destiny upon the small boy by his side. His name was Jesse, and from him would come a shepherd, a king and a worshiper. From his line would come the Messiah, the Lamb of God, the last Adam that would redeem the world from the wages of sin.

Author's Note

My passion to write this book began over twenty years ago in Bible College, and my fascination with Deborah and Jael as women in a patriarchal society, who brought peace to a nation, has grown. As part of our study, we had to write and deliver a sermon. I initially threatened to leave; such was my apprehension toward public speaking. But I was led to this scripture: 'Village life ceased. It ceased in Israel until I, Deborah, a mother, arose, arose a mother in Israel.' Something was birthed within me. My previous degree from a University in London was in Social Science, and I have always been fascinated by how society and people work.

As I began to look at Judges 5:7, I was fascinated. I saw how 'village life' referred to the infrastructure of society, and that the destruction of this foundational community was a powerful force in the weakening of Israel's defences. I naturally thought about how our society has become individualistic and separated into the private and public spheres through changes to society, largely brought about by economic and industrial shifts. We, too, have lost the community that knit us together in previous generations.

I was struck that in the song of Deborah, who was a prophetess, judge and leader of God's people, she attributes her success as a mother. And yet we are not told she had natural children. She is referring to the mother-heart, the heart of a woman, whether single, married, with children or not, in the work place or at home. It is the militant and powerful force that women carry, whether in the work place or in the home. Our compulsion to draw people together, to reach out to those around us with our intuition, wisdom and compassion both emotionally and practically, to those in need, is inherent.

The nature of our economically driven society has undermined the importance of motherhood, both spiritual and natural, and we are weakened by it. It is not a call to change so much as to embrace who we are, and an acknowledgement of all we already do, that is SO vital and often goes without praise. Well done ladies!!

And so, this book is a Biblical, historic novel, therefore, much - including romantic elements of the story and many family members - are imaginative, not scriptural, and are not to be considered as such. However, I have tried to maintain the integrity of the Bible, including relationships and facts by referring to historic archaeological findings and Jewish records and traditions.

Why have you begun the book with Deborah as a child?

Our calling is upon our lives before we are born. Therefore, I wanted to show the possible development of the personality and calling of Deborah as a prophetess, a mother and a judge. I wanted to show, also, how pain and hardship could increase compassion, zeal and wisdom. The question I asked was: *what might have happened in Israel at that time to impassion Deborah to become a leader of Israel?*

I also wanted to look sociologically at the break down of society. To show what happens to society and community when 'each person does what is best in their own eyes/lives for themselves', because it is so applicable to our western society. For this is what Deborah, as a mother, restored: she knitted together the infrastructure of society, loving and encouraging, admonishing and rebuking, but giving them a sense of hope in something bigger than themselves, a future that was good. I believe this message is as relevant today as it was then, and that is what women do: knit communities together.

Finally, I wanted to show what oppression under the Canaanites would have looked like.

Why was Deborah taken as a slave by Sisera, as it doesn't mention that in the Bible?

Archaeological, historical and Jewish views suggests that the Canaanite invasion was centred in the north and may not have reached Ephraim to the same degree. The question then is: *how was it that she was so moved by the oppression in the north that she was inspired to draw together and fight for those who truly suffered?* To support this idea, biblical historians have said that the tribes that did not come to Deborah and Barak's aid were largely those that were unaffected by Canaanite oppression: East Manasseh, Gad and Reuben. Judah and Simeon who would have been more concerned with the Philistine threat.

Other reports suggest that the Canaanites were the first capitalists: they went into an area and exploited it for its resources. Their primary export and economic advantage was the use of Murex, to create purple/blue linen. Hence, the inspiration behind Keret's character, he is representative of 'a Canaanite'. They were also known for their intellect: they are believed to have created the first cuneiform, phonetic alphabet and the Gezer 'agricultural calendar'. They were advanced in military power, not only their chariots of iron, but shipbuilding. Canaanites were also referred to as 'slave-traders', and the Bible tells us that 'they were taken into slavery' and that 'they were oppressed'. It alludes to the fact that this covered all of Israel to some extent.

From my research, I concluded that, whilst the worst of the oppression was based in the north, Sisera's influence on the southern tribes would have been in terms of control of trade, forcing them to be vassals of Canaan until his control of northern Canaan was secure. This theory also helps to explain why Benjamin and Ephraim fought, but why the tribes east of the Jordan: Manasseh and Rueben, did not – because they were not affected.

Furthermore, from my biblical and personal understanding, it is when a person surrenders their life to Yahweh that they are most powerful (it is no longer I who live, but Christ in me and His strength is made perfect in my weakness). These qualities have been sharpened and deepened though times of personal difficulty and hardship in my own life. Hence the question: what happened in Deborah's life to create a woman of such wisdom, compassion and intimacy with Yahweh? I believe what I have written is plausible, given the historic accounts of that period of Canaanite oppression and my understanding of how people react to conflict and suffering.

Finally, I wanted to show the extent of corruption of the Canaanite empire, the child sacrifice and temple prostitution, orgies and slavery, because we struggle to understand why a loving God would command them to be wiped out: the spiritual seed needed to be removed under Old Testament judgement because people didn't have access to spiritual redemption until Christ, but only had the Law and sacrifice.

Why is Shamgar's story included and how did you arrive at his history?

Some biblical critics have suggested that Shamgar was in fact Samson, and that Judges is not chronologically recorded. They argue this based on the fact that both men came from Beit Shemesh and had incredible strength, and killed large numbers of people using unorthodox weapons. Deborah's song clearly tells us: 'in the days of Jael and Shamgar', evidence that they existed at the same time, and I believe they are different people. Samson was named as a judge while Shamgar brought peace. However, due to their supernatural strength, I played with the thought that they might be related; hence the reference to his son as Manoah (Samson's father).

Historians tell us that his father's name, Anath, is not Hebrew but is named after a Canaanite war goddess. Because of the importance of names relating to function in the Bible, and also Shamgar's decision to defeat 600 men with an ox-goad, I have given him a military background.

Yet, because he used an ox-goad, the tool of a farmer, I wondered if he chose a different path to his father, which raised the question: why?

The next question is: If his father was a Canaanite warlord, why did he fight for the Hebrews? I decided that a Hebrew input (bring up a child when they are young and when they are older they will not depart from it) would have been likely to have impassioned and moulded him.

Therefore, the next question is: what happened to make him turn from farming, to killing Philistines?

Despite the fact that these people lived so long ago, basic human responses to pain remain the same, as do the reasons for our passion and motivation to fight for what we believe against ridiculous odds. I am in no way negating Yahweh's call on his life, nor his supernatural intervention. I am only suggesting that He weaves His purposes through the pain in our lives when it is yielded to Him.

Finally, the question is asked of the battle of Barak against Sisera: Why was Judah not condemned for not coming to Deborah and Barak's aid? If Judah, the area previously dominated by Philistia, had known peace through Shamgar, it is understandable why Judah did not come to fight, having had their own battle to fight.

Interestingly, Shamgar is not named as a judge, only that he saved Israel, which would tie in with the fact that he ruled at the same time as Deborah, liberating Judah from the Philistine hold, while the rest of Israel was under Canaanite oppression. The evidence suggests that it was thus; the seven nations that stood against Israel's claim to the land were related to certain areas and their boundaries.

Explain Jael and Heber's Journey and relationship.

We know, biblically, that the Kenites were allotted land in southern Israel, in the desert of Judah - Arad. We know, historically, that the Kenites were metal workers; they most notoriously worked the mines at Timna.

We can assume that there was a life-changing reason for Heber deciding to leave his kin to travel across the other side of Israel. Possibly a disagreement. *But why travel so far?*

So, we know that Heber worked with metal, and that the Canaanites were famous for their 900 iron chariots. We know, too, from the Bible that an alliance was formed between Jabin and Heber.

Why would the mighty king of Jabin, who we know to be a cruel, self-seeking, and ambitious leader, make an alliance with a lowly Kenite from southern Israel?

We also know that the Kenites had an affiliation and loyalty to the Hebrews and their religion, and thus Heber turned away from this in his alliance with Jabin. Kings were seen as godlike and to be worshipped as such.

We know, too, that Jael betrayed her husband's loyalty to Jabin when she killed Sisera.

The Bible says straight after: 'and Heber made an alliance with Jabin: and they told Sisera that the Hebrews gathered on Mount Tabor.' This suggests to me that it could have been Heber who told him.

It is fiction and thus we cannot be sure, but to me, Jael's righteous decision to defy her husband, on a natural human level, and a basic understanding of human relations and responses, suggests that such behaviour is the result of a history of conflict and needing to use wisdom/ trickery because of control, dominance and poor relational habits of the other.

Zimran is a fictional character but represents the fact that, in ancient times, marriages were arranged to pay off debts, and often the bride had little choice – her romantic feelings were not considered. Again, Jael's response to Heber suggests, at best, a conflict of religious loyalties; but possibly alludes to a deeper unhappiness in her marriage, which is based on the choices we know Heber to have made, and the character type that is suggested in these decisions.

Since names have meaning, 'wild mountain goat', is so befitting to Jael and I have built her character around the impulsive, passionate, non-conformist type of woman. Deborah on the other hand, whilst also non-conformist in her own right, is more deliberate, introspective and thoughtful in her character, yet equally strong in terms of her moral code and reliance. Though very different in character, both were used by Yahweh, as they were created to be. Both needed to come to a place of complete surrender and dependence on Yahweh and His Spirit.

Why have you depicted Lapidoth and Barak as the same person?

Essentially, because many Jewish historians seem to believe he was the same person.

There are two theories.

One suggests that Deborah was not married. The term: 'Deborah, the wife of Lapidoth', can also be described as 'woman of torches,' which would make Barak just a military leader. It would also most likely make Deborah a 'mother to Israel', rather than a 'mother in Israel.'

The other believes Lapidoth and Barak to be the same. If I go with this theory, the question then is: what happened to create a name change?

There are many name changes in the Bible, which usually occur with some sort of dramatic occurrence and revelation. Futhermore, in the book of Hebrews, Barak is listed with the other judges, thus implying a relationship with Deborah.

Lapidoth means 'torches'; Barak means 'lightning'. The fact that God used Barak (lightning) to defeat Baal, god of storms, seems to carry a biblical irony that is similar to Moses bringing plagues on Egypt that represented its gods.

The next question is: how did he get the name change/what was the situation surrounding his name change? They always seemed to occur with promise and challenge in the Bible. Again, I asked the question: if Sisera was famous for taking people into slavery, what was the likely event that broke Lapidoth, turning him to complete dependency on Yahweh and changing him from a torch, to lightning? We know, too, that Sisera was famous for making chariots. Who would have made chariots? In the ancient way of things, these jobs were given to slaves.

It also tells us that neither a shield nor spear was seen in Israel. But then, later, we learn that they attacked Sisera and his army with their swords. Where did they get them from? Again, a logical suggestion is that they forged them themselves with skills learned as slaves.

Deborah and Lapidoth meeting as children

I loved the idea of festivals; of celebration, not only of Yahweh and His provision, but of community and relationship. Hence, Lapidoth's early meeting of Deborah was entirely fictional – except for the fact that she knew him as 'Torches'. The fact that she met him again later in Kedesh was purely because she needed to see the plight of the northern tribes; since he was from Kedesh, she needed to meet him and finally to become known as a mother to Israel, who would later gain their trust.

Whilst her separation from Lapidoth involved his name change and re-emergence as Barak, it also allowed me to play with the thought that Deborah had judged Israel alone as a woman. I did not want to diminish Deborah's leadership. I wanted to say: she could have led alone!

Equally, we do not know that she was an actual mother to her own children. I believe it is irrelevant to her ministry because it is Yahweh's anointing and the heart of a woman to knit together, and to have perception to fight for those she loves, and what she believes in. Hence, I have allowed her to lead and be used in both capacities.

Where there was discrepancy regarding points, because of my desire to maintain integrity to the biblical account, I have tried to incorporate both aspects.

Why have you included poetry?

Deborah is acknowledged as producing one of the earliest forms of Hebrew poetry. I liked this quality to her character: it again alludes to her power in her femininity, which is reinforced by her quote: 'Village life ceased in Israel until I, a mother, arose.' She is not suggesting that she is the same as men, but equal and equally powerful in who she is.

Historic and Geographic inclusions.

I also included Ruth and Obed in the story, as they lived at the same time as Deborah, in Bethlehem – they would have been aware, if not affected by both the war of Shamgar against the Philistines and the war with Deborah against Canaan. Of course, the relationships are purely fictional.

In the same way, the battle between the Trojans and Greeks was possibly around this time. Homer's 'The Illiad' and 'The Odyssey' would have been based on events around the same time. I found these facts fascinating and wanted to pass them on as points of interest.

Appendix

Judges 4-5New International Version (NIV)

Deborah

4 Again the Israelites did evil in the eyes of the LORD, now that Ehud was dead. [2] So the LORD sold them into the hands of Jabin king of Canaan, who reigned in Hazor. Sisera, the commander of his army, was based in Harosheth Haggoyim. [3] Because he had nine hundred chariots fitted with iron and had cruelly oppressed the Israelites for twenty years, they cried to the LORD for help.

[4] Now Deborah, a prophet, the wife of Lappidoth, was leading Israel at that time. [5] She held court under the Palm of Deborah between Ramah and Bethel in the hill country of Ephraim, and the Israelites went up to her to have their disputes decided. [6] She sent for Barak son of Abinoam from Kedesh in Naphtali and said to him, "The LORD, the God of Israel, commands you: 'Go, take with you ten thousand men of Naphtali and Zebulun and lead them up to Mount Tabor. [7] I will lead Sisera, the commander of Jabin's army, with his chariots and his troops to the Kishon River and give him into your hands.'"

[8] Barak said to her, "If you go with me, I will go; but if you don't go with me, I won't go."

[9] "Certainly I will go with you," said Deborah. "But because of the course you are taking, the honour will not be yours, for the LORD will deliver Sisera into the hands of a woman." So Deborah went with Barak to Kedesh. [10] There Barak summoned Zebulun and Naphtali, and ten thousand men went up under his command. Deborah also went up with him.

[11] Now Heber the Kenite had left the other Kenites, the descendants of Hobab, Moses' brother-in-law,[b] and pitched his tent by the great tree in Zaanannim near Kedesh.

[12] When they told Sisera that Barak son of Abinoam had gone up to Mount Tabor, [13] Sisera summoned from Harosheth Haggoyim to the Kishon River all his men and his nine hundred chariots fitted with iron.

[14] Then Deborah said to Barak, "Go! This is the day the LORD has given Sisera into your hands. Has not the LORD gone ahead of you?" So Barak went down Mount Tabor, with ten thousand men following him. [15] At Barak's advance, the LORD routed Sisera and all his chariots and army by the sword, and Sisera got down from his chariot and fled on foot.

[16] Barak pursued the chariots and army as far as Harosheth Haggoyim, and all Sisera's troops fell by the sword; not a man was left. [17] Sisera, meanwhile, fled on foot to the tent of Jael, the wife of Heber the Kenite, because there was an alliance between Jabin king of Hazor and the family of Heber the Kenite.

[18] Jael went out to meet Sisera and said to him, "Come, my lord, come right in. Don't be afraid." So he entered her tent, and she covered him with a blanket.

[19] "I'm thirsty," he said. "Please give me some water." She opened a skin of milk, gave him a drink, and covered him up.

[20] "Stand in the doorway of the tent," he told her. "If someone comes by and asks you, 'Is anyone in there?' say 'No.'"

[21] But Jael, Heber's wife, picked up a tent peg and a hammer and went quietly to him while he lay fast asleep, exhausted. She drove the peg through his temple into the ground, and he died.

[22] Just then Barak came by in pursuit of Sisera, and Jael went out to meet him. "Come," she said, "I will show you the man you're looking for." So he went in with her, and there lay Sisera with the tent peg through his temple—dead.

[23] On that day God subdued Jabin king of Canaan before the Israelites. [24] And the hand of the Israelites pressed harder and harder against Jabin king of Canaan until they destroyed him.

The Song of Deborah

5 On that day Deborah and Barak son of Abinoam sang this song:

[2] "When the princes in Israel take the lead,
   when the people willingly offer themselves—
   praise the LORD!

[3] "Hear this, you kings! Listen, you rulers!
    I, even I, will sing to[c] the LORD;
    I will praise the LORD, the God of Israel, in song.

[4] "When you, LORD, went out from Seir,
    when you marched from the land of Edom,
the earth shook, the heavens poured,
    the clouds poured down water.
[5] The mountains quaked before the LORD, the One of Sinai,
    before the LORD, the God of Israel.

[6] "In the days of Shamgar son of Anath,
    in the days of Jael, the highways were abandoned;
    travellers took to winding paths.
[7] Villagers in Israel would not fight;
    they held back until I, Deborah, arose,
    until I arose, a mother in Israel.
[8] God chose new leaders
    when war came to the city gates,
but not a shield or spear was seen
    among forty thousand in Israel.
[9] My heart is with Israel's princes,
    with the willing volunteers among the people.
    Praise the LORD!

[10] "You who ride on white donkeys,
    sitting on your saddle blankets,
    and you who walk along the road,
consider [11] the voice of the singers[d] at the watering places.
    They recite the victories of the LORD,
    the victories of his villagers in Israel.

"Then the people of the LORD
    went down to the city gates.
[12] 'Wake up, wake up, Deborah!
    Wake up, wake up, break out in song!
Arise, Barak!
    Take captive your captives, son of Abinoam.'

[13] "The remnant of the nobles came down;
    the people of the LORD came down to me against the mighty.

¹⁴ Some came from Ephraim, whose roots were in Amalek;
    Benjamin was with the people who followed you.
From Makir captains came down,
    from Zebulun those who bear a commander's[ ] staff.
¹⁵ The princes of Issachar were with Deborah;
    yes, Issachar was with Barak,
    sent under his command into the valley.
In the districts of Reuben
    there was much searching of heart.
¹⁶ Why did you stay among the sheep pens[ ]
    to hear the whistling for the flocks?
In the districts of Reuben
    there was much searching of heart.
¹⁷ Gilead stayed beyond the Jordan.
    And Dan, why did he linger by the ships?
Asher remained on the coast
    and stayed in his coves.
¹⁸ The people of Zebulun risked their very lives;
    so did Naphtali on the terraced fields.

¹⁹ "Kings came, they fought,
    the kings of Canaan fought.
At Taanach, by the waters of Megiddo,
    they took no plunder of silver.
²⁰ From the heavens the stars fought,
    from their courses they fought against Sisera.
²¹ The river Kishon swept them away,
    the age-old river, the river Kishon.
    March on, my soul; be strong!
²² Then thundered the horses' hooves—
    galloping, galloping go his mighty steeds.
²³ 'Curse Meroz,' said the Angel of the Lord.
    'Curse its people bitterly,
because they did not come to help the LORD,
    to help the LORD against the mighty.'

²⁴ "Most blessed of women be Jael,
    the wife of Heber the Kenite,
    most blessed of tent-dwelling women.
²⁵ He asked for water, and she gave him milk;

in a bowl fit for nobles she brought him curdled milk.
²⁶ Her hand reached for the tent peg,
  her right hand for the workman's hammer.
She struck Sisera, she crushed his head,
  she shattered and pierced his temple.
²⁷ At her feet he sank,
  he fell; there he lay.
At her feet he sank, he fell;
  where he sank, there he fell—dead.

²⁸ "Through the window peered Sisera's mother;
  behind the lattice she cried out,
'Why is his chariot so long in coming?
  Why is the clatter of his chariots delayed?'
²⁹ The wisest of her ladies answer her;
  indeed, she keeps saying to herself,
³⁰ 'Are they not finding and dividing the spoils:
  a woman or two for each man,
colourful garments as plunder for Sisera,
  colourful garments embroidered,
highly embroidered garments for my neck—
  all this as plunder?'

³¹ "So may all your enemies perish, LORD!
  But may all who love you be like the sun
  when it rises in its strength."

Then the land had peace forty years.

Footnotes:

a. Judges 4:4 Traditionally *judging*

b. Judges 4:11 Or *father-in-law*

c. Judges 5:3 Or *of*

d. Judges 5:11 The meaning of the Hebrew for this word is uncertain.

e.   Judges 5:14 The meaning of the Hebrew for this word is uncertain.

f.   Judges 5:16 Or *the campfires*, or *the saddlebags*

New International Version **(NIV)**

ABOUT THE AUTHOR

Joanne Szedlak lives in Southampton, England, with her four children and husband. She has degrees in both Christian theology and Social Science. She is passionate about community and the vital, if sometimes overlooked, role women play in knitting together the foundation of our society. She has been involved in church leadership, with this heart, for over twenty years.

Find out more at
www.jascottpulications.com/joszedlak

Printed in Great Britain
by Amazon

23184742R00253